The Eternal Party

H. "DARK END" TOWNSEND

The Eternal Party

Production copyright FurPlanet Productions © 2024

Copyright © H. "Dark End" Townsend 2024

Cover Artwork © Kalahari 2024

Published by FurPlanet Productions
Dallas, Texas
www.FurPlanet.com

eBook ISBN 978-1-61450-618-8
Paperback ISBN 978-1-61450-617-1

First Edition Trade Paperback 2024

For those who are lost,
Because they have lost

Contents

Raindrop Prelude

❦

The manor had always been there. But it was the first time Mila had ever noticed it.

The calico cat stood on the rain-drenched sidewalk, on a spot she passed through twice a day, five times a week, year after year. She stared up at the building she had somehow never paid any attention to before. She didn't remember it, and yet it must have always been there, because she couldn't recall anything else occupying that space and it was too time-worn to be new.

Now that she was looking at it, the building seemed an incongruous inclusion in the city. It was decades — no, centuries — out of date, a manor house straight from a British period drama surrounded by skyscrapers, lit by flickering gas lamps instead of bright streetlights or neon signs, facaded with brick and wrought iron filigree instead of concrete or steel. It seemed untouched by the world around it.

A car zoomed past in the night, kicking up puddle-spray that drenched Mila straight through clothes and fur. The calico shivered, her teeth chattering. Her sodden tail, with its bright oranges and whites turned brown with mud, wrapped around a leg in a desperate attempt to stay warm.

Mila had told herself she could make the trip tonight, that the cold and rain wouldn't matter, that she could take a break from the insufficiently mind-numbing monotony of work that she had thrown her every waking hour into, and the hollow feeling that had been eating away at her mind might be sated for a day or two. But the reality was that the cold and rain did matter, and the manor before her looked so warm and dry.

The entire time Mila had been staring at the house, her hand was shoved into her coat pocket, curled protectively around the petals of the purple hyacinth flowers in a futile attempt to shield them from the elements. She brushed a finger along one and promised herself she would only be a minute. Then she darted up the steps, nearly losing her footing twice on the slick surface.

The door was massive, but it had no bell or knocker that she could see, and when she tried to rap her knuckles on it, the sound was so muted it was inaudible over the constant downpour. Mila wondered if she could stay under the eaves and wait out the worst of the storm, but a burst of wind sent the rain sideways and made her clutch her coat tighter to herself. In a wild hope, she turned the handle and nearly fell in surprise when it yielded easily.

The door creaked open a few inches and out spilled light so bright that the calico couldn't see anything inside. A few receding, repeating chords of a piano could be heard above the storm, but that was all.

"Hello?" Mila called into the half-open entrance. But no one responded. The piano had gone silent. Cautiously she slid into the vacated space and peered around the door.

Warmth and light immediately enveloped her. She was standing before a long hallway that extended to the far end of the block and went up at least two stories. Her jaw went slack as she beheld the amount of money on display. Mila's client list had included the occasional suddenly wealthy heir, who had to be dissuaded from constructing a mansion because they could not comprehend the sheer scope of what that would truly cost them. Did they know how much one genuine hand-woven rug for the front foyer cost to buy? To maintain? Mila did. The calico's eyes flicked from the walls before her furnished with tapestries and larger-than-life portraits, to the ceiling lit by crystal chandeliers, to the marble floors lined with — yes — genuine hand-woven rugs. Mila added each item to a running ledger in her mind, then multiplied by the estimated size of the building — at least four stories high plus a basement and filling the entire city block — and came to a total somewhere between tech-CEO-rich and oil-magnate-rich.

And yet, it was completely deserted. Not a single soul, canine or feline, could be seen or heard.

The door she still stood inside was tucked into an alcove, next to an open coat closet, a pile of towels, and a heat lamp. They were clearly anticipating someone in Mila's state showing up. And the door hadn't been locked. She put on her best I-have-to-talk-to-a-VIP-and-not-get-fired voice and said, "My name is Mila Collins. I am terribly sorry for intruding. I was just hoping to wait out the storm."

The empty hallway did not respond.

"I'll just dry myself off so I don't drip on your floor," the calico said as she reached out for the towels, but she found them frustratingly out of reach. If she stepped away from the door, she would give up her last pretense that she was not actually trespassing but only standing in the entrance. Her arm flailed and her claws snatched at the air, a mere inch from the towels. But it was no good.

The calico sighed, told herself she would make her deepest most humble apology ever to the owners, and stepped away from the door.

It swung shut behind her, the sound of the storm outside disappearing as it latched shut. The calico frantically tried the handle but now it would not budge. "Fuck," she said under her breath, and wondered if she was being pranked: doors shutting just as you stepped through was nothing more than a trope from bad horror movies. Wasn't it?

Mila rested her head against the door in frustration. She realized, after a second, that she was dripping mud and rainwater onto a beautiful rug that cost more than her yearly salary, and she tore off her jacket, throwing it in the coat closet. The heat lamp was already on and the towels were laid out for someone to use, so she reasoned there would be nothing wrong with *her* being the one to use them, but that might have just been the cold making her shiver so hard that she had trouble thinking properly.

The calico dried off as much of her fur that wasn't covered by her shirt and jeans as she could with the towels. She wrapped one of them around the base of her tail and pulled it out towards the tip, wringing water out like a sponge. The sensation made her claws prick out. There wasn't much she could do about her clothes without stripping naked in an absurdly rich stranger's home, so she just dabbed at her shirt and pants with yet another towel to draw out the moisture. After that and standing under the heat lamp for a while, she was almost feeling like herself again. It left her fur standing out in clumps though, and with no brush at hand, she discreetly groomed her pelt down with her tongue.

When she finished, she noticed a basket of dirty towels that she swore hadn't been there a moment before, but assumed it was her mind playing tricks on her. (She also had imagined a thumping sound, as if someone was placing it there.) She told herself that houses did not appear out of nowhere, doors did not lock themselves behind people, and baskets did not reveal themselves just when you needed them.

Mila reached back and tried the handle on the door just to be sure. Still locked. Still unmoving.

The calico plopped herself down into a seat next to the stack of dry towels, took a deep breath, and tried to encourage her hackles to relax. She was reasonably sure she could deal with the owners without too much embarrassment: in Mila's experience, the obscenely rich would tolerate almost anything if you smiled a lot and made it clear that you understood you were not on their level. But there was still a chance things could go wrong.

The old anxieties began to creep back in and Mila slipped a hand into her coat pocket to check that the hyacinth flowers were undamaged. They were fine. Her other hand had instinctively reached into a different pocket and brought out her phone. She had been halfway to making a call, when she noticed she was getting absolutely no reception. Then she remembered that the number she had been starting to dial would never be picked up, and—

From the silence, a high peal of laughter interrupted her quickly degenerating train of thought. Mila's ears flicked to the sound before her head whirled around. Yes, there was definitely some noise there, distant and muffled, coming from a cracked door at the far end of the building. The cat slipped off her muddy shoes and started to creep her way along the hallway on the pads of her feet: she felt like she ought to explain her presence to the owners, but at the same time felt an urge to remain, at the very least, unobtrusive.

As the calico drew nearer, the sound grew from spots of laughter to encompass the full panoply of a very elegant cocktail party: the clink of glasses, the clatter of silverware, the indistinct conversations, and even the soft notes of a piano like the one she had heard on first opening the door. They were playing Debussy, perhaps, or Chopin. The knowledge that there were more people here in this house made her feel better; she wasn't intruding on a single person who expected privacy.

Mila stopped just beside the door and composed herself before she met anyone. She tried to put out of her mind the knowledge that she was still wearing wet clothes, her fur was an absolute mess, and she was walking around without any shoes on; instead, she focused on exuding a conciliatory aura. Whenever she'd needed to bother her boss — or worse, her boss's boss — about anything at work, she adopted the same demeanor: she made it clear that she knew she was being an inconvenience and she was working her hardest to not be one, but it would help her so much if they could just do this tiny little thing that would only take a moment. She stowed away any thoughts of resentment or concern to be dealt with later. So she put on a pleasant express and kept her ears low and deferential as she crept towards the door.

The calico froze when she saw what lay beyond.

At first glance the party beyond the door looked like any other big-city high-society shindig, except that it skewed a little younger. More of the participants were closer to Mila's age in their 30's than were in their 60's. The mix of species was a standard cross-section of urban America: more house cats than lynxes and more wolves than jackals, but Mila still caught the bright pelt pattern of a clouded leopard and the rusty reds of a dhole.

At second glance, it was without a doubt the kinkiest cocktail party she had ever seen.

There was a clear demarcation between the guests and the servants in the expansive ballroom beyond the door. The guests were canines (without exception), dressed in the finest of clothes (without exception), and male (with a few exceptions). The servants were felines (without exception), dressed only in a collar and corset (without exception), and female (with a few exceptions). As she watched, a caracal passed in front of the door, holding out a serving tray just beneath her naked breasts. A wolf selected an hors d'oeuvre and after snacking on it, took a moment to fondle the caracal, who purred so hard that the tray trembled in her grasp.

In a corner, four canines were seated around a table, smoking cigars and swirling drinks as a leopard and cheetah performed an intricate duo lap dance that had them moving from male to male, until one of the watchers grew so randy that he bent the leopard over the table and fucked her right there, to the cheers of his companions and a look of jealousy from the cheetah.

A Bengal cat lay on her back on a table next to the drinks bar. Guests rested filled cups of coffee on her belly, while they added cream or sugar. Though they were placed on insulated saucers, Mila could see the Bengal writhe from the temperature shift, espe cially when a coyote placed his glass of ice water between her thighs, practically nestling it against her sex.

The pianist was a gorgeous lioness who was shifting oddly along the bench as she played. It was only when she leaned over to hit a low note that Mila caught a glimpse of the dildo that had been affixed to the bench and was deep inside the lioness. No, the two dildos on the bench...

The calico tore her gaze from the party and backed away. Part of her wanted to know more. She wanted to ask why corsets were the outfit of choice, even on the few male felines she had seen. She really wanted to tap the Bengal on the shoulder and ask her what being used as a coffee table was like. But a far more sensible part of her was filled with terror at the thought of being discovered. Wandering uninvited into such a sensual party may be worse than intruding on someone in the bedroom, and people this rich could do a lot worse than get her arrested for trespassing. She shuffled as quietly and quickly as she could back towards the door she came in through, determined to get back out even if it meant wrenching the handle off.

Halfway there, she heard quick footsteps and a shout from above. Fear throttled her mind and she ducked to the side, into a stairwell that led down to the basement. Two sets of footsteps filtered down to Mila's ears: one strong and purposeful, and the other meek and quiet. But they both grew consistently louder and Mila slipped down the stairs backwards, attention fixated on the entrance to the stairwell.

A moment later it was filled with the outline of two figures.

Mila cursed under her breath but was grateful that the basement was so poorly lit relative to the hallway above that there was no way she could have been seen. She darted deeper into the basement in search of a hiding spot.

It did not surprise her at all, given what she had seen above, that the basement was a dungeon. It was all one massive chamber, stretching the length and breadth of the block, loosely divided into differently themed play spaces. Japanese paper panels partitioned off a room covered in tatami mats with a dozen bundles of rope waiting along one wall. Beyond that, a bead curtain surrounded a circle of bean bag chairs and a hookah, while the floor was littered with 60's fetish magazines. Beyond that, a rusty iron jail door protected a medieval stockade. Every few feet, there was something new. What little light there was came from dim floor sconces or from a fire whose smoke disappeared mysteriously into the ceiling.

Mila had no time to contemplate the various bondage devices and sex toys that littered the dungeon. She heard the footsteps coming down the stairs and needed a hiding place immediately. She dove past a curtain of heavy metal chains and found herself in a room that vaguely resembled a blacksmith's forge — or at least a Hollywood rendition of one — and found a shadowy alcove formed by a wooden partition that looked just big enough for her to stand in.

The footsteps drew nearer and Mila squeezed herself into the alcove, brushing against unused benches and chairs that had been stored there.

Mila closed her eyes and told herself it would be okay. Her chest heaved with quick, deep breaths, but the sound of footsteps began to recede. As she hid in the darkness and waited, the gnawing loneliness inside her, which had quieted during her initial exploration of the house, started to return. A hand crept into her coat pocket and touched the petals of the flower hidden there, trying to draw comfort from them.

The rattle of the nearby chains made her go as still as she could. But the calico didn't hear an exclamation of discovery. Instead, she heard the sound of lips meeting lips, a chuckle of lustful laughter, a rattle of metal, and then a moan of such need that even the nervous calico found herself squirming to listen in. Then there was a deep silken voice saying, "Don't be nervous."

Mila's heart steadied and her eyes cracked open.

Immediately in front of her was a black cat bound spread-eagled by the ubiquitous chains in the middle of the room. She wore the collar and corset like all the other felines did here, but she also had on a mask of some type: Mila couldn't see the details as the cat was turned away, but she guessed it was a masquerade mask, because it was surrounded by a wreath of feathers that fell over the top of the feline's head in bright iridescent whites. Similar feathers were braided into the fur of her tail, her tail which was the only part of her not chained and which was caressing up between her own legs to draw fur and feathers along her sex.

"Ah, ah, ah," tutted the voice. "Hold your tail up."

The cat in chains whined but brought her tail up to rest against her back. With some surprise, Mila noticed her own tail had taken up a similar position without her even intending it to. The voice had just been so clear and authoritative. It was so easy to do what it wanted.

The bearer of the voice walked into Mila's line of view, standing in front of the black cat. He was a tall German shepherd so muscular and well-built he looked like a football linebacker. He dwarfed the cat, who only came up to his chest, and like the canines above, he wore an expertly tailored suit that had Mila again boggling at the price tag. The watch on his wrist was an Armin Strom; Mila was sure it alone cost at least thirty thousand.

In one hand the dog held a riding crop, which he tapped against his open palm. Mila marveled at how good a view her place afforded, until she realized that a place as kinky as this would no doubt have spots to indulge in voyeurism and she had stumbled right into one.

"Such a needy girl," the dog crooned. "You are so impatient."

Mila knew in her heart of hearts that the dog wasn't talking to her, but she still felt like he was, like he was chastising her the way her teachers had once upon a time. She squirmed in place at the chafing injustice of it, just as the black cat in front of her was.

The dog brought his crop down on his own leg with a quick, loud snap that brought the attention of both cats back to him. He reached out and gripped the black cat's scruff tightly. "You will learn patience," he said.

He pulled the cat forward into a deep kiss. Mila realized that his eyes were tightly shut and she began to stir, wondering if she could make a run for the door, when the dog's eyes slid open, looking straight at her.

The shadows had to be too deep; he couldn't possibly see her. But maybe the dim light from the room was reflecting in her eyes. She stayed stock still, hoping he would think it was just a glint of metal from some stored bondage device.

The dog was making no move and while he was looking hard in her direction, Mila was certain he wasn't looking directly at her. Perhaps he knew she was there or perhaps he was deep in thought.

The dog's reverie was stopped by the black cat, who let out a plaintive whine, with a soft "Please" on her lips after the kiss was broken.

"Patience," the dog whispered back. He took a sauntering step backwards to build some distance between them, and then he one-handedly undid his fly and pulled out his erect cock. "This is what you're craving, I know." He said it as a simple statement of fact, not a question. He knew what she wanted, and he knew he was right.

In her more experimental college days, Mila had bought a canine-modeled dildo online. She'd marveled at the gently tapered tip and the hefty knot at the base. Unfortunately, the toy, much like the dog in front of her now, had been far too large and she had been unable to use it for much other than fantasies before throwing it away a month later in embarrassment. Despite its size, Mila still felt an urge to step out from the shadows and stroke him: she wanted to hold that shaft in her hands and run her pads along it, feel its heat and the pulse of the dog's heart through his skin. Burning hot lust rose unbidden in the calico, but she swallowed back the strange, conflicting desires and stayed hidden.

The black cat was having an even harder time controlling herself. Her hips swayed needily in the air and she bit her lip to unsuccessfully hold back a moan.

"Just one problem," the dog said with a wide smile. "It's too big for you."

"I can take it."

"You want to take it. Not the same thing. I think you could take it, with time and practice and..." He let the syllable hang on the air as he swayed the riding crop back and forth like a metronome as if marking the passage of time. "And patience."

The dog extended a hand to caress a sensual path down the black cat's body, starting from her cheek and winding with deliberate slowness around one breast, then the other, then the first again, before continuing between the cat's thighs. Mila was afforded a perfect view by the cat's lifted tail and spread legs and could see the dog delicately roll the dull side of a claw along her lips as though polishing it with her dew. The perspective also showed off just what a significant size difference there was between the two of them: the dog's massive hand appeared about the same size as the cat's petite hips. As he started to wriggle his finger past her labia and ease into her, the cat mewled in delight, which turned into a shuddering gasp as the palm of his hand started to grind against her clit. Whether from prior overstimulation or natural sensitivity, Mila did not know, but the black cat went up on tip-toes to try and reduce the sensations.

The German shepherd's voice dropped to husky whisper. "You are clenching so hard," he teased. "So tight around just one finger. How am I ever going to fit a second finger in?"

"I can do it," the cat pleaded while Mila watched her body dance and writhe in its bonds from even the slightest movement in the dog's hand.

A part of Mila silently wished the dog would discover her and that he'd fuck her instead of the black cat. She'd be able to take that cock, no problem. Except, she wasn't that much larger than the other cat. She'd still struggle to fit it in. But she wanted it more than the black cat, she knew. She craved it. All she had to do was be patient.

The calico took a sharp breath and shook her head. Where

was this urge coming from all of a sudden? She had to get out of here.

Mila watched as the dog swiped a single finger back and forth over the black cat's labia, edged it aside, and began to push in to join the first finger deep inside her sex. It was slow going. The black cat jumped and grunted whenever the thick digit moved, and then the dog would freeze. His free hand, with crop hanging from a cord about his wrist, stroked up and down her spine while he praised her and offered gentle encouragement. "That's it. You can do it. I know you can. Just relax. We won't go any further until you are ready. But I will get a third finger in you."

The black cat's breathing slowed as she grew more accustomed to the girth inside of her. Mila watched the dog lower his head to lick lovingly along her breasts while she focused on not squeezing her thighs together too much. It wasn't just that it was sexy — it certainly was — but there was also a tenderness in the way he held her, something that Mila herself hadn't experienced in far too long, ever since....

The ground began to quiver beneath Mila's feet, shaking like a particularly heavy truck was driving past. But it kept growing stronger, until Mila was clutching at the walls of her hiding place to steady herself, and items clattered to the floor elsewhere in the basement.

The earthquake abated as quickly as it had arrived. The dog had shielded the cat's body with his own as the building shook, and now that there seemed to be a break, he withdrew his fingers as quickly as he could, undid her bonds, and suggested they return to the main party. Fucking could wait.

Mila remained in her hiding place until she was sure the pair were up the stairs and out of the hallway. Then she darted out and ran for the exit, not caring about the dampness she felt between her thighs. Thankfully there was still no one around, and the couple she had seen in the dungeon were long gone.

But the door she had come through would still not open. There was no sign of a lock, nothing other than the handle itself, which didn't budge. Even when she tried putting her entire weight onto the handle, it refused to move.

Frustration boiled up and was let out in a bare-fanged hiss. She glared at the door like it was deliberately thwarting her.

She turned around to search for another exit, and walked straight into a fox who was standing there.

Fantaisie

Shocked at being discovered so unexpectedly, Mila took a quick step back.

The fox regarded her cautiously and leaned forward on a cane to inspect her closely. He had a mix of black and red fur with a fetching bit of gray starting in around his muzzle and disappearing down his throat. Unlike the dog in the dungeon, he had no excess muscle, but like the dog, he was wearing in an impeccably tailored suit. "Why aren't you dressed?" he asked, with an even stronger aura of natural authority than the dog had.

The question made so little sense to the fully clothed calico that it bounced right off Mila's mind without making much impression. She gathered her wits and slipped back into don't-get-fired mode. "I'm sorry," she said with a small bow of her head. "I think there's been a mistake. I just came in here to get out of the rain. I didn't mean to intrude on your... event"—she silently cursed herself for fumbling even slightly—" but the door locked behind me and I can't get back out."

The fox expressed his surprise in a subtle tightening of his brow and a tighter grip on his cane. "This door?"

"That's right."

"You're sure it was this door, not the front door?"

"I'm positive. I didn't even know there was a front door."

The fox pushed her aside with the cane and tried the handle. It remained unmoving. The tightness of his brow only increased.

"Just let me out. I didn't mean to cause any trouble."

"I can't let you out. The house won't let you leave."

The house wouldn't let her leave? No. This was getting too crazy. She grabbed her coat from the closet and, uncaring that it was still quite wet, began to pull it over her shoulders. "Take me to the front door then. I'll leave that way. I was just on my way to..." Her hand slipped into the coat pocket and retrieved the hyacinth flower that she had been sheltering inside the jacket, protecting from the rain.

The instant her eyes locked onto the delicate petals, the ground shuddered beneath her as another earthquake hit, more sudden and fierce than the last. Mila yelped and pitched forward against the fox, who caught her, but in the process she lost her grip on the flower which dropped to the floor.

What happened next should not have been possible. The flower landed on a groove in the marble floor, and that groove split and widened as though the rock were molten. It became a trench, a crevasse, and swallowed the flower inside it.

Mila reached out, but the marble had already sealed shut again.

"Forget the flower!" the fox said sharply.

The house stopped shaking. The floor was perfectly normal. Mila looked up quizzically at the fox. "What flower?"

The fox sighed in momentary relief, then gripped her shoulder tightly. "Listen to me. Listen to me very closely. You have stumbled into the Eternal Party. This place is magical. It will force you to obey any command given to you by a canine. Do you understand?"

Mila tried to pull her arm away but the fox held tight. She shook her head.

He growled out of the side of his muzzle. "Tell me a secret you would normally never tell a stranger."

"I lost my virginity at nineteen to a one-night stand I've always regretted." Mila's hand flew to her muzzle. "Why did I say that?"

"Because the house forces you to obey," the fox repeated. He leaned in closer and his grip tightened. "This place is dangerous. I can protect you, but you have to say that you are mine."

The calico stared at him. He sounded different. Gone was the sharp piercing authority, but he was just as earnest. "I am yours?"

He shook his head. "You have to say it and mean it. I can't force you on this. It has to be your choice." His ears flicked back as he heard someone approaching down the hall. The fox tugged her into the side of the alcove, where a pillar obstructed anyone's view of her. "Stay here and moan like you are being groped and loving it."

A groan of desire lifted from Mila's throat as the fox pressed in close, hiding much of her with his body and holding his arms in a way that suggested he was fondling her, but without actually doing so. Mila couldn't stop herself, and she tried. She could modulate the pitch of her moans, but she still had to moan. Somehow she knew he was right; she was being forced to obey.

The footsteps approached, slowed, and then turned off to walk in a different direction. Perhaps whoever it had been thought better of interrupting a private tryst.

"You can stop," the fox said, and immediately the moans died in Mila's throat. "Do you understand now? Will you say that you are mine?"

Mila shuddered. She had been completely helpless. And somehow she knew that this strange power extended far further than that. He could make her do anything, couldn't he?

Her heart started to hammer away in her chest, but true panic was kept away by one thought: he could already have made her do anything he wanted, and yet he hadn't. He said he wanted to protect her.

"I am yours, sir," she said, not even realizing she had added the honorific until it had slipped out of her. As soon as she said it, it felt so right, so natural. He was her owner, and she belonged to him.

The fox relaxed for only a moment before his ears shot up.

"Alonso!" a voice called out from across the hallway.

"Quick," the fox said. "Strip naked and toss your clothes away. You no longer feel any shame about being naked around me, but you will still be shy in front of others here, to the point you will have trouble speaking to them."

Mila wanted to protest. Shy? She'd never been shy: she'd always been outgoing and eager to meet new people, but now the thought of meeting more strangers here in this weird place filled her with fear. She wished she could just stay with her owner, that surprisingly handsome fox, and never need to worry about anyone else. Still, he had ordered her and she was his. She quickly peeled off her clothes to please him, noting as she did how sticky her panties were and how they clung to her fur. That only increased her sense of shame, and she hoped no one else noticed how excited she had gotten.

No sooner had she thrown her clothes into the shadows of the entry than three other canines came around a corner: a jackal in a midnight black halter neck dress, and a wolf and a collie in matching three-piece suits. Mila silently hid herself behind the fox.

"What's this?" boomed an approaching wolf. "Did we get a new cat in? I didn't hear any announcement."

"No announcement," the fox said calmly, keeping one firm hand around the calico hiding behind him and the other on his cane. "I think the house was wanting to have her as a surprise for me. I've already claimed her."

The wolf chuckled and nudged the fox with his elbow. "Alonso, you sly fox you. After all these years, you finally picked a cat just for yourself." He glanced to Mila and gave her a quick visual inspection before she could reposition to hide herself from his gaze. "She's a bit... bedraggled."

"There's a storm outside. She got caught without an umbrella."

Mila was mortified by how unkempt her fur was, but at least the wolf was commenting about that and not about her nakedness.

The jackal woman from the trio gave the fox a look of such intense skepticism that Mila felt she already knew everything that had happened. "I'm sure Alonso will introduce her to us all once he's broken her in," she said in a formal British accent that wouldn't have been out of place on the BBC. "Go on and rejoin the party, Miles. I'll be with you in a bit."

The wolf snuck a kiss to the jackal's muzzle and then marched down the hall, laughing arm in arm with the collie.

The jackal snapped her head around as soon as the wolf was out of sight, going from smiling to serious in an instant. "You, cat, did you come in through the side door? Did you cause the housequake?"

"I-I-I..." Mila shivered. Her tongue twisted on itself and her lips refused to move. She'd never had such trouble speaking before, but every time she tried to say something, she imagined the intense gaze of the jackal on her and everything died in her throat.

The fox placed a comforting hand on her shoulder. "She came through the side door," Alonso confirmed. "You'll have to excuse her, Aisha. I made her shy."

"Good thinking," the jackal said, with a note of surprise in her voice as if this was unexpected behavior from the fox. "But we should get her out of the public eye quickly. Your room?"

The fox nodded.

"Follow us," the jackal commanded, speaking directly to Mila. "Keep your head down and do not obey or acknowledge any other canines besides us until you are in Alonso's room."

"You're coming with?" the fox asked.

The jackal rolled her eyes. "She needs things explained to her and you are bad at explaining things." She took a step towards the stairs, glancing over her shoulder to say, "Come along."

The fox and jackal walked out in front, with the calico staying one step behind her new owner. Her *owner*, that still felt so strange and so right at the same time. They made their way up to the second floor via the stairs. Here the marble and crystal decor of the first floor gave way to plush carpeting and lacquered wood, with doors set into the walls at regular intervals. It reminded Mila of a hotel, a five-star luxury hotel like she saw in movies, but it did not seem bound to the size of the city block it was nestled on, because they walked for what felt like minutes. They would occasionally cross paths with other canines or felines, but any questions about "the new cat" were deftly turned aside by the fox or jackal as Mila hid behind Alonso. Not wanting to even meet a stranger's eye, Mila kept her attention fixed in front of her, on the slowly swaying red tail of the fox and the agitated swish of the jackal's black-striped tail. Occasionally they would encounter a couple sneaking a kiss or something more in a shadowy part of the hallway, and they simply opted to give them a wide berth.

Whenever they were out of earshot of anyone else, the jackal spoke in hushed tones. "The enchantment that created this place has two governing rules," she said. "The first is simple: canines command and felines obey. If a canine commands you, you must do as they say. If a canine asks you a question, you must answer. If a canine tells you something is true, it is true for you. In addition to being unable to keep secrets, this means any aspect of your personality or your memory can be adjusted, deleted, or overwritten, at least temporarily."

Mila shivered and thought of how Alonso had forced her to be shy. She tried to push past that and ask the jackal a question, but couldn't manage it, so she directed the question to Alonso instead. "Sir, what's the second rule?"

"The second governing rule," the jackal went on, "is that only those who want to attend the Eternal Party can enter here. This place affords an incredible amount of power over any feline who enters, so the only felines who can enter are those who are so naturally submissive they enjoy that power being used on them. Similarly, the only canines who can enter are those who are domineering enough to make use of that power. Except for reasons unknown to us, sometimes that rule is broken, and people who have no interest in the Eternal Party can enter and become trapped here."

Mila glanced up to see the jackal's penetrating gaze fixed on her and she looked away again quickly.

The conversation lapsed into silence as they passed a group of canines traveling the opposite direction. Although Mila kept her head down, her ears flicked up and tracked the group, catching a fragment of what they were discussing: "—got to try having that cat spanked while she sucks you off. I'm telling you, her throat goes crazy whenever anyone plays with—"

As soon as they were gone, the jackal slid in beside Mila and held her hand. "We will do what we can to help you. That's why Alonso laid claim to you: his ownership weakens the ability of any other canine to command or change you. If I tried to drastically change your personality, the order would not be obeyed, because Alonso would not want that change made. That doesn't mean you can ignore orders completely, but you have a lot more power to resist them. Do you understand?"

Mila nodded. They made a turn somewhere in the twisting hallways of the second floor and Mila was now utterly lost. Thankfully after a few more steps, the trio came to a halt in front of a door with a nameplate on it that read out "A. Hodgson" in swirling embossed script.

"As to why side-door guests like yourself become trapped here at the party, I could not say, but I would wager it has something to do with the quakes that just happened. What were you doing when—"

"No." The fox interposed himself between jackal and calico. "That's enough for now."

The jackal rounded on the fox sharply, irritation etched on her features. Mila guessed she was unused to being told no.

The fox, however, was unmoved. He held up his hands in a placating gesture, his cane dangling in the crook of his thumb. "She's gone through enough for one night, Aisha, and she has a lot ahead of her. She can't leave the house. You can interrogate her more on the subject later."

"Very well," the jackal said. She glanced at the room door. "I'll leave you to it and head back to the library."

"At this hour?"

"We just had the first side-door visitor in a decade, Alonso. I need to research." She bobbed her head to the fox once as a goodbye and repeated a similar, but smaller, motion to Mila, before leaving down a separate path.

Alonso waited for the jackal to vanish from view, then placed a hand on the door. "Welcome to my home," he said before taking Mila in.

Immediately Mila was reminded that they were still deep in the inner city. Wide windows let in the harsh nighttime lights of the street that contrasted with the warm tones she had experienced in the house. The room itself confirmed her earlier impression of a luxury hotel. They were standing in the most sumptuous suite Mila had ever set foot in. On one side of the room was a bed, a massive four-poster with velvet curtains. It was beyond king size. Four people could have slept comfortably on it — or enjoyed an orgy on it, more likely — with room to spare. On the other side of the room was a living area, with a couch, armchair, and coffee table arranged before a fireplace with a television above. Personal touches came in the form of small risqué portraits that occupied spots on the wall or on a single bookcase.

The space in between bed and living area contained a concise collection of bondage implements and toys strewn about. Alonso immediately made his way to them, tucking away the toys into a trunk and folding the furniture into more discreet forms. Mila marveled as a St. Andrew's cross became an end table and a bondage horse became an ottoman. The only item that could not be repurposed was a low cage, which he shoved under the bed before getting shakily to his feet, his ears low. "Sorry," Alonso said, gesturing to the now almost respectable room.

Alonso bashfully looked away, a hand on the back of his neck. Mila rocked on her heels as a million questions vied to be the first one out of her mouth. She plucked up the courage to gesture to where the cage had been hastily hidden. "I'm not going to have to sleep in that, am I?"

"Only if you want to," the fox said and shrugged off his jacket. He still kept his gaze averted from her.

Mila took a step towards the windows.

"They don't open," Alonso said, as if reading her thoughts. He pointed the tip of his cane towards a door next to the fireplace. "You can get cleaned up, if you like."

Mila opened the door to find a sumptuous bathroom with a large shower that could easily fit three people inside with ease. There were also, she noted, some waterproof handcuffs attached to one wall of the shower. At the sink, the calico selected an appropriate comb for her fur length, and began to make herself look decent for the first time since she had left her apartment that evening. Mila worked with deliberate slowness: after all that had happened, she needed a moment to regain her wits. The mortification of being naked among so many strangers was pulled away one brushstroke at a time.

Mila relaxed, but her mind still whirled. She thought of the many rooms she had rushed past in dungeon below. She thought of the Bengal in the ballroom. She thought of the cuffs dangling in the shower not six feet away. She thought about what her owner would like. A dampness returned to her inner thighs that had nothing to do with the rain outside.

When she exited the bathroom a few minutes later, Alonso was sitting on the edge of the bed, tie off and cuffs unbuttoned. The fox offered her a gentle smile and a wag of his tail but said nothing. So Mila explored the rest of the suite. She browsed the

selections on his bookcase and found a good deal of classical litera-
ture in dog-eared, spine-creased books. The portraits that artisti-
cally cluttered the shelves next to the books were all of female
felines wearing the same collar and corset as those in the ballroom.
Behind the bed, Mila found a large walk-in closet that held dozens
of formal outfits, a few informal outfits, and a compact stockade
in the center of the floor. It would have held someone's head at
the height of Alonso's hips, she was sure.

She stepped out, feeling dazed, and collapsed still completely
naked on one of the couches. There was a soft tapping of the cane
on the floor as Alonso moved to sit in the arm chair next to her.
Kindly eyes looked into her own. "Is there anything you need? I
could get you something to eat."

"I need to be fucked, sir," Mila blurted out, and was surprised
by it. But it was true. Even over wanting to get out of this weird
place, she really, desperately, carnally needed a good fuck. She
wrapped her arms around herself tightly. "When I was down in
the dungeon, I was hiding from a couple down there. I don't
think they knew I was there, but the dog's words... may have had
some effect on me."

"That's quite possible." Alonso reached out and snapped his
fingers to command her complete attention. "You are free from
any arousal caused by a canine's suggestion. Is that better?"

Mila shifted on the couch, considering for a moment. "No,
I'm still really horny." The impact of her words hit her a half-
second later and she sat bolt upright. "Wait a second, I *am* still
horny." Mila's eyes were wide and, for a moment, she forgot about
the other person in a room as her hand slipped between her legs
and ran her pawpads softly against her folds. A tremor ran along
her arm and she slid a finger between her labia and against her
entrance. She wanted to keep going. She really, really wanted to
keep going.

So she laughed.

She laughed and laughed, hard, almost breathless laughter,
and she even had to wipe away a tear at one point. She only

stopped when she felt the fox's hand on her shoulder and remembered where she was and who she was with. Her knees snapped together to hide herself and her ears went flat across her head. "Sorry, sir," she said quietly. "It's just that I haven't been honestly horny in a long time. It must have been since..."

There was a warning rumble of the house beneath her feet.

"It's been months at least," she said, quickly diverting the topic away. "I thought something was broken. It's just a relief to know that everything still works, and that I can still want to be bent over and pounded hard. Damn it." She fidgeted in place, trying to give her body something to do so her mouth didn't continue having a mind of its own. "I can't believe I'm talking about this in front of a total stranger, while I'm lying naked on his couch. Sorry, sir. Even though I know I belong to you, I don't know anything about you."

"It's the house. It makes you want to be honest and open with me," Alonso said with a bitter note in his voice. He forced himself to smile and held out his hand to shake. "Alonso Hodgson. My father was a high school English teacher and insisted on naming me and all my siblings after famous literary characters."

Mila shook the hand. "Alonso is a literary name?"

"Alonso Quijano, better known as Don Quixote de La Mancha."

"Haven't read it, sir," Mila said, looking away in embarrassment.

"Nor have I, even though my father tried everything short of threatening me to get me to." He smiled and went on, ticking off facts about his life like were reading from a presentation. "I grew up in a large family, middle child so mostly ignored. I was a good student, but not exceptional. I considered military service, because I wanted to fly a plane, but instead ended up as a commercial pilot for many years, mostly working international routes. And then I found my way here." He crossed one leg over the other and leaned forward. "I don't know anything about you either, not even your name."

"I'm Mila, sir." She didn't mention her last name. She had a suspicion that if she thought too hard about it, the house would begin to shake again, and as if to confirm her thoughts, there was a little shiver in the floorboards under her feet. "Besides that, not much to tell. I grew up in the city. Supported myself going to college through odd jobs, but I'm doing well right now — or at least I was before I got trapped here — because I work in finance." She shivered on the couch, still aware of her nudity and arousal. She curled a tail between her legs to press against her mound.

Alonso noticed. "If you would prefer, I could remove your arousal."

"No!" Mila surprised herself with the strength of her denial. "I'm liking it. It's just... you know... this place and you and all of this. I don't know how it works. I don't know what I'm feeling. I don't know how to feel about how this place works. An hour ago I could not have imagined a place like this even existing. Everything is so strange."

"It's a lot to take in, but perhaps this will help." The fox reached out and rested a hand on the calico's forehead. "Your stress and anxiety is fading away."

It was as though there was a knot in her stomach and Alonso's words tugged it until it straightened out. She relaxed. "Thank you, sir." She found herself squirming a little more on the couch. Without the stress in the way, the need was only hitting her harder. She fiddled with her hands over her belly, resisting the urge to finger herself. Even if she was naked next to a (near) stranger, she wanted to preserve a little dignity.

The fox tapped a finger on his cane. "I'm surprised you haven't asked me yet."

"Asked you, sir?"

"To fuck you."

"Oh, um..." New anxieties appeared. She sat up straight, feeling like she'd made a terrible faux pas. He was her owner after all. "It's not that you aren't attractive, sir. And it's not that the idea doesn't have some appeal..."

"But you're still overwhelmed."

Mila nodded.

"I fully understand. Perhaps in that case, I will ask you some questions to gauge your comfort. Would that be all right?"

Mila squeezed her thighs together and tried to put some more insidiously needy thoughts — like how well-endowed Alonso was, or if he would mind if she finger-fucked herself senseless, or how that stockade in the closet might be used — out of her mind. "Okay." Then she tried to push back against the submissiveness she was feeling. "But I can ask you the same questions in return."

"That's fair." The fox sat back and laid his cane across his knees. "You said you saw the dungeons below, and you didn't run away screaming, so I'm guessing you are at least aware of kink. And you already told me you are not a virgin — sorry for prying into your privacy on that one. Would you consider yourself interested in sex generally?"

Mila laughed. It seemed like such a silly question. "Yes, sir. You?"

"Of course. Are you straight?"

"Mostly, sir. I'm not attracted to all women, but for the right one... Someone like Jeta Horowitz maybe," she said, mentioning the bombshell action actress.

The fox nodded knowingly. "There are very few people alive who could resist Jeta Horowitz. Would you—"

"Wait, I get to ask you questions too, remember? Are you straight?"

"Yes. Now, would say you are experienced sexually?"

"In what sense?"

"Let's say number of partners."

"About ten. What about you?"

"Prior to arriving here, only three. Since then, dozens, possibly hundreds by this point. But with your partners, did you have sex often?"

"Yes," she said with a nod.

Mila intended to add a question of her own, but Alonso

started to shoot off questions in rapid succession. "Have you ever given head?"

"A few times."

"Ever received?"

"A few times," she repeated.

"Anal?"

"No, sir."

"Bondage?"

"No, sir." She was compelled to answer, but she held up her hands to ward off more questions. "There were a lot of things I'd wondered about trying, but I just never found the time. I don't have that kind of experience."

The fox drew a claw along one of his whiskers thoughtfully. "Would you consider yourself submissive?"

Mila's mind flicked back to the party she had seen earlier in the grand hall below them. Certainly, the position several of the other felines had been in felt enticing, but she also thought of the other servants she had witnessed demurely serving drinks or letting themselves be used as footstools. "I don't think so," she said, "but I also don't know if I understand all that that entails."

He nodded and his stroking claw continued its progress back and forth along his whisker unabated. "Would you be interested in trying some of those things, now that you are here?"

"There are a lot of things I'd be willing to try right now if it meant getting a dick in me." She tried to secret a hand in between her thighs to rub gently against her sex. "Am I going to keep blurting out how horny I am?"

"Quite likely. You are now stuck in a magic house designed to perpetuate a never-ending kink party. Ignoring your current arousal, would you be interested in experimenting?"

"With the right person, slowly, carefully, yes."

The fox's tail wiggled so the tip brushed against the coffee table. "And what do you think of me?"

"I am so, so grateful for a voice of sanity on a crazy night, sir."

"Thank you, but I meant what do you think of me physically."

"I think you're probably not as well hung as the German shepherd from the dungeon."

He chuckled and shook his head. "It's good that you are already realizing that you can tweak the intention of the orders you are given and the questions you are asked. But I am not letting this go until I get a direct answer. I am your owner. You belong to me. We are almost certainly going to have sex, unless you are emphatically against the idea. What do you think of me as a potential partner, knowing in addition that this place gives me the power to rewrite your thoughts?"

It was like a barrier had been broken in her mind. He had asked her a direct question and she had to answer. It all came spilling out of her at once in a jumble. "You're handsome in a rugged sort of way, and I'm hoping that streak of silver extends farther south than just your muzzle. I would never have thought of you in a sexual way if we'd bumped into each other on the street, but then I haven't been thinking of anyone in a sexual way in so long. Now that I am, I'm hoping you'll push me onto my back and fuck me senseless and hold me close and tell me I'm beautiful while you explore every inch of my body with your hands and then whisper all the kinky things you're going to do to me because I feel like I can trust you and I feel like I can trust you because you had the chance to make me do whatever you want and you haven't so maybe that means you won't and fuck I think that dog from the dungeon made me impatient on top of everything else so now I want to try everything I never had a chance to before even though I'm a little scared you'll still turn me into some sort of mindless sex toy and is that enough, sir?" Mila took a deep breath and swallowed. She'd done that last bit in one go.

"Yes, that's enough. And before we go any farther, let me assure you I have no interest in turning you into some mindless sex toy or rewriting your personality on that level."

"Thank you, sir," Mila said with some relief. "So if you don't want a mindless sex toy, what are you hoping for in a partner?"

"I'd be satisfied with keeping you happy while you are here."

"Now who is avoiding the question?" The calico couldn't help but grin, her tailtip twitching.

Alonso chuckled and thumbed the head of his cane. "Fair point. Truth be told, I'm not used to explaining what I want. With the felines here, I just give commands. The other canines don't care what I want or do." He lapsed into thoughtful silence, as though the most pressing questions had already been asked.

But there was one more that Mila needed to ask. It was the most important one of all. "Uh, sir?" She found her throat going dry. Now that the time came to it, she was having trouble putting the question into words, shaping sounds around that secret fear. "Am I... Am I acceptable, sir?"

His expression fell; his whiskers drooped. "What do you mean, Mila?"

"Physically? Am I all right? Do you like the way I look?" She had to turn her head away, unable to face him in case the answer was no.

The hard tip of his cane touched her far cheek and pulled her back towards him. "Mila, you are far more than just acceptable. Perhaps you would like me to demonstrate just how acceptable I find you?" There was a predatory lust in his golden eyes and a gleam from a fang that shone through his smile.

Her concerns temporarily allayed, lust started to bubble up within her again. "O-okay, sir," she said. "Just go easy on me." Except she didn't really want him to go easy on her. She wanted to get Fucked with a capital F.

The fox reached out and caressed along her jaw. The soft intimate touch was delightful and she pressed into it. For a moment, nothing else happened, and Mila simply relished the moment of calm. "You're still feeling so shy, Mila," the fox said in a low voice. "You're unused to being naked in front of others. But as much as you are embarrassed, you love the feeling of me looking over your naked body. It makes you feel so good. You want to be on display for me."

As the words took hold, Mila's tail curled over her hips, hiding her sex, and an arm lifted up to hide her breasts. Her eyes squeezed shut. She couldn't believe herself. Sure, she was in a magic house, but that was no excuse for her being so casual with being naked in front of someone she had just met today. She shuddered and cracked open an eye.

Alonso still had his hand on the calico's jaw, stroking her, but his gaze was down, on her tail-covered sex.

Mila gasped quietly. She squeezed her thighs together and writhed on the spot. Her sex felt so hot and she could feel her juices dripping out onto her now sodden tail. Maybe it was okay to let him look.

Slowly, she began to move her tail aside. But first she had to unwind it from her leg, where it had coiled up tightly. With conscious effort, the tail began to relax and uncurl. Seconds ticked away as she delayed revealing herself until the last possible moment. And when her tail, sticky and wet, peeled away at last, the fox nodded and said, "Good kitten."

Then he continued. "You love being called that. It feels like a tingle of raw bliss being poured into your body and it is so hard not to just purr in response. Good kitten."

Mila wriggled on the couch and hard as she tried, she could not keep the purr down.

"Good kitten," he repeated.

Mila's eyes fluttered shut and she sighed in contentment.

"Now, are you going to show me your breasts too?"

Mila bit her lip. "Do I have to?" They were simple words, but they had to fight to be heard around the purr that seemed to be constant within her now. She could feel the fox's gaze locked on her chest.

"Don't you want to?" he asked.

She bit her lip harder, steeled herself, and then tore her arm away in a sudden motion to reveal them.

"Good kitten," he said.

Mila's hips swayed against the couch, grinding the bottom edge of her lips against the soft fabric there. He didn't even need to say the words to make her feel good, the feeling of him so focused on her breasts like they were the most precious things in the world was enough reward on its own.

"Good kitten," he said again.

His hand dropped from her jaw down to the curve of her neck and then from there to her waiting, expectant breasts. But he didn't grope or squeeze them, as she expected, but drew his claws along them from base out towards the nipple, to get her to push her chest forward, and then he pressed gently on the underside so she lifted them up. Then he did the same on the other breast, until her chest was at the perfect angle for him to ogle.

"Good kitten."

The purr was so loud now, Mila almost couldn't hear the fox's words. She just felt like she was drifting on a rolling tide of happiness.

"Show me just how aroused you are."

Mila obeyed without hesitation. She scooted her hips forward until they were almost on the edge of the couch. She leaned back and spread her sex wide in a V. A finger dipped just past her entrance and pulled back, showing off the drops of excitation that came with. His ears perked towards her and the attention he paid to her sex made her more needy than ever before. Her tailtip twitched in anticipation.

"You're ready to be fucked, aren't you?"

Mila nodded eagerly. In trying not to drop a hand between her thighs and finger herself deeply, she felt her claws extending and sheathing over and over again.

"Let's test your creativity, shall we?" the fox said half to himself. He rested a hand on Mila's hip. "You said there were lots of things you wanted to try but never had the time. Now is your time. Think of one, and if you truly want to experience it, then seduce me into trying it out on you."

The desire which called out to Mila was not the one she expected. Sure, she had seen many fascinating possibilities since entering this house, but the curiosity she felt latch onto her thoughts was a much older one. There was no question of whether she truly wanted to experience it or not. She was not going to let this opportunity pass by.

The calico let out a needy moan as her body undulated. She ran her tongue along her lips and stretched in a way only felines could, making sure that the motions showed off each part of her naked body to its fullest. At the same time her claws pushed out and her hackles went up

"Wait."

Mila froze in place, claws digging in to the couch. Even her mind seemed to lock up, unable to process anything as she waited for her owner.

"What part of that command is making you resist?"

"The seduction part," Mila answered simply, without any tone or emphasis. "I do not want to seduce you or anyone else. Never again. And please do not ask why, sir."

"I won't," he assured her. "Instead of seducing me, would you be comfortable...convincing me?"

"Yes, sir."

"Then I amend my previous orders. Do not seduce me. Continue from where you left off and simply convince me."

The new command clicked into place far better. The tension dissipated, the claws retracted, and the hackles lowered. The calico had no time to process how easily the fox had manipulated her because she was already sidling closer to the fox and inspecting him more intimately than she had at any point before. She noticed that there was now a sizable bulge tenting the front of his pressed pants. "Are you sure you actually need me to convince you of anything?" she said offhand, and then she reached out to rest a hand on his chest. She could feel the rise and fall of his breathing in tight compact loops. "May I?"

He rested a hand on her hip. She silently thrilled as his gaze once more slipped down over her form. "Go on, kitten."

She undid the top button and spread the shirt open just enough for her to lean in and nuzzle at the top of his collar bone. Her muzzle stayed nestled into his fur as she undid two more buttons to give herself more access. Mila leaned back and gave a small cheer of triumph: the silver along his muzzle did filter down to the black and red fur on his chest. He was turning out to be as handsome as she had hoped.

Despite the need churning within her, Mila continued working one step at a time, undoing every button and easing the shirt off so that it would not irritate the fox's fur. Once it was off, though, she tossed it aside without a second thought and wrapped her arms tight around Alonso. For a moment she just breathed and felt the warmth and presence of the fox so close to her, his coarse fur against her own silken fur. Underneath his kindly exterior, she could feel worry knotting his muscles. He felt like a spring coiled up and ready to release.

As she began to tug his belt open, she mused, "You said you had a lot of experience with sex, sir." Her tone modulated more formal, as though she were making a presentation to her boss and needed to convince him of something.

Alonso laughed a little. "I have spent many years at an ongoing kink-party-slash-orgy."

She tugged his belt out and let it drop to the floor before falling to her knees to get his socks and shoes off. "And what sort of experience do you like in your partners? Do you want them to be as experienced as you?" She let the question hang in the air as she got back to her feet, deliberately pressing forward to angle her breasts up to his view, thrilling at the way he was distracted by them. "Or do you prefer your kittens to be more... virginal?"

"Sometimes one, sometimes the other."

Mila took her place in his lap and started to undo his zipper and button, purposefully fumbling her actions so that she had more excuses to brush her fingers along the now throbbing erection trapped by his clothes. She heard him take a shuddering breath when she finally pulled his shaft free and she pulled away enough to look at her owner's cock for the first time. No, it wasn't as big as the German shepherd from the dungeon, but it was good for his size, and given how similar in shape the fox and calico were, she thought it would be a pleasantly sized shaft for her, although the knot would certainly never fit. She caressed his balls idly in one hand while tugging his pants off to leave him as naked as she was.

"Well, if experience is what you are looking for, you could slide this right into my sex." She cringed internally at the terminology, but her mindset was still that of a business presentation, and she wouldn't say "pussy" or "snatch" there. Of course she wouldn't be naked and talking about her sex either.

His hands held her waist steady as he ground his shaft into her touch. "I sense an 'or' attached to that."

She gave the politest smile she could manage. "Or if you wanted to try something brand new. You could be the very first one to take me from behind. Think about it, sir. You could truly claim me as your kitten by doing something no one else has ever done." She put the saleswoman's pitch on her words. She practically had to stop herself from saying this was a limited time offer.

The speed and strength of Alonso's response surprised her. He spun her around in his lap so he could wrap his arms around her chest. His shaft pressed hot and hard into the fur of her backside, pinned by their closeness. She felt tension in his body again, coiling tighter than ever before. He felt ready to burst and hadn't even entered her yet.

"I take it my offer is acceptable?" Mila's tail was trapped between them, but she tried to caress it back and forth as best she could. Her voice dipped out of formality. "You don't need to hold back, sir. I'm yours."

The fox snorted and his voice came out low and raspy. "I have to remember who you are."

She returned his almost-growl with an almost-purr. She

swayed her hips back and forth to brush against his cock. "I am yours and I'm desperate for you to fuck me." She took hold of one of his hands and guided it down her body until it slid over her slit. "Can't you feel how needy I am, sir? That's me, wanting you."

He trembled and then shoved her to her feet in a sudden motion. "Get on the bed," he rasped out. "Head down, ass up."

"Yes, sir," she said with a quick mock salute. She sauntered over to the bed, glancing over her shoulder to see if he was watching, but he was distracted by opening a hidden compartment in the coffee table, pulling out a bottle of lube and greasing his shaft thoroughly. By the time he looked up, she was already on the bed, wriggling her butt.

He stepped around the couch, pausing for a moment to lean his cane against the wall with reverence, and crawled up on the bed. Mila distantly realized that he had no limp or anything. He must have just liked the cane and the air of dignified age that it gave him. But then she was distracted by the weight of the male pressing down atop her, his hot length pressing against her backside. His hand gripped her scruff tightly, which made her stop all wriggling and hold perfectly still.

She felt him guide his tip into position and tensed as she felt it press against her hole. It was one thing to want this, quite another to actually do it, and she had no idea how it would feel.

Thankfully, Alonso went slow. The fox kept his grip tight on her to stop her from moving as he leaned forward and used his weight to ease into her. The tapered tip spread her open and made her whimper softly.

"Relax as best you can," he whispered in her ears.

She obeyed. Of course she obeyed her owner. As she did, the painful tightness gave way to a feeling of fullness that was familiar but missing a key component to make it truly satisfying. Being so near to contentment but not achieving it only made her more needy. Even the tight grip to her scruff was no longer able to keep her from squirming and she shivered on Alonso's shaft.

His knot pressed gently against her entrance and his grip on her neck finally loosened. She groaned and reached down to rub over her sex, which was feeling even emptier than it had a moment before.

"Hands off," Alonso said in her ears, and Mila obediently but reluctantly placed her hands back by her head. "You are my kitten. Tonight you will only touch yourself when I give you permission."

"Yes, sir," she said with a groan. He was just holding himself in her, driving her mad with need. His shaft would occasionally throb and shift that feeling of fullness and remind her once again of how empty her sex was. "Please, sir."

Alonso nuzzled against her shoulder and playfully ran his teeth against her skin. He stroked along her back, running upwards against the natural flow of her fur and making her wriggle from the sensation. His fingers worked in lazy circles and whorls over her body, tracing the outlines of the splotches of orange and black on her pelt. His hand went around the curve of her shoulder to her underside to grope and tease at a breast before making his way down to her crease.

The feeling of his claws brushing over her labia was electric and Mila nearly bit her tongue from stifling the moans. One finger found its way to her clit and began circling around it. The pleasure built and built inside, hastened by every circuit around her spot of pleasure until she couldn't hold back any more and came hard.

She felt the fluids dripping out of her sex down her inner thigh and trembled. It had been way, way too long since she had had a climax like that.

Alonso languidly ran his hand over her belly, cleaning off his fingers on her fur. "It sounded like you quite enjoyed that."

Mila nodded dazedly, still lost in the afterglow. "Yes, sir."

"Good kitten," he said to a shiver of delight from the calico. "Now it's my turn for pleasure."

She felt a pushing sensation as the shaft slipped out and

then it eased back inside. It wasn't as directly pleasurable to her as having a cock in her sex, but it was nice all the same. But what mattered more to her in that moment was that her owner was using her for his pleasure. He was enjoying himself and it wasn't like she even had to do anything. She purred and tried to push the purr deeper inside her so he could feel it against his shaft.

Alonso's thrusting sped up until there was an audible slap each time he hilted. She kept feeling his knot press against her with every thrust, but he thankfully didn't seem to have any interest in tying with her. Instead he gripped her and sped up until Mila was having trouble staying in place, because he was bouncing her so vigorously. His claws raked through her fur and dug against her skin. His breath came with a hitch. There was little warning that he was close until he slammed forward so hard he pushed her flat to the bed and his shaft spurted inside her. His load was big, or maybe that was just her being unused to anything like that under her tail. She could feel it filling her with sticky warmth and she purred again. "Now I'm truly yours, sir, claimed by you."

The chuckled, a little out of breath, and rolled to the side pulling her along with him. He rested his muzzle in the crook of her shoulder. "So what do you think of your first experiment with anal, kitten?"

As the haze of afterglow began to recede, Mila felt a pang of guilt, even betrayal, at having so quickly jumped into the arms of this fox, but those feelings were pushed aside by the knowledge that she had been a good kitten for her owner. "It was lovely, sir. Although I wonder if I would have enjoyed it so much if you hadn't made me like it."

He kissed her cheek. "I didn't."

"Sir?"

"I didn't make you like it. I only made you want to try something. Your enjoyment was all your own."

"Oh," the calico said, and then repeated, "Oh."

He ran a hand over her naked belly. "Does that change your opinion?"

She paused and considered. She knew she had to answer him. A canine — her owner, no less — had asked her a question. But she felt like she had time to come up with an appropriate response. "I think it was a fun change of pace, but not my preferred way to have sex. But listen to me. I haven't even thought about sex in a year and I'm talking about a change of pace. I already feel like I could have fuck you again right now."

"You could," Alonso said. "Part of the magic of this place. It protects you from illness and injury and you can go nonstop without sleep, food, drink, or even using the bathroom, if you wanted."

It was tempting. "Speaking of bathrooms, maybe we should clean up, sir? I'm very sticky."

Alonso caressed in between Mila's thighs, as if testing her fur for how sticky it truly was. "Yes, I suppose you are. Let's shower together."

They did not get up immediately though. First the fox withdrew from her, easing himself out in a way that left another moan tickling the back of Mila's throat. If she hadn't already suggested getting clean, she might have suggested a second round first.

Alonso took her hand and guided her into the shower, which came on at the perfect temperature for them, not too warm or too cold. Alonso worked the water in under her fur, starting at her head and working his way down until he was soaping away their combined fluids from her fur. As he took care of her, Mila was distracted by the sight of the cuffs dangling there. Although her recent orgasm had blunted her need, it hadn't stopped her mind from dreaming up all the sexy possibilities this equipment presented. When Alonso finished cleaning her, she in turn took care of him, spending longer than was absolutely needed cleaning over his shaft and sheath and balls. He didn't seem to mind.

But they went no further than that. Tiredness had started to creep over Mila's mind and Alonso seemed to recognize that. He toweled out her fur, then his own and guided her back to the miraculously clean bed, where she collapsed, staring at the ceiling. "I suppose I should figure out how to get out of here."

"It won't be easy," Alonso said, resting beside her with a hand on her thigh.

"But that jackal said someone else came through the side door a few years ago. How did they escape?"

Alonso looked at her sadly. "They never did," he said. "I'm still here."

Polonaise

Mila woke up.

The calico cat panicked briefly as she did not know where she was. The bed was far larger than her own and the curtains around it dulled the searing morning light to something bearable. A man's arm laid across her naked belly.

No, not a man's arm, her owner's arm.

The strange events of the previous night snapped into clear recollection in her mind and she jerked upright, rubbing the sleep from her eyes.

The fox beside her yawned and sleepily asked, "Are you all right?"

"You mean besides being trapped by a magical house that's forcing me to obey you?" She was snippier than she had meant to be; that wasn't the sort of tone she should use with her owner. She needed coffee.

"Yes, besides that," the fox said, still with his head buried in the pillow.

"I'm..." She considered and felt over herself with a hand. She was nervous, yes, afraid, yes, completely naked in the arms of a man she had known less than a day, yes, but beyond that was remarkably fine. "I'm okay," she said.

"Good." Alonso yawned and stretched. He shook his head, then shook it again as if to dislodge something. "It's a lot to take in, I know. It was for me too. But you'll be all right. I'll make sure of it."

She nodded, unsure how much she could trust a promise like that. At least he believed it and that was some comfort to her.

Alonso gave a long, drawn out sigh. "I suppose if you're up at this hour, I can get up too."

Mila wrapped the blanket around herself, but when she thought of how it would feel for Alonso to open his eyes and see her on display, she let it fall back down. Beams of morning light turned her naked tricolor body into a stunning prism of oranges, whites, and blacks. "Aren't you a pilot?" she teased. "I thought pilots were used to getting up at all hours."

"Brat," he commented. "I haven't flown since I got here. I've been enjoying the early retirement and the lack of morning alarms that comes with it."

She couldn't resist needling a little further. "I thought you said we don't need to sleep. So why do you need to sleep in?"

The fox blinked and his golden eyes slid over to her, lingering on the curve of her breast. "I don't *need* to sleep or sleep in, but it still feels really good."

The calico quietly thrilled at being stared at while she contemplated a few years spent without Microsoft Excel. As much as the house scared her, that thought brought a smile to her face. Still, there were accounts that needed oversight and coworkers relying on her.

"So how are we going to get out of here?" she asked.

The fox's ear flicked and he got up, placing a hand on the calico's thigh. "Mila, I know you want to get out of here as soon as you can, but you need to be prepared for the possibility that it may be months, even years before it will happen."

Mila swallowed and nodded. "Is there anyone else like us trapped here? Has anyone else made it out?"

The fox blinked sleep out of his eyes. "At the moment, no. It's just the two of us. But there have been others and they have escaped. Aisha, the jackal you met last night, could tell you more: as our librarian here, she's also the Eternal Party's unofficial historian."

Mila's growing nervousness was squelched when Alonso leaned over and whispered, "Good kitten," into her ears, so close that his whiskers brushed her fur. The calico shivered in delight. "Thank you, sir," she said.

Alonso yawned, stretched, and pressed his hands against his lower back as if working a kink out of his spine. "We should figure out what we are doing today," the fox said.

Mila felt the new shyness taking hold. "Can't we just stay here?"

"We could. But eventually you'll need to leave the room, and it would be better if we haven't spent the whole time acting like we've been trying to hide you."

"Even if we are trying to hide me?"

"Exactly. It avoids a lot of questions we don't want to answer and potentially orders you don't want to obey. So let's see what's on the agenda for the day." The fox swung himself out of bed, slipped into a robe that hung nearby, and paused for a moment to scratch the base of his tail with a yawn. Then he ambled over to the door of the room and picked up a sheet of paper that had been slid underneath. Exquisite calligraphy decorated the page. After a moment of squinting at the looping letters, the fox plucked out a pair of glasses from a pocket of his robe and read.

"Well?" Mila asked after the fox had been at it for a while.

"I don't think you'd be interested in most of this."

"Maybe I would be," she said, forcing a hint of defiance in her voice.

Alonso tapped a claw on the first item. "Brunch with a variety of pastries made by our resident chefs Devon and Theo."

"Brunch sounds nice."

"I know this event. All felines will be eating out of bowls on the ground like proper pets."

"On the other hand, I've always been a solid breakfast-and-lunch type of woman."

Alonso smirked and ran his claw further down the page. "There are a number of demonstrations in the dungeon later this morning. 'Ropework for beginners: the first knots.' 'Spanking appreciation club.' 'A short, sharp introduction to knife play.' 'Benefits of bi-curiosity.' 'Fellatio and him.' 'Cunnilingus and her.' Ah, and there will be some movies shown."

"Oh?"

"Vintage pornography."

"Oh."

"After lunch there will be a board game get-together."

Mila put her head in her hands. "How did they make board games sexy? Let me guess: strip poker?"

"No, no," Alonso said with barely suppressed laughter, clearly enjoying himself. "They rarely play strip *poker*. And it looks like later this afternoon the French speaker's club will be meeting."

"Something about cunning linguists?"

"They genuinely just practice their French."

Mila frowned. "I don't know any." She'd learned some Chinese in school, under the presumption that people getting a business degree should do that. It ended up not being much use, and the tiny bit she had learned was quickly forgotten.

The fox frowned. "Normally there are a lot more general interest activities, but it appears very little is scheduled for today. We have everything from an anime club to a model railroad club. I myself am partial to our wine-tasting group." Alonso's claw continued down the page until it reached the bottom, and then he paused. He tilted his head one way and then the other while his tail swayed behind him. He was strongly considering this one. "Looks like a masquerade ball happening this evening."

Mila barked out a laugh. "I can't go to that."

"Why not?" The fox asked, putting his glasses back in the pocket.

"There will be people."

"And?"

Mila found herself tugging the bedsheet up to her shoulders. "They'll see me."

Alonso was nonplussed and stood for a second, tapping a claw against his wrist, until he realized the problem. "Sorry. Mila, my command to feel shy yesterday is now finished."

The calico blinked. She could tell she felt different, but the transition had happened seamlessly. If she hadn't been paying attention, she wouldn't have noticed the change at all.

"Now, would you like to go to the ball?"

"No," Mila said, just as firmly as she had before.

"Why not?" he asked again.

The calico swallowed. He'd asked her a question. She had to answer honestly. "I don't belong out there. I'd look out of place."

Alonso dropped the invitation on the end table that had once been a St. Andrew's cross. He sat on the edge of the bed and had to lean over until he was almost horizontal to touch Mila's hand. "What do you mean?"

The calico's tail tip flicked in mild agitation. "Look. I peeked into the ballroom last night as I was sneaking around. I saw what everyone there looked like, and I don't mean sexy."

Alonso pulled himself closer, his hand staying on hers. He stayed persistent. "Then what do you mean?"

Mila thrust her arms out as she fumbled for words. "They... They looked fancy! They looked gorgeous."

Alonso's touch slid from her hand to her leg and worked up until it was just next to her sex. But he didn't press any farther. "And you think you are not?"

"I'm pretty," Mila said defensively. "There's a difference." When Alonso gave her a look she sighed and explained. "I look good in a t-shirt. I've been told I look very good in a t-shirt that's a little too small. I can do pants and shorts just fine. But every time I've ever tried to wear a dress, to wear jewelry, to style my fur, to get *fancy*, I look like an idiot. If you take me to the ball, everyone is just going to laugh at me."

"You were worried last night if you were acceptable to me. Is this related?"

The calico bit her lip and tried to hide her muzzle in her arms. "Yes," she muttered, miserable.

This made Alonso think, a finger tracing a lazy circle on her thigh as he did.

"Sir," she said with a note of warning.

"You will go to the ball," Alonso declared, and as he said it, Mila knew she would have to go. Her owner was choosing for her. "However," the fox said, "you will only go if I can convince you that you will be just as gorgeous as anyone else there."

Mila grumbled under her breath. "I suppose that is allowable," she said, as if she had any choice in the matter. "I'd much rather try to get out of here though."

"I know," he said. "Believe me, I know." He pulled away from her and sat further along the bed, staring into nothing. "Mila, I spent my first month here obsessed with getting out, and all it did was run me ragged. I was very nearly suicidal, not that I am sure if you even can kill yourself inside the house. I don't want that to happen to you too. Do you understand?"

"Yes, sir," Mila said with soft whine of frustration, even as she was thankful that Alonso was trying to steer her away from a self-destructive path. She forced herself to be more cheerful. "Is it weird that the one thing I can't stop worrying about are the work emails I need to respond to?"

Alonso chuckled and looked over his shoulder at her. "Maybe a little."

Mila tried to laugh off her own comment. She knew she had been throwing herself into her work a little too hard the last few months, but she hadn't expected to find herself unable to muster a care for anything else.

Alonso continued, unaware of Mila's internal turmoil. "But you don't need to worry about that at all. The magic will take care of it." He gestured around him as though the magic was in the air itself.

"But these are some very important accounts."

"And this place has very powerful magic," the fox countered.

Mila wanted to doubt that, but she reflected on everything that had happened to her since she arrived last night. Alonso, a complete stranger, had been able to make her strip naked just by ordering her to do so. He'd made her — her of all people — try to be seductive, and she couldn't stop him.

The fox, sensing he had won the argument, patted her on the shoulder. "Think of it this way, being trapped here is a lot like having gone on vacation overseas and run into passport issues on the way back. You're stuck somewhere unexpected and it isn't your fault, so people will understand if you can't fulfill your obligations. You can't fix all the passport issues yourself. Might as well spend some time kicking back and enjoying the benefits of living abroad."

"Like the incredible sex with handsome foxes?"

The fox's eyes slid away from her as if mildly embarrassed. "At the exact moment, I was thinking of our world-class tailor." He gestured to his own wonderful silk bed robe. "I'm sure he can make something for you that will meet even your own high standards." The fox arched an eyebrow, as if asking whether she agreed.

Mila considered. What was the worst thing that could happen? That the tailor wasn't up to the job? She found herself nodding to Alonso.

"Good. But we should at least get you properly attired to leave the room. Clothes, please." The last words were directed towards a nearby wall.

Thump.

Mila jumped at the sound. It sounded like something heavy had fallen against the wall. No, it sounded like something heavy had fallen *inside* the wall.

"That'll be the house delivering your clothes."

"Collar and corset?"

The fox nodded. "It's traditional for felines here. Aisha told me it dates to the founding of the Eternal Party."

Mila touched her sides. "Going to have to figure out how to breathe in one of those," she said, more to herself than the fox.

"Oh, no worries about that," he said as he slid off the edge of the bed and opened a hidden panel on the wall. He handed her the corset that had been placed into a nook there. "It's fitted to your form and doesn't constrict. It's more decorative than functio..." The words died on his lips as he looked back to the nook again. His mood turned on a dime. He slammed the panel shut hard enough to make the walls rattle. His voice was a deep growl. "Pick. A. Different. Design."

Mila's heart thudded in her chest and she tried to pull away, holding up the corset to hide herself.

Thump.

Another sound of something falling in the wall.

Alonso opened the door tentatively and picked up the collar there. He inspected it and nodded.

"What was that about?" Mila asked quietly.

"Don't ask me about that," the fox said. An order, firm and solid and unyielding in her mind.

"Yes, sir." She looked down at the corset in her hands. "Can you help me into this?" she asked, trying to change the subject as quickly as she could.

Alonso snapped his fingers and pointed to the space in front of him. Mila obeyed the unspoken command, rolled out of bed, and stood naked before him.

He took the corset and wrapped it around her midriff, sealing it shut along her spine. Just how it sealed shut she had no idea: it had no zipper or laces and all Alonso had done was press it together. She didn't know what it was made out of either. It was shiny like latex, but had the texture of leather, and yet it moved with her like Lycra. If she hadn't felt it go on, she would have had no idea she was wearing anything at all. Magic, she had to remind herself. It had to be magic.

"I think I can figure this one out," the calico said as she reached for the collar, but Alonso pulled it away. "What's wrong?"

"Mila, who is your owner?"

"You, sir," the calico said, wondering where this was going.

"And how important is my ownership to you?"

"Very, sir," she said, surprised at her response, yet knowing it to be true all the same. "You are the most important person in my life."

He nodded. "That is how the house directed your thoughts after you submitted to me."

Mila frowned and tried to search through her own feelings. "I think I can tell, but only if I really think about it. But that doesn't change that I still feel that way."

Alonso held up the collar between them. It was a simple band of leather with a silvery tag at the front proclaiming its wearer to be "Alonso's kitten." "To many here, this is the physical embodiment of our relationship and should be treated with the same respect as the relationship itself. And I know that we came together out of practicality, but that doesn't mean it should be treated casually."

"So what do I do?"

"Stand still," he said with a smile.

The fox stepped around Mila and placed his hands on her shoulders. He started to massage her, working his thumbs against her collarbone, as he whispered in her ear, "Good kitten." Mila staggered at the hit of pleasure and threatened to go limp under his ministrations, especially when he kept repeating the trigger phrase over and over. He had to wrap an arm firmly around her corseted middle to have her stand upright.

"*My* good kitten," he whispered again as he drew the dull side of a claw along her throat.

"Yours," Mila murmured against the sweeping tides of pleasure.

"Mine," he said more firmly, holding his hand over the front of her neck.

Mila could only nod and purr in response. Mila had already pledged herself to him, had felt the magic of the house connect them, but this felt like he was pledging himself to her. As much as she was his kitten, he was her owner, and that meant something too. The calico had felt a range of emotions since being trapped in the house, but what she didn't expect to feel in that moment was safe. That was the overwhelming impression she was left with. She was safe. Even if there were a hurricane outside, here she was safe. Even if the world might be going to hell in a handbasket, here she was safe. Even if she was trapped in a magical house that forced her to obey, here, with Alonso, she was safe.

He lifted his arm from her belly and steadied her before sliding the loop of leather gently around her neck. He adjusted it, brushing down her fur so it fit comfortably, and then cinched it shut at the back. "Good kitten," he said once more.

He turned Mila around to face him, and the calico face-planted into his chest, burying her nose into the fur there, and holding tight to his robe. For a while, Alonso simply stood there and let her be close. Only after several minutes had passed did he start to wriggle out of his clothes. Mila pressed in more to his naked body and that touch of silver in his fur.

"Mila, I should get dressed before we go."

"I just want to stay here."

Alonso caressed behind her ears. "How about this? If our tailor can't make you look up to your standards, we'll come back here and you can hold onto me all night. Fair?"

"Fair," she said with reluctance and peeled herself away from the fox. She contemplated saying that she wasn't satisfied with the outfit, no matter how good it looked, but she suspected she could not get away with that.

Alonso ruffled the fur over her head playfully before getting dressed himself. Mila was a little jealous of him being able to wear proper clothes that actually covered his nakedness. He fetched his cane and approached the door, but Mila said, "Wait. What about breakfast?"

Alonso paused and turned an ear back to her. "Are you actually hungry?"

Mila held a hand over her stomach and felt the new corset there. "No. I should be, right?"

Alonso shrugged. "The house takes care of you. Most people don't eat unless they really want to."

"People were eating when I peeked into the ballroom last night."

"It would be a poor party if no delicacies were served." Alonso put his hand on the door and tilted his head. "Come along. Stop stalling."

Mila grumbled a little but kept close to the fox as they stepped out into the hallway. It wasn't quite empty, but the few there seemed even more sluggish and tired than Mila felt without her morning coffee. Mila found herself getting stared at a lot: the felines offered a friendly smile as they passed, but the canines were all appraising her.

The fox found her trembling hand and squeezed it as they walked down the hall.

After their second turn, a door opened and a widely yawning wolf stepped through. "Oh, morning, Alonso," he said. "Who's the girl?"

The calico tried to act natural, but it was hard. Thankfully Alonso took the lead. "This is Mila. She'll be getting introduced at the ball tonight."

The wolf chuckled and ogled her in a way that made her ears lay flat. "I look forward to meeting you appropriately later then."

"If we go," Mila said under her breath.

Alonso coughed a little at Mila's out-of-turn remark. "We made a bet," he explained.

The wolf had a twinkle in his eye. "Did you? Brave girl to be making a bet with Alonso."

"Really?" Mila suddenly felt much less confident.

"Last girl who tried that ended up getting the jawbreaker treatment." He made a little bow. "Good luck to you and see you at the ball tonight." He winked and ambled down the hallway in the opposite direction.

As soon as he was out of earshot, Mila hissed out in a whisper, "You didn't actually break someone's jaw, did you?"

"Of course not!" Alonso actually sounded hurt that she would suggest it. He sighed as he caught sight of her glare. "Look, she lost the bet fair and square, and since she was a mouthy brat who liked to be punished for being a mouthy brat, I shoved the biggest ring gag I could fit into her mouth and had her spend the night in a harness that kept her muzzle locked to my hips: she had to deep throat me all night."

"Fuck."

"Don't get me wrong: she loved it. She spent the next month trying to lose a bet to me again."

"This place takes all types, I guess."

"It really does."

They came out of the endless hallways into the entrance foyer of the house. Seeing it, Mila wondered how she could have ever believed the door she had come through was the front door. *This* was an entrance. The door itself was made of solid cherry, stained dark with an embossed design that looked like a stylized version of the collar and corset she wore. The foyer went up four floors with a staircase spiraling the outer wall the whole way up.

Mila's gaze was drawn up to a massive art installation hanging down through the center of the foyer. Shards of glass were hung on strings and arranged with mathematical precision so that when viewed from one angle, they took on the image of a diving osprey, and when viewed from a different angle, they took on the image of a leaping salmon. "A Clemenza," she whispered.

"What? The glass?" Alonso was insufficiently amazed for Mila's taste.

She put her hands on her hips. "That is a Clemenza hanging

glass sculpture. There's one in the Atlanta airport. It cost them three million dollars to install, and you have one hanging here that is twice the size."

Alonso looked up at the floating shards of glass as if seeing them for the first time. "Really? Would you like to install a smaller one in my room for you to enjoy?"

An undignified kittenish squeak escaped Mila's throat.

Alonso placed an arm on Mila's shoulder and started to walk, deliberately holding himself between the calico and the sculpture so she couldn't keep staring at it. "Wealth has a very different meaning here. There's no reason why we couldn't all have diamond rings dangling from every finger, except that we all know how ridiculous we would look like that."

As they walked along the staircase, Alonso quietly explained the layout of the house. The basement held the dungeon Mila had seen the previous day. The first floor consisted of social rooms, like the ballroom. The second floor consisted of lodgings, with personal rooms for all the canines along the exterior walls and rooms for the felines along the interior. The third and fourth floor held a lot of the professional rooms where people worked, like the tailor they were going to see, as well as the library. There was also a rooftop observatory and a greenhouse.

They turned off the staircase on the third floor and found a lot more activity here than they had seen on the second floor. Over a dozen people were there, milling about. The canines wore sleepy expressions: one was even still in his pajamas. All of them held onto a leash which connected to the collar of a feline who was on all fours next to them.

"They must have arrived early for the brunch I told you about," Alonso whispered in Mila's ear.

At first Mila felt a wave of sympathetic embarrassment over how her fellow felines were behaving, but then she looked back to the canine still in his pajamas. He was holding the leash up and stroking absently behind the ears of an Abyssinian who was pressed up against his leg and purring loudly. Embarrassment turned into a touch of envy: she loved being touched there but it was usually considered too intimate to do in public. There was no sign of concern for social mores on the Abyssinian's face, only raw contentment.

Alonso fended off questions about Mila from the more awake of the brunch-goers, and the pair of them quickly moved past. Thankfully, the third floor lacked the magically extended, maze-like corridors of the second and they quickly found the tailor's room.

It was like walking backstage on a top-tier Broadway production. Costumes and fabrics hung in gigantic racks all around, with higher shelves of parts and tools accessible by step stools.

Mila felt disoriented. The calico was used to walking into a room and understanding the price of the items it contained, but her knowledge encompassed most finished goods and few raw materials. She could do a rough appraisal of a house at a glance, but would get stumped by a two-by-four. Her tail flicked behind her as she scowled at the room's contents.

She would have stood still, unwilling to go further into the room, were it not for Alonso's hand applying gentle pressure to the small of her back. So they walked on past row after row of sumptuous coats, dresses, hats, and other clothing items. In the center of the room was a small clearing with a husky humming merrily as he did some modeling on the most realistic cheetah mannequin that Mila had ever seen. His ears perked at the sound of newcomers and he turned with a wide smile. "Ah, Alonso, who is this beautiful jewel you bring to my doorstep?"

Alonso smiled at the kitten at his side. "This is Mila. She's new here. Mila, this is Erik Lauderdale, our resident tailor."

The calico held out her hand to shake and the husky, oblivious, picked up her arm and began inspecting her pelt pattern closely, gnawing on a wooden pencil absently as he did so. "New, hm?"

"Mila and I have a bet going," Alonso went on. "She doesn't think your skills are up to the task of getting her ready for the ball this evening."

"You'll lose that bet," the husky muttered around his pencil. He let go of Mila's arm and clapped his hands sharply. "Tricia, bring me some color samples."

Behind him, the mannequin moved.

Mila screamed and jumped behind Alonso.

Alonso held her protectively. "It's all right," he said. "She was just in doll mode."

Doll mode? No, no, she'd dealt with too much crazy in the last twenty-four hours. She was not going to ask. "Sorry," she said, taking a look around Alonso's side. "She surprised me."

The pencil tip swirled in the air as the husky masticated the other end. "Very new," he muttered to himself. "Oh well. Tricia, activate conscious mode."

The cheetah, who had been picking up something from a shelf, stopped with her arm suspended in midair and shivered. Her head flopped down to hang loose on one side like a broken-down animatronic. Then, like a switch had been flipped, the cheetah sprang to life and squealed. She bounced off the step stool she was standing on, covered the intervening distance in three quick strides, and give Mila a bone-crushing, breast-squashing big hug. "Hiiiiii there," she said in a voice so bubbly and sweet it outdid most sodas.

"Um, hi," the calico said, feeling a little confused.

"I'm Tricia," she said, drawing out the last syllable of every sentence and hanging onto it for at least a full second. "I'm Master Erik's assistant. You must be here for a costume. You're so lucky! Master Erik doesn't dress just anyone. I mean, he dresses me every day. But that's just us."

The cheetah broke her hug and bounced on her heels next to the husky.

"Nice to meet you," Mila said, feeling like her mother was over her shoulder and reminding her on how to be nice to strangers. "I don't think I've ever met a... living mannequin before."

"I prefer the term robo-girl," Erik said. "She has many modes. This is merely her fully conscious mode. She spends almost all of her time in mannequin mode."

"Or in sexdoll mode," the cheetah added with a giggle.

"Almost all of your time? Don't you ever sleep?" Mila asked.

"Dollies don't need to sleep," the cheetah said with a wink.

Erik waved his hand. "We could explain the details of the process or we could get started with dressing you."

"Oh! Oh! Oh!" The cheetah waved her hand in the air like she was trying to get the attention of a teacher from the back row of class, despite being no more than five feet from anyone in the room. "Master Erik! Master Erik!"

"Yes, Tricia?" He had on the patient smile of someone who knew he could silence all this with a word.

"Can Mila and I both be dollies for you?"

The husky gnawed on his pencil a bit more. "If her owner consents."

Mila ducked behind Alonso as the fox stroked his chin thoughtfully. "It would keep the reveal of your outfit for her a surprise. I like it."

He turned to Mila who was making her best you-cannot-be-serious face, and placed a hand on her shoulder. "I'll be right here the whole time. I won't leave you alone. Now, go blank."

The world faded around her. It wasn't that she couldn't see it, but rather it had lost all meaning. There were colors and movements, scents and sensations, but none of it mattered. The only thing that mattered was the sound of her owner's voice as Alonso spoke in her ear, instructing her. At his command, her legs eased into a wider stance, and she unfurled her arms straight out to either side. It was a position that should have been immensely tiring to hold, but tiredness, like the shapes around her, had no meaning anymore.

Things moved, sounds were made, but nothing required her to see or hear, so she didn't. Everything blurred together.

Fabrics were touched to her fur, measurements were made and tested, paints were applied to her fur and then stripped off before they set. Her body was moved into different poses and wherever it was moved, it stuck without any effort on her part.

Then something happened that required her to react. A finger was slid into her sex and a voice commanded her to grip it. She did. She clenched without thought and with barely any reaction. Then the voice commanded her to relax and she did. The finger was extracted and a separate small vibe was slipped into her. Again she was told to grip. The control for the vibe was slipped into a holster on her hip, set to a low power. No command came to relax.

Pleasure still had meaning. Pleasure was its own meaning.

Thrumming, wet, throbbing, slick pleasure flooded into a brain devoid of all other sensations. Time lost meaning as all of Mila's existence focused in between her thighs, a nexus of delight.

The vibe was turned off. A voice spoke in her ear, and suddenly things had meaning again. Suddenly she could think. She nearly collapsed against Alonso as the long-term teasing of the vibrator caught up to her all at once. "Fuuuuuuuck."

"Eyes forward, hands at your side," Alonso commanded. "No spoiling the surprise early."

Mila squirmed, but was forced to obey. "How is it possible to feel this horny without feeling aroused?" she said under her breath. While she had to keep her eyes forward, she did notice that the light was hitting the room differently. Shadows were in a completely different place. "How long was I out?"

"Several hours."

"What?"

The fox ignored the outburst. "How do you feel?"

"I feel like I just woke up from the best sleep of my life. I feel so mellow."

Alonso leaned forward and whispered. "Now imagine how hyperactive Tricia was before she became Erik's doll."

Despite herself, Mila giggled. This was all so surreal.

Alonso coughed softly. "Erik?"

Mila, having been told to stare ahead, couldn't turn to look at the husky, and she had to nudge the fox to let her see him.

The husky was leaning back against a table with the cheetah bobbing her head in his lap. Except there was a mechanical repetitiveness to her movements, which again reminded Mila of an animatronic. When Alonso's next cough caught the husky's attention, he slipped himself out of the cheetah's mouth and covered himself up, but the cheetah kept moving in the same way, oblivious, with her lips in a near perfect O.

The husky clapped his hands together. "Ready for the big reveal?" He rolled over a full length mirror covered with a curtain and tore the cloth away with a flourish.

For a brief moment, the calico did not recognize herself, so complete was the transformation.

The biggest change was her fur. Almost everywhere that was visible had been painted in some way. But rather than completely erasing her calico colors and starting over, Erik had used them as a starting point. The sharp changes between whites and oranges and blacks had been softened by blending the colors into each other. Highlights of red and purple ran throughout her fur to accent the edges of these transitions, and through them all were little specks of glitter that twinkled like stars. In fact, the whole effect was like looking at a picture of some deep space galaxy: swirling pinpricks of stars on a multi-colored background. The corset was still there about her middle, a nexus of darkness around which the colorful galaxy of her pelt seemed to swirl. The sci-fi theme extended to the new clothing she wore. She had on latex gloves that went from her fingertips up to her elbow and stockings that went from her toes to her knees. They started black at the tips, but sharply swapped to whites in an asymmetric pattern that actually balanced out the lopsided colors of her pelt. Behind her, a cloak flowed from her neck in brilliant sparkling purple, and a separate high collar, which almost touched her ears, came up behind her head. (The collar Alonso had slipped on her that morning was still there, gleaming at her neck.) Were it not for her naked breasts and sex, she looked ready for a role in some high-class sci-fi production as Queen Hibernia, Conqueror of Space Sector 225, or something like that.

Oh, and somewhere along the line, her nipples and clit had gotten pierced.

"So, do I win the bet?" Alonso asked.

"Yes," Mila admitted, and then quickly diverted the topic, "but when did this happen?" She touched the nipple rings with a touch of anger in her voice. She half-expected them to be fake. But no, they were securely lodged in her flesh.

"While you were being a mannequin."

"Why?" She did her best to keep her voice even and neutral, but when Erik looked away, she stared daggers at the fox.

"I thought they'd look good on you." He made a gesture with his hand, slowly lowering. The implication was clear: "cool down."

The implicit command had its desired effect, putting a lid on the simmering irritation Mila felt. She supposed that her owner wanting it was a good enough reason. The calico took a deep breath. "I'm just surprised they're fully healed already."

Alonso slipped a claw through the loop of a nipple ring. He began to curl his finger and Mila braced herself for a painful tug, but none came. The ring slipped free to dangle from the fox's claw. Except... Mila's eyes darted from the ring to her nipple and back again. The ring was a perfect loop. Her nipple was unpierced. Alonso reached out to push the ring against her nipple again, and suddenly it was reattached, as though she had been wearing the ring for months.

"How?"

"You're in a magical house that can force you to obey any

order I give but you're wondering how the nipple rings work? It's like I told you: no injury or illness while you're here."

"No pain either."

His ears flicked. "Pain isn't the same thing as injury. It can hurt, if I want it to. But that's not my style."

Mila looked back to her reflection, to the whole ensemble. So she'd gotten piercings. They were magical temporary piercings. Nothing to panic over there, or get angry with her owner about, which meant there was no longer anything holding back her initial wave of emotions.

She was beautiful.

Mila turned to the husky and bowed her head. "I don't know how to fully thank you, sir." It was true. She didn't know how to thank him.

"The best thanks you could give me is to return. I had so many ideas and alas you can only wear one outfit to the ball tonight. The second best thanks would of course be sex."

"Another time," Alonso interjected.

"Of course," Erik said in full sympathy. "You have to make sure your cat is well adapted to your desires before you loan her out." The husky tilted his head and gave a sidelong glance to the fox. "I will say I am a little surprised how much you let her back-talk you. I would have thought that wasn't your style."

The fox shrugged. "We're starting slow."

The husky gave a curt nod. He glanced back at Tricia and a smile flickered across his face as he reached down to adjust his pants. "If you will excuse me..."

They made their goodbyes and left, heading back towards his room on the second floor.

Now that it was midday, there were far more people in the halls, but the tenor of the looks she was receiving had changed. She was catching people's attention. Eyes roamed the curve of her cloak, not the curve of her breast. At least one mouth hung open as she passed by. Several felines, hanging on the arm of canine owners just like Mila was, whispered of how it had been too long since they had gone to visit Erik and weren't they about due for a new outfit.

It made Mila puff out her chest a little with pride, even though she still was half-naked.

Just imagine the look on BD's face if he could see her right now.

BD's face...

The house wasn't fast enough this time.

The image of his face, stuffed full of tubes and so weak that it hurt him to even smile, flashed across her mind and jabbed an icicle of cold pain into her stomach. She was never going to see him again. She was never going to hold his hand. She was never going to rest her head against his shoulder and pay no attention to a movie they were watching because she was too busy listening to his heartbeat flutter whenever she ran her thumb over the back of his hand.

He was gone.

The floor twisted under her feet as the house shook. It sent her flying into the arms of the fox and she clung to him, claws out, as hot wet tears tried to counteract the freezing sensation inside.

Alonso held her tight. "Don't cry," he said in a soft, nonjudgmental voice, "or you'll ruin your make-up."

It was an order, but it was an order that carried a choice. She didn't want to ruin her look, not after Erik spent so long on it. The tears dried up instantly. But the calico continued to cling to Alonso and that feeling of safety he provided, trying to chase the painful memories away. She knew her claws were tearing up his jacket, but he said nothing, so she didn't care.

Even though she wasn't crying, she was still sobbing, and her whole body shook uncontrollably. She kept her grip tight until the image of the face began to fade.

Mila's whole body went tense as she felt the presence of another person beside her. She blinked and saw a Dalmatian dabbing at her wet cheeks with a handkerchief. He worked delicately so as not to smudge Erik's design. When he was done, he looked directly into Mila's eyes with an inquisitive expression and moved his hand in a quick pattern that the calico realized belatedly was ASL for "O-K?"

She gave a slow and unsteady nod.

Alonso loosened his hold of Mila and signed back with far less skill. "S-U-B-D-R-O-P."

The Dalmatian nodded in sympathy and gave a thumbs-up to Mila before heading on his way.

As Mila watched him walk away, the thing she kept thinking about was how he checked in with her, not her owner.

Prior to that moment, Mila had thought that the danger of the Eternal Party lay in its guests abusing their power over her. But this Dalmatian hadn't shown any prurient interest in her. He simply wanted to make sure she was okay. The danger wasn't from malicious actors misusing their authority but from fundamentally decent people with the wrong set of expectations. They thought she was like Tricia, eager and willing to obey, and any protests she made would be assumed to be an act. It was like Alonso had said earlier: she might as well be stuck while traveling abroad and was dealing with a clash of cultures.

Mila's claws retracted slowly. "I'm sorry, sir," she said, quietly. "It's just—"

He put a finger on her lips. "Mila, you never need to explain your tears to me."

Mila couldn't properly express how gratified she was at that. It had become an awful cycle, hearing the same questions, telling the same story, and receiving the same false sympathy or hollow condolences. It was a relief to not need to justify her feelings. "Thank you, sir."

"Are you good to continue?"

Mila's ears flicked as she heard a piano down the hall, a gentle uplifting melody that soothed her, but Alonso didn't seem to have heard it. His attention was fully on her. As quickly as the song arrived, it faded away. "Sir, is there a music room up here?"

"Not nearby. Why?"

"Thought I heard something," she said. She remembered hearing a piano like that when she first entered the Eternal Party. On reflection, it couldn't have come from the ballroom; that was too far away. So what was she hearing? "Let's get back to the room, sir."

She held tight onto his hand all the way back to Alonso's room. Step by step, the haunting memories receded. Step by step, Mila began to feel like herself again.

By the time they were alone again, Mila was standing tall, and the horniness that had come from wearing a vibrator for hours had returned in full force. "Sir, when Erik said he wanted to have sex with me..."

"He almost certainly meant as a doll, yes."

"Earlier today that would have seemed so weird, but I just spent several hours as a mindless mannequin and it honestly wasn't that bad. And I am still really needy." She pinched the bridge of her muzzle as she fell backwards onto the bed, doing so delicately as she could so as not to ruffle her new clothes. "We're back to me declaring my eagerness and availability again."

Alonso took a seat next to her. "Are you actually interested in Erik's offer?"

The calico thought about it for a moment. "No, sir. I might not mind trying the doll idea with you, but not him. I just got back on my feet, sex-wise, and I don't want to rush straight into having sex with everyone I meet. Also, not sure about the idea of having sex as payment."

"Understood," he said. It made Mila feel a little better to know he was listening to her and wanting to hear her desires as well. "We still have some time before the ball. What do you want?"

Mila sat up. "I really want to do something unrelated to sex, just to prove I can around here. I know you said we don't need to eat, but we can still get some food, can't we?"

"Of course. What do you like?" The fox jumped from the

edge of the bed and stood next to the wall, at the same spot where Mila's collar and corset had been delivered earlier.

"Some comfort food. Pizza and ice cream."

"Better specify a flavor of each before you get something random."

"Oh," she said, not having expected to need to give a full order so quickly. "Sausage, onion, and arugula pizza with strawberry ice cream for dessert."

Thump.

The fox opened the panel on the wall and the smells of freshly cooked pizza hit her hard.

"Wait, is that...?"

"Montero's from the look of it." The fox picked up a pizza box and handed it over. There was also a large bowl of ice cream and a spoon.

The two ate in silence for a bit, with Mila sprawled out over the bed and eating directly over the box with a knife and fork so she didn't mess up her costume at all. As she was starting in on the ice cream and purring softly at the cool flavor of strawberry on her tongue, she asked, "What else do you have for entertainment around here? Is there TV? Movies? I mean normal movies," she added, remembering the vintage pornography display Alonso had mentioned earlier.

The fox took a big bite of pizza, and as he chewed, he picked up a remote from the bed stand and made a screen descend on the other side of the coffee table. The screen covered nearly the entire wall. "We can get any TV channel you want and we have all the streaming services. We've even been known to turn the ballroom into a movie theater when a big new release comes out. We also have Internet, but it's more limited: read only."

"Really?"

"One of the weird rules of this place. Things can enter, but few things can leave."

"Like us."

"Like us." He wrapped an arm around the shivering feline.

She shook herself and tried to put on a braver face than she felt. "Well, that explains why my phone had no reception last night."

He nodded and tried to move the topic of conversation on to other things. "What show do you like to watch?"

"Stuff about antiques? Sometimes I like to see if I can guess the price of an item before they reveal it. I also like to watch cooking shows. They always feel so wholesome and comforting, even if I couldn't make any of those recipes to save my fur."

The fox seemed to prefer the second idea and swapped the channel over. It was one of those cozy midday shows with a woman baking a meal for her friends who would appear at the end of the hour. Mila still had no idea what the difference between sauté and sear was, but she enjoyed herself nonetheless. She tried not to get too emotional at the end of the show, when in came the horde of friends to partake in the meal. Friends had stopped coming by Mila's little apartment; she'd stopped going out to dinner with them.

They watched a few shows one after the other (without a single complaint from the clearly bored fox) before a chime from a clock reminded Alonso that the ball was approaching.

"Do we have to go?" Mila asked.

"Yes, we do. I won the bet. And besides." He ran a finger over her chin. "You look absolutely stunning and I want to show off how lucky I am to have you."

She nodded meekly and tried to use the cloak of the costume to hide herself a bit.

"Now, now," he said. "I want to show off all of you." He ran a claw down her neck and over her chest to caress around a breast. "I want everyone to know this is mine."

She nodded again, a little more this time. At least if she was clearly his, she might not get as many propositions from strangers. She hoped.

Besides, there was another part of her, a part that had been taunted and teased for how she looked all through high school, that desperately wanted to strut all around the ballroom.

Alonso changed his coat into an identical one, minus the clawed holes that Mila had given it earlier. "One more thing," he said. "Around here they follow some old school notions about submissives and dominants. Just know that around here, if you make a mistake in front of others, they will assume it is a fault of mine, as I am responsible for you."

"That's supposed to make me feel better?"

"Yes. Think of it this way: no matter what mistake you make tonight, no one will think any less of you."

A knot tightened in Mila's gut. "But you're my owner. They'll think less of you."

"I can handle myself. Don't worry about it."

There was a sharpness to his words. It was a command. Immediately the knot undid itself. "Yes, sir."

"Now come along."

As the pair of them made their way down to the ballroom, they were joined by more and more canines and felines. It was the big event for the day and it seemed like the entire house was turning out for it. At first, Mila enjoyed the appreciative looks the other felines gave her, but then they got close enough to see the tag hanging from her collar, the one proclaiming her to be Alonso's kitten, and their expressions hardened. Mila pressed against Alonso as people crowded around her, holding on tight to his hand.

The ballroom itself was radically different from how the calico had seen it the previous night. Then, it had mostly been a wide open space with a small stage for a pianist to play from. Now the stage was hidden by a massive curtain. A coyote in a carnival barker outfit stood at the entrance to the room. "Felines to the left, canines to the right," he called out.

Mila felt her stomach drop. She clutched tighter to the fox's hand as they drew closer. She wanted to ask him not to leave her alone, but there were too many people here. She would be overheard.

The fox's hand squeezed hers back. "You'll be fine," he said.

She still had a death grip on Alonso when she stood right in front of the carnival barker coyote. He gave a fang-filled smile and tipped his hat. "Right this way, little kitty, back behind the stage."

"Go," Alonso said.

Mila's hand released unwillingly and she took a step towards the stage. She looked back over her shoulder and saw the fox give her an encouraging smile. The order compelled her to look away, to step past a parted curtain and arrive backstage. Alone.

Grande Valse

Mila only had a second to look around the backstage area. In the middle of the space were chairs and couches for everyone to relax on, and along the walls were mirrors with vanities for people to finish off the detail on their costumes. Mila's sci-fi queen outfit was about in the middle as far as elaborateness went. Some felines took the masquerade ball theme seriously and were wearing dresses that called to mind Venetian Carnival parties. Others had costumes that would leave cosplay enthusiasts drooling. One lioness walking past was wearing some kind of faux magic battle armor that weighed more than Mila did. The common themes throughout the room were that everyone's costume was sexualized in some way and that no matter how simple or complex the outfit was, it still contained the house's collar and corset.

Then, after a second had passed, Mila was swarmed.

"So they were right. Alonso did select a feline of his own."

"I told you. Didn't I tell you?"

"She's brand new."

"Can't have been here more than a day or two."

"How did she manage to snag him so quickly?"

"Maybe he just has a thing for calicoes."

"Ladies! Ladies!" One of the few males in the group, a silver cat wearing a fantasy mage robe that was a mostly transparent blue, jumped up in front of the others. "Let's give her a bit of space. She's had a hectic day. Go on. Shoo. You can all gawk at her some other time." When that failed to get a reaction, he got sterner and said, "Shove off, or I'll tell Alonso."

With a mix of groans and sighs of disappointment, the crowd dispersed, although many of them still kept their eyes fixed on the newcomer.

Once the two of them were relatively isolated, the silver cat turned to Mila. "Wasn't sure if that would work. I'm Alex, by the way." He held out a hand to shake.

"I'm Mila," the calico said. When the group of felines had descended on her, she had wrapped herself up tight in the cloak to hide. She extricated a hand to shake Alex's. "I wasn't expecting so much jealousy just from having Alonso for an owner."

"Eh," Alex waved dismissively in the air and with his outfit it looked like he was casting a magic spell. His floppy-tipped pointy hat bent down over his eyes and had to be brushed aside. "It's less jealousy than you think. Mostly just surprise. Some girls here have been pining after Alonso for years but he's never shown any indication of wanting to collar anyone, and then you show up and he's got you wearing his collar before anyone else has really met you. Everyone wants to know your secret."

Mila flushed and opened her mouth to say something but the silver cat waved her off again.

"I'm not worried about it. I never had a shot with Alonso, being male and all, and besides Master told me to look out for you. He said you'd had a bad case of subdrop earlier today."

Mila remembered the deaf Dalmatian she had encountered. "Thank you. And thank him for me too."

"It's nothing. If you have any questions, or need any advice on how to deal with the Feline Faction," he gestured to the many cats behind him, many of whom were still watching her, "let me know."

Most of what Mila wanted to know was about how to escape this strange place, but there were some things she thought he could help with here and now. "I could use some help understanding context."

The silver cat's ears perked expectantly, which nearly sent his hat toppling off his head.

Mila reached up and touched her throat, fingers brushing over the edge of the leather there and feeling the memory of when Alonso placed it on her. She shivered, relishing in the phantom feeling of his protection. "So I know what this means to me, but what does it mean to everyone else for me to be wearing Alonso's collar?"

The silver cat tilted his head and put a finger on his chin in a dramatic thinking pose. "It means that in the eyes of the Eternal Party, you are committed to each other: partners, boyfriend and girlfriend, that sort of thing. How deeply committed you are is up to you. For some collared couples here, they might as well be married. That said, most people here are pretty open in their relationships. Any canine with no sub of their own can use any uncollared feline they want, but they'll generally get permission first before playing with someone else's sub; and a canine with a sub won't play around with other subs quite as much." Shrewd eyes roamed over Mila's form. "Alonso seriously collared you without explaining all of that?"

Mila's first thought was an echo of Aisha's from the other night: Alonso really was bad at explaining things. Then she realized that by asking her question, she'd made Alonso look negligent. The calico felt an urge to protect him. She forced a little laugh. "My fault," she said. "I was a little too quick and eager to be collared."

The silver cat bobbed his head. "Well, not to worry. You got Alonso, and he's great. Seriously, you don't know how lucky you are."

Mila glanced around the room. Jealous looks still followed her, and a quartet of felines headed up by a particularly irritated-looking lynx stared daggers at her across the room. "I don't feel particularly lucky right now."

Alex turned around and followed her gaze, his floppy hat bouncing around his ears. "Oh, that's Vivien. Don't mind her. Focus on yourself. I mean look at you: you look fantastic," Alex said. "Master Erik really outdid himself on you."

"Thank you. And you look great too."

"This old thing?" Alex brushed his hands down the mage robe. It was diaphanous, so that the silver of his pelt underneath seemed overlaid by the blue of the robe. It did very little to hide the lithe body underneath, or the collar and corset that were just as prominent on him as they were on all the female cats. "I usually only pull this out for role play nights."

"Roleplay like tabletop?"

"Like 'Oh no, the fierce barbarian is immune to my spells, and now I am helpless to prevent him from ravaging me,'" the gray cat waggled his eyebrows in a way that made Mila giggle. "It certainly might involve going down on a tabletop."

The calico burst out laughing. "I could use another bit of help."

"Name it."

"Well," Mila pulled out the syllable as she looked around. "I don't know exactly what it is we are going to do tonight. I thought this was supposed to be a masquerade ball. Why are we all backstage?"

"Let's find Natalie. She can explain better than I can. After all, she set this up. Hey, Nat!" The silver cat spun on the balls of his feet, robe billowing out, and sprang up on tip-toes to see over the heads of the other felines nearby. He gestured for Mila to follow him and they walked up to a vanity along the back wall where a cougar was hurriedly putting on some finishing detail to a harem costume she wore. Her body was draped in silks with threads of gold underneath, and they all joined up at nodes that were high-lighted by topazes the same color as her sandy fur.

"Sorry," the cougar said, turning in her seat as the calico and silver cat approached. "Spent so long setting up the stage that I barely had time for my costume. What do you need?"

Mila's eyes dropped to the cougar's hips and she started. There, underneath a piece of silk so thin it hid absolutely nothing, was a very sizable sheath. Mila stared at it without realizing until the cougar waved her hand in front of Mila's face.

"Oh, I'm so sorry," Mila said.

To Mila's surprise, the cougar, Natalie, laughed lightly. The most admonishment she gave the calico was a small roll of her eyes. "No, no. I get that reaction a lot. Let me guess, you're trying to figure out why you are so completely sure what my pronouns are."

The calico nodded. "I wanted to ask, but it was like I already knew the answer."

Alex grinned and folded his arms in a rather triumphant pose. "It's one of the neat side effects of the house's magic. You already know the right pronouns to use. No misgendering here. Oh!" He gave the cougar a pleading look and bounced on the balls of his feet. "Can I tell her the story? Please, can I?"

The cougar's eyes slid to the calico conspiratorially. "The only reason I let him is because he really does tell it better than I can. Go ahead, Alex."

The silver cat hunched forward and lowered his voice as if he were telling a particularly juicy piece of gossip. "So this is how Nat realized she was trans, right. Picture this. It's been a long day. Nat and two canines just finished a marathon of really hot and heavy fucking. Everyone's exhausted. So the doms kick back and relax with Nat on footrest duty. Her mind is wandering but she catches little bits of conversation from the other two. She hears them discuss a particularly elegant dress Erik was showing off. Then she zones out and misses that the conversation has shifted to bondage gear, so when one of the canines talks about how good that item would look on Nat, she thinks they are talking about the dress still and not a pair of cuffs.

"Cue the moment of panic. Nat's thinking that she doesn't

belong in that dress. That dress belongs on a beautiful woman. Then it hits her: she wants to be that beautiful woman. She's trans. Except the magic of the house means the moment she knows it, everyone knows it. Those two canines had been continuing to discuss her while she was having this realization, and they end up swapping the pronouns they use for her mid-sentence. Both of them ended up giving her the exact same look you were just a moment ago."

Mila's ears flicked back self-consciously. "What happened next?"

"You mean after I shifted pronouns without a clutch?" The cougar grinned and took over the story from here. "I panicked, I cried out of complete embarrassment, and then we all had a very long, very good heart-to-heart. They were completely understanding. Mistress Aisha even insisted on taking me to a doctor the next day. Just initial steps to start." Natalie nudged the much smaller cat with an elbow. "Anyways, how can I help Alonso's new kitten?"

Alex jerked a thumb towards the calico. "Mila here wants to know what's expected of us tonight."

"Oh." Natalie sat up straighter. "Not too much will be expected from any of us. You can relax back here until they call your name. Then you'll go out on the catwalk one at a time, walk down it..."

A sudden ringing filled Mila's ears. Her throat felt tight. She clutched the cloak around her and fell to her knees, trying to be as small and unobtrusive as she could. She felt the silver cat and cougar kneel down beside her. "I can't!" Mila exclaimed. "I can't do that. Everyone will be looking right at me."

"It's okay, Mila. We can take you off the roster if you need us to," the cougar said in a coaxing tone.

Mila took a shaky gulp of air. She'd wanted to show off her outfit, but she'd hoped to catch a few eyes at once, not be the one person everyone in the room was staring at.

Natalie was gently rubbing at her shoulder. "Let me guess,

some body image issues?" she asked once Mila had calmed down enough.

The calico nodded. She looked up into the understanding eyes of the cougar. "Had some personal experience with that?" she asked.

"Oh yeah. It took me a very, very long time to believe that other people would find me attractive. So, can I give a piece of advice?"

"Sure," Mila said, with more assurance than she actually felt.

"Look, lots of people show up at the Eternal Party and expect the magic here to solve all their problems. It doesn't. But what it can do, if you give it a chance, is give you the space and the time for you to solve the problems yourself."

Mila thought of the floorboards trembling underneath her. Natalie was perhaps more right than she knew.

The cougar continued, "That's what it did for me. Now, you don't have to go out if you don't want to, but my suggestion is to take a leap, while you have people to catch you if you tumble."

The calico took several deep breaths to recenter herself. "Okay," Mila said. "I'll do it." Part of her still didn't want to, the thought of all those eyes on her still sent her stomach churning.

The cougar grinned and tapped Mila's shoulder in thought. "Let's see. You've never been down a catwalk before. You don't know how to strut, do you?"

"On it." Alex winked and darted off into the throng of felines, coming back a few moments later with a tall, stony-faced jaguar who was wearing a costume of similar regality to Mila's own. Alex introduced her as Ingrid and quickly explained what Mila needed. The jaguar's imperious stare made Mila worried she was about to be on the receiving end of yet more jealousy, but then she caught sight of the tag hanging on the jaguar's collar: her owner was someone named Zuberi.

Natalie resumed touching up her costume and Alex sat back to watch as Ingrid scrutinized the calico. "The most important thing to do is hold your back straight and your head high," the jaguar said and demonstrated the posture.

"I don't know that I can—"

"Back straight! Head high!"

Mila swallowed and extended her head up to match the jaguar's posture.

"Better. You are a queen and are dressed as such. A queen must hold herself so. That way commoners must look up to her."

Mila glanced down at her half-naked torso. "I don't feel very queen-like."

"Head high!" the jaguar repeated sternly. "A queen does not have time for such doubts." When Mila followed the directions, she went on. "Now to movement. Poise and grace are key. To achieve poise and grace, you must be deliberate in all action. Move as slow as you need to achieve the desired result. Think of a cloud: it does not need to move fast to catch our eye and command our attention in its journey across the sky. You must do the same. Now, we step."

As one, Mila and the jaguar extended one leg and stepped forward.

"Recenter your weight over your forward foot and bring your back foot in. Return to having your back straight, head high. Pause. You may pause, for you are a queen. It is commoners who rush. Then step again."

A high giggle made Mila turn her head. The lynx who Alex called Vivien was passing by. "What's this? Does the new girl need walking lessons?" The other felines around her joined in the giggling laughter before disappearing into the crowd.

Natalie had ducked down with one hand held up to partially hide her face out of shame. "I am so sorry, Mila," she said. "I will talk with her later."

Ingrid dismissed Natalie's apologies and Mila's concern with a snort. "Feh," Ingrid said. "You are royalty. Ignore the laughter of the chattering classes. You have no need for their gossiping ways."

"Right," Mila said and practiced taking another step forward.

Thinking of the lynx as one of the "chattering classes" made her feel a little better.

"Much better. But you do not know where to look. Pick one thing, pretend it is the only thing of importance in the world. Focus on it and direct all your energy towards it. That will be enough." There was the ring of a bell and a voice calling for the felines to come to order.

Natalie stood up. "I'll go speak with the director and have you go last, Mila."

Ingrid bowed her head. "A good idea. You should go last and watch the others. Take what ideas you can. Discard the rest. You will succeed." The jaguar tilted her ears forward and departed without explanation.

Alex snuck back in beside Mila now that Ingrid had gone. "What did I tell you?" the cat said with a grin. "She knows her stuff."

"I wouldn't be surprised if she was a queen," Mila muttered.

Alex gave a noncommittal shrug. "Rumor is she's noble of some flavor, just never managed to figure out what flavor that is."

"Huh." She saw Natalie conversing with the coyote from before and gesturing back to the calico.

The coyote caught Mila's gaze and nodded. He was running his final checks and as soon as he appeared satisfied, he stepped out from behind the curtain and onto the stage. A microphone amplified his voice both in the ballroom and backstage. "Greetings one and all and welcome to tonight's festivities. We will be delighting you all with a presentation of the felines. First up, Abigail!"

Mila found her way off into the wings of the stage, barely hidden from view from the audience but able to see a good chunk of the catwalk. Several of the felines who went out were happy enough to walk down to one end, pose, and then walk back. Others made more of a show of it. Mila thought a few of them must have been professional models by how they held themselves so naturally. Ingrid too simply strutted to the end of the stage, waited a moment looking almost bored at the attention she was receiving, then strutted off. Alex just had fun. He dashed to the end of the runway, waggled his eyebrows with a suggestive roll of his hips, and ran back. Seeing such varied performances made Mila feel at ease: it didn't matter what she did, someone would like it. Watching Natalie felt best though. The cougar seemed to be so at ease with herself, doing a seductive dance at the end of the catwalk, it made Mila think that she could have that confidence too. Someday.

Then there was Vivien again. The lynx flashed Mila a dangerous smile before performing a whole gymnastics routine to make her way down the runway. At the end, she stood on one leg with the other pointing straight up into the air, parallel to her spine. She paused a moment to slip a hand down between her thighs and spread her labia wide to a hoot and holler from the crowd. Then she cartwheeled back offstage, deliberately bumping past Mila as she did so.

As each feline did their part, they filtered out from the edges of the stage to go mingle with the crowd. Before long, Mila was the only one left.

"And finally, we are proud to introduce the newest attendee of the Eternal Party. Please welcome Mila!"

There was applause, actual applause before she had even shown her face. She stood just beyond the curtains and tried to remember everything Ingrid had taught her. She needed a focus out in the audience. Her eyes swept through the crowd, and she saw Alonso there, just beyond the end of the stage. Him, she could focus on, and so long as she focused on him, it was as though the rest of the eyes upon her didn't matter.

She barely paid attention to her movement. She only knew that she was moving towards him. When she reached the edge of the runway, she paused and slowly turned to survey the crowd. One hand lifted into the air and waved in a queenly fashion.

Mila, buoyed with confidence, turned back towards the stage, where Alex and Natalie gave her a thumbs-up from the wings.

The coyote announcer's voice boomed out over her ears. "Take a good look at the tag on her collar, ladies and gentlemen. That's right, she's been collared by our very own Alonso. Congratulations, Mila."

A gasp went through the entire room. She heard, rather than saw, people leaning over in their seats to whisper to one another. About her.

From the wings, Alex was frantically waving for her to come towards them, and Natalie was mouthing, "You can do it," over and over again.

She tried to remember the brief lessons Ingrid had offered, but they felt like fragments drifting away from her grasp. Until she remembered what she had said about the chattering classes. Mila was supposed to be a queen. She shouldn't have to worry about them.

The calico lifted her head high and stepped forward, marching offstage while trying to hold onto that feeling as best she could.

Alex and Natalie had their arms out and pulled Mila offstage like she had just been walking a tightrope. "You did it!" Alex said with a fist pump.

"Yeah. I did," Mila said, dazed. She could feel adrenaline lingering in her system, making every muscle tense.

The coyote ducked back behind the curtain and shook Mila's hand. "A pleasure to meet you. I'd suggest you find your owner as quickly as possible. He will likely want to be in charge of your introductions past this point."

The thought of being back in Alonso's embrace made the lingering anxiety of being on stage ebb away. Maybe that was the magic, soothing her mind and encouraging her to relax into the embrace of her owner, but if so, she welcomed it this time. She thanked the coyote before slipping out the side with Alex and Natalie helping to keep her upright. Already the runway was being stored away, to leave a spot for dancing in the middle of the room.

Thankfully, Alonso was waiting there to meet her when she came out, one hand leaning on his cane and the other outstretched to invite her into a hug. The calico fell into the embrace, listening to Alonso's whispered praise and approval that made her spine tingle in delight. "Alex, Natalie, thank you for looking after my kitten."

Natalie leaned in and placed a lingering kiss on the side of the fox's muzzle that made Mila feel momentarily jealous. "Of course, Alonso. I hope to get to spend some more time with you again someday."

The little silver cat struck a heroic pose in his mage robe. "Always happy to be of serv-eee-hee-hees!" The cat broke down into frenetic giggles as his Master, the Dalmatian, hefted him up over one shoulder with little effort. True to what Alex had said before, the Dalmatian had dressed up like a barbarian, loincloth and all.

He looked to Mila and signed O-K with a questioning look.

The calico fumbled an O-K sign back. "Thank you," she said.

Alonso cleared his throat and made a show of touching his chin and then extending his hand forward.

Mila quickly made the same gesture.

The Dalmatian grinned, glanced over to the wriggling cat on his shoulder, and made an apologetic gesture to suggest that he had to be excused to go fuck his feline roughly. He waved goodbye and left, while Alex, realizing he was being carried away, shouted his goodbyes from the Dalmatian's shoulder.

"If you'll excuse me," Natalie said, "I'm hoping to find some fun this evening." She departed as well.

Alonso gave Mila a squeeze and kept her close as he began to walk through the crowd. She recognized very few of the canines, and even after being introduced she could hardly remember their names or faces afterwards. After a while, Mila noticed how Alonso was deliberately running ahead of the typical questions Mila might be asked. Without prompting, he discussed where and how they met (a made-up version of course) and what attracted them to each other. It meant there wasn't much reason for anyone else to question Mila and accidentally find any problems in her story due to her inability to lie to a canine. On the few occasions Mila had to speak up, she adopted her best speaking-with-the-boss voice. They seemed to like that.

The one canine they met that Mila she did recognize fully was Aisha. The jackal wore a backless dress that elegantly showed off the stripe of black and silver in her fur there. She smiled as the fox and calico approached. "May I speak with your kitten for a moment alone?"

"Only for a moment," Alonso said and pressed against the small of Mila's back to encourage her to step off to the side with Aisha.

The jackal found a secluded spot next to the floor-to-ceiling windows that looked out over the street. She sipped once from her wine glass. "There was another housequake earlier today. You wouldn't happen to know anything about that, would you?" She spoke in a voice that was quiet without being hushed, a clandestine voice.

Mila bit her lip and her hands worried the edge of her cloak. "I really don't want to talk about that right now," she said, trying her best to keep the image of BD's face out of her mind's eye.

Aisha's supporting hand was on her shoulder. "No, not right now," she agreed to Mila's relief. "Now is a time for revelry. Although, to be honest, I didn't expect to see you out here so soon. I only came down for a break from my research." She paused for another sip of her drink and brought her head a little closer, her voice a little lower. "Are you doing all right?"

"I am, ma'am," Mila said, causing a slight frown to tease the edge of the jackal's muzzle. "Last night was... very stressful, but Alonso has been showing me the nicer side of the house today." The calico spun on the spot. "Look at this. I never thought I'd be able to look this amazing."

"Indeed," the jackal said, her eyes drifting down to take the calico in. Then there was an almost audible snap as the jackal's muzzle wrenched upwards and her ears laid flat against her skull.

Mila replayed the last few moments in her mind. She'd been spinning slowly and Aisha's gaze was roaming up and down to take in all the details of Erik's work. Then, briefly, the jackal's head had canted and she ran a tongue against her lips as she lingered on the curve of Mila's breasts. Aisha had been viewing her with the same sexual intent so many other canines at the party had, and then had almost immediately yanked herself away.

Aisha was embarrassed. She was the one other person at the Eternal Party who knew that Mila didn't belong there, and she had just been treating her like she was any other feline here.

This collided with the realization that another woman was finding her attractive. "It's all right," Mila said. "I-I don't mind you looking."

The jackal's ears shot up, suspicious and alert. "Really? You don't sound certain."

Now it was Mila's turn to hold her ears flat. She tried to sort through the new feelings. "I can't say I've ever had a woman check me out like that before. It's... different. But not bad," she hastened to add. "It's just that the closest I've been to another woman has been late-night fantasies of being wrapped up in Jeta Horowitz's arms, you know."

"Oh, I know." The jackal shook her head with a laugh. "I've met plenty of women who tell me that they would be straight were it not for Jeta."

Mila rubbed at an elbow nervously and went silent as another couple passed by them within earshot. "So you can look, if you want."

The jackal considered, resting her cheek against her fingers. "Do you only want me to look?"

Mila stammered and tripped over her words, stopped only when Aisha's hand touched her own. "Tell me if you become uncomfortable," the jackal said, and it was a true canine command. Mila had to obey.

Aisha sipped her wine and took a step around the calico, keeping her hand on Mila's arm. It trailed up from her wrist to her elbow to her shoulder. Mila found herself hyperfocused on the simple movement of Aisha's claws along her fur, so that she was completely oblivious to the incoming kiss until the scent of wine-sweetened lips hit her nose and whiskers brushed along her own. By the time she had processed that enough to want to return the kiss, Aisha had already pulled away, and Mila's muzzle met only air.

The jackal continued her slow circumnavigation of the calico, her attention drifting along Mila's body. She found herself adjusting her posture to give the jackal a better view, holding out a shoulder, puffing out her chest, and then cocking her hips. Aisha's gaze lingered there, staring at her folds, taking sensually slow sips of her drink as she did.

Aisha's touch returned to Mila's hip, and the calico was surprised to find how warm she felt just a few inches away from those fingers. She was relieved when Aisha decided to move her hand upwards rather than to explore the nearby sex. Mila still wasn't completely sure she was ready for that. Even then, her fur went out on end when those claws drifted up to the underside of one breast and caught on the piercing hanging there. "I am surprised you opted for these right away."

"I, uh, didn't. Alonso decided on them for me."

The jackal's hand flinched away. "Tch! That man." She scowled down into her wine and took another heavy drink.

Mila felt the moment passing. Aisha's mood had soured and was not returning. "You are indeed beautiful," the jackal said, "but there are more important concerns facing us. I need to get back to my work, and if you are not otherwise engaged tomorrow, I'd like you to stop by the library, so we can get you out of here as soon as possible."

Mila bobbed her head. "I will let Alonso know."

"Good girl," Aisha said, although it did not prompt the same sort of pleasure overload that Alonso's praise did. "Perhaps we can continue this exploration then. For now, hurry back to your owner." She pointed in the direction he had gone.

She followed Aisha's pointing finger to the far wall of the room. While the central floor was now being used by couples who danced to classic waltzes and modern tangos, many conversation spots had been set up elsewhere, separated by planters whose broad leaves and flowers muted sounds and gave the illusion of privacy. A few felines were wandering with trays to offer snacks or drinks or sex toys to the seated guests. Mila quickly located Alonso. The fox was in attentive conversation with a few others. He smiled as Mila came close.

"There you are," he said. "Everyone, you've already seen Mila, my new kitten. Mila, this is Noel." He gestured to a maned wolf sitting across from him who, in contrast to the typical style of the masquerade, was wearing a Stetson hat that would have been over-sized if not for his lanky frame. The wolf tipped his hat to Mila. "This is Zuberi." Alonso gestured to a painted dog who had opted for a leather harness visible underneath his dinner jacket. "And this is—"

"Ingrid," Mila said, recognizing the jaguar. She flattened her ears a little at interrupting her owner. "Thank you for your help earlier."

The jaguar was kneeling besides the couch in front of Zuberi. She coughed and extended her neck slightly to show off her collar and the tag on it that declared her to be Zuberi's.

Mila was confused until she remembered what Alonso had told her earlier. Her actions reflected on her owner. She gave a bow to Zuberi, "And thank you for... letting her help me." It was a lame ending, but the painted dog did not seem to mind.

Alonso moved his cane from where it had been resting on the circular couch next to him. He patted the now vacated spot until Mila took it.

The maned wolf tracked Mila closely as she sat down. "So you finally did it, old man. Wondered if you'd ever pick a feline of your own. And she is quite a treat, I must say." His tongue ran over his lips. "Don't suppose you'll loan her out soon?"

"Not soon, I suspect," Alonso said. "I still have to do a lot of work to get her to where I want her."

"Naturally. Keep me in mind once you get her there."

Mila tuned out as the two canines began talking in greater detail about some issues of sports which she didn't care much about. Alonso's hand had crept under her cloak and was kneading delightfully at a spot just above the corset. She mewled in pleasure and melted back against the fox.

Her attention was drawn to Ingrid, still posing, chest thrust forward, kneeling before the painted dog. He was caressing her just between the ears and it seemed to be having much the same effect on her as Alonso's touch was on herself. The jaguar was trying to maintain that regal demeanor, but each scritch over her head threatened to make her lose her posture. As the calico watched, Ingrid's eyes kept drooping and staying closed longer each time. Then, one time, they remained shut even as he kept rubbing that spot. Slowly a purr issued forth from the jaguar and she went limp, posture dripping away.

The jaguar, moving languorously, turned around and began pushing herself up just high enough for her lips to meet the painted dog's. He broke the kiss, whispering softly to "his princess," before she began making her way back down his body with her muzzle, exploring the contours of his chest with delicate, loving movements.

Despite expecting it, Mila was still surprised when Ingrid undid the painted dog's fly and pulled his shaft out into her muzzle. She buried her nose in the fur of his groin, swallowing around the whole length with ease.

"You needn't wait on my behalf," said the painted dog in a rich baritone voice with a strong Swahili accent.

Mila thought he was talking to her, but no, he was addressing Alonso. The calico turned slightly and saw the fox smirking down at her and also noticed a very prominent bulge in his pants. It was one thing for her to prance around semi-naked in front of so many people, and it was one thing for her to enjoy it, but did he honestly expect to fuck her in front of them too?

"Into my lap, kitten," her owner commanded. And she was compelled to crawl up there, facing him. She tried to express her concern with her face, but she needn't have worried. The fox didn't seem to have any desire to fuck right there, despite what his erection suggested. He caressed her cheek and spoke to the other canines. "I'm going slow with this one. Her desires run deep but her experience is limited. I'm enjoying breaking down her barriers one at a time."

Noel chuckled. "If it were me, I'd have her deep-throating me and loving it, like Ingrid there."

The jaguar gave no sign that she recognized she was being spoken about. Her nose was so tightly pressed into Zuberi's belly that Mila wondered if she could even breathe like that. She was swallowing loudly around the painted dog's shaft.

Zuberi himself only shook his head at Noel's comment.

"If I had done that," Alonso added, "I would not have been able to experience that tremor that ran up her spine the first time she exposed herself to another at my command. I prefer the slower approach."

"Maybe, maybe," the maned wolf said. "But I'd be having a hell of a lot more fun. Oh, hello there."

"Greetings Master Alonso, Master Zuberi, Master Noel," said the newcomer, in silken smooth tones that spread a chill of ice down Mila's spine. The calico turned her head to see Vivien the lynx standing there. "Master Noel, you are lacking a partner this evening. May I offer myself?"

"Fuck yes," the maned wolf said and without any ceremony revealed his own cock. "Get over here and ride me."

The lynx practically sprang into the wolf's lap and within two seconds had his shaft sunk deep inside her. Mila flinched at the thought of such a quick, unlubricated entrance, but Vivien looked up, caught Mila's eyes, and grinned.

That bitch, Mila thought. The calico couldn't stop her claws from extending and pricking through Alonso's fur.

The fox knew that something was wrong and he whispered in her ear. "Calm down."

That did calm her down, rather forcefully, but her distaste for the lynx remained. She glanced to the side and saw Ingrid still lost in her own little world, happily servicing the painted dog's cock with her mouth. She tried to look into the shadows of other booths along the rim of the ballroom and saw more figures copulating happily.

So fucking was typical in these spots, and although Alonso had given good enough reason for the other canines why they weren't, here was Vivien shoving it into the calico's face that she wasn't doing what was expected, that she wasn't serving him as he ought to be served.

That thought more so than any other burned in her mind. No, Mila wasn't as kinky or as open as anyone else here, but the thought that she wasn't worthy of Alonso for that reason stuck in her craw. It was as though she were back in high school again and being mocked and teased for her asymmetric pelt any time she tried to date a non-calico. Suddenly it no longer mattered that she had an audience, because Vivien was in that audience and Mila was not about to let the lynx get the last laugh.

Careful this time to keep her claws retracted, the calico drew her hands down Alonso's chest in a circuitous path down to his belt. The fox cast her a questioning glance and got a stern look of resolve in response. She fumbled with his belt and zipper. A moment of hesitation hit her when she felt the warmth of his shaft under his boxers, but then she remembered Vivien's eyes on her and she yanked the stiff member out into the air and positioned it to her entrance.

The calico shoved herself down onto the fox's length and grunted at the sudden penetration: thankfully, the no-pain side of the house's magic also extended to shoving a full size dick into herself without preparation. There was a touch of discomfort but nothing more. Besides, if Vivien could do it, so could she. She lifted herself up and sank back down, still giving no thought to her own pleasure but trying to make it feel good for him. His expression was pleased at least.

After five or six anger-fueled thrusts, Mila began to relax and actually enjoy herself. She was wetter than she could ever remember being: maybe the house's magic was compensating for the lack of lube. While Alonso's shaft felt good under her tail the previous night, this was a much better fit. The next time she sank down a little moan came out on her breath, and she found herself licking lips that were dry.

Mila wrapped her arms around his chest to steady herself and he gripped her under her thighs to take up some of the pressure of lifting herself off. After a few readjustments, she finally found a good position for her legs. Then she began to bounce more eagerly in his lap, causing shivers up her own spine as he kept hitting deeper within her. The swift thrusts also caused her new piercings to make themselves known again. They tugged at her most sensitive spots in unfamiliar yet delightful ways and the only thing that held her back from giving full voice to her pleasure was the knowledge that she was still surrounded by several complete strangers.

The calico glanced over at Vivien, feeling smug, but that smugness drained away when she saw the maned wolf with his head back, tongue lolling out, and the lynx bouncing with a wet slapping sound as she dropped down over his knot and then back off on every single bounce.

Fucking hell, the calico thought. She glanced down at the knot on Alonso's own shaft, performing a furious mental calculus. Maybe it just looked big and wouldn't actually feel that big. She bit her lip and, the next time she dropped down, tried to press a little farther to no success. She lifted up and tried again. Nothing. She winced from the effort and strain of trying to fit him in. Fear began to trickle into her thoughts: how badly would she injure herself if she did manage to take the entire knot? Each time she pushed down now, her muscles clenched tight as if to seal herself off.

"Shh," Alonso said, trying to soothe her. "You have taken enough for today."

Behind them, there was a giggle from the lynx.

Alonso looked over Mila's shoulder. "Something funny, Vivien?"

"Yes, Master Alonso," she said, still giggling.

"And what is that?"

"Uh." The lynx's vigorous fucking of the maned wolf came to a sudden halt. "It was just something that was funny to me. Nothing you need to concern yourself with, Master Alonso."

"I asked you a question, feline."

The tone sent a shiver down Mila's back, because it easily could have been said in anger, but there wasn't any anger in Alonso's voice whatsoever. Instead, his words just dripped with disappointment. Mila felt she could die of second-hand shame for the lynx, and she didn't even fucking like her.

It was suddenly very quiet in their corner of the room.

"Yes, you did, Master Alonso," the lynx said.

"Then I will ask the question again, and this time I expect the full truth. What was funny?"

"I was laughing at your girl's inability to take your knot, because anyone you own should be able to please you just as you desire. I was hoping you would realize she was not appropriate for you and reject her."

"Stand at attention, Vivien."

The lynx slowly, sadly pulled herself off the wolf's lap. Before she could stand as directed, Noel reached out and smacked her ass hard enough to get a yelp of pain from the lynx, then he sat back with a growl.

Vivien carefully raised herself to her full height in the center of the circular arc of the couch. She stared into the distance, not looking at any of the canines. "Master Alonso, I—"

"Be silent," the fox commanded, and the sounds died in the lynx's throat.

Alonso's hand touched Mila's hip. "Get off and sit beside me."

Mila did as she was instructed to, but she held onto Alonso's hand for a moment, squeezing it and looking meaningfully into his eyes. He squeezed it back and his touch lingered for a moment as though he were trying to tell her that things were not as bad as they seemed.

Alonso stood up before Vivien, the fox not even bothering to tuck away his erect shaft before he did so. He stood before the feline, whose ears were now flat against her skull and whose eyes were trying to point anywhere but at the fox. "I thought you respected me, Vivien."

The lynx blinked away some tears. She opened her mouth, ready to protest, but no sound came out.

"Speak," the fox said simply.

"I do respect you, sir. You're my favorite dom in the whole house. But I don't want to see you unhappy because you rushed into ownership of a clearly inferior feline."

Mila rolled her eyes at that, but Alonso spoke in the same deeply disappointed timbre he had used before. "A clearly inferior feline?"

"Yes, sir."

"That's what you think of *my* choice?"

"Yes, sir." Vivien looked utterly miserable and she sounded like it too.

"And yet you claim to respect me."

"I do, sir, but—"

"But nothing!" The fox jabbed a finger in Mila's direction. "I have already made my decision. I chose her. Nothing you say or do will change that. Now either accept that or stop lying to yourself that you respect me as deeply as you say."

Even from where Mila was sitting, she could feel the force of the command. It had to be obeyed, but just as Alonso had done with her earlier, he had given the lynx a choice. Which would win out? Her devotion to Alonso or her dislike for Mila?

The lynx's shoulders tightened for a moment, as if she was fighting off the need to answer either way and being compelled to by the house. "Mila is yours," she said with finality. "She is your property. You are her owner."

Alonso held her gently by her shoulders as she squeezed her eyes shut and lowered her head. The fox even placed a delicate kiss on her forehead. For a moment, nothing was said, and even Noel and Zuberi seemed to be holding their breath. (Ingrid, oblivious to it all, was still enraptured by Zuberi's shaft.) "You do want me to be happy, don't you, Vivien?"

The lynx nodded, not willing to speak.

"Even though I'm with Mila, you want me do be happy, don't you?"

The lynx nodded again. "Yes, sir. I understand she is yours now."

Alonso cradled the underside of Vivien's muzzle in a hand, lifting it and waiting until she opened her eyes again. "You want me to be happy with her, don't you?"

The lynx looked confused. "Sir?"

The fox tilted his head one way and then the other. "I'm sure you've noticed she's a little inexperienced. But you want me to be happy with her, don't you?"

The lynx blinked once or twice then nodded fiercely. "Of course, sir. You should love spending time with the kitten you've chosen."

"You know how to serve me so well, Vivien. Think of how much Mila would benefit from your knowledge and skill. Assist her in serving me better, or risk that I will be unhappy in my choice of submissive."

Mila again felt the soft tug of a command, but this time there was no resistance from the lynx. She was already being led down the track. This was just the final push she needed.

"Of course I will help her, sir. You can rely on me! And I'm so sorry for forcing you to interrupt your playtime with your kitten. Please don't wait on my account a moment more." Vivien trailed a hand up Alonso's inner thigh and cupped his balls, which still hung out of his pants. "You know how much she'll love feeling your seed inside her." She gave the balls a gentle pat and then stepped back to the wolf who, after many apologies from the lynx, allowed her to resume her position in his lap.

Alonso slid into the seat next to Mila and guided her back into his lap as well. "Don't look so surprised," he ordered.

Mila shivered. She'd been expecting something quite else, something like the jawbreaker treatment she'd heard of earlier, or something with lots of crops and whips being used painfully, or maybe Alonso drastically rewriting the lynx's personality. Instead, it felt like he'd changed very little. Vivien still thought of Mila as a clearly inferior feline to be serving Alonso, and the lynx still appeared to worship the very ground Alonso walked on, but now that meant she would help Mila instead of trying to sabotage her. All he'd really done was make it clear that she couldn't change his mind.

Mila caught the lynx's gaze as the calico was repositioning herself with the tip of Alonso's cock against her sex. There was a meaningful look in Vivien's eyes, and she began to descend deep onto the wolf's shaft before nodding to the calico. It took Mila a second to realize that Vivien wanted her to follow her lead. She did, despite her residual distaste for the other woman.

Once they were both equally deep, Vivien swayed a little from side to side, rolling her hips with her. The lynx gradually slowed the movement of her upper body, until it barely moved at all, but her hips kept up the same motion. Mila tried to replicate the effect, and she nearly failed once or twice with Alonso's cock threatening to slip out of her, but soon she was doing it just like the lynx and earning a pleasured murr of contentment from the fox.

Alonso touched her throat with a single finger, which he trailed down her body in a zig-zag fashion until it was just above his thrusting cock. There the bar through her clit was still sending shocks of undefinable ecstasy through her body. Her breath caught in her throat as she felt that finger slowly approach the piercing. When they met and he gently flicked the bar, it sent electric bolts of pleasure through her that had her knees squeezing him and her spine flexing and her mouth biting down on a finger to keep from crying out.

Her ears perked as she suddenly was aware of the wolf and fox talking. "You see what I mean?" the fox was saying. "She has never had such attentions before and I get to experience her very first reactions."

"It is truly a pleasure to watch you work," the maned wolf said back. The painted dog next to him was nodding in agreement.

"You could be just as skilled," Alonso said. "You just need to work on your subtlety."

"I know. But sometimes there's such a cute butt on a disobedient feline and I just need to give it a firm slap to correct her." The wolf pushed Vivien forward in his lap to admire her backside and raked his claws through her fur.

Alonso chuckled and groped Mila the same way, but there was a gentleness in his touch that was missing from Noel.

Mila kept mimicking Vivien's actions, learning little motions and how they could be used to pleasure her partner. But after a while, it became clear that the maned wolf had needs of his own. He gripped the lynx tight and started to pummel his shaft into her sex, eagerly popping his own knot into and out of her as she shivered in delight. He growled low, and that growl turned to a deep low howl as he climaxed while hilted balls-deep. Mila silently marveled at how so much seed was being pumped into the lynx that it had to spill out in copious amounts.

Whoever worked as a janitor here had better have been paid a ton, she thought.

The lynx purred sweetly at the maned wolf. "May I go assist Master Alonso and Mila?"

The wolf, who had gone nearly limp with his tongue lolling out, lifted one weak hand and made gentle shooing motions.

Vivien stepped off of him and knelt down before Alonso and Mila, not caring that she was dripping cum from her sex or that, so far as Mila could tell, she had yet to climax herself. For a while she just watched as Mila's sex slid over the fox's shaft with an expression approaching reverence on her face. Then her ears shot up. "Master Alonso," she purred out. "Since this is the first outing with your kitten, why don't you paint her?"

Paint her? Mila thought. Even more so than Erik already had?

The fox gave a squeeze to Mila's hips. "Good idea. Kitten slide off me and kneel before Vivien."

The calico obeyed with a touch of regret. That shaft was feeling quite good inside her and her desire was no longer suppressed by being surrounded by so many new faces: she wanted to get off. She slipped down to kneel facing the fox and he stood up so his shaft was level with her face.

Mila wasn't quite sure what was expected of her, but she thought she understood the common porn tropes. She opened her mouth.

"No, no, close up."

Unsure, she did, and then she remembered what Vivien had suggested. Painting...

The calico shivered and watched as Vivien took a firm grasp on the fox's shaft. Her fingers danced over it in complicated patterns that Mila felt she should be learning, but instead the calico was focused on the head of that cock, pointed directly towards her face. It twitched and pulsed on its own accord as much as from Vivien's stroking. Behind it, Alonso's hips were starting to shudder. It did not take long before he came and several ropes of sticky seed covered her face, dripping down onto her chest. She reached up to brush a glob off that had landed just behind her nose, but Alonso waggled a finger. "Leave it," he said in between quick panting breaths.

Her hand slipped away and she looked up at him with her ears cocked to the side. Then she looked down at his shaft, still standing proud before him, messy with the remnants of sex. There wasn't a towel around. Mila swallowed, opened her mouth, and began to move forward, only to be stopped by Alonso waving her off.

"Vivien, why don't you clean me off?"

The lynx slipped around Mila's side and pulled the fox shaft into her mouth, stripping it clean with her tongue. She pulled off with a swirling motion of her head and a last flick of her tongue across the tip of his cock. "Thank you, sir."

Mila felt a surge of warring emotions well up within her: gratitude that she did not have to clean off a cock with her mouth semi-publicly, but also frustration that the privilege had gone to Vivien instead. He was Mila's owner. She was his kitten. Surely that meant it was her responsibility, right?

Alonso, unaware of the conflict within the calico, gave Vivien a doting pet on the head, then pulled Mila up beside him. "Let's head back to my room," he suggested and Mila nodded.

Mila's ears perked at a high, keening sound and she turned to see Ingrid staring with desperate need at the painted dog's shaft held just out of reach in front of her. She was straining at his iron grip on her scruff, and only with soothing rubs over her ears and whispers of "My princess," did she calm down and resume her regal kneeling position. Zuberi let go and shifted forward, not to slide his shaft back into her mouth, but to clean it off on the fur of her muzzle, before tucking himself away. He gave one last pat to Ingrid's head before standing before the fox.

"Alonso, a pleasure as always." As the painted dog and fox shook hands, Mila marveled at Zuberi's voice, refined and charismatic: Mila would have happily listened to him read the dirtiest of porno scripts just to hear him speak. When he turned to address her, his handsomeness caused Mila to feel a pang of jealousy for Ingrid. "And a pleasure to meet you as well. Should you ever desire a tour of the more exotic parts of our dungeon facilities, please let me know."

Mila thanked him, feeling slightly too dazed to comprehend his offer or consider what the more exotic parts of the dungeon might contain.

Then they left, but first Alonso seemed interested in saying his personal goodbyes to everyone there. As they went, Mila caught almost every one of them staring at her and the fox cream coating her. Alonso whispered a command into her ear to masturbate gently and she found herself rubbing a finger along the edge of her clit piercing even with the gaze of these canines on her.

There was something different in the canines they spoke with and how they regarded Mila. They looked at her with approval now, and Mila was trying to understand what had changed. The only new thing was the seed that marked her, but a voice inside her pointed out that if she was wearing his seed, it had meant that she had pleased him. She'd done a good job.

Mila felt oddly pleased with herself.

But even with that, she gave a sigh of relief as they left the ballroom. Some privacy was what she wanted now, and privacy especially so that she could finally get off after feeling teased throughout so much of the day.

Back at the room, Alonso slowly helped Mila undress. Although here at the house, undress meant "down to collar and corset." She was shocked they were left on as Alonso guided her into the shower, but they appeared to be waterproof at least, and they felt so comfortable and natural that soon she had forgotten they were there. The fox's fingers began to work out not only the seed from her fur but also the paints that Erik had applied to her earlier.

"Hands up. On the wall."

Mila rested her hands on the wall and looked back over her shoulder at him.

"You did very good today, kitten," he said as a hand came up under her tail and a finger pressed deep into her sex. Mila panted softly. "I hope you had fun too."

"Uh-huh," she said with a shudder. She was so pent up that

the finger was already getting her needy. It curled and twisted inside with sharp motions that brought gasps to her lips.

While Mila was content to enjoy that one digit, Alonso brushed gently over the bar through her clit while plucking at the nipple ring like it was a guitar string. It was all Mila could do to keep herself upright under the cacophony of pleasurable sensations.

"Going to cum for me, kitten?"

"Uh-huh."

"Orgasm hard, right now."

It was a climax unlike any other Mila could remember. Sure she had been horny all day. Sure she had been enjoying being pounded by fox cock not that long ago. Sure there was currently a finger twisting expertly within her, but it was his words, his command, that pushed her over the edge. It was as though his words had removed the need for foreplay and action and just pressed straight on the button in her brain which initiated an immediate orgasm.

Mila's claws extended, scrabbling for purchase on the sheer surface of the shower wall as she came. He seemed to have found a special spot inside her, and he delighted in grinding his knuckle against it. It prolonged her orgasm in a rolling wave until she quietly begged him to stop.

Alonso's finger stilled within her but his thumb brushed across her clit piercing. "Would you like these taken out?"

Mila's voice was momentarily incoherent as the sensations coming from her clit made it impossible for her to do anything but mewl. She finally managed to whisper out, "Please," in between teasings.

The fox pulled out the three piercings with deliberate slowness. When he had removed the ring back in Erik's room, it had felt like nothing at all, but now he was working them out in ways that made Mila clench down on that finger still pressed deep within her. She breathed a sigh of relief when they were gone, even if it meant that Alonso pulled that finger out. She double-checked that there was no lasting holes, still unable to believe the magic was capable of that.

Later, dried and happy, they cuddled on the bed. "Is every day going to be like this?" Mila asked.

"Some are," Alonso said, a finger brushing the fur down along her neck. "The house has different events and not everyone likes them all. Some are big gigs like tonight, with virtually the whole house in attendance, others are smaller affairs which might only draw a dozen or so people at once. And of course, there are private spots."

"But it feels like it's all sex all the time."

"Mostly sex, most of the time."

"But doesn't that get boring?"

The fox laughed softly and pet her cheek. "I have been here ten years and while I have experienced many emotions, boredom has rarely happened."

Mila found that hard to believe, but she'd experienced so much just in her one day here than she'd even thought really possible. If people who were well aware of all these kinky possibilities could stay here for years with no problem, it could probably keep her entertained for a long time as well.

The calico shivered. She was thinking like she was going to stay here forever. She had to get out of here. And soon.

Sonata

⌒⌒∞⌒

Mila woke up the second day much like the first, forgetting where she was. But this time, she accepted the reality of her position much faster and with less immediate panic. She shifted out of bed slowly so as not to wake the fox. The calico didn't want to go exploring the house on her own, not when any canine she met could command her obedience, but there was, off to the corner of Alonso's room, a small reading nook next to a window, hidden by a curtain.

When she pulled the curtain aside and slipped into the nook, there were things waiting for her there: fresh brewed coffee, a few croissants, and a copy of "Two Times the Danger," a thriller novel she had half-finished before getting trapped here. A bookmark had even been tucked into the novel at the same place she had left off.

Magic, she reminded herself. The calico curled up and started reading again.

Mila made it through three more chapters before she heard the fox stirring. She didn't move the curtain or call out. She just waited to see what would happen.

Alonso shuffled around, sliding into his silk robe and a pair of slippers. There was a pause during which she guessed he was looking around. Then he stepped closer to her hiding place and gently parted the curtains. He glanced down at her there, with the book propped open on her lap. "Good morning," he said in a voice still bedside quiet as if he didn't want to disturb her. "I see you found my favorite spot."

"Who do I thank for the book?" she said.

"Thank the house."

"Really?"

The fox nodded and stifled a yawn.

"Oh." Mila looked around, but there didn't seem to be an appropriate face of the house for her to approach. So she caressed the windowsill. "Thank you for the book. Even if you did trap me here."

There was a slight shiver in the woodwork.

Mila felt something tight in her chest. "Trapped," she repeated.

Alonso sensed her rising panic, knelt next to her, and closed his hand over hers. "Relax, kitten. We'll get you out of here," he said.

The calico's ears perked suddenly. "Oh, I forgot to mention. Aisha said she wanted to see me today to work on getting me out." Just as suddenly her spirits deflated. "But hasn't she been trying with you, for ten years?"

The fox massaged his thumb into the back of her hand. "To be honest, I haven't tried hard to get out in quite some time. It felt like we hit a wall and couldn't make any progress. But now you're here. We have twice as much knowledge. And no one knows the house or its magic like Aisha does."

"Okay." She felt a little better at that. "So we'll go see Aisha right away?"

"You'll go see Aisha."

"But—"

The fox held up a hand to stop her. "There's no one else here that I would trust you alone with. And you need to get comfortable with not being at my side all the time here."

"So I'll go figure out how to get us out while you literally fuck around?" She forced herself to smile. She meant it as a joke.

The fox set his head to one side, looking sheepish. "Only a little fucking around. I should spend some time with Vivien."

"Why her?" Mila couldn't help but have a little pout in her voice. "She was such a bitch to me yesterday, and you were giving her treats."

"Treats?"

"You let her suck you off at the end. I thought I was supposed to do that."

"Treats," he repeated, with a wry smile. "She cares for me deeply, Mila, and even though I can't explain to her why I chose you instead, she needs to know that I still care for her as well."

"I guess." She sighed and set the book aside. "Just seems like you're going to go have fun while I have to work."

"I'm sure Aisha will make it fun for you too. But for now, breakfast?" Mila had only eaten one of the croissants and offered the others to Alonso. The fox picked one up with a bemused look, as though he had never had a croissant with breakfast before.

They spent a few minutes together in silence as the sun crept up over the horizon and bathed the room in warm yellow light. Alonso kept a hand on Mila's leg the whole time. When it came time for them both to get on with the day, he gave her reminders on how to get to the library and whispered a few extra instructions into her ear that she didn't remember consciously but felt were there to keep her safe if she encountered anyone else.

Then he commanded her to go to the library. So she set her book aside, finished off the dregs of coffee, and left.

The halls were busier than they had been the previous day, although mostly with felines preparing for various events. They gave polite greetings, and even the ones who had seemed jealous of Mila the previous day were friendlier now. Perhaps wandering around last night with Alonso's seed all over her face had convinced them she knew what she was doing, or perhaps without Vivien there to stoke the flames, everyone else had cooled off. Mila didn't know, but she was glad either way.

Halfway to the foyer, the calico encountered a sleepy dog who took one step out of his room, saw her, and commanded her to get on her knees. Mila excused herself, saying she was under orders from Alonso, and was silently grateful for whatever he had put in her head that morning. She hurried off and tried to get to the library as fast as she could.

Back on the third floor, she walked past Erik and Tricia's room and several others like a wine room, several music practice rooms, and the kitchen, before arriving at a pair of double-doors that had a large sign above them announcing they led into the library. Tentatively, the calico opened them and stepped inside.

Mila was rapidly growing used to the grandeur of the house, but she nevertheless felt her breath pause for a moment at the sheer spectacle of the library. The room itself extended up two stories, with every bookcase reaching all the way to the ceiling and accessible by glass-floored catwalks at various levels. One wall was full of windows that let in bright light straight down the aisles, while another wall held a warm fireplace whose flickering glow just reached a pair of cozy reading chairs. Besides those chairs, everything in the room was bespoke.

"Aisha?" Mila whispered into the room, but the sound disappeared into the plush carpet and soft book covers. Cautiously, the calico stepped into the room, checking down each aisle of bookshelves and expecting to see someone, but the library was surprisingly empty.

As she wandered down an aisle, Mila read the spines of the books she passed. There were many well-loved paperbacks — romance, science fiction, thriller, horror, murder mystery — and just as many musty old tomes that looked like no one had bothered to open them a single time. Several had been bound by hand, with delicate artistry along the spine, and Mila felt a small gap in her monetary knowledge. She tried to think of the library as a whole, comparing it to a full community library, and estimated this room with all its contents would cost on the order of ten million dollars. If it contained as many unique books as she thought, then maybe she needed an extra zero.

Mila finally found Aisha on the far side of the room, leaning over a reading desk that was covered in open books. She would scan a line, compare it to a different line in another book, then to a third book, and then jot down her observations on a notepad. The jackal moved with such speed and precision that Mila wondered if she was actually able to read everything, and Aisha did all this while still wearing a stunning black dress that was subtly different from the one she had on last night, with a slit that ran up both legs all the way to the hip.

"Aisha?"

The jackal lifted an ear in acknowledgment but did not turn to face her. "I am finishing up here. Please stand still and silent over there until I am done." She indicated a spot with the tip of her pen.

Reluctantly, Mila moved to the indicated point and folded her hands together. She had hoped, after last night, for an opportunity to further explore being with another woman, but it seemed that Aisha was not in the mood.

Minutes dragged on and Mila's impatience grew. She was bored; there was no other way to put it. Her folded hands started to fidget and her tail lifted and swayed in wide arcs for want of something to do. The calico cleared her throat. "Aisha?"

"First of all, my preferred term of address is Mistress Aisha," she said, not looking up. "Not Mistress, not Ma'am, not Madam, not Miss or Mrs. Njeri, and certainly not Aisha. Is that clear?"

Mila was momentarily taken aback, but she nodded all the same. "Yes."

The jackal let out a puff of air, like a sigh she hoped to hide. "As you are both a newcomer and a side-door guest, I do not expect you to know or follow the rules I have laid out for felines here, such as how to greet me properly. But I do expect a minimum level of respect."

Mila licked her lips. "Which is...?"

The jackal did not move except with her eyes, which swiveled to fixate on the calico. "You should use my title whenever you speak to me."

Mila blinked. The jackal had been looking mildly irritated with her ever since she arrived. Was this why? "I understand, Mistress Aisha. I'm sorry. How should I greet you properly?"

The jackal's eyes swiveled back to the desk in front of her. She lifted a finger for silence as she finished writing down her thoughts, then she put the pen down and turned to Mila. She looked mollified now. "You're not ready for that, dear, but your interest is appreciated. However, I asked you to remain still and silent, and you did not. Why?"

"Um, I got bored, Mistress Aisha. Sorry."

The jackal sat back and crossed her arms. "Being asked to serve as furniture is quite a common request around here you'll find."

Mila remembered the story Alex told about Natalie the other day. She had been serving as a footrest, he had said.

"While your lack of knowledge of the scene is understandable — for many guests, arriving at the Eternal Party is their first real exposure to BDSM culture — your lack of enthusiasm is not. That, more so than anything, will make you stand out." The jackal narrowed her eyes and scrutinized Mila, who felt a sudden urge to stand up straighter. "I assume Alonso has not been enforcing any protocols while in private? I understand, I sympathize, but I ultimately do not agree. You need practice blending in."

Mila nodded.

"So let's try this again. I would like you to stand there, still and silent, until I am finished. And if it helps," she added with a smirk, "think about how we might have carried on last night."

Mila shivered at the suggestion, but she did her best to stay as still. Within seconds her tail was twitching and her fingers were itching to do something, anything at all. She took a deep breath and tried to calm herself down. Her thoughts drifted to the topic Aisha had recommended. Key moments from last night stood out in her mind: the scent of wine, soft lips touching hers, and a strong grip on her breast. What had she wanted to come next? A kiss, a proper kiss this time, with her lips meeting Aisha's and the cautious exploration of tongues. Then the jackal's touch on her thigh, stoking that gently building flame between her legs.

Mila was aware she was starting to fidget again, so as quietly as she could, she slipped both arms behind her back and gripped her tail to keep it from flicking about. The scenario with Aisha replayed in her mind, until she realized how selfish she was being expecting Aisha to give her attention without returning any. Here, Mila's fantasies ran into a brick wall. It didn't matter how she approached it, whether she thought of Aisha shimmying out of her dress, or of herself reaching out to caress the jackal's body, or going down on her, her mind always hit a point where she couldn't picture what would happen next.

"That was much better, Mila."

The jackal's voice made Mila jerk to attention. Her eyes had fallen shut as she had fantasized and now opened to see the jackal smirking at her. "Thank you, Mistress Aisha," she said. "How long did I hold it for?"

"Nearly twenty minutes."

The calico blinked in surprise.

"Must have been a very nice fantasy you were having."

"Actually no, Mistress Aisha. I think I'm getting teased by my own lack of knowledge."

The jackal nodded in sympathy. "That can happen."

"May I ask what you were working on, Mistress Aisha?" The calico pointed her muzzle to the books strewn about the desk.

"Searching for a way out for you and Alonso," Aisha said,

turning her attention back to her notes, which she scrutinized for a moment as if reconfirming what she had just written down.

Mila felt a bit relieved. "I hope you'll be able to help, Mistress Aisha. Alonso said no one else knows the house like you do."

"That's only because I read more than anyone else." The jackal flung an arm out to indicate the bookshelves that surrounded them. "There's far more here than just gripping page-turners and steamy romances. The library also houses the entire recorded history of the Eternal Party, including journals of prominent guests. There's even a few tomes on magic."

Mila blinked as the full import of that hit her. "Does that mean you can do magic?"

The jackal gave a quick irritated glance to the calico. "Try that again, dear," she said.

Mila held her ears flat. "Does that mean you can do magic, Mistress Aisha?" she corrected herself.

The jackal did not give a verbal response. Instead she tilted her head to the side and beckoned the calico to follow her. Less than four steps later, they stopped and Aisha fixed her with an impatient stare. "Mila, let the dominant lead," she said sternly.

"Sorry, Mistress Aisha." Mila, who had been walking shoulder-to-shoulder with the jackal, took a step back and followed behind until they were in the very center of the library, facing the entrance doors.

There the jackal widened her stance, focused her eyes and ears on the door, took a deep breath, extended her hand, and whispered something too low for Mila to hear.

Nothing happened at first. Then Mila saw the handle begin to jiggle. The jackal started shaking too, her whole body tensed up against an unseen force. Seconds ticked away and Mila started to get worried: the jackal was holding herself so tightly she wasn't even breathing.

Then, with a click, the lock on the door turned, and Aisha nearly collapsed. Mila had to support her under one arm. "That's amazing, Mistress Aisha."

"No, it's not," the jackal said fiercely and pulled her arm away. "That barely deserves to be called a parlor trick. I nearly pass out if I try to lock a door from across a room and yet she," Aisha pointed to a portrait that hung above the door, "was able to make this whole manor and all the magic it contains with a single spell — with a single word no less — and it apparently was the easiest thing for her."

Mila gaped up at the portrait. "What, her? But—"

"All the damn tomes are in code. And it's not just a substitution code either. It's a whole new language."

"Aisha, how could she—"

"I've only managed to get this far because they have diagrams — very poorly drawn diagrams, but diagrams at least."

"Mistress Aisha!"

The jackal stopped raving and raised herself to her full height. "Yes, Mila, what is it?"

"What do you mean she made the house?" She indicated the portrait that hung above the entrance. It depicted a regal looking snow leopard in an early 19th-century dress with wide-puffed sleeves and elegant decorations on the hem. She sat on a bench, facing the viewer, one arm against an unusual black railing.

"That's Lady Yasmin, the mage who built this place."

"But... her? Really?"

The jackal crossed her arms. "What's so strange about that?"

Mila gaped at her for a second then pointed to the corset she was wearing. "I thought this place had been made from the teenage bondage fantasies of some perverted male canine." She realized she'd been forgetting something and added a quick "Mistress Aisha" to the end of her statement.

The jackal cocked a hip, staring at the calico. Mila swore she even heard a quiet harrumph of dismissal. "Mila, if the Eternal Party had been intended to be a dominant fantasy, the house would have taken in any feline that was passing by and not cared how they were treated. Instead, it only allows in — at least in theory — those felines who want to be here, and only allows in those canines who would use, but not abuse, that power. Lady Yasmin was a natural submissive and wanted a place she could be submissive safely."

"I guess, Mistress Aisha," Mila said, "but why the corsets?"

The jackal gave a small laugh. "The Eternal Party deliberately caters to all flavors of sexuality, but the one thing she insisted on were the collars and corsets. I think Lady Yasmin may have had a uniform fetish."

Mila glanced up at the portrait again. Sure enough, the snow leopard wore a corset over her dress. She looked so aristocratic, but still, Mila could imagine her kneeling at the side of some canine and staring lovingly up at him, like Ingrid had.

"Still, I think it's pretty neat that you can do magic, Mistress Aisha." Mila had hoped the compliment would please Aisha, but it had the opposite effect.

Her whiskers twitched. "I should be able to do so much more, but we are missing too much." The jackal threw up her hands in frustration. "That's the problem with this place: no one bothers with the paperwork. I'm only the librarian because no one else wanted the job. I'm also the Eternal Party's historian, accountant, and protocol officer. So of course no one took any decent records, whether for magic or anything else. Just look at this!" She stormed down a nearby aisle and, having been ordered, Mila followed helplessly behind. The jackal grabbed a small leather-bound book from a shelf. "See? This guest was here in the 1910's and kept a record of every meal he ate while he was here. But was there any record of what other options there were? No. For all we know, all his meals were privately made. Useless." The jackal crammed the book back onto the shelf. "And all the records are like this. I have to piece together facts from a dozen different records. But that means scouring daily journals on the off chance someone mentions the same event someone else did."

The jackal rested her head against a bookshelf, and her voice dropped low in sympathetic sadness. "What I can tell you is that others have come through the side door like you and Alonso, but

I couldn't tell you if there's been a dozen or a hundred others. I could tell you that all the side-door guests that I have records for made it out, but not how. I can also say that the housequakes have accompanied them, but not what caused them." Her eyes swiveled to stare at the calico again. "But then again, I think you already know what is causing them."

Mila wilted a little under the gaze. "I-I'm not totally certain, Mistress Aisha."

"But you do have an idea?"

The calico nodded.

"I won't force you to tell me, Mila. I know things have been hard for you, but I am working at a deficit of information here as you can see. Anything you can tell me might help to get you and Alonso back home quicker."

That got her. If it had just been about her own escape, she might have held off longer, but it was the fox relying on her too.

Mila took a deep breath and rested her head on a nearby shelf, mimicking Aisha's earlier posture and feeling the cool wood against her. "It's the house," she said quietly, "trying to prevent me from thinking about something. Any time I get close to it, it shakes to distract me."

"I need more to go on than that," the jackal said, encouraging Mila without ordering her.

Why was this so hard? Mila thought. She'd talked about BD plenty of times since his death.

Yes, another part of her answered. And it hurt like hell every single time.

Aisha turned to look at her with wide eyes. Her whole body seemed tense, ready to spring into action. She could feel the floor beginning to stir as well.

"It was my husband," Mila said quickly. "Whenever I think about how much I miss him, it—"

A full housequake started again. Mila and Aisha flung their arms out to the shelves to steady themselves as books rocked and threatened to spill out over the floor.

The jackal's voice rang out over the noise of the quake. "Stop reacting emotionally."

Immediately the shaking stopped. "Yes, Mistress Aisha," Mila said in monotone, straightening herself.

"Interesting," the jackal said. "No emotions, no quake." She paused a moment to compose herself, running a hand over the shelf and realigning the spines of the books after the quake had discombobulated them. "Mila, if you had your emotions, would you be comfortable continuing to describe what caused the quakes?"

"No, Mistress Aisha," the calico said, still in monotone, "but I would do it if it meant helping myself and Alonso escape."

Aisha nodded. "There were three housequakes since you've arrived. Tell me what happened right before each occurred."

"Yes, Mistress Aisha. The first occurred while I was in the basement. I was watching a couple playing while I was trying to hide from them. The canine was caressing his partner lovingly and I was missing my husband holding me like that. It was just as I was thinking about that when the first quake occurred.

"The second quake happened shortly after I met Alonso and was trying to get out through the side door, but I do not remember the moments before the quake.

"The third—"

"Wait. You don't remember what happened before the second quake?"

"That is correct, Mistress Aisha."

The jackal's eyes narrowed suspiciously. "Mila, you can now remember whatever Alonso told you to forget that day. Now resume from the second quake."

"I cannot remember, Mistress Aisha. My owner commanded me to forget."

The jackal crossed her arms. "Very well. Continue from the third quake then."

"The third quake occurred yesterday on the way back from the tailor's room. I was thinking how much BD would have loved to see my outfit, and that triggered a memory of seeing him in the hospital bed, which was when the quake happened."

"BD is your husband, I take it?"

"Yes, Mistress Aisha. Bernard Collins, but he hated the name Bernard so everyone called him BD." Mila swapped topics without pause. "There was also a fourth quake that happened just now. I was trying to discuss him without thinking about him, but failed."

The jackal tapped a finger to the tip of her muzzle. Mila watched without any concern for the passage of time. After a while, the jackal came to a decision, nodded in agreement with herself, and turned to look directly into the calico's eyes. "Mila, until you leave the house, you will not feel any emotional reactions to the death of your husband unless you choose to. Otherwise, regain all your emotions."

Mila blinked and shivered as her ability to feel things came back. The last few moments had not been the pleasantly relaxing lack of focus that being a doll had been. It was as though the world had been drained of all color and life, and the sudden return left her momentarily stunned.

It took a few seconds, but then she started crying, sniffing hard to hold back the sudden flow of tears and snot.

"Mila?" The jackal's hand was on Mila's cheek, her tone full of concern.

"It's okay. I'm happy. Really." She sniffed again, hard, and tried to look away. "I just haven't been able to remember him without it hurting in so long. I can think about our wedding again." Her voice was cracking a little. She was relieved when the jackal first handed her a handkerchief and then, a moment later, a cup of tea procured from the ether (even if the tea did have milk in it).

The jackal walked Mila over to the comfy armchairs in front of the fireplace, supporting her weight as best she could. She stayed close until Mila had finished the tea and taken a shaky breath afterwards. "Do you think that information will help?" the calico asked when she had recovered.

"Mila, please remember how I asked you to speak in my presence." There was an edge to Aisha's voice that surprised the calico: this was about more than just making sure Mila was acting appropriately around other dominants. She seemed to be holding back something, but Mila had no idea what.

The calico's tail curled unconsciously about a leg. "Do you think that will help, Mistress Aisha?"

"I do." The tension released. "As I said before, the records here are sparse and incomplete, but they do exist. Other side-door guests are mentioned, but, of course, the records don't bother to address why they were here or how they got out. Still, if it has something to do with your husband, I can start cross-referencing to similar ideas and see if something comes up. But I can already eliminate one possibility," Aisha said, sitting back in her own armchair. "It's not simply the loss of a loved one that has you trapped."

"How can you know that, Mistress Aisha?"

The jackal sighed and glanced into the fireplace, watching the flames flicker. "Because when I was a girl, I walked in on my eldest brother right after he had blown his brains out all over the bedroom. I'm the youngest of seven siblings and I've watched them all die one by one. My father..." But what exactly it was her father was or did was never said, although it was clear to Mila that Aisha hated him. The jackal took a moment to recompose herself, smoothing down her hackles and letting the edge drop from her voice. If Aisha had been feline, Mila suspected she would be seeing claws slowly retracting. "If it were as simple as losing someone you cared about, I should be trapped too."

"Do you think Alonso—"

"Alonso has never discussed what he thought caused the quakes after his arrival with me. And as his friend, I have not pried on that point."

Mila nodded, wondering privately about the fox. "But, Mistress Aisha, how do you know you're not trapped?"

The jackal cocked an ear. "Mila, I leave the house every week. I want my mother to know I am well, and the only way to make an outgoing call is to leave."

Her mother, Mila noted. Not her father. "Oh. I just thought... I haven't seen anyone enter or leave..."

"You've only been here a day and a half, Mila. We have some permanent residents, some who only stop by the house for a day or two a year, and everywhere in between. Some people only visit the house once, while others return time after time. We're a very popular vacation destination for those in the know. Come to think of it..." The jackal stroked her chin for a moment then stood and gestured for Mila to follow.

The calico noticed how she hadn't been ordered to follow, but suspected that it was expected of her, nonetheless. This time she was careful to stay a step back. She remembered staying behind Alonso as they had walked up to his room that very first night. It had felt so natural. Why was this so much harder for her to remember with Aisha?

Down another path, between the bookshelves, was a table that had a few useful items on it, most notably an old rotary phone, which Aisha picked up. "Jay," she said into the receiver, not having dialed anything.

A pause.

"Good morning, Jay."

Mila thought she heard a voice on the other end of the line say, "Good morning, Mistress Aisha."

"Are you available? I need your assistance on a discreet matter in the library."

Mila heard a sound of assent on the other side.

"Thank you. I will see you shortly."

Then the jackal hung up. "Now, when she arrives, you are not to recognize her until I give you permission."

"Yes, Mistress Aisha," Mila said, although she had no idea what the order meant.

Aisha waited impatiently, rapping claws on the table, until she stood up sharply and went to make more tea for Mila, just so she had something to do. Mila sipped it as delicately and slowly as she could, and was grateful when the handle of the library rattled and was followed by a knock.

"Go and get that, will you?" Aisha asked.

"Yes, Mistress Aisha," Mila said, before heading for the door. She was worried that the lock would stick, after the jackal's magic before, but it yielded easily.

Striding into the library came the pinnacle of feline feminine beauty — so far as Mila could define it — a tigress with stripes so sharp you could cut yourself on them, standing 6'2" with a stunning curve to her figure and the muscles of a gladiator. She wore a corset and collar as all felines at the party did, but hers had been etched with stripe patterns that matched her own pelt perfectly. There wasn't a strand of fur out of place on her entire, nearly naked body: it somehow looked luxuriantly soft while also showing the definition in the muscles underneath. She could probably dance a tango to perfection and then bench press her partner.

Mila could feel her heterosexuality weakening by the second.

Her imagination now had none of the trouble it experienced thinking about Aisha before. Sexy scenarios didn't just present themselves, they barged into Mila's consciousness armed with an air horn and marching slogan, demanding to be heard. She wanted to kiss the tigress. She wanted to fondle her. She wanted to follow the outline of her stripes with delicate licks until she found the one that would point her right towards the tigress's snatch. She wanted to be stalked down the bookshelves, pounced upon, and ravished.

The tigress glanced to the calico, smiled benevolently, and then read the tag on her collar. "Oh, so Alonso finally took a girl of his own. You lucky cat." Her voice had a European lilt that made Mila feel weak at the knees.

"Thank you for coming so quickly, Jay," Aisha said. "I have a request of you that requires the utmost discretion."

The tigress turned to the jackal and dropped into a formal bow. "Of course, Mistress Aisha. I will tell no one."

"Mila, please lock the door again."

Mila couldn't help but stare at Jay's breasts and marvel at how they seemed to float. The calico fumbled for the lock several times before tearing her eyes away from the tigress.

The jackal gestured to the calico. "This is Mila. She came in two days ago, through the side door."

The tigress's eyes widened and her tailtip flicked with agitation. She turned to Mila and enveloped the calico's hands in her own, cradling them in a soothing embrace. "Are you all right?"

Mila managed a small nod. Her throat felt strangely dry looking up into the face of the tigress who was oh so close. "I'm doing okay," she said, managing to prevent her voice from squeaking. "Alonso and Aisha have been looking out for me."

The tigress nodded and kept her hands on Mila's while she turned to look at the jackal. "You want me to check in on her things, Mistress Aisha?"

The jackal nodded.

"Check on things?" Mila asked.

"Normally it would not be necessary," Aisha said. "The spell on the house does an amazing job of making sure your presence will not be missed outside."

"Oh, yes," Mila said. "Alonso said it was like being on vacation, Mistress Aisha."

Aisha perked her ears, waiting for Mila to go on, but when she didn't, the jackal asked, "Was that all he said?"

Mila had been feeling like she was beginning to understand things and that was now slipping away. "Yes, Mistress Aisha," she said bashfully.

The jackal rubbed her temples. "That man is terrible about explaining things."

Jay laughed politely.

Aisha shook her head. "Here are the basics. The magic will work to excuse your absence from the world with as minimal an inconvenience to you as possible. If you stay here long enough to miss a rent or bill payment, you will return to find that a clerical error has meant you didn't need to pay. Your friends will just assume you're out on holiday. Even your job will be waiting for you as if you just stepped out for a day, and you'll be collecting paychecks all the while."

"That sounds too good to be true, Mistress Aisha."

The jackal smiled. "As official Eternal Party accountant, my duties include managing the general fund which all guests are required to pay part of their earnings into, rather than just becoming obscenely rich. In fact, that's how I learned Alonso was trapped here: he couldn't leave to set up the deposit. But there were other ways in which the magic affected him differently. Some of his neighbors were suspicious about his extended absence, which has never happened with other guests. So we need to make sure your life is taken care of."

"In case I'm trapped here for years like him?"

"Yes."

Mila felt a shiver run over her shoulders, but it was turned aside by Jay squeezing her hands tenderly. The tigress smiled down to her and Mila melted a little more.

The jackal disappeared for a moment and came back with a pen and pad of paper. "Mila, please write down your full name, home address, work address, and any other places you would want Jay to check in on."

Mila took the items and considered what else she might want to write down, when she noticed that once again Aisha was giving her a look. "What did I get wrong this time?" she asked.

"When you are given an order, you should respond."

"Sorry. Yes, Mistress Aisha." She ducked her head down to try and avoid Aisha's gaze for a while. She quickly wrote down as much as she could think of, including a request for Jay to check in on her plants, or at least give them to a neighbor who could take care of them. The only part of the command which gave her pause was when she had to write down her name. Mila Collins. Her married name. But for once it didn't spark any pang of regret inside. The command from Aisha to feel no emotion had been quite thorough.

The calico paused, considering what else she might need to add to the list. While she thought, she decided to ask a question that had been bugging her for a few minutes, "So, Jay, you can also just come and go as you please?"

The tigress flicked an ear at being called Jay: not her usual name then. "That's right," she said. "I come here for about a week every few months. It's a great vacation." Now that Mila was hearing more of the accent, she guessed it was either Polish or Hungarian, probably a few generations removed because it wasn't terribly strong, similar to the East African tones mostly hidden under Aisha's British pronunciation.

"A vacation? Here?"

"Of course! A week of the best sex of my life with handsome men and women who fulfill my wildest fantasies? It is so relaxing. Better than yoga, meditation, or tai chi. I should know. I've tried them all. This is by far the best. I walk out of here at the end of the week with a clear head."

The calico glanced down at the tigress's absurdly perfect breasts. "I can't imagine having sex with handsome men would be any challenge for you."

"Nor sex with beautiful women," the tigress said, a purr rippling through her words.

Mila flushed pink in her ears as she saw how intently the tigress was looking at her and felt another bit of her heterosexuality give out with only a sliver of protest. Aisha's gaze last night had made her feel good: Jay's gaze was making her feel hot. Flustered, Mila tried to refocus her attention on the paper in front of her and tried not to think of how she wanted to feel the tiger's tongue grooming through her fur.

"But it not just about availability," the tigress said while running that tongue over her lips as if she knew exactly what was on Mila's mind. "It is also about style, and the men here have so much of it. You are Alonso's kitten. You know this better than most."

Okay, Mila had to admit that was a good point. "But if you enjoy it so much here, why leave?"

"Because I also enjoy my job and my family. I could not give them up forever."

Mila nodded and folded up her note, handing it to Aisha. "That should be everything, Mistress Aisha. But she can't get into my apartment without my keys and those were in my jacket."

"Did the house take your jacket?"

"Yes, Mistress Aisha."

The jackal reached out and rapped a knuckle hard on the table. "Keys," she said.

There was a loud thump of a book falling over from behind them. It was so sudden that Mila jumped.

"Go and get them," Aisha commanded.

The calico crept over to the fallen book. When she lifted it up, she found her keys were underneath. She came back and held them out to the jackal, who sighed again, harder than before. Mila's ears flattened at the way Aisha looked at her. She was fucking something up again. "Oh come on," she said, letting more of her frustration into her voice. "Is there really a wrong way to hand someone something?"

Jay intervened before Aisha could say anything. "Perhaps, Mistress Aisha, Mila would benefit from a practical demonstration."

The jackal's gaze slid over to the tigress. "Very well."

Jay stepped up to Mila and took the keys from her, her fingers, Mila thought, lingering just a little. Then the tigress stood tall, bowed low, and extended the keys in both hands. Aisha picked the keys out with a nod of her head.

"Mistress Aisha," the larger feline said before Aisha could redirect any attention to Mila again, "may I greet you properly?"

The jackal woman considered with a tilt of her head. "Go on."

"Yes, Mistress Aisha," the tigress said and she slid down to all fours with sinuous ease, padding up to the jackal's legs and bending her head low to kiss the arch of the jackal's foot. She began to raise herself, pausing every inch or so to give another audible kiss as her muzzle worked its way up the jackal's leg. When she reached the slit of her dress, the tigress reverently lifted it aside and continued her way up to the jackal's inner thigh. Mila was unsurprised to see that Aisha wore nothing under the dress and that the tigress's lips soon made contact with Aisha's sex. She lavished her tongue over the clit before dipping down and nuzzling in between the folds. The first lick was quick and drawn over the labia: the second went in deep. Mila could see how the tigress was straining to reach as deep as she could.

The jackal ran a hand over the tigress's head as the feline withdrew her tongue. All the subtle signs of stress had disappeared. "You're getting better at that every time, kitty. One of these visits you're going to manage to make me orgasm from one lick alone."

The tigress remained where she was, purring adoringly up at the smaller female.

The calico, who had been watching this all in increasing embarrassment, shied back as Aisha looked to her once more. "I'm sorry," she said, and crossed her arms over her chest, feeling a sudden desire to be clothed far better than she was. "I'm fucking this up. I just don't understand it all, and I know I'm going to keep making mistakes. I'm sorry," she said again, babbling.

Aisha glanced down to the tigress who made a discreet flipping motion with her hands. That brought a bemused smile to the jackal's face. "Jay, dear, what does your schedule look like today?"

117

The tigress's tail flicked as she thought. "My flight is tomorrow, Mistress Aisha, so if I want to check on Mila's things, I should leave this afternoon."

The jackal tipped her head in acknowledgment. "Would you be all right with Mila knowing who you really are?"

"Yes, Mistress Aisha."

"Recognize her," the jackal commanded simply.

And Mila did.

Of course she did. The tigress had featured prominently in a poster that had hung in Mila's dorm room. Several posters in fact. "Jeta Horowitz!"

Theme and Variations

"You're Jeta Horowitz," the calico repeated.

Jeta — for it was impossible to continue thinking of her as Jay now that Mila knew the truth — nodded. "That's me."

Mila's tongue ran circles around her mouth, while her brain chugged in place. Eventually she said the only thing that came to mind. "You're famous!"

"I suppose that I am," the tigress said with only a hint of patronizing.

"You've won an Oscar!"

The tigress considered. "And an Emmy."

Finally the dam burst in Mila's mind. "But you're a millionaire. You're one of the highest paid, most in-demand actresses in the world. You live in a mansion. You're tailed by paparazzi wherever you go. You have a bodyguard. Why are you here?"

Jeta giggled softly. "I am, I am, it's not actually that big, I am, I actually have two, and I told you, nothing relaxes me quite like this. Besides, it's a cheaper habit than picking up cocaine. I stop here in between projects."

"But you're here, with me," Mila said. The reality of her interactions with the tigress before hit home. "Oh fuck, and you flirted with me too."

Jeta purred, leaning forward so her sizable breasts swung in the air. "I was hoping you would flirt back."

Mila's eyes slipped down from the golden gaze to follow the line of stripes that seemed to be pointing straight to the tigress's nipples. The calico felt like her own college-age fantasies were coming true. "Oh no," she babbled. "There's no way. I mean, what would I even say to you?"

"That is where I come in," the jackal said. She stood in front of the calico and rested a hand on each shoulder. "For now, while the three of us are in this room, you, Mila, are an honorary canine. You may command felines as we do. And Jeta, since she is an honorary canine, you are to obey her just as you would any of us. Understood?"

"Yes, Mistress Aisha," said the tigress, but Mila just stood staring at her.

The jackal gave a thin smile at the calico's dumb-founded expression. She rested a hand on the kitten's hip. "Good, as a fellow canine, you don't need to recognize my authority any more. I am a fellow dominant."

"You mean we could have been doing this all along?"

"You're still a feline. Any canine could still command you. This just changes how Jeta will react to you."

"This...feels weird," Mila said. Even though she had not been in the house long, the unspoken rule of "Canines command and felines obey" had still felt like a natural part of the atmosphere. But here she was now an honorary canine with the power of command.

"I expect it would. But this is your chance to explore the other side of the coin. Everyone is different in what they expect, and that includes you. You're now functionally a dominant, and you have before you one of the world's most beautiful women who you can command to do anything your heart desires. Will you make her crawl on all fours, turn her into a fucktoy, treat her as a lover?"

Mila looked down at Jeta, who was purring quietly on every

breath, not looking away from the calico. "I can't possibly have that kind of power over her. That's not how this place works."

"Try it out," the jackal suggested, and Mila felt that it was truly a suggestion, not a command. But it was perhaps a good suggestion.

Mila forced herself to look into Jeta's eyes and not look away. She considered what sort of order she could give that would prove that the tigress was really under her control and not just playing along like the actress she was. "Orgasm hard, right now," she said, replicating Alonso's command from last night.

The tigress's spine went rigid and her eyes went wide. Her whole body shivered and her hips juddered in place as she tried to keep still. Even as Mila watched, juices dripped out of her sex and onto the floor. The calico was convinced: that part was hard to fake.

"Wow..."

The tigress purred and her body swayed in its kneeling position.

"I just made Jeta Horowitz orgasm." Mila's mind wheeled around that fact and it made her feel slightly dizzy.

"Yes, you did," Aisha said. She leaned in close and lowered her voice. "Remember, Mila, unlike you and Alonso, Jeta is here because she wants to be. She enjoys this, and she clearly fancies you. Don't hold back for her sake. Now enjoy yourself. I'm curious to see what you will do." The jackal actually sashayed as she stepped away and took a seat in one of the armchairs.

By this point Jeta had mostly recovered and was kneeling upright, chest thrust out.

Mila thought about what she'd want to do with her. If she was completely honest with herself, she'd fantasized about Jeta — or at least the characters the tigress had played — before. One movie she had loved watching and rewatching was "Sister Black." Jeta had played the eponymous bounty hunter Sister Black, sent to kidnap Carmen, the daughter of a crime syndicate's leader, but ultimately ends up protecting Carmen from warring factions. In one scene, after a fraught battle, Jeta was wearing nothing above the waist but a super-tight shirt and she was hugging Carmen in against her chest. That one moment had spawned a lot of self-exploration of Mila's own breasts and questions about what it would like to be pressed up against another woman like that.

Looking down at the still heavy-breathing tigress prompted a dozen other half-forgotten fantasies to spring to recollection again. Mila had trouble choosing between them.

So instead, she opted for none of them.

"Jeta," she said, her voice still tentative and lacking the suaveness of Alonso's voice or the natural superiority of Aisha's. "I want you to treat me as you would Aisha. Greet me properly, but just know," she interrupted before the tigress could move too much, "I haven't been with a woman before."

The tigress nodded and smiled. "Yes, Mistress Mila. I will make your first time one to remember."

The calico could hear the pounding of her heart as Jeta fucking Horowitz slid out onto all fours, lowered her head and kissed the top of her foot. As the tigress began to lift herself up to move along Mila's leg, the calico suddenly understood why the kisses had seemed so intimate: Jeta was running her rough tongue over the fur, mixing a kiss with a grooming motion that felt electric. The position Jeta was in meant that she was often licking across the fur, instead of with it. By the time Jeta had reached Mila's knees, the tigress had to hold the calico's legs steady.

Mila began to tremble. The closer Jeta got to her sex, the harder it was to keep still. The tigress seemed to be slowing down, teasing her with how close she was getting. But she never stopped or turned back and when her cool nose touched Mila's clit at last, she gasped, and then she gasped again louder as that warm tongue slid along her clit and parted her folds. She had to hold onto Jeta's head for balance as the tongue began to push inside her. Jeta adjusted her position so that she took more of Mila's hips in between her jaws, all to get her tongue just that little bit further in.

But then it was receding. The awesome build-up of pleasure crested and started to fall back down.

She gripped the tigress's head tighter. "Don't stop," she commanded, a desperate note in her voice. "Keep doing that until you make me cum."

The tigress obeyed. She had to, of course.

Mila closed her eyes and just relished in the sensations of that thick tongue moving in and out, curling and flexing as it did so and lighting up sensations within herself she hadn't realized were physically possible.

She didn't last long. It only took twenty licks to get the pent-up calico to cum. Her thighs squeezed around the now purring tigress who didn't pull away until Mila could stand on her own once again. Jeta had a satisfied smile on her face as she licked the last of Mila's juices from her muzzle. "How did I do, Mistress Mila?"

Mila didn't answer. "Stand," she said, and the tigress stood. Mila buried herself in that warm fur, pressing herself in with her head between the two breasts with her arms wrapped around the bigger woman, just like in "Sister Black." Jeta's own arms held Mila gently. "That was fantastic," she whispered. "Thank you."

"You're very welcome, Mistress Mila."

"Now, uh, why don't you go down to the kitchen and get Aisha and I some... tea?" Mila's mind had spun trying to think of something for the tigress to fetch, and in a moment of panic had opted for the same drink she'd already had twice that morning. She was going to be bouncing off the walls from the caffeine high, unless the house prevented that too.

The tigress stepped back, bowed deep and low, said, "Of course, Mistress Mila," and stepped quickly to the door.

Mila, feeling still somewhat unsteady on her feet, staggered into the chair next to the jackal.

"You sent her away," the jackal remarked laconically.

"I needed time to think. It's not that I don't want her, I'm just so unused to being with women I don't know how to proceed."

"Jeta has lots of experience in that department. I would suggest making use of it. Ask her what she would do if she had met you outside the house."

"I can't do that." Mila's hands fidgeted and twisted in her lap. "She would have just ignored someone like me."

"Oh I don't think so. But I'll make you a deal. If you ask and get an answer you dislike, I'll wipe your memory of it."

"Do you do that often?"

"I wouldn't say often." The jackal's thin shoulders shrugged. "Memory play can be fun, watching someone struggle to remember their own name, for instance; it can also have a practical side, allowing dominants a second chance to get things right without letting our mistakes be remembered. One of my first times with a feline here, I was so tongue-tied I ended up resetting their memory to restart the scene four times in short succession until I could say hello without stuttering."

Mila didn't think four times would be nearly enough to give her the time to address Jeta Horowitz with confidence. "I'm not sure that will be necessary." Mila looked the jackal up and down. She was calmly waiting. "Should we call someone else for you so you aren't left out."

The jackal offered a small but sincere smile. "Thank you for thinking of me, but I am quite enjoying watching you at the moment."

"And getting more tea was okay?"

"Mila, dear, it's fine."

Mila nodded and fidgeted as she waited for the tigress to come back, which she did after a few minutes — just enough time to steep the tea. The tigress held the tray one-handed with an arch to her back which thrust out her chest. She knelt down between the jackal and calico and set the two cups of tea on the table before setting the tray to the side. "Your drinks, mistresses."

Mila followed Aisha's lead, as the jackal made no verbal acknowledgment but instead just tilted her head in thanks. They both sipped their drinks slowly until Aisha arched an eyebrow in a way that practically screamed, "Get on with it."

Mila set her tea aside and Jeta immediately refocused her attention on the calico. "Jeta, I want you to imagine a scenario for me. Let's say you didn't meet me here, but instead met me on the set of one of your movies. Maybe we got coffee together and chatted."

The tigress nodded.

"Would you be attracted to me at all?"

"Oh yes, Mistress Mila."

"Uh, why?"

"Because you're obviously interested in me, Mistress Mila, in a very physical sense." The calico tore her gaze away from the tigress's chest to see Jeta smiling knowingly back at her. "At the same time, you aren't as stupidly egotistical as so many of my coworkers are: you don't think I'm just some air-headed bimbo with nice tits. You're also attractive enough I would probably go to bed that night fantasizing about you, if I didn't have anyone else to occupy me."

"You would really fantasize about me?"

"Yes, Mistress Mila."

The calico considered for a second, a lump in her throat that wouldn't go away no matter how she swallowed. "Aisha, how did you do that thing before, with the keys?" she asked.

The jackal took another delicate sip of her tea. "You just state what you need. Make sure you direct your voice towards the house or some object within it."

Mila knocked her fingers on the small table between the chairs, as if she were trying to get the house's attention. "Pillows," she said towards the table. There was a thump from the next bookshelf over. "Big ones." Another, louder thump from the same spot. "And very fluffy." A quieter thump. "Really big, at least person-sized." Another thump.

"Dear, you'll confuse the poor house."

Mila nodded meekly and then checked in the direction of the

thump. In between the shelves, she found a pillow just to her specifications. The calico paused and, curious to test the limit of the house's ability, leaned in to whisper to the books, "A diamond." A very soft thump made her ear flick to a nearby novel, which she pulled out to reveal a stunningly cut gem. Alonso was right: wealth had a very different meaning here.

The calico picked up the pillow and found it was surprisingly heavy. So she had to ungainly haul it on her back. She laid it out in front of the fireplace with a sigh of relief. "Lay down," she said to Jeta.

"Yes, Mistress Mila." The tigress stretched out over the pillows as instructed, propping up her head on her hand while her naked body splayed out.

"Close your eyes and imagine we are continuing from the earlier scenario. You had a nice coffee with me during the day and you've been unable to keep me out of your thoughts since. You are now at home, in bed, fantasizing about me. Act as you would then, but also narrate your fantasy aloud."

"Wait." Aisha reached out and touched Mila's arm. "Remember what you are for a moment. Be as respectful of her fantasies as you would want us to be of yours. They are not to be told to outsiders."

"Yes, Mistress Aisha," Mila said. Then her honorary canine-ness returned and she looked down at the tigress. "Go on."

The tigress nodded. "Yes, Mistress Mila." Her eyes slid shut and she stretched out as only a big cat could, claws unsheathing and pricking the air before she returned to relaxing on the pillows. One finger traced patterns into the thick fur of her belly. "You looked so cute during coffee, checking me out like that. It made me want to tease you more. I'd invite you over for drinks one night, then show up at the door in tight shorts but a super loose shirt. I'd greet you all tipsy-like, pulling you into a hug that was more intimate than you expected. And then I'd keep teasing you in little ways. Finding excuses to lean forward so my shirt would fall open and you could see right down to my naked breasts beneath, or to bend over with my ass high in those tight shorts. I'd drop double entendres into the conversation but be seemingly oblivious to it, until I have you squirming constantly.

"Or maybe..." The tigress's hand wound its way along her belly until she was pressing against her clit. Her claw extended just a little brushing back and forth over that spot. "Maybe I'd find some way to bring you here, have Aisha or one of the others get you used to being with another woman. And when they are done, your final test would be to go down on me."

Mila squirmed in her spot, especially with the way Aisha's gaze had slid over to her. "Stop."

"Yes, Mistress Mila."

"Start the fantasy over, but this time, you want to have me in a more, uh, dominant position."

"Yes, Mistress Mila." Jeta pulled her hand back to her belly and began drawing in her fur once more, her puffy labia left ignored. "I invite you over for drinks," she says again, "planning to tease you with my body. But when I open the door, you aren't surprised at all. You expected this somehow. I'm confused but I keep trying. Nothing seems to work until I lean over in front of you and your hand darts into my shirt to grope me." She trails her hand up to caress over a breast and then grips it roughly. "I try to pull back but you tweak my nipple and make me gasp. You call me a slut. I try to protest but you tweak my nipple again." She mimicked the action on her chest, tugging her stiff nipples in a way that made her groan.

"Wait," Mila said, and the tigress froze in place. "I thought you said you didn't like people who only thought of you as an air-headed slut. Why are you like that in your fantasy?"

"I love being a slut, being made so horny I can't think of anything but sex. I hate people who think that's *all* I am capable of being. You're not like that. You know that when I'm acting slutty, it's just that, an act. You know that I can speak three languages, can play the viola, and got a degree in geology because I love it so much."

Mila didn't actually know all of that, but she guessed the tigress was referring to the version of her from the tigress's fantasy. "Okay. Keep going."

Jeta resumed groping her breast as if nothing had happened. "You push a second hand down my shirt. You tell me you know I'm a slut because if I weren't, I would have left by now. But you've seen how desperately I flirt with everyone. You know how sex-obsessed I am. And I can't deny it. You slide into my lap and start to undress me and I don't want to stop you." Jeta's hand ran from her hip up to her neck in a gesture that reminded Mila of pulling a shirt off, then down from her hip to her leg as though she were pushing her shorts off. "Then I'm naked underneath you and you can see how hard my nipples are and you can smell how needy I am. You tell me to finger myself and I obey you without question. I'm masturbating under your orders and loving it." She slid her hand between her thighs and slipped a finger inside.

"Wait," Mila said again. "Don't get yourself off yet. But tell me what happens in the fantasy after you do get off."

"You move in," the tigress said with a purr. "My mansion should belong to a proper woman, not some slut, so I give it to you and you keep me there as your personal fuckgirl. I never wear clothes at home any more. You keep me on display like a trophy, showing off my body to all your friends, and you have me masturbate for your enjoyment at least three times a day, but even that isn't enough for me. You make me so horny I want to masturbate all the time."

"Stop." Mila was shivering in her seat, squirming at that. "Thank you, Jeta. You can stand up now."

The tigress stood up, her eyes opening for the first time in minutes. She kept her gaze respectfully lowered before the two dominants before her.

Mila was lost in thought, idly preening her whiskers as she tried to focus and keep out the idea of Jeta Horowitz as a live-in plaything.

After a long pause in which Mila's tea grew cold, Aisha said, "Did that inspire some thoughts?"

Mila started at being addressed. "Uh, yes. Just trying to process all this."

The tigress reached out and touched Mila's foot. "If it helps, it is just a fantasy. I don't actually want to give you my house. It is, to borrow an on-the-nose analogy, just a role I would enjoy playing with you."

"And," Aisha put in her thoughts as well, "even if I am hoping you will experiment and learn something, your own comfort is important too. Don't push yourself into something that would make you unhappy."

The thing that ultimately decided it for Mila was Jeta's tail. The tigress did her best to appear calm and restrained, but her tail was flicking behind her with barely contained energy. The fantasy had really gotten her going, and she was looking at Mila still.

The calico turned in her seat to address Aisha, trying to keep her back straight so she looked prim and proper. "Would it be possible for me to give Jeta a different collar?"

"You are not allowed to claim her as your own."

"No, I just need something different."

The jackal considered. "Allowable, but I will be the one to place it on her."

"Okay, house, I need a new collar for Jeta, one with something I can tug."

A thump from a nearby bookcase, and the calico got up to retrieve a fairly standard collar but with an attached leash that drifted down to hip level. Aisha took it from her and began removing Jeta's current collar with ceremony and reverence before bringing the new one around her neck with as much respect.

Quietly, Mila asked the house for two formal dresses, one for her and one for Jeta, each in the same style as Aisha's. Jeta slipped into hers on Mila's orders, but Mila found herself feeling weird as she wore hers. She'd spent most of the last two days either naked, nearly naked, or dressed in a way that was designed to attract every eye in the room. Wearing a dress felt almost stifling after that. Jeta, understanding part of what was expected, made sure the leash of the collar was outside the dress.

Mila tapped the table once more. Tea had already been the theme for the morning, so she went all in on it. "House, I need a full food spread for a proper British afternoon tea — scones, jam, the usual — and make it all extra fancy." A louder thunk and this time Mila had to get the items from a cupboard hidden under a bookcase. It wouldn't have fit on the shelves.

Then Mila had to request a table to put it all on and a third chair, but she insisted on setting it all up herself, much to Aisha and Jeta's amusement.

The calico wanted her idea to stay a little surprise from Aisha, so she leaned up on tiptoes to Mila could whisper directly into Jeta's ears and craft the scenario directly in her mind, employing a temporary memory erasure command so the tigress would not consciously remember the orders. Then Mila slid into her spot opposite Aisha at the table.

Jeta remained impassively where Mila had left her until the calico snapped her fingers. Then the tigress stood to her full height, adopting a formal bearing and looking down at the two women. "Ladies," she said, her voice as elegant and erudite as Ingrid's. "Thank you for inviting me to tea."

Aisha lifted a questioning eyebrow at Mila, who simply nodded. "Of course," the calico said. "Please, join us. Aisha was just telling me that you know a lot about how the house works."

The tigress slid gracefully into a seat. "I do not think anyone truly knows how the house works, but at Aisha's request, I have been investigating. Oh, thank you." She graciously accepted a scone and butter knife and passed along another scone and utensil to the jackal, who was watching with interest.

"And what have you found?" Mila asked, taking a sip of her tea.

"That to anyone who has not been welcomed into the house, it simply does not exist. I—"

Mila reached in and without the tigress even being aware of it, gave a little tug to the leash on Jeta's collar, just enough to add some pressure to the back of the tigress's neck. The tigress's only reaction was to have her ears go flat for a second, before perking back up. "I'm sorry, what was I saying?" She looked confused: the great actress had misplaced her lines.

"You were saying the house did not exist."

"Right, of course." The tigress adjusted her seat, as if trying to get comfortable and took a delicate bite of her scone, wiping her lips clean with a napkin after. "I've asked people just outside to tell me what they think of the building, and they can't see it. If I point towards it, they always look to the side. To them it simply does not exist."

"Fascinating," Mila said. She knew she wasn't a good actress, but she hoped she was decent enough for the current purposes.

"Tell her about the block," Aisha suggested.

Just before Jeta could speak, Mila tugged the leash again. Down went the tigress's ears and they stayed down as her seat-adjusting motion looked a lot more like a squirm. "I'm sorry, could you repeat that."

"Tell her about the block."

Jeta nodded. "Right. My apologies. It doesn't exist, according to the city. There is no space between 15th and 16th street and between Oak and Hedge. When I really pushed hard on it, all they said was that there must be a decorative partition there."

Mila faked a tittering laugh as she pulled on the leash, now with enough force to make the tigress's body move about an inch.

Jeta fanned herself. "It feels so warm in here today."

"It's fine to me," the jackal pronounced with a predatory smile.

"Same here," Mila agreed.

"If you say so." There was a quaver in the tigress's speech. She rolled her shoulders, took a quick breath, and started repeating what she had said before. "This space doesn't exist, according to the city."

"You said that already," Mila pointed out.

"I did?"

"You did," Mila said while tugging the leash again.

The tigress let out the quietest of groans this time. "I'm sorry, ladies," she said. "I think the most recent stunt work has tweaked my back a little."

Mila glanced down and saw that the tigress had looped her tail over one leg, with the tip of it disappearing underneath the slit of her dress. "What about the house? Anything else you can tell me?"

"What else would you like to know?" The tigress tipped her head slightly to sip at her tea, and Mila flushed when she caught the tigress's eyes roaming over her form.

"Aisha said that the house would prevent people from noticing that I'm gone. Is that true?"

"Oh yes." After another gentler pull on the leash, Jeta slid her arm under her breasts. Her breathing was a little more energetic: her chest moving back and forth to brush against her own arm. "I, uh, when I visit here, every thinks I'm on vacation, which is true, but no matter who you are, people will excuse your absence."

"Can you be more specific?" Mila began to wind the leash along her finger so that it pulled steadily harder on the tigress's collar.

A soft moan crept into Jeta's voice. "Specific?"

"About how people will excuse my absence?"

Mila wasn't letting go of the leash and Jeta took a deep breath, letting it out with a trembling sigh. "I'm sorry, could you repeat the question?"

Mila tutted in mock exasperation. "Aisha, I thought you said Jeta was an erudite speaker. You said she knows three languages."

"I do," the tigress protested with a needy whine in her voice.

"Uh-huh. Which ones?"

A sharp tug stopped her initial comment and she started again saying, "E-English, and—" Another sharp tug stopped her from speaking again. When she finally stopped squirming enough to speak, she said, "And... And... I forget." She whined like a kitten who wasn't getting her dessert.

"I don't know what to tell you," Aisha said, understanding the role they were set out to play. "I bet she was lying about being a geology expert too."

"She probably couldn't even tell us the chemical formula for quartz."

"I can! It's—" A tug on the leash. "It's... I forgot again."

"She seems to be doing that a lot."

"Well, what do you expect when she's so distracted by sex all the time?" Mila said with a shrug.

"I am not!"

"She's been moaning since we sat down," Aisha pointed out.

"And she thought we wouldn't notice she's been grinding against her tail for the last few minutes."

"I am not! I would never!"

"Then show us your tail," the calico said with a giggle.

"T-that's not fair."

Aisha leaned in slightly and spoke low and commanding, in tones that Mila felt she would never be able to replicate, even with practice. "Show. Us. Your. Tail."

Slowly the tigress's long tail extracted itself from under the dress and held itself up in the air, clearly wet with her own arousal.

Mila touched her chest with feigned indignation. "And to think, such a common slut tried to join proper ladies for lunch." She had to stifle a giggle at calling herself a proper lady.

Despite being so much larger than the calico, Jeta looked small now. Her shoulders were hunched and her head was drooping. "I'm sorry," she said. "You were just so beautiful. I wanted to be with you." Her hands were fidgeting just above her lap, as if she were trying to occupy them and not give in to her lewd desires.

Mila gave several quick tugs on the leash in rapid succession, each time breaking down the willpower of the tigress a little more until Jeta spread her legs apart and slid a hand under her dress to start fingering herself. She looked so embarrassed.

"Disappointing," Aisha commented, taking a bit of a scone. "She clearly does not make a very good lady, but perhaps she could still be a useful slut."

"R—really?" Jeta's eyes were wide, her ears forward. She looked so desperate and hopeful. "Do you mean it?"

"Mmhmm." The jackal chewed and swallowed another bit of scone. "Don't you think so, Mila?"

"I do," the calico confirmed, "but first of all, she needs to get out of that ridiculous dress. That belongs on a woman of poise and dignity, not on her."

Jeta looked down at herself, seemingly oblivious to the hand still lewdly grinding over her crotch. "I guess. If you think so."

"I know so."

The tigress swallowed and pulled her hand away so she could shimmy out of the dress. Mila was still silently awed by the fact that she had functionally just made Jeta fucking Horowitz of all people strip herself naked.

"Is that better?" the tigress asked with a soft whine in her voice.

Part of Mila wanted to say, "Oh hell yes," but she wanted to continue the scenario she had built up. "You're still at the table," the calico pointed out. "This is a place for ladies of refinement."

"Under the table," Aisha suggested. "That's the better place for her."

Meekly, the tigress slipped down and disappeared under the edge of the table. A second later the sound of wet fingers diving into a wetter sex could be heard along with a constant stream of moans.

There was an extended pause in the action. Mila realized how famished she was looking at the delightful food and decided to really dig in, her earlier breakfast feeling like the tiniest of snacks now. She found herself following Aisha's lead on this. The jackal didn't need to act refined: she simply was refined. She understood the conventions and had the natural grace to enact them. Aisha would sip her tea, then Mila would sip hers. Aisha would clean any crumbs off her muzzle and then Mila would, dabbing at the same spots in the same way.

But Mila did not understand why the jackal had adjusted her position on the seat until she noticed that the sound of finger-fucking under the table had stopped and been replaced with a loud, constant purring.

The calico glanced under the table: Jeta had repositioned herself with her head between the jackal's thighs. She had one finger buried within the jackal and, based on the way the arm was moving, she was gently flexing it. Meanwhile the tigress had her head pressed to the jackal's hips, tongue softly swirling over the jackal's clit.

Mila moved herself into a similar position in her chair, adjusted her dress to make sure her sex was revealed under the table, and made a soft coughing to attract the tigress's attention.

She could only feel and hear what happened next. The soft sound of licking and kissing stopped. There was a pause, then a barely suppressed squeal of joy before a hand slid up her leg, to her naked sex and slid a finger inside. A moment later warm lips wrapped around her clit and suckled.

Mila felt a tingle rush down her spine to the tip of her tail, making the fur stand on end. She gave out a soft groan and then straightened suddenly when she saw Aisha's amused gaze on her. The jackal was calmly stirring her tea as if nothing whatsoever was happening under the table, although from the way Jeta's shoulders were angled against Mila's knees, the calico guessed Aisha was still being fingered too.

Mila tried to ignore the sensations building between her legs. That one digit was curling and extending, twisting and turning in a delightful manner while the tigress's tongue was giving occasional swirls over her clit. Mila concentrated on the fork in her hand, slicing off a piece of cake and skewering it with as much refinement as she could manage under the circumstances. It was impossible to push all sensations away, but she managed to contain it to stifled moans on her breaths. When she felt an urge to grind her hips or squeeze her thighs, she channeled that into flexing her feet, curling her toes, sheathing and unsheathing those claws.

"You know," Aisha said slowly. "A proper lady should be able to be fucked without anyone being aware of it." She tapped a thigh gently. "Jeta, focus on me, get me off hard and fast."

A moan burbled up through Mila's throat as the lovely tongue and finger slipped away from her in an instant. They were replaced a moment later by the tigress's tail, brushing its way up over her sex then back down again. The fur was so soft and delicate. It felt like silk being caressed over her labia. Mila had to stuff a huge bite of cake into her mouth to silence her cries of delight.

Aisha, however, hadn't changed her posture or given the slightest indication that Jeta was doing anything to her, even though the sounds of eager slurping from beneath the table suggested she was. Jeta was working so hard that she had to pull away every few seconds to suck in a gulp of air before diving back in. Mila watched, dumb-founded as Aisha calmly sipped her tea. "Could you hand me another scone? They really are quite lovely."

The calico placed two on a plate and passed it across the table.

The jackal delicately nibbled on one and considered. "I think it could use a touch more orange peel. I shall have to recommend that to the house next time."

There was a squeal of delight under the table and the tail went rigid against Mila's sex. Then the tigress was panting heavily. "Oh, thank you. You taste so fucking delicious."

Mila blinked. "You came?"

The jackal nodded before taking another bite. "As I said, a proper lady should be able to be fucked without anyone being aware of it. Jeta, dear, come out here for a moment."

The tigress crawled out and knelt beside the table, still panting, her breasts bouncing with each heave of her chest. Mila noticed that her muzzle was still quite wet.

The jackal set down all her food and pushed it slightly away. "I think we may have had two impostors at this table. Jeta, you should test Mila to see if she deserved to sit here too." She then leaned over and whispered a few instructions into the tigress's ear.

Jeta nodded obediently and stood, crossing over to stand beside Mila. Before the calico could protest, she had been lifted from her chair and pressed against the flat side of a bookcase, the tigress's strong arms holding her up so the two were at eye level to one another. "If you ever want me to stop, the safeword is 'red.'" Then they were kissing, and the tigress's big tongue was playing over her lips and against her own tongue. Mila could taste and smell Aisha still on Jeta, but she didn't care.

With the warmth and strength of the tigress so close, Mila began to run her hand over the tiger's form. Her fingers explored the much thicker, more luxurious pelt of the bigger feline, starting with the rough fur over her hips, then up to the soft, plush fur over her belly. Her fingers crept up to the edge of the ubiquitous corset that all felines in the house wore, skipping over it to run her hands over the edges of Jeta's breasts.

The tigress seemed to understand the unconscious yearnings of the calico and lowered the other feline down so Mila's head was now level with her breasts.

Jeta held her still and just breathed, deep and slow, giving the calico time to work up her courage up until she was holding the breasts in her own hands. Except holding was probably not the right word. Two hands around one breast still wouldn't be enough to hold it. She was gently lifting them, feeling out their weight and their girth and the texture of them. The tigress let out a gentle purr as Mila's fingers brushed over stiff nipples.

Tentatively, Mila leaned in and brushed her muzzle against the breast. The fur was thick and rich against her nose and not only did it smell so strongly of the tigress, but there was also an underlying scent, a scent of grasses and flowers, maybe lavender. She opened her lips and gave a kiss to the breast, then another when the tigress responded positively.

Mila thought of how she enjoyed having her own breasts played with and tried to do that. She lifted one breast up and brought her mouth in to kiss right over the nipple, letting her lips slide over it and graze her teeth lightly after. The purr grow louder and louder in Jeta's chest until it seemed to be the only thing Mila could hear. The calico continued her loving kiss and caress of the breast in front of her heedless of all else, until Aisha intervened, gently prying her off, and making Mila finally let go of the nipple which she had been eagerly suckling.

The calico held her ears down and looked up shyly at the jackal.

Aisha tapped the tigress's shoulder. "Give her something to remember you by, Jeta."

The tigress grinned and wrapped the smaller feline in a bear hug that smothered the calico in the tigress's chest. As Jeta nibbled on her ear, her hand slipped down the calico's squirming flank, claws out, tearing the dress Mila wore to shreds. The tigress flicked her fingers and that was enough to remove the last tatters of the dress from the calico's body. Now with nothing in the way, she rubbed a finger against Mila's waiting slit. Mila tried to wriggle out of the grasp but Jeta was far too strong. Her arms were pinned to her side and she couldn't even manage to work them around to her front so she could reciprocate the pleasure the tigress was giving. It was futile; the purring tigress wasn't giving an inch.

Mila felt Jeta spread her labia wide. A claw traced over the entrance to her sex in a lazy circle before slipping in with a quick motion that barely let her register its entrance before it exited again. Then that same finger pressed against her clitoral hood, rolling over it for a moment before returning down. The tigress repeated the circuit from entrance to deep inside to clit and back, growing faster with each pass, until the rub on her clit became more like a strum, and the swirl of a claw over her entrance disappeared almost entirely, and Jeta alternated between a quick dive into Mila's sex and a quick flick along her clit.

Mila gave full voice to her pleasure as her orgasm crashed into her, but it was muffled by the thick fur of the tigress.

When the bear hug finally loosened and Mila could stand on her own feet again, she launched herself up as high as she could, wrapped her arms around Jeta's neck, and pulled the other feline into a fierce kiss. "Thank you," she said, when she finally broke the kiss, "that was wonderful."

"Yes, you were, Mistress Mila," the tigress agreed.

The jackal clapped her hands once, bringing both felines attention to her. She stood at a slight distance, eyes sharp. "Mila, you are no longer an honorary canine. Jeta, give your honest opinion on Mila's performance as a dominant."

The tigress took a slow step away from Mila and bowed slightly. "Yes, Mistress Aisha. Mila was a good dominatrix but I believe hampered by her inexperience both with women and with dominance. She did well to listen to my desires and craft them into an interesting scenario, and the idea with the leash dumbing me down with every tug was hot, but it was a set-up without a conclusion."

Aisha nodded, and with little other movement, her eyes slipped to look at Mila. "And what did you think of being a dominant?"

"I..." Mila's voice quavered. Assisted by the magic forcing her to answer a canine's question, she pushed aside the complex boil of lustful emotions and tried to think clear-headedly. "That whole scenario was really hot, like once-in-a-lifetime ecstasy, but I don't think that was who I am most of the time, Mistress Aisha."

"Once-in-a-lifetime ecstasy," the jackal repeated slowly. She mouthed the words an additional time. "I suspect you'll look back on this moment fondly for years to come in that case. A true dream come true, you might say." There was something strange about the slow plodding tone in Aisha's voice. "So tell me, Mila, how would you have reacted if half-way through, Jeta had voiced the opinion that the entire scenario was stupid?"

Even imagining the possibility felt like a punch straight to the calico's gut. Jeta herself flinched at the idea. "That would have been miserable, Mistress Aisha," Mila said, feeling as though that did not come close to adequately describing it.

Aisha gave a single slow nod. "The dream would have become a nightmare. Instead of being a moment you would have looked back on fondly for years, it would be a source of embarrassment for just as long, impossible to think about without your gut knotting up. You had an expectation for how events would go," she said while reaching out to touch first Mila's chest and then Jeta's, "and it was up to her to match those expectations, or else risk ruining the whole thing. That is, in part, what the duty of a submissive is. That is what *your* duty is now in the Eternal Party."

Mila thought back to how she had reacted when she had handed the keys over to the jackal and cringed. If Jeta had whined like that it would have felt awful. "I think I get it now, Mistress Aisha, but," she interjected quickly, "how do I know how people want to be treated? Everyone is different."

It was Jeta who answered. She leaned down and purred softly into Mila's ear. "Make them feel the way I made you feel."

"I can't do that!" Mila said quickly and gesticulated towards the tigress's body. "I don't look like you."

"Of course you can. I made you feel desired. I didn't need big tits for that, not to say they didn't help though." She grinned and gripped her breasts, holding them out and making Mila squirm.

Mila glanced at the jackal, who was regarding the two felines thoughtfully. Mila tried to put herself in the jackal's position and think about what she wanted. The small cat stepped to her and leaned in to return the kiss on the muzzle that Aisha had given her the previous night. "Thank you, Mistress Aisha," she said in a low voice, "for all that you have helped me with."

"Of course, dear," the jackal said, "and that is much better. Now—"

"Wait. Sorry, Mistress Aisha." Mila turned to Jeta. "We haven't gotten you off properly in all this. I don't think the order to climax should count."

"Don't worry about it," Jeta said with a smile.

"Why not?"

The tigress turned to the jackal. "Mistress Aisha, could you ask me that so Mila knows I am telling the truth?"

The jackal agreed. "Jeta, why do you not want Mila to make you cum now?"

The tigress caressed Mila's side. "Because I enjoyed this scene and I want this arousal and these fantasies to last all the way until I get home, by which point I'll be so eager, I'll get to a screaming orgasm using my favorite vibrator thinking about you."

Mila knew it was the truth, but she still couldn't believe it. Jeta Horowitz was going to fantasize about her? "Are you doing this for me?"

"Not just for you." The tigress rested a hand on the bookcase over Mila's head. She seemed to loom high over the calico. "But if you know that I'll be thinking of you, then perhaps you'll be thinking of me." She leaned in and whispered directly into Mila's ears. "And when we meet again, I'll want to know all the fantasies I inspired."

Mila blushed so hot in her ears she thought she could hear them sizzle.

After cleaning up from their impromptu meal, Aisha returned to the problem of research. The jackal employed Mila and Jeta as assistants, sending them to procure whatever books she thought would be helpful. Mila had a surprising amount of fun clambering over the glass walkways of the library to reach the upper shelves.

After several trips fetching books, Mila was surprised that the jackal next sent calico and tigress together to get a single book. But as soon as the pair were out of earshot, Jeta pulled Mila in to a quick but deep kiss that made the calico feel like she was back in high school and sneaking touches and sometimes more behind the bleachers.

"You know why she pushes you so hard to get it right, don't you?"

The seriousness of Jeta's question cut through the haze of fantasies crowding Mila's mind (which were currently centered on fumbling gropes under tight shirts, except now with Mila as groper rather than the groped). She looked at the tigress with a confused mew on her lips. "You mean Aisha? I thought it was so I would fit in better."

"That's part of it." The tigress stood back, hands on her hips. Were it not for the corset, she would have looked like a warrior. "But it's also for her sake. How many other canine women have you even seen here?"

Mila tried to count them all. She held up nine fingers.

"Exactly. Most of the dominants are male, and while the house does a good job of keeping prejudices at bay, it's not perfect. Add to that that she's a librarian doing stereotypical women's work..." Jeta's voice trailed off.

Mila wondered if the tigress were understating the case. She'd been on the receiving end of enough teasing just for being a calico that she knew just how cruel people could be over even small things. Besides being a dominatrix and librarian, Aisha was British, a jackal, possibly Muslim if her name was anything to go by, and she spoke with a subtle East African accent: each difference was another target to some people.

There was also what Alonso had said. If Mila misbehaved around a dominant, the rest of the party would assume it was the dominant's fault, not hers. Each time the calico acted casually around the jackal, it was undermining her authority.

"Is that why she has that 'greeting properly' thing?" Mila asked. "So that it's reinforcing she is the one in charge?"

Jeta nodded. "You got it."

Mila considered, head on her hands. "I don't think I'm up for doing that yet."

"You don't have to be." The tigress wrapped an arm around the smaller feline's shoulder. "You just need to show respect, especially when you are around others."

"I will." Then Mila said it again. She and Jeta then went and found the book they had been sent for and brought it back to Aisha. Mila presented it to her in both hands with a slight bow. The jackal acknowledged this with a small smile and tilt of her head, and nothing else.

Aisha employed the pair in other ways after that. Most often she had them scanning books for specific words or phrases. It should have been monotonous, even impossible work, but a few suggestions from the jackal had them able to casually flip through the books with ease and even enjoy it all the while.

It should have worried her that Aisha kept having her look for any reference of dead partners, but it didn't.

Even though she seemed to have every book she needed, Aisha would still occasionally send them out for more, just to give the two felines extra time to explore one another.

Mila was hardly aware of the passage of time until Aisha clapped her hands and declared that they should have lunch. Mila didn't feel hungry, but she supposed the jackal was doing this to give them a break and Mila another touch of normalcy. She didn't complain about the lovely toasted sandwiches and salads, nor about the conversation. Jeta was happy to regale them with behind-the-scenes details of her movies.

"Can I ask something of both of you?" Mila put in during a lull. When both other women gave her expectant looks, she went on. "So you've both heard about my time entering the Eternal Party and how crazy it's been, but how was it for both of you? I mean, how did you even know to come here?"

"There's a sign," Aisha explained. "People will be walking past the house and, if the magic thinks they are appropriate, they will see an invitation written out for them. Most people see something like a marquee sign, complete with sliding letters. Some guests, those who bring something unique that the Eternal Party needs, are greeted with more elaborate signs, including some who get a sign made from wrought iron. Although Jeta's sign might have been the most unique."

The tigress laughed, a deep belly laugh that made her whole body shake. "Oh yeah," she said. "I'm guessing that the house ran into a problem with me: it thought I would have a great time here, but I was never passing by this way. The closest I came was a hotel five blocks from here."

Mila leaned forward to listen more closely. "So, how'd you find it?"

"The house used a billboard," the tigress said, grinning. "It was huge, probably fifteen stories high so I could see it over the other buildings, and it had a picture of me in an armbinder with the words 'Jeta Horowitz, you slut, come on over.'"

It was a good thing Mila wasn't eating anything, or she might have choked.

"I'm not kidding! The only reason I wasn't frantically calling my agent was because I knew that couldn't have been a picture of me. I'd never worn an armbinder before. So I slipped out of the hotel, came over here, and found another sign welcoming me in."

"And...?"

"To start with, everyone was as starstruck as you were." Jeta winked. "Then the canines realized that if I was there, it must be because I wanted to be and so there was an impromptu orgy in the foyer. I swear, I must have sucked twenty dicks in a row." Her eyes seemed to glaze over with happy reminiscence. Then she nodded to the jackal, "What about you, Mistress Aisha? I bet you got the wrought iron sign."

The jackal shrugged. "I don't know."

For a moment, Jeta was too stunned to say anything, and when she finally did, she forgot, for the first time so far as Mila could tell, to use the jackal's title. "What do you mean you don't know?"

Aisha shrugged again. "I tended to walk with my muzzle down a lot. I didn't see the sign that was there for me. I was just passing by on the sidewalk and then I was suddenly here. Or rather, I was right about there." She gestured down a different aisle of bookshelves. "So far as I can tell, I am the only person who has ever been forced to enter the house. Even the side-door guests have voluntarily entered."

Mila and Jeta glanced to each other. "Why do you think that is, Mistress Aisha?" Mila asked.

The jackal sat back in her seat in what Mila had come to think of over the course of the day as her thinking pose. "The magic of the Eternal Party, before anything else, is designed to help keep the Eternal Party, well, eternal. It will do its best to make sure key roles in the house are filled, but that's not a complete explanation for why I am here. The only key role I play at the Eternal Party is that of accountant, but I wasn't the accountant for over a year after I arrived. The best I can guess is that the magic needs someone in the house who can pick up the basics of magic in case something goes wrong with the spell, a magical repairwoman, if you like."

Jeta did not seem surprised by the casual reference to Aisha doing magic, so Mila guessed her earlier demonstration wasn't something special for Mila herself. "Has something gone wrong with the spell, Mistress Aisha?" Mila asked quietly.

"You're here, aren't you?" Aisha sighed and crossed her arms. "There should be a proper, fully-trained mage in residence that I could ask. There was one for over a hundred years after Lady Yasmin died. Even after the last mage in residence, the Eternal Party kept contact with other magical conclaves, but one by one they've either ceased communication or vanished. A group of gay mages visited us in the 1980's, and since then we've heard nothing. For all I can tell, the Eternal Party is the last bit of magic in the world, and I'm the last mage." The jackal's fist clenched so tight it shook. "And all I can manage is to lock a door from across the bloody room."

There was little more to say at that point. The mood had

turned somber. They cleaned up lunch and continued as they had before.

Eventually it was time for Jeta to go, as much as Mila wished she could stay. "I do have to stop by your apartment," the tigress reminded her.

"Wait." Mila realized something and suddenly felt a burst of laughter well up in her throat. She managed to contain it down to a mere squeak. "Jeta Horowitz is going to show up at my apartment and no one is going to think that's odd?"

The tigress grinned slyly. "I put on a chest binder and some padding in my shoulders and you would be surprised who struggles to recognize me. I've even fooled my own agent before." They shared one last kiss together, which the tigress encouraged to linger. "I'll check in on you next time I'm here, although I hope you'll both make it out before then. Also, whenever you and Alonso do get out of here, you are always welcome to visit me."

"In the mansion and everything?"

"In the mansion and everything."

Mila practically skipped back to Aisha and got to work on whatever the jackal requested of her while thinking of the tigress. Hours passed by with ease, until Mila stopped in the middle of a commanded skimming of a journal. "I've got it."

"You do? What is it?"

The calico read aloud from the book. "George and I spent the evening consoling a feline who was distraught. Apparently she was a widow, having lost her husband some time before her arrival at the Eternal Party, though the grief has never fully left her. We could only sympathize so much — as George and I are both unmarried — but she was grateful all the same. It is a rare evening here where I feel I have done good simply by listening."

"Interesting. What year was that?"

Mila checked. "1876."

Aisha flicked through her notes and groaned. "No good. I don't have any record of a side-door guest during the 1870's." She tore out a sheet of paper, starting a new list, with the reference in the journal at the top. Mila was worried this had meant her discovery was worthless, but Aisha assured her finding a part of a clue was still finding a part of a clue, and they persevered.

Eventually, Mila found two more references to guests who had lost their husband or wife before entering the party and one of them did overlap with the description of a known side-door guest well enough that Aisha was convinced they were one and the same.

Mila wasn't sure whether to feel elated or despondent, but again Aisha simply looked determined. The hardest part of solving a jigsaw puzzle was getting that first connection, she said.

By then the sun was setting. Aisha muttered something about insufficient hours of daylight, but told Mila they were done for the day and that she should return to her owner.

Mila took a step out into the hallway and recoiled. "It's dark," she exclaimed, which was putting it mildly. About one foot past the door, the bright light of the library was suddenly sucked away. All she could see was the vague outlines of objects. It was disorienting; as a feline she was used to being able to see at least a little in the dark.

Aisha glanced over her shoulder. "Strange. Didn't think that was on the schedule for a few nights yet."

The calico extended her arm out towards the darkness, and when it passed over the threshold, her fingers disappeared from view. She yanked her hand back and stared at her own hand in wonder.

"We call it the Midnight Dance, but of course, it's more for sex than dancing."

"Of course," Mila said.

"Even in a place like this, there is still a thrill to anonymous sex, so during the Midnight Dance, anyone in a public space can't tell who they are with. That darkness isn't just for your eyes: it'll hide your scent as well. But it will leave just enough of your senses left for you to make your way around and tell that you actually have a partner." The jackal turned to the nearest wall panel. "House, we need two candles."

There was a pair of thumps from a nearby bookcase and Aisha retrieved the candles (powered by small LED bulbs, not flames) and handed one to the calico. "So long as you hold onto this, you'll be able to see, and you won't be a target for anyone else's affections. Goodnight, Mila."

"Goodnight, Mistress Aisha."

The calico watched as Aisha shut the door, held her candle in front of her, and stepped into the darkness. Immediately, she was swallowed up by it, becoming nothing more than a faint outline of a canine, no longer even readily discernible as a jackal.

Mila held her light the same way, and took a gentle step into the darkness. This time there was no strange disappearance of her fingers. She stayed whole and visible to herself. The candle seemed to act like a bubble, providing a small sphere of protection from the darkness just for herself.

Mila made her way back with one hand along the wall, because even though she held a light in one hand, there was still that worry that it would go out and she'd be plunged into darkness and vertigo without a good reference point. Progress was slow for two reasons. For one, she was still not fully used to the house's twisting hallways and trying to find her way in the dark involved a lot of back-tracking. For another, she would occasionally hear laughter or the sounds of sex from those enjoying the Midnight Dance and gave them all a wide berth.

This left Mila's mind with plenty of time to wander. She felt like she had learned so much over the course of the day. As the calico took slow measured steps, she tried to recall everything that had happened. Her thoughts lingered often on Jeta, but then, as she rewound events further, a few other events stood out in her mind: there was the way Aisha had pointed out that she hadn't asked Alonso much about his history, and then, almost at the start of the day, there was the strange way Alonso had reacted when the house had shown him a collar. Curiosity bit at the back of her thoughts. She wanted to know what had been wrong with the collar, but she couldn't ask him about it. He had forbidden it.

The feel of the wooden wall under her fingers made her think about all the house had been able to provide at a simple verbal command, springing out from hidden panels and nooks. Alonso had only forbidden asking him about the collar. She paused and considered, before whispering, "House, can you show me the original collar design that Alonso rejected?"

Thump.

The thump had happened practically under her fingers and she found a small hidden door in the wall which revealed a secret compartment. Inside was the collar. Mila held it up and inspected it under the dim light. It looked almost identical to her own except that there was a cross-hatched pattern over the leather on either side of the name tag. She tried to think of why that would be significant and it took some time to remember that Alonso's cane had a similar pattern on it. Conclusions silently began to form in Mila's mind.

She slid the collar back and slipped away downstairs, arriving at Alonso's room only a few minutes later.

The fox was in his robe, reading a book. The cane was resting against his leg. "Well, you were out late," he said, marking his place in the book with a claw. "I hope that means you were successful."

"Only a little," the calico admitted as she put the candle down.

"And did you manage to have some fun?"

Mila rocked on her feet for a second, trying to hold back the squeal of delight boiling within her. She was unsuccessful. "I got to meet Jeta Horowitz!"

The fox smiled and nodded his head knowingly. "She is quite a wonderful person."

"And you weren't going to mention you already knew her when I brought her up the other day?"

"She enjoys some amount of anonymity and privacy. We've

had a few incidents of overzealous fans even here. But I hope you did more than just talk with her all day."

Mila put her hands on her hips. He knew full well they did far more than just talk. But then she saw the glint in his eyes. "Yes, we did. We were helping Aisha most of the day. She wasn't able to find much, but we are pretty certain we know the cause of the housequakes now."

The fox slipped a bookmark into his novel and then set it on a nearby table. Alonso leaned forward with a hand on his cane, ears perked and attentive. "Go on."

"It was me. I was causing them without realizing it. Whenever I thought about my husband and whenever I felt the pain of losing him — he died a while back — the house started shaking, like it was trying to distract me."

It was here that Aisha's earlier command revealed an unfortunate side effect: when something causes no pain to oneself, one can forget that it can still cause pain to others. So Mila plowed into her next question without even thinking.

"Did the house also shake for you when you thought about the person you lost?" she asked.

The fox's hand closed tightly around the head of the cane, as if hiding the cross-hatched pattern from view. He stared deep into her with a blank expression and spoke with a voice cold and distant. "What, Mila, makes you think I lost someone?"

I Want What I Have Not

"I asked you a question."

Mila fumbled. She tried to resist answering, and anywhere else she could have. The calico could have blustered and made up something to cover up the fact that she had said the wrong thing. But this was the house. This held the Eternal Party. A canine had asked her a question.

She tried to remember how Vivien had stalled at the masquerade. "Yes, you did, sir."

"Answer me now, kitten."

Even the use of the pet name did not alleviate the feeling of the command ripping the answer from her. "I figured it was likely that you had lost someone too because Aisha said that similar housequakes had occurred when you first arrived and that you had never discussed why they happened and then there was the collar you rejected for me which matches the design on the cane you use even though you don't need it to walk so I guessed it was a memento from someone you loved and your anger at the house for providing that collar was because you didn't want it to look like I was taking their place." As soon as the magic would let her, her jaw slammed shut with an audible clack.

The fox barely moved. He stared at a point on the far wall, over her shoulder. "How did you know about the collar?"

"You said I couldn't ask you about it, so I asked the house to show me."

He closed his eyes and lowered his head.

"Sir?"

He didn't move.

"Sir, I'm sorry."

"I am not ready to talk about this yet," he said, his voice half whisper and half growl.

And then Mila made it worse. She tried to force a laugh and say, "No problem then, sir. You can just erase my memories, right? Make it like I never thought of it at all."

The fox's hand gripped the cane so tight that his knuckles stood out in his fur. "Get out," he growled.

It was an order. She couldn't disobey. Even as she began to turn, she pleaded with him. "I'm sorry. I shouldn't have said anything. Please don't make me leave." Her feet were pulling her towards the door. She could only constrain the steps to be short ones. She couldn't stop them entirely. "Please, Alonso. Please." Her tone rapidly became more pleading. "Don't leave me alone."

She opened the door. She stepped through. She closed the door. And she couldn't, no matter how hard she tried, make herself open the door again. But she could bang on it and she did, pounding on the wood as hard as she dared without drawing attention from anyone else. "Alonso, let me back in. I can't get back in unless you let me. Please."

There wasn't a single sound from inside. He wasn't even moving.

The sense of safety and security that came from being Alonso's kitten shattered in an instant. She was alone, she was trapped, and she was unprotected.

"Fuck!" she yelled and slammed a fist into the door.

A sound behind her. In the shadows of the Midnight Dance, a canine head was poking out from a nearby room to ask what all the ruckus was about, but before he could say more than a word, his head was jerked back and the door slammed shut in his face, wrenched out of the canine's grip with a yelp.

All along the hall, doors made a clicking sound as its occupants were being locked inside.

The house. The house was protecting her.

Maybe it would help her too. "Open this door," she pleaded to the wood. "Open it."

Nothing. The house was as unresponsive as the fox had been.

She felt tears trying to well up and she pushed them aside, replaced sadness with anger so it hurt less. "Fine. You heard him," she said to the walls. "He told me to get out. Now let me out."

Mila ran as fast as she could for the front door. Ahead of her, doors slammed shut and locks were turned, keeping her path clear of all other canines and felines. The candle in her hand remained the only source of light; deep shadows full of nightmares chased her down the halls.

Something else was chasing her too. For the third time since entering the house, she heard a piano which seemed to come from nothing. Deep, quick bass notes pounded away just behind her. The floor writhed and twitched in time with the beat, as though the notes themselves were trying to snatch at her heels.

When she reached the main foyer, the piano cut off suddenly as light burst around her. Unlike the halls shrouded by the Midnight Dance, here it was as bright as it had always been, so bright that it stung her eyes. But thankfully it was deserted. Mila barreled down the stairs two, three steps at a time before skidding to a halt in front of the main door and taking a firm grip on the massive iron handle.

No matter how hard she tried to open the door, the handle wouldn't budge.

Mila took a few steps back and charged the door, intending to ram it with her shoulder, but the moment her fur made contact with the wood, it deformed like putty and absorbed the entire blow.

"Fuck. Come on," she growled. "I've had enough of this place. Let me out. Now." Nothing. "I want out! Please. I don't belong here." Then she spoke in a quiet voice, pleading now where she had been shouting before. "Why are you doing this?"

Mila clapped her hands over her ears as the strange piano music returned, pounding away on the high notes so that it sounded like the keys were shrieking. She staggered under the aural assault that seemed to bypass her every attempt to protect herself from it. Then the notes suddenly dropped in a quick glissando towards the bass, and just as it was about to hit the lowest note on the piano—

THUMP!

The sound hit Mila right in the chest and knocked the cat to her knees.

In the aftermath, a haunting silence filled the foyer, broken only by the sound of Mila's frantic panting. As she got back up to her feet, there was a creak from a small coat closet next to the main door, as though it were protesting a large weight suddenly placed inside it. Mila stared at it for a moment, then tentatively reached out and gripped the handle of the closet door. It turned easily in her hand.

Inside was a gravestone. In a plain and simple font, it read, "Here lies Bernard 'BD' Collins, beloved husband, brother, and son. Always in our memory."

It didn't hurt; Aisha's command saw to that. But once again a white-hot anger filled the space where the pain should have been. Anger at the world. Anger at fate. Anger at the house. Anger at BD for dying. Anger at herself for being angry at him. "Don't you think I know that he's dead?" she spat. "I know he's gone. I know nothing will bring him back. Not even your magic."

She waited the span of a breath in the tiny hope that the house would try to prove her wrong.

It didn't.

She clenched her hands into fists held impotently at her side.

"He'll stay just as dead with me in here as with me outside. So why shouldn't I leave?"

The closet door squeaked as it eased itself shut.

Thump.

Mila sighed and reached for the handle again.

Thump.

She jerked her hand away.

Thump thump thump.

The closet door was shivering as whatever was inside continued to bang against it. It grew louder and louder, like a monster trying to claw its way free from inside. Then, it was suddenly silent.

When the echo of the thumps finally died away, Mila reached out and cracked the door open.

The contents spilled out, slamming the door fully open and burying her in... something. She fell underneath the tide, sucked into an undertow. Mila flailed as she was swept off her feet and tried to find some purchase, any purchase. At least she could breathe, but she was still panicking. Her tail bumped into something solid and she reached out in that direction with her feet, finding the floor and pushing off. She breached the surface, gasping.

Photos. She was swimming in a giant pool of photos. They covered the foyer down at least seven feet deep. And on each and every photo was a picture of herself standing before the gravestone. The images surrounded her, smothered her, threatened to drown her.

"All right, all right. Fuck, I get it. You don't do subtle well, do you?"

The ground shivered lightly beneath her and the photos began to slip away as if a drain had been opened underneath them. Mila touched down on solid ground again and watched the last few photos disappeared through cracks in the floor.

Mila's anger abated as quickly as it had arrived. She was suddenly cold. She wrapped her arms around herself and shivered.

"I know I fucked up. Can I just go somewhere to be alone for a little while?"

The main doors into the halls of the manor eased shut and instead a small side door opened with an inviting squeak.

"Thanks," she said softly.

The calico silently climbed the stairs and made her way to the door. It led to a small staircase the wound up to the top of the manor parallel to the main stairwell. She guessed it would have been a servant's passage before the house was a magical kink wonderland. Another squeak of an opening door guided her up higher, past the third floor, past the fourth, and to the rooftop observatory. Thankfully, the Midnight Dance did not come to any of these spaces and she dropped off her candle in an alcove that seemed designed for it.

The observatory itself was on two levels. The entrance was a few feet down from the rest of the room, connected by a gentle slope. The bulk of the room was filled with telescopes of all shapes and sizes, tables of star charts and arcane astrological tables, and a few chairs, more worn down — or perhaps that was, more well-loved — than any furniture Mila had seen elsewhere in the house. Mila knew the price point of only a few of the items, because only a few of the items were made in the last few decades. At least two telescopes looked like they dated from the early 19th century. Mila took it all in and then looked up.

On the other side of the glass geodesic dome that made up the roof, a swath of stars cut the cloudless night-time sky, reflecting off the windows of the adjacent skyscrapers like the world's largest kaleidoscope. It was amazing. She had lived in the city for so long, but she had rarely ever looked up at the stars.

The door creaked shut behind her and a warm brush of air encouraged her to continue up the slope. She reached the top and saw that amongst all the observatory miscellanea was a table, which held a warm blanket and a freshly steaming cup of cocoa alongside a few cookies. Snickerdoodles. Just like her mom used to make.

"You know," she said to the house, "when you aren't terrifically aggravating, you're actually kind of okay."

Mila spread the blanket out over the largest clear spot on the floor. It was soft and fluffy and warm and perfect for laying back on and stargazing. She propped herself up on an elbow every now and then to sip her cocoa or nibble on a cookie, and the house made sure that her drink was always topped off and her plate was never empty.

With each slow breath of chocolate-cinnamon scented air, the feeling of safety returned. It was more delicate than before, held together with chewing gum and painter's tape, but it was there. Even if Alonso wasn't going to protect her, it seemed like the house would, in its own twisted way.

Hours later, when Mila's anxiety had started to wane and sleep threatened to claim her, she heard the door creak open and turned an ear back.

Then she heard the tap of a cane.

Her ear snapped forward. Her whole body was turned away from the door, lying on the blanket. She wasn't going to give him the dignity of acknowledging him.

"Mila, turn around and look at me."

The calico was forced to roll over and she hated it. Given the sunken entrance, her head and his were almost level, only a few feet apart. She returned Alonso's furious stare with one of her own.

The fox raised the cane and waved the tip threateningly at her. "You are *never* to do that again," he hissed. "I don't care what the hell you think I want, or how badly you think you've fucked up, you will never offer up your personality or memories like that again. They are the most important things you have in this place. They are the only things that make you still you and not just another faceless toy. Do you understand?"

The last words were bellowed out, and Mila pinned back her ears in shock as the weight of Alonso's command tightened around her thoughts like an iron cage. But what surprised her most wasn't the force of the command, but the certainty that for all the bluster in Alonso's tone he wasn't angry with her. He was angry with *himself*.

Alonso had been so careful with her. Not just with her, but with Vivien too, even when she was trying to embarrass Mila. He had changed the lynx as little as possible to stop her from further antagonizing Mila when he could have just ordered her to believe Mila was her friend. The calico had just waltzed into his room tonight and casually offered a violation of her own mind, against all his ethical beliefs. He was angry with himself because he had been tempted by her offer, she realized.

"I understand, sir," she said softly.

The fox drew back and rested his weight on his cane. For the first time, it seemed like he really needed its support. Alonso was panting hard, as if he had been running all over the house looking for her. "My room is yours to do with as you like. I'll only return to it if you permit me. I can make my excuses and stay elsewhere for as long as you need."

Mila felt an urge to say something, to apologize. It had been partially her fault. She'd stepped on a live wire of Alonso's personal morals. "It's okay," she said.

"It is not okay!" he yelled suddenly. "It is not okay. It is not fine. It is not fair. This whole damn place is unfair. It lets me rip into your most intimate thoughts without any concern. It even encourages me to do it. And then I have the gall to be insulted when you ask a single question about my life."

The fox gripped his cane in both hands and swung it against the nearby wall so hard that Mila was surprised it didn't leave a dent. "Show me the photo, you stupid house. You know the one."

There was a muted thump from a nearby cupboard and the fox went to fetch the item he had requested. He stepped to the edge of the upper level and put the photo before her, propped up against the cocoa mug. Then he backed off.

Mila drew herself up to a kneeling position and reached out for the photo.

She had expected the wife.

She hadn't expected the kids.

Four smiling foxes looked up at her from the photo. A much younger Alonso, without that fetching bit of gray, had his arm around the shoulder of a white-furred fox, while two teenaged kits, one boy and one girl, mugged for the camera before them.

"The kits too?" Mila asked.

Alonso drew a cautious breath and nodded. The fox suddenly needed so much support that he had to lean up against a wall. "Her name was Lily, my high school sweetheart," he said. His voice was low and distant, as if he were narrating events that had happened to someone else a long time ago. "You know the kind of couple we were: everyone knew how in love we were but us. We thought we were just friends. Then graduation started to approach, we considered life after school, and we realized how much we still wanted to be together." He laughed thinly. "It was the most unromantic proposal you have ever heard: we had a free period after lunch, so we were chatting about nothing important at a cafeteria table and I toss out the idea that we should get married that summer. She said yes but only if I proposed to her again and for real this time."

He lapsed into silence for a moment. Then he shook himself and went on. "Ended up that it took us over a year after graduation to actually tie the knot. We kept talking about kids, and I knew that meant I needed a better job. I'd always imagined myself as an Air Force pilot, but that's no way to raise a family, I thought. So I went for a commercial pilot's license instead. Lily was an art teacher. She should have gone into painting professionally, she had the talent for it, but she insisted she wanted to help others.

"Then, one day she welcomes me home after I pulled a red-eye all the way from Paris and tells me she's pregnant. A few months later Ethan was born, and the year after that we had Val." Alonso's voice cracked. As he worked to regain his composure, he wrung the head of his cane in his hands for something to busy himself with. "I had hoped they'd want to share the sky with me. I wanted so much for them to join me, but they took more after their mother. The stage was their calling. Ethan was an actor — boy, could he sing — and Val did tech. In Ethan's Junior year, they both got a chance to go upstate to a big competition. Lily insisted on taking them both. The kids practiced for months: Ethan did that soliloquy so many times that even I practically knew it by heart."

The fox drew himself up and lifted his cane like a sword as he quoted: "'This fool, he takes me for a thief, as if a heart could ever be stolen. A heart can only be happily given away.'"

The cane dropped. Alonso sagged once more against the wall. His voice became almost monotone. "They were set to drive back Sunday, while I was flying in from Tokyo. We touched down, taxied, disembarked, and I go to call her, same way I always did after a long flight, but no one picks up. Someone, I forget who, pulled me aside and told me: Lily had hit a patch of ice on the drive. There was an accident. No survivors."

He breathed heavily and shook his head. "I don't remember much of the next few days. There was a funeral, I'm sure. But then... I was just sitting in the house, and I couldn't stop thinking about how big it was." Alonso swallowed a lump in his throat. "It had never seemed so big before. And there were so many things in it that I had never really looked closely at before. Why had Lily bought that particular painting and put it right there? Why had she..." His voice trailed away, lost in reminiscence for a moment.

"I had to get out of there. I got back in the air as soon as they would let me. But then the complaints started. I thought I was just focusing on the job, but I was scaring the tail off every copilot I had. They called me death on wings, half-expecting me to snap mid-flight and crash us into a mountain or something. I don't know. They made me go in for a psych eval, and concluded that I was just depressed. 'Don't worry. You'll get over it soon.' And then on the next psych eval, they said I was still depressed. 'Don't worry. You'll get over it soon.' And the same on the next psych eval, and the next one, and the next. But I never got over it.

"Then, one day, I'm wandering through the streets when I see a house I'd never noticed before. The door was open with a sign saying 'Guests welcome.' People were laughing inside, and it felt so inviting. I went in and I've been trapped here ever since.

"And yes, to answer your question from before, the house shook whenever I thought about Lily, just as it did for you. At least at first, when the pain was sharpest." He held up the cane and ran a claw along the hatched pattern. "She made this, you know. Picked up woodworking from her dad. For a long time, I thought the house was telling me to get over her and give up my attachment, but..." Alonso roused himself and walked over to a nearby window, which permitted itself to be opened a crack. In a quick motion, he flung the cane out into the night, but it disappeared midflight.

Thunk.

Alonso opened a cabinet and retrieved the cane. "It wasn't that simple. Or maybe I just haven't gotten over her. Even now, I keep wishing I'd just had a chance to say goodbye. Maybe if I had, it wouldn't have hurt so much."

"It wouldn't have helped."

Alonso spun around at Mila's words, his expression first angry, then surprised.

Mila swallowed. Talking about this should hurt. Even thinking about this should hurt. But it didn't, and that was somehow even worse. "BD, my husband, he got pancreatic cancer. By the time we discovered it, it was already too late. It had already spread." She hated how her voice sounded without any pain in it, almost like she was relating a comedic anecdote. Aisha had said she could feel the pain if she wanted to, so she let a bit of it in. Immediately her throat seized up and a few tears dotted her eyes. She wiped her nose on the fur of her arm and continued, "We thought we had a little time after the diagnosis, so we planned a quick bucket list of places to visit: Scotland, London, Amsterdam, Rome, Istanbul. We bought a ticket barely a week out at a horrifically exorbitant price, but we never made it. His condition worsened too fast. Too sick to fly. Then too sick to move. Then he was in the hospital all the time.

"He had a routine, even then. Whenever I had to leave him, or whenever he started to fall asleep, he told me how much he loved me and he said good bye, just in case he wasn't there to say it again. He wanted to make sure my last memory of him was of that. He did it every day until... until he was too weak to say it anymore. So I said for him and told him how much I loved him and said goodbye." She shook her head. She could still feel the immense weight of her pain hovering just out of reach, threatening to break her. "I got to say my goodbyes, Alonso. I said them every day for months, and each and every one hurt more than the last. It wouldn't have helped you."

The fox's ears turned away, then his eyes. "Maybe we each should have gotten one goodbye. Maybe then we wouldn't have been stuck here."

She laughed wryly at his optimism. "I don't think it's that easy either. When I asked the house why it wouldn't let me leave, it said—"

"Wait." Alonso held up a hand. "You asked the house a question?"

"Yes."

"And it answered?"

"Yes. Not in words, though. More with symbolic objects."

"Mila, the house has never answered questions before. It gives us what we request, but it doesn't speak, in symbols or otherwise."

Mila shrugged. "I don't know. It did with me."

The fox stared at her in disbelief. "Well," he said after a moment, "go on."

Mila straightened up. "When I asked the house why it wouldn't let me leave, it told me, well, it basically told me that I was drowning in sorrow. And I get what it meant. Before I came here, I was always obsessing over his death. I didn't let myself do or even feel anything else. It suggested that if I left, I'd just go back to that again."

Alonso nodded. He tapped the cane against the ground as he thought. "It was similar with me." He turned to address one of the nearby walls. "House, why can't I leave?"

Silence greeted him.

"It's not working," he said.

Mila sat back and crossed her legs, thinking. "It's a magic house. Maybe you have to ask the question in just the right way."

"Like hopping on one leg during a full moon while yodeling the alphabet backwards?" he suggested. "We could be testing different ways of asking questions forever."

"But we know it hears the questions, just like it hears the requests for items. Maybe we just need to trick it into giving us an answer."

"Trick it?"

"Like with those old logic problems: you know, one guard always tells the truth and one always lies, but you can only ask them one question. You have to think laterally. Let's try this. House, if we ask you a question and the answer is yes, give us, oh, one dildo. And if the answer is no, give us two dildos, but — this is important — give them to us about a second apart."

Alonso's face brightened for the first time since he had entered the observatory. "One thump or two thumps."

"Right. House, do you understand?"

The calico and fox waited with fur on end.

Thump.

"Is my name Denise?"

Thump. Thump.

"I think it's working, sir."

Alonso pressed in close to the railing that separated the upper level from the lower, getting as close as he could to her without vaulting over it. "Go on, kitten," he said, his voice soft and quick with anticipation.

Mila nodded. "House, is there a way for you to let us both out?"

Thump.

"Are you not letting us out now because if you did we'd both be 'drowning in sorrow' outside?"

Thump.

"So if we could get over that, and be outside without drowning in sorrow again, you'd let us out?"

Thump.

Mila felt her heart flutter, and then she heard the pounding of feet as Alonso raced up the slope, took the corner onto the upper level at a dead run, and swept the calico up into his arms. He spun her around through the air while hugging her. "You did it! My wonderful, beautiful kitten. You did it."

Mila couldn't help herself. She giggled as she was twirled through the air, and though she didn't want to forgive Alonso so readily, she felt that sense of security rebuilding itself as he held her close. "I haven't gotten us out yet."

He set her down and peppered her in kisses all over her head. "But you figured it out. You know why we can't get out. Now all we have to do is..." his voice trailed off and he took a step back.

"Sir?"

"I just realized. After all those years of attending stupid psych evals, now its the house playing psychologist."

She smiled lightly. So did he.

He planted one more kiss on her cheek. "Shall we see what it takes to actually get out now?"

The calico pressed her head in against his chest and felt the warmth of him there. "Okay. But this is going to take playing twenty questions with a magical house. Uh, house, is the way we leave the house by being together?"

Silence.

Mila's heart skipped a beat. "Did we break it already?"

Thump thump.

She relaxed a little. "That's good. But why didn't it work?"

"I think I know. House, is there more than one way for us to get out?"

Thump.

The fox nodded to her. "You said 'the way.' But there's more than one way. It probably can't deal with nuance." He held up a finger and thought for a second. "Is one way for us to leave by dying?"

Thump.

"Are there ways for us to leave that do not involve dying?"

Thump.

"Good to know. Mila, would you like to continue?"

"Yes, sir. House, are there ways for us to get out that involve us needing to be together?"

Thump.

That was better, Mila thought. "House, are you trying to make us forget our old partners?"

Thump thump.

"There's your theory confirmed, sir."

He nodded.

"Could you let one of us leave but not let the other one leave?"

Thump.

"So it's not something we do together. It's individual."

The fox tapped a finger on his chin thoughtfully. "House, are both of us closer to overcoming our sorrows than we were when Mila arrived?"

Thump.

Mila blinked. "Wait. I'm closer to getting out already?" The house's singular thump was drowned out as Mila continued to talk. "But I've barely been here, and most of what I've been doing the past few days is... well... fucking. And the same with you! How is this helping us get out?"

No response from the house.

Mila started listing off all the events that had occurred since she entered the house, and asking if they had helped her get closer to getting out. The answer to all of them, outside of simple, everyday stuff like eating meals, was that they were helping. Even getting thrown out of Alonso's room earlier had helped, according to the house. "I don't get it."

"Maybe the house is taking a holistic view," the fox suggested. "When I, uh, asked you to leave, that wasn't on its own helping you to get out, but it led to us being here, which is helping you to get out."

Mila groaned and dramatically flopped backwards. "I do not want to try and wring answers out of the house right now."

"Then we won't."

"But—"

The fox pressed a finger to her lips to quiet her. "Mila, you've had a long and stressful evening and I am at fault for that. You don't need to fix every problem right now. You've done enough. You have made me believe I might finally get out of here, and that is far, far more than enough." He pressed in close enough to brush his whiskers against her cheek. "Thank you, Mila."

She nodded and returned the affectionate touch, resting her head on his shoulder. "And thank you, sir, for telling me about your family."

He hesitated, a tension in the muscles of his shoulder. "Do you want me to go?"

"No. Please stay."

He smiled and began to kneel down to join her on the grand blanket, when her ears shot up.

The piano was playing again.

Alonso looked at her strangely. "What is it?"

"You don't... hear that?"

His ears turned in the direction hers were turned in. Then they slowly panned out, searching. "No. What is it?"

"Music. I've been hearing a piano every now and then since I entered the house." She felt uncertain and directed her voice down to the floor. "I am hearing music, aren't I?"

Thump.

"Can Alonso hear it?"

Thump thump.

The fox looked at her with an unreadable expression. He wrapped an arm around her and asked, quietly, "What does it sound like?"

"It's—" The response died in Mila's throat as the piano was joined by a voice. She struggled to describe it for several moments before telling him it was a song. The words were in a language she didn't know, but the meaning beneath them was clear all the same. The music was floating and elegiac, a song about grief and loss. It seemed to capture the precise emotion Mila had felt the day after BD had died: the feeling that the world was unreal and it would never be made right again.

She told Alonso that she thought the house understood what they had both gone through.

The fox said nothing. He waited for Mila to tell him that the song had ended, quietly pulled her in against himself, and told her to sleep.

Impromptu

Mila woke to sun stabbing her in the eyes in a way only the city was capable of: a dozen bright reflections from the skyscrapers meant there was no escape no matter where she turned.

She rolled over to be facedown, pressing up against the warmth of Alonso next to her.

Then she sniffed the air. She smelled bacon.

Her first impulse was to wake Alonso up for breakfast. Her second impulse was to slap herself. He had abandoned her last night. Was she so desperate to move on from BD that she'd allow herself to be mistreated like that? Was that what the house was trying to get her to do?

She tried to banish the dark thoughts from her mind. She trusted the house, a little. She trusted Alonso, a little. But she wasn't going to trust either of them fully. Not yet.

The calico carefully slid out from under Alonso's arm and crawled over to where the scent of bacon began. Two small bed trays lay at the edge of the blanket. Each had a card with the name of the intended recipient leaned against a cloche. The calico peeked under one cloche to find bacon, yes, and an omelet with herbs beautifully spread over top, two slices of toast, and a selection of jams in small jars. Next to it was a full pot of steaming coffee.

Out of curiosity, Mila peeked underneath Alonso's cloche and nearly burst out laughing. "I think you pissed the house off."

There was a groan from behind her and she turned to see the fox rubbing his eyes as if he could squeeze the bright sunlight out of them. "Why do you say that?" he grumbled after a few more moments of fighting against being awake.

"Because I got served a five-star hotel meal, and you got served something from a Victorian poorhouse."

He stilled. "Packet oatmeal and packet tea?"

"Now that you mention it, I think so."

"That's what I typically get."

"Seriously?" Mila took a bite of her omelet. She'd never had one so good. "Why not ask for something better?"

Alonso pulled himself up to a sitting position then crawled over to his own tray, taking a long draft of tea. "Habit," he said. "I used to get sent out on a lot of late flights and then have to get up early for the first flight out. I started bringing a packet of instant oatmeal and a tea bag with me. Could make them both with hot water from the hotel room coffee pot while I was showering. Eat and drink quick then be on my way. Even at home that's all I wanted for breakfast. Save the fancy meals for lunch and dinner." Then he added, "Lily thought it was silly too."

It occurred to Mila that Alonso had likely not spoken about his wife to anyone in ten years. He seemed tense, but at the same time relieved. "Did she keep trying to make you eat a proper breakfast?"

The fox looked at her askance. "For years. I think she only stopped when Ethan was about six or so, and even then, she always made a big show of making one more serving than she really needed, which Ethan would inevitably volunteer to eat so it would not be wasted."

The two of them continued eating breakfast in silence for a

few minutes more, until Mila worked up the courage to speak more. "Sir, would you be honest with me?"

He looked up. "As best I can."

"Last night, would you really have erased my memories?"

He looked down. "The house is designed to continue the Eternal Party. You've felt the influence it has on you, making you announce how horny and needy you are. It affects dominants too, although we don't talk about it. It makes us want to use you. So yes, I would have. That's why I got you out of there before I did anything I was going to regret."

"Was that what was happening my first night as well?"

Alonso coughed and choked on a bit of oatmeal.

"I'll take that as a yes," Mila said, prodding her omelet with a fork idly.

"Yes," he agreed after a gulp of tea.

"So?"

"So?"

"What were you thinking about that night?"

Alonso turned to look at her directly and Mila felt a shiver of magic-induced delight run down her spine as her owner focused on her. "Honestly?"

"Honestly," she confirmed.

"Well..." He set his spoon down. "You were taking to anal so well already, and were talking about claiming you in a way no one else could, so I was considering getting you some piercings. There's a type of bar piercing that can go across your labia and be a sort of chastity device, preventing all access to your sex, except of course by your owner, who could remove them at any time."

"Oh."

The fox held up his hands to ward off any accusations. "I swear I was not this kinky when I first arrived."

They shared a brief moment of quiet and a shared smile. Then, as they returned to their food, Mila asked. "How was it for the not-that-kinky you on your first days here?"

"Not as bad as yours have been," he said with a grimace. "When a canine first arrives, there's a lot of glad-handing and back-patting to welcome you in. I had no idea what was happening, so I just smiled and went along with it. I didn't want to let on that I was different and couldn't leave.

"Turns out that first night was an art exhibition: felines and one or two canines bound up in various poses, situated for viewing around the ballroom. The rope and the leather did nothing for me, but it was a room full of beautiful, naked, eager women and I quite enjoyed that. It stayed that way for a long time: I learned how to work with various kinks for my partners, but it was years before I enjoyed bondage for its own sake. So I started to develop a reputation for scenes that had more texture to them than the typical canine. I had to make it enjoyable for myself after all. I became a highly sought after dom within just a few weeks."

"That's it!" Mila flushed a little under Alonso's inquisitive look. "Ever since I became your kitten, other felines have been looking at me a little jealously. Even Jeta Horowitz sounded like she wanted to be in my position."

"Sorry about that."

"If that's the cause, maybe we can bleed off some of that jealousy by doing things together with other felines." Mila blinked. "Wait, did I just offer myself up for a threesome."

"I think you did. The house, remember?"

"Yeah."

Alonso scooted closer along the floor and held a comforting arm around Mila's shoulder. She felt an urge to push it off, but she didn't. There were warring impulses within her: the house telling her she could trust her owner implicitly, while her own anxieties were telling her he was completely untrustworthy. She had to remind herself they were both wrong: he had messed up, but he did appear to be trying to correct that.

She pondered what to ask the house next about how to get

them out. When she had formulated her next question, she found that Alonso was staring wistfully out into the sky. She nudged him.

"Oh, sorry, I was just thinking" he said, stating the obvious. "When I first realized I was trapped, I made myself a promise on what I'd do if ever I got out of here. Thanks to you I might be able to do it."

"What's that?"

"Go to the diner down on 9th street and get a patty melt."

"You've been trapped here for a decade and the first thing you want when you get out is a burger?"

Alonso gave a crooked smile. "The house can make a decent burger, and don't tell Devon and Theo I said so, but their attempts to improve on it have been bad. I want a proper diner burger. Something so juicy you feel the urge to lick your fingers after every bite."

Mila laughed a little.

"What about you? What are you going to do after getting out?"

"Oh, well, I..." she fumbled.

"You don't have to answer."

A small wave of relief swept through her. "But we are trying to be more honest with each other, aren't we?" she said, talking herself into giving an answer. "I'm planning to get a dildo. Don't give me that look. I've had no libido for a year and I'm happy it's back, that's all."

He looked back down at his food, but the smile never left his muzzle. "Canine or feline?" he asked after a bit.

"Canine," she admitted.

"Vulpine?"

She nodded.

"Bigger than me?"

"Same size. You're a good fit, all but the knot." She prodded the remaining bit of egg on her plate with a fork. "I'll have to be content with the real thing until we get out."

He chuckled. "It won't be long now. I'm sure of it. We just need to let the house play psychologist a little longer. Wait, what's wrong?"

Mila had suddenly turned away from her tray, staring at a spot on the ground hard as she thought. "Why isn't the house shaking?" she wondered aloud. Then she tried to spell her thoughts out more clearly to her owner. "The house is keeping us trapped because we would drown in our sorrows outside, right? And the house shakes to jolt us out of thinking about those same sorrows. Those thoughts were there all the time when I was outside the house, but they've only been here and there inside the house. Why?" She thought she knew the answer but she wanted confirmation.

"I don't know. I've kept pretty busy since I arrived."

"Busy and distracted. Ever since I arrived, I've either been in the middle of doing something or anticipating what would happen next. I think that's part of the reason why the house is keeping us trapped. Because in here it can distract us and keep us happy."

"But it also seems to think it can fix us so we can get out at some point." The fox got a suspicious look and ran a claw over his chin in thought. "I wonder if it's trying something like exposure therapy."

"What's that?"

"My psychs tried it with me. If something causes you discomfort, you try exposing yourself to little amounts of it at a time. You get used to it, so you can take a little more and then a little more and then soon it doesn't bother you at all. Maybe the house is trying to do that, but for happiness: getting us used to being happy so that we can be happy without its intervention. House, is that right?"

Silence.

"Probably too open-ended a question, sir. But I think that's the right idea. After all, the house has said that even I have been getting closer to getting out since I arrived. House, does all this exploration of sex I've been doing helping me to be happy on my own?"

Thump.

"And if I could be happy on my own, you'd let me out?"

Thump.

"So would experimenting with things more help me get out?"

Silence.

"Damn, probably too open-ended again."

"There's good and bad ways of exploring sexuality," Alonso pointed out. "That might be the confusion. But if you'd like to try more, I could—"

Mila leaned forward and put a finger to his lips. "I don't trust you. Not completely. Not after last night. And not even with me wearing this." She extended a claw and tugged her collar partway out from her neck. But the movement made her feel suddenly naked and she let go, smoothing down the fur around it.

"That's fair." The fox sat back with a distant expression. Then his ears perked forward and he took the calico's hands in his own. "Mila, from now on, whenever you are alone with me or Aisha and you are given an order or suggestion you find greatly repulsive, distasteful, or dangerous, you will instead just say, 'Red,' and otherwise ignore what you were told to do. Understood?"

"Yes, sir," she replied automatically. She understood why he had to add most of the caveats he did: no other feline would have a safeword, so it had to only be usable around Alonso and Aisha. "But why emphasize greatly repulsive?"

"Because something finding something mildly distasteful isn't that different from not having tried it before. And if you are going to try new things..."

"Got it. Can we test it to make sure it works?"

"What's something you find repulsive?"

Mila felt her stomach do a quick flip. "Blood and gore."

"Mila, you want me to use my claw to draw a cut across your palm."

"Red!" Mila felt a tension within her mind, as though her thoughts were being extruded from a toothpaste tube. Then it passed. "It worked. I don't want you to do that."

"Good, now let me think how to phrase this next one." He brushed a claw along his whiskers in thought. "Mila, if you are alone with me and I give you an order of a sexual nature without getting permission, either explicit or implicit, from you first, you will instead slap me on the muzzle and otherwise ignore the command. Understood?"

"Yes, sir."

"Now finger yourself."

Mila's hand had connected a firm strike to his cheek before she had even fully processed his words. "Sir!"

"I'm all right," he said, smiling at her. "No injuries inside the house, remember?"

She nodded gently, still in disbelief. She'd gotten in a solid blow.

"Now, with those two commands, you have to choose to initiate anything and I can't accidentally push you past any hard limits."

That finally made Mila's sense of security feel stable again. She leaned against Alonso, nestling into the fur of his chest, and let him enfold his arms around her. The calico just stayed there for a while, being held and letting herself enjoy it. It wasn't perfect. It wasn't the way it had been before, but she could trust him a bit again.

"Okay," she said. "You're the teacher. I'm the student. Let's try something." She emphasized the last sentence, deliberately giving him permission.

He nodded and leaned in, whispering so close to her ear that she could feel the movement of his lips and the tickle of his breath. She didn't process the words consciously. She didn't need to. She could simply let the magic of the house do its work.

But nothing happened. Mila tried to figure out what Alonso

had done with no luck. The fox did nothing to suggest he had even made a suggestion, other than wear the most cocksure grin the calico had ever seen. He had adjusted her memory again, she realized, but only in a way to make the effect of his suggestions a surprise. The suggestions must have been all right despite that, because she hadn't used the safeword.

Feeling a bit thirsty, Mila reached out for her coffee and took a sip, but her nose wrinkled. The flavor was off. It was missing something. "Oh sir," she called out in a singsong voice while one hand began to trail up his legs and over to his groin. "It looks like the house forgot to give me enough cream for my coffee. Don't suppose I can have some of yours?"

She didn't wait for a full answer, but set her coffee down and started to open up his pants. His boxers were drawn away to reveal a half-hard length springing into the air. A bead of pre was already forming at the tip and she caught it on a finger and tasted it, rolling the little drop of liquid around in her mouth. "Mmm, strong notes of sexy male. My favorite,"

Her hand dove back for his groin and wrapped around his shaft, starting to pump it eagerly, while she fished out his balls to tease and caress.

Mila flattened herself low to the ground, her breasts resting on the blanket, and held her muzzle out towards the shaft. But for a moment, an old nagging fear crept into her brain. It was amazing how some things from her teenaged years could still haunt her, and there had been her "friend" Lucy who had informed her with the certitude of gossips everywhere that felines couldn't give blowjobs. Sure her tongue was a little rougher than a canine's was, but it wasn't anything like the ancestral felines of old. Despite that knowledge and despite the many blowjobs she had given BD over the years, the fear that she couldn't perform nagged at her nonetheless.

She put her lips to the cockhead and gently lowered herself down, doing her best to keep her tongue still. She wasn't comfortable taking his whole girth orally either, but she could wrap her hand around his knot and let her nose bump into her hand. Her inner teenager cheered at showing that know-it-all Lucy what felines were really capable of. Alonso's shaft pulsed in her mouth with clear eagerness.

Alonso did not intercede in any way, letting Mila tend to him how she liked. He only whispered down to her after a few minutes to let her know he was getting close.

She fetched her half-empty coffee cup and held it near the tip of his shaft while stroking him in earnest. The calico was licking her lips in anticipation, eyes fixated on the slit of his shaft and the yummy goodness that would soon come out. Then he climaxed with a grunt and a thrust of his hips. The first jet of his cream landed beyond the far rim of the cup, but the rest, to her delight, fell right inside. She kept stroking him lightly, using a thumb on the underside of his shaft to push the rest of his seed out. She used a spoon to make sure it was thoroughly mixed then took a long sip, holding the cup to her chest as she let out a purr of delight. "Just how I like it. Thank you, sir."

"Of course, kitten," he whispered into her ear. "Reset."

Mila quivered as the change Alonso had made to her personality left her. "Making me like the taste of your cum, eh, sir?" she said once her mind was back to normal.

"Seemed a good place to start experimenting."

"I don't know. I think you were playing it a bit too safe." She raised the coffee cup and slugged back the rest of the drink.

Alonso gaped at her with such bug-eyed astonishment that Mila nearly spit the coffee back out. The calico forced herself to swallow before breaking down into giggles. "That was worth it just for your reaction," she said.

His face went from shocked to mildly reproving. "I take it you didn't enjoy it?"

"Jizz and coffee will not be the new taste sensation sweeping the nation, no, sir." She set the empty cup aside and nestled in against him. "I don't mind the taste of you, but I'd prefer not to get it that way in the future."

"Mmph." Alonso caressed down her form until his hand was on the curve of her ass. "You know, any other dom here would punish you for playing a trick on me like that."

She flitted her tail from side to side playfully. "Is that the sort of punishment that is meant to be enjoyed?" She winked.

He grinned wickedly down at her.

The next thing Mila knew, she couldn't see. It was the deep blackness of total darkness and she was afraid. Then she remembered she was still in the house, she was still with Alonso, and she began to relax.

There was something on her head and she tried to move her hands up to take it off, only to find her hands were bound as well. They were pinned behind her back so tightly that she could do little more than lift her shoulders and wiggle her fingers. Her elbows touched and her wrists were close to one another, but beyond that all she could tell was that her arms were held straight along her back, sheathed in something leathery.

She tried to turn an ear to listen for something around her and found both ears unable to move. A hood over her head was not only blinding her but holding her ears rigid. And stuffing them, she noticed. She wasn't hearing anything. Even the sounds of her own movement and breathing were dampened.

At least she could still smell. There was a lingering tang of coffee and breakfast, the musk of a male fox, and the slight musty smell of the observatory. She hadn't left the room, then.

Mila jumped when she felt a hand on her shoulder, unable to tell who it was, but then she noticed a finger of the hand was tracing out letters on her fur. A... L... O...

Mila sighed and relaxed. The hand was Alonso's. It moved up her collarbone and ran over the edge of her collar before coming to the front and dropping away. A second later, she felt a tug. A leash. Okay then. That was only fair after she had leashed Jeta the other day. He pulled forward and so Mila extended a questing foot so she could take a blind step.

As soon as the calico had moved, the remaining additions of her new outfit made themselves known. First was a weight inside her sex. She realized she was clenching and could not relax around the intruder. It bounced and rolled in a delightful way within her. Second and more prominently was a feeling on her nipples. There was a gentle pinch to the tips, maybe from a clamp or from a new piercing. Either way, they were attached to something that swayed in front of her body, a weight of some kind. It wasn't heavy enough to produce a painful pull, but it still jostled around and tugged her nipples in a chaotic variety of directions. Third, the sensations on her nipples were echoed on her clit. Something there was also persistently and erratically tugging, but without the constant downward weight.

The feline felt the pull of the leash increase. She was delaying and Alonso wanted her to keep up. She tried to move slowly, but he wasn't having that. The pull became more and more insistent until she was forced to shuffle along at a steady walking pace. No matter what she tried, Mila could not make the various toys hold still. The whatever-it-was in her sex kept bouncing forward and back and the weight between her breasts seemed to move in a new direction on every step.

Mila just tried to focus on not tripping over herself as she followed Alonso in the dark. The path forward was dipping down. The calico thought it was the walkway to the lower level of the observatory, but it kept going down, and down, and still ever down. She must have been on the third floor already. Mila wondered if the house had smoothed the stairs up to the roof into sloping ramps to accommodate her inability to see. It was surprisingly considerate.

The calico managed to distract herself enough that when Alonso came to a halt, she walked straight into his flank without recognizing that he had stopped pulling the leash.

She took a half-step back from him and waited.

Alonso rested a hand on her shoulder and tapped twice. Okay, that was a signal for something, but wh—

Two strong, rough hands gripped her breasts, roughly rolling them and making the weight between them go wild. As quickly as they came, they left, and the weight continued its erratic bouncing with even more enthusiasm.

Mila ran a tongue over dry lips — at least her muzzle had been left free — and shifted her stance. The calico had never thought of her nipples as such a focal point of pleasure before. Normally pleasure was greatest between her legs and her breasts were a lovely accompaniment, but today the opposite was true. The constant teasing that she couldn't prevent or anticipate was getting her going impressively well. She wished she could get a little more direct stimulation. On a thought, she tried Jeta's idea from the other day and brought her tail around, intending to rub it between her thighs. But her tail seemed to come to a dead stop about an inch away from her sex. She thought something might have gotten in the way, so she tried approaching from a different angle, only to run into the same problem.

Fuck, she thought to herself, he told me I couldn't use my tail, didn't he?

The calico felt a pull on the leash and started forward again. She still didn't know quite where they were, but by what she knew of the house and the feel of the carpet and marble under her feet, she guessed she was in the hallways of the first floor. Mila took a deep breath through her nose and tried to use scent to help orient herself, but the problem was how many distinct scents floated through the Eternal Party. It wasn't just the mass of bodies or the mix of sex, leather, and latex; there were distant notes of many foods, pungent spikes of alcohols, acrid bites of chlorine from a pool, soothing wisps of fresh-cut flowers, and — most unusual to Mila's thoughts — the toe-curling tangs of violin bow rosin.

Only a few moments went by before they stopped again.

Another touch to her shoulder, warning her, before someone new played with her breasts. This time instead of the merciless groping, the touch was delicate, claws raking through her fur and just barely touching the flesh underneath. They kept going as they approached the nipple, so that they drew lines of sharp pleasure right across the exposed skin. And they continued from the edge of the areola, to the nipple, then along the sides of the stiff nub until all the claws from one hand could meet right at the tip. Mila drew a shuddering breath and tried to cross her legs to hide her dripping arousal.

Despite the claws, the touch was so gentle that by the time it was finished, the weight had grown completely still, but because the raking claws had drawn so much attention down to the very point of her nipples, the calico knew that the next time she took a step, she'd feel the weight all the more.

They left that person behind with Mila now moaning lightly with every step. She could feel their direction changing and guessed they were moving from the hallways into the grand ballroom. Mila felt more and more people surrounding them, from the warmth of their presence and the feel of their footfalls on the ground. The air was heavy with the scent of canine now. Each of them took the time to grope her, but they all had a different style. Some went slow, some fast. Some caressed over the whole of her breast, some just tweaked the nipples quickly. Some sought to relax her, some to excite her. There was always a pause between what they did, giving her time to feel the jostling of the weight over her increasingly sensitive nipples. It didn't matter if they tried to still it. At this point, she was breathing too hard to keep it still any more; her heaving chest threw the weight forward and back. The only reprieve was that the device in her sex had stilled and no one seemed particularly interested in whatever was on her clit.

The calico started to pant. Her mouth was open and her tongue hung out. Her arms were struggling against their bondage. Her tail kept trying to make the trip to her sex but was impeded every time. Beads of arousal dripped down her inner thigh. Mila opened her mouth, wet her lips once more, and whispered out, "Please."

The hands currently on her breasts paused, but only for a moment. Then they picked up where they had left off.

"Please, sir," she said, trembling. "I can't take any more."

Something pressed to her lips and without thinking she opened her mouth, letting a faux shaft slide fully into her muzzle. The phallic gag was secured with a strap around the back of her head, and it pressed far enough in to her mouth that she could do little more than grunt or squeal.

More and more hands started to play with her entire torso. There was no escape from their constant teasing. When she tried to back away, Alonso pulled the leash tight. When she tried to push against him, he placed a hand on her hip to keep her away. When she tried to bend forward and cover her chest with her body, his hand was on her shoulder, pulling her back upright. Even distractions were no good: running her tongue over the phallic gag just made her want to bounce her head on Alonso's lap, and rolling her hips to make the toys inside her jiggle around only made her hornier without providing any relief. There was nothing to do but take it and get needier and needier with each passing minute.

At last, some relief. The hands began to leave, one by one, each giving some different way of saying good bye, whether by one last squeeze or one last flick of her nipple. Then the leash was pulled, turning her around and guiding her back out of the ballroom.

But the first step of the stairs made her realize it wasn't over. Unlike the gentle ramp down, the jolting upwards motion of the stairs rocked the weight on her chest and the toys in her sex even more. The weight bounced so sharply that her clit was finally receiving the attention it craved, and yet it wasn't nearly enough to satisfy her. Mila closed her eyes under the blindfold and tried to power through it, telling herself that Alonso was taking her back to their room and then he'd release her from this wonderful torment. But no sooner had he gotten her to the top of the stairs, then he turned her right around and marched back down again.

Mila let out the longest, hardest whine she could, which dissolved into whimpers of pure need. She thought she might honestly start to cry. He couldn't keep teasing her this badly. He just couldn't. Her tail was lashing behind her.

They stopped after the next step. Alonso slipped an arm around her waist, stilling her trembling body. After the last of the sounds of lust left her throat, they turned together and headed for his room. The moved slowly, steadily, with him holding the weight on her chest away so that it stopped bouncing. Mila's breathing began to slow.

She lowered her head, pressing her muzzle in against Alonso's arms and curling her tail about his leg, the only ways she could express her thanks while being so tightly bound.

Inside their room once more, he had her stand in the middle of the floor and peeled back the hood that covered her head just enough to uncover one ear. For the first time in at least an hour, she could hear again. And what she heard was Alonso's smirking voice whispering into her ear. "I need you to stay perfectly still for me, kitten. Can you do that?"

Mila nodded frantically. She'd do whatever he said so long as he fucked her after.

She felt his hand slide down her body, skirting around the edge of her overstimulated breasts and coming to rest just outside her sex. "Release," he whispered huskily in her ear, and she stopped clenching tight around the toys inside her. They slid out, one after the other into his hand.

Mila couldn't help herself. Her legs quivered and her hips shook at her sex's sudden emptiness.

"I asked you to stay still," he reminded her.

She whined through her nose.

He tutted quietly and placed his hands on her breasts, so gently it didn't worsen the need within her. He placed his thumbs against her nipples, there was a pinching feeling, and then the weights were suddenly gone. He repeated the process at her clit. The calico breathed easier.

Her tail tried to curl to press against her sex, but was still impeded from doing so.

"Not just yet," the fox chided her. Alonso began easing the rest of the hood off. She had a disconcerting feeling of pressure equalizing as her second ear was uncovered. He kept the blindfold pressed close to her face for a moment and let the light creep in one small step at a time, giving her time to adjust.

Then she could see. The first thing she noticed was Alonso. The fox had undressed at some point since entering the room and he was fully erect. She could barely tear her eyes away from his shaft, so desperately did she want it. But she did enough to see what he was holding, the clamps and chain that had connected her breasts and clit. The weight she had been feeling was a cardboard sign, which read, "Tease my needy tits so my owner can fuck me gushing wet."

She shivered. She was definitely gushing wet. And he was going to fuck her.

He set the sign aside and held up a pair of metal spheres. "Ben Wa balls," he said. He rolled them on his hand and demonstrated how moved in erratic patterns. That was what had been in her sex.

The fox gently set them aside and began to undo the gag she was wearing. He worked it out bit by bit to give her jaw time to adjust.

When the head of the vulpine-shaped shaft left her muzzle, she swallowed once and said, "Please, sir."

His ears perked. "Please, what, kitten?"

"Please fuck me. Please fuck me. I need to get fucked so bad. I've never wanted it this badly before. Not in my whole life. Please just fuck me."

He took hold of her leash and drew her forward to the bed. She had expected the feel of the Ben Wa balls jostling inside of her as she moved, and almost missed them. The fox laid down on his back, his shaft pointing up into the air above him. She crawled forward on her knees (her arms still tightly bound behind her) and positioned herself with her sex right over his shaft.

"Wait."

Mila froze, groaning with impatience.

The fox reached down and touched her clit softly, as if he were casting a magic spell on it. "You can't cum until I give permission."

She whined louder than ever. "Sir!"

"You can't cum until I give permission, kitten. But you wanted to be fucked so started getting fucked."

Her body moved to obey. Immediately she dropped her weight and took in almost the entirety of the fox's shaft inside her sex. She was so slick with her own natural lubrication that she almost didn't feel him entering her: it was as though one second she was empty and the next she was filled with nothing in between. She squirmed in delight and understood why he had ordered her not to cum. She probably would have from that thrust alone otherwise. But Mila couldn't stay and enjoy it. He had commanded her to get fucked. So she started to lift up and then drop down again.

At least he had let her set the pace. Her eyes fell shut and she simply relished in the consistent rhythm of their hips meeting over and over again. It didn't matter how unused she was to the cowgirl position: she didn't grow tired at all. The house did most of the work and the calico could just enjoy the feeling of that shaft pummeling her. Each time she fell down, she felt that knot press against her. She gave an extra grind of her hips when she sank down deep, to pleasure it a little bit more.

"You're going to take it tonight," the fox said firmly. "I won't let you cum until you do."

Mila froze. "Red!"

Alonso scrambled to sit up. He gripped Mila under her shoulders and assisted her as she pulled off his length. "What's wrong?"

"I can't do it," she panted. The fear that had sprung up when she first tried to take his knot had blossomed into terror. She could feel the magic of the house holding her back from hyper-ventilating. "You'll split me open."

The fox sat back slightly with a queer look on his face. "Is that all you're worried about?"

She stared at him, open-mouthed. "Isn't that enough?"

Alonso reached up and caressed along her cheek, gently rubbing his palm into her fur. "Take a deep breath and relax, kitten."

She obeyed.

He kept his hand on her, but turned his head to the side, addressing the wall. "House, show us the largest dildo Mila could take inside her without injuring herself here."

There was a soft thump, muted by plush comforters and sheets, and Alonso pulled them back to reveal one of the largest dildos she had ever seen sitting on the bed. It was longer and thicker than the fox's forearm, textured into a smooth cylinder with a tapered tip. She gaped at it. "No way," she said. "No way could I take that." But so far as she knew, the house hadn't lied to her. Maybe it wasn't even capable of lying. "Could I?"

Thump.

The fox nodded in agreement with the house. "I've seen someone smaller than you take something about that size. No injuries can happen here, remember? While you are in the house most of your physical limitations don't mean much anymore. I suspect the only reason you couldn't take something even larger is because your bones would start to get in the way." He pulled the sheets back over the monstrous dildo, and then thought for a second. "House, just to confirm, could Mila take something that size right now without hurting herself if she were outside the house?"

Thump thump.

Mila glanced down to Alonso's shaft and the knot at the base of it. It was half the diameter of the dildo, but still looked far too big.

"You can take it," the fox insisted. "Can I show you?"

Mila felt a warmth in her chest. He was again putting control in her hands, even though he was her owner. The fear receded; she knew he wouldn't let her be hurt, because he'd done so once and would be careful not to make the same mistake twice. She looked him right in the eyes and nodded. "Go slow, sir."

He nodded. Instead of lying back as he had before, Alonso stayed sitting up, pulling in some pillows to support his back. Then, with her in his lap, he lifted her so she was lined up with his shaft once again. He gently lowered her until he was halfway inside her. "Relax your sex completely and keep it relaxed."

He ordered: she obeyed. She felt muscles she wasn't even aware of go utterly limp.

"Now I'm going to enter you fully."

Mila tensed a little as the knot neared, but this time he kept pushing her down even when she felt the knot at her lips. There was no instinctual clenching that pushed it back out: she couldn't under his orders. So it spread her and entered her and soon she had engulfed it completely, panting. Nothing had ever before stretched her so wide.

"You can use your muscles again."

Her sex squeezed suddenly and they groaned as one. Mila shivered from tailtip to eartip. "I did it. I actually did it." She nuzzled the fox. "Can I cum now, sir?"

He smiled and carefully rolled onto his side with her. "You will cum the instant I do, kitten." He started to thrust in deep short bursts, never pulling back far enough for his knot to escape. She was grateful for that: she wasn't sure she could bring herself to take it in a second time.

Mila's moment of panic had calmed her raging libido, but only for a moment. With Alonso in and humping hard once again, she found herself skyrocketing towards orgasm, only to hover magically on the edge. Her muscles tremored in pre-climactic anticipation. The part of her mind not enraptured by the pleasure was keenly aware that he had to cum for her to, and so his orgasm became the focus of all her desires. It flustered her and excited her to be paying such close attention to the subtle shifts in his body, like the way his shaft had started to twitch and strain after every thrust. She wanted to clench down and squeeze him inside her, but she was already so tight around him. There was no need. He shuddered, sank deep within her, and came.

All at once Mila's orgasm crashed into her. She yowled in delight and squeezed her legs against Alonso to hold him tight. She felt warm shots of his seed fill her and add to the heat burning inside.

As the afterglow settled over them both, the fox slid a hand behind her back and started to undo the straps of the binder holding her arms together. When he had finally tugged it off and she had shaken some life back into her extremities, she wrapped him in the biggest hug she could, purring as hard as she could to let her happiness be known.

After a few minutes, Mila worked up the courage to try and slide off that massive knot.

"Wait." Alonso put a hand on her hip. "Wait for me to shrink."

"How long will that take?"

"With the way you keep squeezing me, quite a while."

Mila nuzzled in at his chest. "You goof," she said gently. "You just like having your bone buried in me, sir."

"Can you blame me?"

"No," she said, and felt the purr rise from her chest. "It's not a bad way to spend an evening." She nestled into him and felt his shaft throb in continued excitement. When she next looked up, she saw him gazing distantly out of the window. "Sir?"

He nuzzled back at her then directed a question to the wall. "House, are we closer to getting out than we were after breakfast?"

Thump.

"That's good to know," Mila said. "But how?"

He looked over to where the phone sat on the bed stand nearby and looked to be judging how he could get over to it while remaining tied with Mila. "As ever, we should talk to Aisha. But we can leave that until morning." He shifted his hips and felt the tug of Mila's firm grip on his knot again. "I suspect that jackal will be ecstatic."

She wasn't. She was furious.

Etude

"You threw her out? You son of a bitch!"

In retrospect, that was the wrong part of recent events to bring up first when they spoke with Aisha in Alonso's room the following morning.

Before fox or calico could react, Aisha had taken a swing at Alonso. Just as her fist connected with his jaw, she whispered something and the air around them grew hot and thick for an instant. Then the punch landed with a clack of teeth snapping against teeth, and the fox crumpled backwards.

Mila tried to run to him, but Aisha caught her arm in a vice-like grip. "Get up," she spat at the fox. "Get up, you arse. I want to hit you again."

Aisha yanked Mila around behind her, interposing her body between the calico and her owner. The tone of her voice was one of rage, but the expression in her eyes, so wide they were almost bulging, was one of fear and terror. She was digging her claws into Mila's skin without even realizing it.

Mila's mind whirled to try and catch up. What had Aisha said the other day in the library? All her siblings were dead and the reason was... "Alonso isn't your father, Aisha," she said, trying to project calm into her voice.

The jackal's head snapped around so she could stare directly at the calico.

"It's all right. Things went wrong, but we've fixed them. I'm safe now."

The painful grip on her wrist loosened. Aisha's hackles fell. Her eyes resumed their narrowed, focused glare. "If this should ever happen again—"

"It won't," Mila insisted.

"If this should ever happen again," Aisha repeated, as if it were a near certainty that it would, "go to my room. You will always be welcome there, and I'll protect you as long as needed."

Mila put a hand over Aisha's. "It won't be needed," she insisted calmly.

The jackal stared at her a moment more, then twisted her arm out of Mila's weak embrace. She took one step towards the fox, still curled up on the floor, and extended a hand.

He took it, cradling his jaw in his free hand, and let himself be pulled to his feet.

"Make sure it isn't," the jackal said curtly.

Alonso nodded and winced. He pulled his hand away to glance at it. There was blood on his fingers.

"Sir!" Mila rushed to his side. "You're hurt. How?"

Aisha snorted and stepped aside. "I told you, I've been trying to get Alonso out of here for years. The first thing we tried was to disrupt the magic of the house. Damp towel and ice pack." The last words were directed to the wall, and after a thump, she retrieved the items and handed them to Mila. "I can manage it, but only in a small space, not much larger than my hand. The magic of the house doesn't like being interfered with. I can only manage enough to get the handle on the side door to turn while Alonso isn't there, or disrupt the injury prevention on a good right hook."

Mila dabbed away the blood on Alonso's jaw. He winced lightly every time she did and snarled at the cold when she pressed the ice pack against the spot.

The jackal dropped into one of the armchairs in Alonso's living room space, unconcerned with Alonso's injury. "Now what is it you wanted to tell me? I presume that wasn't it?"

"No, we —" Alonso began and then winced harder than before at the movement along his lips. He gestured to Mila and then waved in Aisha's direction.

Mila, after making sure one more time that Alonso was all right, turned to the jackal. "We can talk to the house."

"You can what?"

"We can ask it questions, only simple yes/no questions for now, but... yeah."

The jackal leaned forward. "Tell me."

Mila wasn't sure Aisha realized she'd given a direct order. The jackal listened with ears perked to all the events of the previous day, including how she had successfully taken Alonso's knot and the house confirming that had helped them get closer to getting out. The only part that Mila left out was the strange piano music. It unnerved her that she was hearing something that Alonso could not. Alonso seemed to notice, but he said nothing.

As soon as Mila finished, Aisha stood up. "I need to test this. I will be a few minutes." Instead of leaving though, she walked into the corner of the room next to a bookcase and directed her questions at the walls of the house. She kept her voice low so as not to disturb the others, but the constant thumps of the house's replies carried all the same.

Mila tended to Alonso's muzzle once again. On closer inspection, it looked like she'd clipped his lip quite well. It was cut and bleeding on the inside of his mouth. It would have swollen badly were it not for the quickly applied ice. As it was, it probably looked a lot worse than it was, and Alonso appeared more shocked than pained.

Mila dabbed away the blood with the towels before it could crust up in the fox's fur. There seemed to be little else to do while waiting for Aisha.

Eventually they moved to sit, with Alonso taking the farthest spot from Aisha that he could. Mila cocked an ear to the far corner to try and get a better feel for what the jackal was asking. Aisha was peppering the house with questions that reminded Mila of her Introduction to Computer Logic course in college. The jackal then asked about the house and its history, modern events, previous residents of the house, and the journals she had up in the library.

When Aisha finished, she stepped back to her seat and sat down stiffly, her eyes unfocused as she remained deep in thought. "You are extremely lucky," she said.

Mila sat up straight. She felt like she was the one being addressed. "How so, Mistress Aisha?"

"Because the house is not in the habit of answering questions." The jackal spread her hands wide and took a deep breath as if preparing a formal lecture. "The house can act of its own accord at times: it trapped you both here without being directed to do so, and it can often provide things we want before we think to ask for them. However, the house is not conscious or intelligent in any way we might normally define consciousness or intelligence, so how can it do this? My best understanding is that the magic that animates the house is not logical in nature, but emotive. It reacts to what we feel. We wake up craving a tasty breakfast and one is provided. We feel sleepy away from our room and a pillow appears. So it was that your fears after being abandoned" — Aisha glared at Alonso — "resonated with the house. That's why it acted to protect you in that moment. Your desperate cry for answers from the house was so heartfelt it literally enabled the house to answer you. So, as I said, lucky."

"I'm lucky because in a place designed to make everyone happy, I was incredibly unhappy, Mistress Aisha?" The calico gave a sympathetic look to Alonso, trying to communicate the complicated roil of emotions still within her.

"That's about right. No one, so far as I can tell, has thought that the house was capable of communicating in the last two hundred years. But you, due to chance, knew that it was, and so you could set up this ingenious way to ask it questions." She took a deep breath and sighed. "Unfortunately, as I said, the magic is not logical. The house gets confused by complicated grammar or ambiguity. It struggles with probability: in my brief testing, I have not been able to get it to really understand what 'maybe' means."

"But now we know why we are trapped."

"Yes," Aisha agreed, "that is a very good start. Let's try to dig deeper on that. House, there have been others who you have brought in and trapped for similar reasons to Alonso and Mila, correct?"

Thump.

"And some of them managed to get out?"

Thump.

Alonso coughed, winced, and interjected in a quiet voice. "Without dying?"

Thump.

Aisha gave him a look that suggested she did not appreciate being interrupted. "Did at least fifty percent manage to get out?"

Thump.

"At least seventy-five percent?"

Thump.

"All of them?"

Thump.

A wave of relief washed over the fox and calico. But Aisha still seemed concerned. "House, did any of them stay here as long as Alonso did?"

Thump thump.

The fox sighed. "So apparently I'm just exceptionally fucked up?"

Thump.

"That wasn't directed at you!"

Mila couldn't help herself. She managed to mostly hide the burst of laughter in a snort, but it was clear to everyone what she had intended. The tension that had been gnawing at her since she had been thrown out released in a tide of unstoppable giggles. She kept right on going, and soon Aisha joined in, the jackal chuckling to herself and looking smugly at the fox.

"It's not that funny," he insisted. "Ow. Damn it."

Mila's giggles and Aisha's chuckles both turned into full blown laughter, and though Alonso tried to hide it, he was starting to crack a smile too. When the infectious humor in the air finally made its way to him, he got caught in a looping cycle of laughing, wincing at the sudden movement of his jaw, which only made the others laugh harder at his misfortune, which made him laugh again.

Mila clutched at her chest. "Oh crap, it hurts to laugh."

"Serves you right," Alonso accused in between bursts of short laughter. "Oh, house, is she fucked up too?"

Thump.

"There. Confirmation! And Aisha, her too?"

Thump.

"See? A room full of fuck-ups."

The laughter began to fade as people tried to catch their breath. Then a serious thought occurred to Mila. "Wait, if the house thinks Aisha is messed up, why isn't she trapped here too?"

The jackal considered, suppressing the last of her laughter. "That is a good question. Maybe the house doesn't think my problems are serious enough, or maybe they aren't the right type of problem, or maybe they aren't a type of problem the house can solve, or maybe... House, was holding people here what Lady Yasmin intended when she made you?"

Thump thump.

"Thought so. The spell that made this house is so intricate it's managing to interface with technologies that weren't invented for a hundred and fifty years after the spell was cast, and it has a mind of its own after a fashion. It's no wonder it has developed idiosyncrasies."

The fox leaned forward, a serious expression on his face. "So, do you think you can ask the right questions to get us out of here?"

"I do, but not today."

"What?" The outburst made him wince again.

"Alonso, our working hypothesis is that the house is trying to heal you both from some old psychological wounds. I am curious how you expect to do that if you are running yourself and Mila ragged trying to figure out how to get out?" In Aisha's words, Mila heard an echo of what the fox had told her on her first morning, how he had been so obsessed with trying to escape that it had nearly turned him suicidal. "It is difficult to heal in high stress environments. So instead, I want you both to relax. Let me work on things on my own."

"I don't take orders from you," the fox said with a surly note in his voice.

"Except when he does," Aisha said, winking to Mila.

"That was one time."

"Six," Aisha corrected. "Besides, I'm not giving you an order, Alonso. I am just expecting that you will do what is best for yourself and those you are responsible for." Her last words were tense and cut across the air of the room like a dagger.

Alonso glanced at Mila, then back to Aisha. He nodded.

Mila herself interjected with a question, "So what's the best way to relax around here, Mistress Aisha? Please don't say it more sex."

The jackal sat back and steepled her fingers. "Most activities you do at home you can do here as well. However, I've also found that the freedom of the house allows guests to explore the things they always wished they had the time to do. Is there a skill you've wanted to cultivate?"

The calico considered for a moment. "I always wanted to learn how to cook properly, Mistress Aisha."

The jackal tilted an ear in acknowledgment. "The kitchen would be a fine place for you."

Alonso nodded. "I suppose they would. Very well." He turned to look Mila straight in the eye, and despite his relaxed posture, his gaze was commanding, controlling. "Mila, when you are feeling ready, you will report to the kitchen and ask for a cooking lesson. You are also under orders from you owner to not engage in any sexual activity with anyone else for the remainder of the day."

"Yes, sir," she said, accepting his will completely.

Aisha stood and brushed off a stray piece of lint from her otherwise immaculate dress. "I will return to the library then. But Alonso, I will be keeping an eye on you."

Alonso thumbed the head of his cane. "Good," was all he said, and then Aisha left.

The fox and calico ate a simple breakfast together. Once finished, Mila's orders kicked in and she excused herself. She remembered passing the kitchen on the way to the library the other day, so retraced her steps there.

The kitchen was the first room in the house that Mila encountered that was not so grand and opulent it took her breath away. It was instead quite a functional room. The pots and pans that hung from hooks overhead, the ingredients that lined the shelves, the equipment that filled the countertops — none of it was the most expensive options available, but instead the most functional. The one extravagance was a lever-operated espresso machine.

In the center of the room was a heavy wooden table where at the far end sat a lion, dicing vegetables. He had his mane trimmed down quite short, which gave him a youthful appearance, and he looked up with a winsome smile that made Mila's heart flutter. "Hello," he said and then reached out to tap the table. "We have visitors," he announced.

There was a wet shlurping sound and out from under the table came a bright-eyed corgi who wiped something wet and sticky off his lips. "Hello! Nice to meet you," he said and held out the non-sticky hand. "You must be Mila, Alonso's new girl."

Mila guessed the gossip on new arrivals spread quickly. "Yes, that's me. Nice to meet you too, sir." She modulated her voice back to meet-a-VIP mode as she shook the corgi's offered hand, remembering the lesson Aisha had taught her in the library.

"Oh, no need for that sir business. We're light on ceremony around here. I'm Devon, and the fine hunk of meat behind me is Theo."

"Hi," the lion said with a wave. He stood up from his cutting board and Mila noticed he was, like herself, completely nude below the waist. He also had a full erection absolutely dripping with saliva.

"Sorry for interrupting," Mila said with a blush. She let her voice return to its normal tones and was glad for it: she wasn't sure she could keep it up all day anyway.

"Don't worry about it," the corgi said. "I can suck him off any day, but we get guests in the kitchen so rarely. Does Alonso need a special dish?"

Mila shook her head. "He sent me here for a cooking lesson."

"A cooking lesson? From us?" Devon looked utterly thrilled by the idea. "She wants a cooking lesson from us, Theo."

"I heard."

The corgi clasped his hands before him in a prayerful gesture. "First, we must know what we are dealing with. What is your knowledge with cooking?"

Mila embarrassedly scuffled a foot against the floor. "I've successfully made bread catch on fire in a toaster, and I know how to make things explode in a microwave."

The corgi was frozen for a moment and his gaze stared straight through Mila. "You present me with a challenge, but I accept," he said at last. "Now, let's see..."

Before he could complete his thought, the calico tapped him on the shoulder. "Alonso also ordered me to not engage in sex with anyone else today."

The corgi tilted his head to one side and grinned. "No worries from me there. You lack the desired equipment. Theo, on the other hand..." The corgi gave the still erect lion a critical look. "All arousal off," the corgi said.

It was like watching cold water being poured over someone. The lion's cock wilted and shrank, with Theo giving it a quick clean with a towel before it slipped back into his sheath. He gave a slight groan of disapproval but otherwise did not complain.

"Now, Miss Mila Microwave," the corgi said, "let's crack some eggs."

/

And crack eggs they did. Devon got a pair of bowls from the house and requested five dozen eggs. Mila had never seen so many eggs in one place before. Devon had Theo demonstrate the proper egg-cracking technique, then told Mila to try it.

It exploded in her hand, covering her fur with shards of shell and sticky whites.

"Drop it in the bowl, clean your hand on this towel, and let's go again," Devon said, while offering a wet towel.

Theo once again demonstrated, and Mila tried to replicate. This time she brought her hand down and nothing happened. Not even a crack on the egg. She tried a second time, and it exploded.

So it went, with Mila trying and failing over and over again. Whenever they ran out of eggs, or whenever a bowl was full of the shattered remains of shell and white, Devon would pause the proceedings to fetch new eggs from the house or shove the dirty bowl in a cupboard. Mila wondered why not put them in the sink, but the next time Devon opened the cupboard, the bowl was gone. The house was as good at cleaning up what wasn't wanted as it was at providing what was wanted.

Time passed, and Mila got so focused on the precise motion of cracking eggs she didn't notice that someone else had entered the kitchen until Alonso coughed by her side. She flicked around and barely avoided tossing egg yolks on her owner. "Sorry, sir," she said, trying to clean herself up.

The fox chuckled. "You've been busy. What have you made today?"

"Oh, uh, nothing actually made. Just practicing working with eggs. It's still early."

"It's nearly five p.m., Mila."

The calico glanced out of the kitchen windows at the shifting light outside. Then she looked at the old clock hanging above the sink. "I guess it is."

"You've been cracking eggs all day?"

Devon wiped his own paws off and came up to Alonso. "We are working almost from scratch here, but don't you worry, I will have her cooking with the best of them before too long."

The fox tilted his head in acceptance. "I'll send her back first thing tomorrow then, if she would like that."

Mila's heart fluttered and she nodded eagerly. She was actually looking forward to coming back.

"But for now, Mila, if you are done for the day — ah." Alonso brought a hand up to his injured muzzle and held it gently.

The corgi squinted at him, "Alonso, are you all right?"

"Fine, I'm fine. I hope. I unfortunately volunteered for one of Aisha's experiments."

"Oh." The corgi seemed quite satisfied by that answer. "Be careful with that."

"I will," the fox promised. "Mila, if you are done for the day, please accompany me."

Devon bobbed on his feet. "I think we can call it here. Just remember to practice those motions." He mimicked the act of tapping the egg to the table.

The calico gave Devon a little bow and slipped out.

The fox waited for her, his arm held out for Mila to slip hers in beside it. "Had fun?" he asked once she was in close and he could whisper.

"Yes, sir."

"I trust Devon and Theo were good companions?"

"They are quite nice, sir. Not what I expected to find here at all."

Alonso tilted his head curiously. "What do you mean by that?"

"Other than Theo wearing the collar and corset, you almost couldn't tell he belonged here. Devon doesn't seem interested in the whole canine command thing either."

"You misjudge them, Mila. The house opened itself to them. It would not do so if they were not meant to be here."

"But Devon didn't order me once the whole time I was there and I don't think that's because he's gay."

"He rarely orders anyone besides Theo."

"He didn't even do that today, except once at the very beginning."

Alonso was silent for a moment, a bemused smirk on his face. "I suggest you watch them more closely tomorrow."

"Yes, sir."

Alonso gave Mila's hand a squeeze as he walked with her to a glass display case that was on the wall. It was a larger version of the daily itinerary of events, listing all that was happening in the Eternal Party that day. She hadn't bothered to read it before she left and it looks like Alonso hadn't examined it closely either.

The calico leaned against the fox and was content to let him decide on what to do that evening, until her eyes alighted on one line. Suddenly she was jabbing at the glass barrier. "There! Can we go there?"

Alonso squinted. "Are you sure?"

"Yes!"

On a screen in the small theater, a game show played.

"If you can guess the price of this new dining room set — complete with table, chairs, tablecloth, and all this lovely dinnerware — to within one hundred dollars, it is yours to take home," the host announced.

The heavy-set bulldog held out a microphone to the contestant, who hemmed and hawed before saying, "I'll go with an even five thousand."

In the theater, seven sets of eyes turned from the screen to Mila, who sat in the middle of the room, one leg crossed over the other, grinning like a Cheshire. "Six thousand, four hundred, and twenty-two dollars; and seventy cents, although they never tell you the cents," she said.

There was a dramatic countdown on screen as they awaited the reveal. Then the number flicked on. Six thousand, four hundred, and twenty-three. On screen, the unlucky contestant received gentle applause as condolence while the host talked about her consolation prize. Meanwhile, in the room, seven figures applauded Mila in stunned silence.

The theater was technically Sports Room B and throughout the year would host viewing parties for football, soccer, baseball, hockey, and basketball, depending on the season; however, whenever there wasn't a game to watch, other groups took over the theater for their own uses. Apparently there was a contingent of felines who excitedly watched Korean soap operas here every afternoon, and once a month it was rented out by the Bad Movies Club, which got together to drink and laugh at some of the worst films ever made. There was also this group surrounding Mila now: they were mostly older canines who preferred to wind down before the evening, not with an hour in the dungeon, but instead watching their favorite game shows. "How the hell does she do it?" one wolf, whose muzzle was pure white, asked Alonso.

Mila turned to face the wolf and puffed herself up, her tail practically touching her neck in pride. "The same way I can tell you that your cufflinks are about a hundred and fifty each, your tie pin comes to about sixty-five, and your shoes are one-thousand and two-hundred, unless I've misjudged the model."

The wolf looked at each item as she called them out, then back at her with a shrewd expression. "About? Around? What happened to getting it right down to the cents?"

Mila shrugged. "Shows like this tend to get their stock from the same places. If you stay up to date on the latest catalogs, which I do, it's easier to be accurate. On the other hand, I think your shoes are Santonis, but I can't be sure. If you really want to test my knowledge, we should put on an antique show or something about home remodeling after this: those are a lot harder."

The wolf looked ready to query her again, but the host had brought up another contestant and everyone's attention went back to the screen, waiting for a new opportunity for Mila to demonstrate her ability — everyone's attention except Alonso's, whose gentle eyes stayed fixed on his kitten all evening.

"So what is it you want to be able to cook?" Devon asked, the next morning, as they set up the egg-cracking station once again.

"Anything," Mila said, and she said it honestly. "Anything more complicated than an instant microwave meal or a bowl of soup on the stove." She sighed and rested her elbows on the central table. Her pride and exultation at demonstrating her ability during the game shows last night was now giving way to the rank humility of her cooking skills. "My mom was always a perfectionist about food when I was growing up and barely let me in the kitchen. After that I was in college and eating in the cafeteria all the time. When I started a job, I didn't have the time to learn. Then..." It didn't matter that Aisha had pushed away the pain. She still felt a void in her life.

Devon was right by her side, a hand over hers. The corgi smiled sympathetically. "You don't have to tell us if you don't want to."

"No, I think I should talk about it more." She took a deep breath. This was the reason why the house had trapped her here, wasn't it? "Then I married."

"Oh." The corgi's face darkened just a little at the tone in Mila's voice. "He didn't hurt you, did he?"

"No!" Mila said with surprising emphasis. "No, he was great. He just..." It never got easier, no matter how many times she had to say it. If anything, it got worse. "He died. Cancer."

Mila was suddenly aware of the presence of the lion on her other side, holding her other hand as comfortingly as Devon did. Two faces wide and open, all focused on her. "I'm so sorry, Mila."

She nodded. "It was a few months ago. I guess I'm still trying to process it all. But he always liked to tease me about how I couldn't cook. I was the breadwinner in the family, so I think he liked having something simple he could point to that showed I wasn't the best at everything. He even—" she was cut off by an unexpected laugh from her own throat. "He even bought a gag gift for our first anniversary: a box of stupid pancake mix. He always made sure it was prominent in the pantry so I could never forget it." She squeezed the hands holding hers. "I told him I would make pancakes for him one day. But it didn't end up happening."

Devon added a supporting touch on her shoulder. "Would you like us to teach you how to make pancakes?"

"I'd love that."

"Pancakes it is then."

They started the same way as the previous day, cracking eggs. Mila had, as Devon suggested, been practicing the motion since yesterday: whenever no one was paying attention to her during the game shows, when she had crawled under the bedsheets but not yet drifted off to sleep, while she was reading and waiting for Alonso to wake up, and even a few times randomly in the middle of the hall, to the curious looks of passersby. The calico began her day in the kitchen with bright new resolve, which initially caused her to start exploding eggs in her hand for the first few times, until she could control herself. Then, with almost perfect precision, she cracked a dozen eggs perfectly in a row.

"Excellent work, Mila," Devon enthused as the corgi swept

around the kitchen and prepped a second task for her: whisking. He set out a simple copper bowl with three eggs inside for both her and Theo.

Theo was acting a bit different today. The lion was admiring his own reflection. More than once, he checked to see if his mane was properly combed. It was a surprising amount of vanity that she hadn't noticed before. When his eye caught hers, he smiled roguishly and winked at her.

Mila laid her ears back and focused her attention on the whisk that Devon was pushing into her hand. He was instructing her on proper technique, not, as he said, to whisk faster, but to be able to sustain whisking by hand for a long time.

She would have picked up the skill quicker if it weren't for how distracting Theo was being. Every time she glanced at him, he seemed to be subtly hitting on her. There would be a little arch to his eyebrow, or his tongue would be snaking along his lips, or his tail would be positioned to draw her eyes down to his naked hips. The lion had a toned athleticism and Mila felt herself going a bit hot under her fur at his intense gaze.

Before lunchtime they swapped to separating yolks from whites, and Mila swore she had cracked a hundred more eggs all under Devon's hawk-like gaze before they stopped.

Thankfully around lunchtime, they took a break from that and turned to measuring and weighing ingredients. Devon was lecturing on the importance of weighing some ingredients by weight, some by volume, and which would be which. Mila was surprised by her focus and recollection, even of some of the most trivial details. The determination to finally make some pancakes burned in her mind, but determination did not make her memorize things better. Then, she realized that Devon was using the natural commanding power of the house as a canine to make her pay attention and make her remember. He was constantly telling her, "Don't forget."

Meanwhile, Theo, who was quite well aware of all of these things, was lounging back against the far counter. The lion had his head turned to the side, once more admiring his reflection in a hanging pan. Once or twice, Devon would notice what he was doing and the lion would turn to him, licking over his lips slowly and adjusting his naked sheath. Devon occasionally turned and mock-admonished him for not paying close enough attention.

What was going on?

The pancake batter came together with surprising quickness, once Mila had a recipe in front of her. It was a spreadsheet, with instructions; she knew how to deal with that.

But then came her nemesis: the stovetop.

Dealing with all the dials, and heat, and the right choice of pan would have been enough on its own, but Theo's preening had become a major distraction at this point. The handsome lion was at the station beside her, not close enough to be constantly touching her, but definitely close enough that his flirtatious tail sways kept brushing against her leg. Whenever she looked knowingly at him, to try and give him the hint to stop, he smiled like an adorable himbo and just did it again. She would have complained to Devon, but the corgi was admiring the hunk as much as she was.

In fact, he seemed to be really enjoying the show he was putting on.

Something clicked into place in her mind.

"You altered him," she said.

"What?" lion and corgi said in unison.

"Devon, you altered Theo's mind."

Lion and corgi shared a look, then Devon spoke. "Yes, of course I did."

"Sorry. Let me start over." Mila put her hands on either side of her muzzle and took a deep breath. "I was commenting to Alonso yesterday that you two seemed different from everyone else we've met here. You don't even seem to give any orders. But he said I should pay closer attention."

"Ah," Devon said, looking satisfied. "Well, all canines here, myself included, tend to enjoy something that reinforces our position here at the house. For most of them, that comes in being called a title or having felines be deferential to them or more outright physical reminders like leashes and bondage. We do things a little differently." The corgi touched the lion's back and smiled up at him. "I like to just go in and make a little tweak to his personality. When I see him acting it out, that's the reminder that I'm in control. That's all I need. And it helps that Theo is really into it too."

"It's true," the lion said with a cocksure grin.

"Next time, could I watch?" Mila asked.

Devon's look once more went quizzical.

"I mean, when you alter him next, could I watch? I'm still learning what all goes on here. And I'd like to watch how you do what you do."

"If Theo's all right with it."

"Sure!" the lion said with a broad grin. "I love it when cute girls watch me."

Mila flicked her ears down at being called cute. At least it was easier to believe coming from Theo than from Jeta Horowitz.

The corgi coughed and spoke in low conspiratorial tones. "I'll check with him again once he's back to his primary personality. Just in case."

Hours later, when Alonso next arrived to pick up Mila, he was presented with a plate of pancakes, after a fashion. There was a single pancake, which was somehow burnt only on the left side.

"I don't know what to say." Devon rocked on his heels. "I'm half convinced you took ownership of a gremlin. However, I will point out that this is a substantial improvement over how she began."

"That's good," Alonso said in tones so forcibly neutral that not a single emotion showed on his face.

"We will continue to make progress tomorrow."

Alonso tilted his head to the corgi before turning to the calico. "Come along, Mila."

Mila's ears drooped as she followed the silent fox out to where the daily schedule hung. "I'm sorry, sir," she said in a low voice.

His whiskers twitched and he looked down at her. "What for?"

"For not being a better cook. I can tell you were disappointed."

The edge of his muzzle lifted in the lightest of smiles. "Mila, I have tea and oatmeal for breakfast. I am hardly one to complain about cooking."

"But you can cook, can't you?"

"Burgers and steaks, sure. You know, man food," he said it with a fake deepness in his voice that brought a laugh to the calico. Then he dropped down so he spoke in a whisper, not looking at her as he did, "I usually left the cooking to Lily."

They read the schedule in silence for a while. Alonso nudged her arm and said, "May I pick the event for tonight?"

"Of course, sir."

Mila stared at the earplugs in her hands. "What are these for?" she asked Alonso quietly.

He pointedly did not answer but instead watched the demonstration happening in the center of the room. They were in a space on the first floor that Mila thought had once been a study, if the house had ever been a true manor house before it had been the Eternal Party: there were a few desks and leather chairs that had been moved to the side, and the shelves on the wall held some old books, miscellaneous paperwork with a heavy patina of dust, and bottles of liquor with eye-watering prices. She'd wanted to try one of them, just to see what $750-a-shot whiskey actually tasted like, but couldn't bring herself to ask.

The demonstration consisted of a female cross fox being suspended by rope to a hook fixed in the ceiling. Her assistant, a male Sphynx cat who did the actual work of tying her up, remained silent and let her do all the narration. "Now," she said with a voice that rang out like a shot. Her narrow eyes scanned the room and made it clear she was addressing every single person in there. "We have had some issues in the Eternal Party with lax safety. Here if you cut off someone's circulation with a too tight knot, the worst that will happen is they go numb. Here if you put too much pressure on the chest and your partner can't breathe, the worst that will happen is that they will temporarily lose consciousness. But I do not care. You will all follow proper safety instructions or you'll feel the strike of my crop. Again."

The last word was growled out as the cross fox glared at Noel, the maned wolf Mila had met at the masquerade. He pulled his always present Stetson down to avoid the boring glare of the fox.

Mila watched the fox sway a bit and fingered the earplugs Alonso had given her. "Are they for balance? Disorientation?"

Alonso continued to avoid answering and put a finger to his lips to indicate she should be quiet.

"I'm glad to see so many new faces here," the cross fox went on, nodding to a few people in the room, including Mila herself, "as well as veterans, and others." Again these last words were growled out as she stared daggers at Noel. "Don't worry. You're not expected to follow everything that Mason is doing right now. We'll be doing a quick step-by-step tutorial later this evening and will have more advanced lessons on specific techniques or variants in upcoming days and weeks. For the moment, I want to show our newbies my favorite aspect of suspension bondage."

She nodded to the Sphynx cat, who Mila assumed was Mason. Alonso bumped Mila's shoulder gently so the calico leaned in to watch more closely.

Mason gave the cross fox a gentle push so that her whole body swayed a few inches back and forth. He kept one hand on the ropes midway between the fox and the hook for added control. The Sphynx stepped into position so that at the high point of the fox's swing, her naked sex brushed against his sheath. They remained there until the cat's growing arousal caused his shaft to slip out and start plunging into the swinging female.

She in turn started to grip the ropes and jerk them at just the right moment to speed her swing towards the cat. The feline's shaft kept growing and kept growing. Mila was shocked, and a little jealous, of how big he was. When the Sphynx had finally reached full mast, he kept his hips moving with the motions of the swinging fox so that she never slipped fully off of him.

On a silent cue, Mason stepped forward with a sharp thrust of his hips. The fox shrieked in delight and was bounced up and away. They began to fuck in short sharp powerful thrusts that meant their hips met with a hard slap. Mason let go of the ropes and held on to the hook above them both. All that was needed to keep the fox swinging in those short sharp arcs was the strength of his thrusts.

The cross fox seemed to be unleashed. "Oh yes. That's it. Fuck me! Harder! Harder! Yes. Yes! YES!" Her voice rose in speed, pitch, and volume, until the bottles of $750-a-shot whiskey started to shake on their shelves.

Mila slipped the earplugs in.

When Mila arrived the next morning, she found Devon and Theo in an animated discussion that quieted as soon as she came in.

"Have a seat," Theo offered. There was a musical lilt to the lion's voice and he was slightly more animated than usual. Mila wondered if she was meeting the real Theo for the first time. "We were just pondering some ideas for today's play."

Devon nodded. "Since you are so new, I thought we could show you something a bit more out of the usual. So many canines here can fall into a routine."

Mila slipped onto a stool and leaned onto the table. "All right. What did you have in mind?"

"Making Theo dominant."

"Oh, like an honorary canine thing? Mistress Aisha did that with me." Even when the jackal was nowhere nearby, Mila made sure to add the honorific. Devon and Theo seemed nice enough, but she wanted to make sure the two men knew for sure that she considered Aisha as worthy of her respect.

"Not quite. That's for having felines be dominant over other felines. We were thinking of having Theo be dominant over me."

"So you'd be an honorary feline."

"Again, not quite. When you're acting as an honorary canine, you can command felines the same way we do, but there's nothing that can make a canine be as receptive to commands as felines are. I'd just be adjusting his personality to be more controlling, but he couldn't actually use the house's power to command me."

"Believe me," Theo put in. "We've tried."

The corgi shrugged melodramatically. "Oh no. We'll just have to live with me being able to assert incredible magical control over you to fulfill our kinky desires."

Mila giggled a little. "Okay, but I thought the rule of the house was that canines had to be in command."

"And ultimately I would be," Devon said. "I could stop or start it any time I choose, or even adjust his thoughts mid-scene if I want to be dommed in a different way."

Mila nodded and accepted a cup of coffee from the house, settling down to watch.

Devon and Theo started by holding one another's hands, looking into one another's eyes. There was a subtle motion from Devon. He extended his thumbs over the back of Theo's hands and pressed in against them. The lion's gaze drifted out of focus. "There we go," Devon said. "Emptying your thoughts. Emptying who you are. Ready to be filled with a new you for the day. A new, dominant you. A new, assertive you. A new, controlling you."

As Devon went on, broad strokes outlining this new persona and how it would relate to Devon (in control of) and Mila herself (assertive towards but not directly in control of), before filling in the details, specific actions he would take or things he would like and how these related back to his overall outlook.

"Pause," Devon said, and the lion's ears went flat. The corgi then looked to Mila with a wag. "Give me something to add to his persona."

Mila was about to protest that she didn't know what to do, let alone feel comfortable getting in between the two lovers. But that had clearly been a command from a canine.

The corgi winked as the realization set over her.

Mila considered as she sipped coffee again. "How about he likes groping you in an effort to make you gasp or moan unexpectedly?"

The corgi smiled and added that to the growing network of ideas in the lion's head, attaching that concept to a few others in an effort to increase its hold on the lion's psyche. Then, as he relaxed his hands, he leaned in for a kiss.

The lion began to kiss back, gently at first, and then with rising passion, lifting a hand to pull the corgi closer. When he broke it, he glanced once over Devon's form before giving him a critical stare. "You know better than that," he said sternly. "Strip."

The corgi backed away from the table with a small smile and began to undress. Mila was fascinated. She'd of course seen Alonso naked, but the typical experience in the house was that canines remained clothed unless actively engaging in sex, and they often didn't bother fully undressing for that. The corgi looked quite cute naked, and his smile faltered for only a second when he looked to Mila, returning in full force when he slid his attention back to the lion, who was gazing over him appraisingly.

Theo made an appreciative nod and turned his attention back to Mila. "Sorry about him. You know how some subs can be. So forgetful."

The calico bobbed her head. "Of course... sir?"

"You don't need to be that formal with me, Mila. Devon is my sub. You're a guest. Just remember whose kitchen you are in."

"Of course."

"Devon," the lion said sharply. "Help Mila out with her pancakes. And keep that cute tail up. I want to be able to watch your ass any time I want."

"Yes, sir," the corgi said and ducked in next to Mila, pulling out the necessary ingredients and the recipe list from before. From there, the day began to proceed much as it had the day before, but for as much as Devon had only altered Theo's personality, there was clearly a difference in him as well. He held himself a bit straighter whenever the lion watched him. His voice was quieter and more deferential, even when whispering cooking tips to Mila.

Mila did the prep faster than ever before and brought the bowl of batter over to the stove.

"Now remember, Mila. The key thing to look for are the formation of bubbles on the—"

The corgi's voice went silent all at once.

Mila turned sharply to see Theo walking away with a small smirk on his face and the corgi staring at a spot on the wall just above the stove. Seeing her suggestion take hold sent a little thrill through her. She could see why Devon liked it.

"Anyways," the corgi said. "Remember to look for the bubbles forming on the top of the pancake, that's when you'll know to flip it."

Mila began making pancake after pancake under the close watch of the corgi. Every now and then he would seize up and freeze as Theo continued in his attempts to make him gasp or moan. Mila noticed that as time went on, the canine's arousal was more and more evident, with a half-hard shaft starting to push out from his sheath.

It was curious for Mila being so close to a naked and aroused male but not feeling any particular reaction to that fact. Perhaps because Devon was gay and clearly not showing interest in her, it was easy to treat him as a companion rather than an object of her own affection. She was still turned on, but more by the constant antics the corgi and lion got up to.

Theo finally managed to get a proper reaction out of the corgi when, instead of just groping him, he got behind the corgi and slid a finger deep under his tail. Not only did Devon go silent, but he gripped the oven door and bit his lip, stifling any sound. Theo would not be denied. He twisted the finger inside his partner, which made Devon's shaft slip out fully and bob in the air. The corgi let slip a groan of contentment, which rose in pitch as the lion pulled out. Theo winked to Mila, then settled in against the windowsill with his own shaft standing proud before him.

After several more tries, Mila got a pancake looking the way she thought a pancake should look, and so the corgi instructed her to start from the beginning, but this time he did not offer corrections midway through, letting her make mistakes and only realize something had gone wrong when she finished. It was a frustrating process that made Mila feel like she had lost a lot of the progress she had made. But she persevered and finally had something she had made from start to finish with only the recipe, and it looked perfect. "There, Devon, what do you think of that?"

Devon wasn't looking at the pancake though. He had gone slightly cross-eyed and was moaning out. Over his shoulder, Theo gave a wink and then directed her gaze down so she could see him reaching between the corgi's thighs and squeezing the corgi's sac.

"Well," the lion said, "I think they look great."

"Mmhmm!" the corgi offered in a half moan.

Theo let go and began to pull back when the corgi reached out and snatched his hand, pressing his thumb on top the same way he had that morning. Immediately the lion's body slumped. "You're horny," the corgi said in a firm but quiet voice, trembling with its own need. "You can't wait any longer to fuck me." Then he let go.

Theo stood up and his shaft throbbed in the air. "Excuse me a few minutes, Mila," he said.

He gripped the corgi's hips and roughly turned him to face the stove. "Hands up," he commanded, and the corgi reached up to grip the edge of the vent over the stove. The lion worked with surprising slowness and delicacy, turning off each burner on the stovetop with a click, setting the pots and pans aside, then standing behind Devon, cock pressed against the now-wagging tail. "I told you to keep that up," the lion said with a playful growl.

Immediately the corgi's tail pressed against his own back, but it still didn't stop wiggling back and forth. The lion gripped his hips and pressed them in close. Mila watched a drool of pre drop onto the corgi's fur.

"Lube," the lion commanded, and held out his hand to the calico.

Mila looked around. They were in a kitchen. Where the hell would lube be? Then she remembered herself and asked the house to provide lube. She pulled the provided stuff out of the drawer and handed it to the lion, who quickly slathered his cock in the fluid before putting his tip to the corgi's hole. He gripped Devon's shoulder firmly and began to ease himself in.

And as he did, he turned to look at Mila.

The calico flushed, remembering that one of the things that Devon had implanted in him that morning was a bit of vanity, a desire to be watched. Mila's embarrassment, feeling that she was intruding on a private moment between the lovers, melted under the way he looked at her, as if he were sizing her up for a second fuck once he was done with Devon.

While Theo was a symbol of masculine calm, Devon was beginning to wriggle and moan out louder than ever before. The lion returned his focus to his partner and growled in his ear. "Are you already getting close, you horny thing?"

"Uh-huh," the corgi barked out in between thrusts that almost lifted him off his feet.

The lion thrust hard one more time and then coaxed the corgi's hands from the vent, turning him to face the calico. Devon was enjoying himself too much to even notice the presence of the third person in the room, his face slack in pleasure. Theo pressed himself in deep from behind, gripping the corgi's hip to ensure they stayed together, as he reached around and started jacking his partner off. Devon huffed and whined but before long his shaft was jumping and spurting his seed to splatter onto the floor.

"Good boy," the lion cooed in his ear.

Theo helped the drooping corgi get down onto his knees and then fall forward onto all fours. The lion knelt up behind his partner and resumed fucking, once more showing off for Mila as he did. He flexed his arms and showed off his charm and Mila felt another flutter in her heart as she watched. When his thrusts grew deep and the corgi moaned in unslaked lust, Mila found herself wishing she were in Devon's place.

The lion growled, gripped the corgi's tail hard, and climaxed. He panted for a moment, then pulled out and began meticulously cleaning himself and the corgi, even wiping the floor clean of Devon's seed. Seeing Mila's perplexed look, he shrugged and explained, "We try to keep things reasonably clean in the kitchen. Jizz doesn't taste good in any batter that we've found."

Or coffee, Mila thought to herself, and she giggled.

When Devon recovered, he praised Mila's progress — her perfectly made pancake now cold on the counter — and declared that they should try different kinds of pancakes. He summoned a sampler platter from the house that contained many types he and Devon had baked before, not just buttermilk pancakes, but chocolate pancakes, and pancakes with bacon bits, and pancakes with roasted apple slices and whipped cream, and so much more. "You made all these?" Mila asked, astonished.

The corgi beamed. "Oh yes. Most are based on existing recipes that we've put our little spin on. It's the house, you see. It can make anything it's seen before but it can sometimes struggle to make something new, especially when it comes to food. So we make as many different things as we can, so future guests will have a wide variety to choose from."

Mila sliced off a piece of bacon-infused pancake, dipped it in some delectably soft honey butter, and ate it, purring all the while. "You should open a restaurant."

"That's the plan. Theo and I—"

Theo coughed.

The corgi looked momentarily stricken. "Sorry, sir. You explain."

The lion rolled his eyes. "Subs keep forgetting their place. Anyways, yes, the plan is for us to open a restaurant. We're using our time here at the house to develop and perfect our recipes, so that when we are ready to leave, we can take the local food scene by storm."

"Well, I look forward to visiting."

Theo nodded with a smile and gestured to the array of plates on the table before them. "Which would you like to try making first?"

Mila ended up selecting the pancakes with bananas foster, and spent the next several hours learning to make that. But she felt a buoy of confidence, from having finished a proper pancake for once.

This time, when Alonso arrived, he was presented with a full plate of fluffy golden-brown disks topped with sliced bananas, walnuts, and an ooey-gooey sauce.

"She's improved greatly," Theo said. "She made that with little assistance beyond a recipe."

The fox stood, resting a little weight forward on his cane and considered the plate. He seemed completely unperturbed by Theo's more dominant tone or the fact that Devon was still completely naked. Either he was well aware of the cooks' proclivities or he simply didn't care. "Mila," he said, after a moment, "why don't you make a set of four so that we can all have pancakes for dinner? Provided, of course, you are interested." He addressed this last comment directly to Theo.

"It will be a good test of her abilities," the lion said and took a seat to converse with Alonso on news while Mila whipped up three more batches. Theo insisted Alonso dig into the first plate before it got too cold.

They all came out quite well, if Mila was any judge (and she was rapidly becoming a better one). She felt immensely proud of herself but also worn out, and she requested to Alonso that they just go back to his room and relax for the evening. He agreed.

The fox and calico decided to watch a movie, and Mila selected a light-hearted 60's comedy about mistaken identities. The wordplay in the dialogue went a mile-a-minute and soon Mila was having trouble hearing the film because of how hard she was laughing. The thing that finally made her stop was the realization that Alonso wasn't laughing. He wasn't moving at all.

At first she thought the fox had fallen asleep, so she fumbled for the remote and muted the film. But when she looked up, she saw the fox staring at the screen. In the dimness of the room, the moving light from the screen cast strange shadows over his face.

"Sir?"

The fox opened his mouth to say something, then shut it and shook his head. "Never mind," he said. "You don't need to hear me talk about Lily so often."

"Do you want to talk about her?"

"All the time."

"Then I'll listen."

Without looking away from the screen, the fox let his paw drift up over Mila's back until it was caressing her neck around the edge of her collar. "She loved these old movies, the history of them. She wouldn't stay quiet during a film because she always had to tell me how this movie impacted the future of movie-making. I've been expecting to hear her chime in for the last thirty minutes or so. I miss... I miss learning from her."

"I'm afraid I don't really know any movie trivia."

"You're not her!" the fox said firmly. "And I don't want you to be her. But... thank you for thinking of that."

Mila's tail curled around her leg. "Maybe there's a good director commentary for this? We could watch that afterward."

Finally the fox looked away from the screen and he pulled Mila up to nuzzle against her neck. "I'd like that." He paused and considered. "Was there something... some movie that you and your husband liked to watch together?"

Mila grimaced and pulled back. "That would be a bad idea. The kinds of movies we liked to watch together were typically the ones where you cry at the end. I think I've had enough tears for a few years."

They fell into an awkward silence. Mila knew Alonso was trying to do the same thing she was: help the other deal with the awful grief while dancing around the fact that they were actually doing so. Alonso eventually broke the silence by unmuting the movie.

At least, Mila noted, this time he started to laugh.

The next day there were even more pancakes with Devon and Theo. Mila made chocolate pancakes and wheat pancakes and buttermilk pancakes. She topped them with thinly sliced strawberries or hand-made honey butter. She made pancakes so thin they were practically crepes and pancakes nearly an inch thick. She tried, exactly one time, to make art on the surface of the pancake by cooking a design in the batter. The resulting cat emoticon she made would not have impressed anyone over the age of six. (Devon admitted that neither he nor Theo had the knack for it, and he didn't ask her to do it again.)

When Alonso arrived that evening, he was presented with a flight of four different pancakes. Devon had given her tips on proper plating, and she felt the dish actually would have looked presentable at a restaurant. "I'm impressed," Alonso said. "But I do hope I'm not going to be feasting on pancakes every day."

Devon nodded. "Of course. Next week, we plan to do waffles only. Kidding! Kidding! Sorry, Alonso, I'm only kidding."

The fox rolled his eyes and shook his head.

The four of them enjoyed Mila's pancakes and they discussed plans for her to continue learning how to cook and what dishes they might work on next. After that, Alonso escorted her out, but instead of going to the schedule, as they had the last two days, he started pulling her in a different direction.

"What's going on?" Mila asked.

"Not here," he said under his breath.

Together they went downstairs, all the way to the first floor and to the opposite end of the house from the ballroom, where there were a series of smaller rooms. They entered one, which had little more than a chair, a chaise lounge, and a wonderful view of the city street outside, a simple lounge room with just enough space for two people. Alonso locked the door behind them.

The fox fell into the chair and wrapped his tail over into his lap, leaving Mila to settle herself into the chaise. Mila expected him to start speaking, but he just stared out the window. She coughed.

He jerked in his seat and looked down at her. "Sorry," he said. "I spoke with Aisha again earlier and the news wasn't the best: the house isn't going to tell us how to get out."

"Damn." Mila felt her claws extending for a moment. She had to will them to sheathe once more.

"It's more like the house can't tell us how to get out. How did Aisha put it?" He made some vague motions with his hands as if remembering how she had gestured would help him remember what she said. "It's not like climbing a mountain. With a mountain, you follow a path and you will always end up at the same place. However, we aren't trying to reach a place, but a state of mind. Your state of mind may depend on why you were following that path. So even if the house knew things we could do that would get us out, it wouldn't tell us, because it would change why we did those things and they might no longer work."

Mila sighed. "That makes sense, but it is frustrating." She gave him a meaningful look.

"What?"

"Didn't Aisha say we should be trying to do relaxing things and not focusing on how to get out for a while?"

Alonso threw up his hands. "I've been trying," he said.

"Really, I have. While you've been getting cooking lessons, I've read books, gone to the gym, taken naps. I've even done a damn jigsaw puzzle. But Mila, you have to understand, I have been here for ten years. I feel like I ought to be doing something, anything, to get out. Every time I tried to relax, I just got more anxious. I eventually went up to the library to ask Aisha what I should be doing, but she just threw me out."

"At least she didn't hit you this time, sir."

"A small blessing that." He touched his muzzle gingerly.

"Um, sir." Mila swallowed as she shifted the topic. "If I may ask..."

"About Aisha and me?"

The calico nodded.

He sighed and shrugged. "It's like I told you, when I arrived, I wasn't that kinky. I was exploring things. At one point I thought about trying to be submissive. Aisha was a good teacher, and I gave it a good shot, the same as I would for any kink a feline partner enjoyed, but I found it wasn't really my thing."

"And afterwards?"

"Aisha really prefers her partners to be submissive, so it didn't work out between us after that."

"I meant after she threw you out today."

"I convinced her to let me stay and help with her research if I promised to relax with you afterwards."

"Is that why we're here?" The room was, Mila noted, quite bare, as if it had no clear purpose or perhaps that people brought their purpose to it.

"After a fashion. We're here because I wanted to show you Lily." He turned to face a closet that was built into one of the walls, one hand on the handle.

Mila swallowed uncomfortably. "Lily's dead. Isn't she?"

"She is," he said, and opened the door to show her.

Mazurka

Lily was there, wearing a bridal gown with a wind-tossed veil lightly concealing her face. The vixen held a bouquet of flowers in one hand and was laughing at some unheard joke. Behind her was a simple altar and pulpit in an outdoor pavilion.

It was a painting, life-size and so life-like that Mila at first assumed it was a photograph.

"Our wedding day," Alonso explained, "captured as best I can remember it. We were pronounced man and wife, I kissed her, there was a cheer, and then I leaned in to whisper in her ear." He chuckled in remembrance. "I told her that now we were married, all the sex we were having was official and we both needed to up our game."

Mila looked up into the vixen's laughing face. "Seriously? You said all that at the altar?"

"Oh yes, and she gave as good as she got. She told me it was good we had to up our game because I really needed to improve." Alonso grinned wryly. "Family asked what we were whispering about, but I claimed honeymoon privilege."

Mila stepped forward and, with a claw extended, gave the painting the gentlest touch, as if to confirm it was real. "You made this? It's beautiful."

Alonso shrugged. "She was the real artistic talent in the family. She could make just about anything in just about any medium with just about any style, and I mean that. Once, for a class she was teaching, she wanted to demonstrate the ubiquity of art. She let students write down ideas, tossed them into a bucket, and drew out a random assortment. She ended up having to paint the Statue of Liberty in blue and black paint, using only a notched drywall trowel. Oh, and it was Cubist too." The fox reached out and touched the painting just over Lily's hand.

"I had a habit of scribbling in the margins of my notes in school, little comics or caricatures of teachers we really didn't like. When we started dating, I'd often draw cartoons of the two of us on napkins or whatever was at hand. When we got married, she showed me she'd kept the first one I ever did. It's probably still back in a photo album at the house somewhere. She encouraged me to keep drawing, even gifted me a very nice sketchbook for the purpose, but there was work and then there were kids, and it just never happened."

Mila leaned in against the fox's arm and thought how much that sounded like her and cooking. "Well, I think it's great."

"Good kitten."

Mila shivered from her nose to her tailtip at the phrase. "Did you make all the pictures I saw in your room too?"

"I did." He reached in past the painting of Lily and came back holding an easel, a pad of large paper, and a kit with some art supplies. "And if you're all right with it, I'd like to draw you tonight."

The calico felt the familiar rush of embarrassment over her body and tried to push it aside. "Okay. What do you need me to do?"

Alonso pointed to the chaise lounge nearby. Mila sat down, adopting what she hoped was a photogenic pose. After setting up the easel, Alonso knelt down in front of Mila. He began to position her, his touch more delicate than Mila had ever felt as he made the most minute adjustments. "You will stay in the position

I place you," he commanded. "When you need to talk or stretch, you may, but you will return to this position after."

Mila tested this out. She stretched one arm and when she relaxed again, it just slipped back into where it had been before. It felt unusual, but the magic of the house prevented it from feeling tiring.

The fox made frequent adjustments to Mila's posture, sat down, ran his eyes over her form from that perspective, got up to make a few more changes, and did this all several times before being satisfied. When done, Mila was sitting forward on the edge of the chaise lounge, one knee drawn up. Her elbows rested on the knee and her chin rested on her hands. Mila was relatively sure that the position was designed to hide her nipples and sex from view.

He picked up a selection of pencils from his kit and began to sketch in gentle broad strokes. She followed the trace of his hands and tried to imagine what he was working on. The long sensuous line down the page was probably the curve of her flank and leg. The quick up and down may have been her ears. He seemed to struggle with getting her muzzle just right because he kept adjusting and readjusting the line.

Mila found the act of being drawn very relaxing. The constant repetitive motions of the kitchen had left her feeling stiff despite the protective magic of the house, and the command Alonso used to hold her in place required no effort on her part, so she could sink into position and nearly fall asleep.

"And done."

Maybe she had fallen asleep, because Alonso's words came as a shock to her.

"You're free to move again, Mila. Come take a look."

The calico stretched into a yawn and then stepped around behind Alonso's chair. He'd used only pencil, highlighting her form in sharp black and varying grays on white paper, with the only color coming from an orange pencil he'd used for some of her fur, and a bit of green for her eyes. It was unmistakable as being her, and yet, it also had an artistic commonality to it, as though Mila were just standing in for calicoes in general. The sketch would not have looked out of place in a high end gallery. Her cleverly concealed nudity would be no concern in such places.

"It looks beautiful," she said, feeling that something needed to be said but also feeling all her words were inadequate to the task.

The fox nodded in acknowledgment of the compliment, but there was a tension in his face suggesting he saw all the flaws she did not. "This has become one of my favorite ways to blow off steam besides sex. I've probably drawn every feline in here more than once and a good chunk of the canines too. I keep telling Aisha she's going to need her own portrait in the library one of these years and I should be the one to make it."

"Can I see some of them, sir?" Mila asked, bending over the back of the chair to bring her muzzle in close to his.

He looked up at her and nodded, tapping his cane on the ground once. "House, my full collection out of storage if you please."

There was a louder thump than usual in the nearby wall and Alonso opened the closet to reveal a huge stack of paintings, more paper sketches, and several notebooks of smaller doodles. The painting of Lily was nowhere to be seen. He pulled a large sheaf of papers out to show Mila, and she recognized most of the felines inside from around the house, although a few were, she guessed, people like Jeta who only stopped by for short periods. She saw a full painting of Jeta in the stack in fact, along with several sketches.

"She's very happy to model," Alonso said. "And she liked them so much she's taken two of the most risqué back home with her to decorate her bedroom."

Mila was somehow unsurprised that the buxom tigress would decorate her bedroom with nude paintings of herself.

The calico browsed some of the other portraits. She was surprised how many of them were tasteful, simple headshots.

There apparently was a punk lioness somewhere in the house who just enjoyed making exaggerated faces. But there were also a lot of art so lewd that it almost felt too dirty for the house itself. Her eyes were particularly drawn to a picture of Zuberi and Ingrid, the painted dog and jaguar couple, which appeared not only to be mid-coitus but mid-orgasm, with a snarl on the dog's lips and a gush of fluids dripping from their joined sexes. "That one took a while," Alonso admitted. "They were very keen to replicate the pose nightly until I could get it just right."

Alonso pulled out a folder of large pencil drawings and carefully added Mila's to the mix, putting it and all the art supplies back into the wall.

The hour had grown late, but Mila found herself springy and full of energy after what she guessed had been a waking nap on the chaise. She bounced all the way back to Alonso's room. She was even looking forward to being taken to Alonso's bed and the potential fun that could happen there, but for once he didn't even offer the possibility. He cradled her in his arms, turned on some more cooking shows (which Mila found herself studying with renewed interest) and fell asleep long before the calico did. When she got tired enough, she turned off the TV, pressed her muzzle into the silver-tinged fur of the fox's naked chest, and drifted off to sleep.

Mila's cooking lessons the next day were about breakfast staples: waffles, just as Devon had teased, but also omelets, bacon, hash browns, and a few other ways to prepare eggs. She drew the line at one item however. Despite Devon's insistence that juicing oranges by hand resulted in the best flavor, Mila just said, "There are some things I want the supermarket to do for me."

Alonso was in comparatively high spirits when he came to

collect her at the end of the day, and not just because he didn't need to have pancakes for the third day in a row.

"Aisha has deputized me," the fox said down in his little painting room. He had posed Mila this time with her looking out the nearby window, eyes bright and ears perked as if she saw something unexpected coming down the street. "She's not getting any more straight answers out of the house and is trying to dig back into its history. Thankfully the house's memory is good and she's starting to be able to piece together things she wasn't able to before, but the process is slow, and she has me going through the old references to those who came in through the side door to see if I can find anything new."

"And are you?" Mila asked, before she was drawn back into the pose.

"I'm finding a lot that Aisha calls interesting but very little that seems immediately useful to us. She has repeated, to the point I am almost tired of it, that academic study is a careful process and we should not expect answers within a day or even within a week."

"I'm not minding this so much."

"The cooking lessons or being my model?"

"Both."

Alonso looked her way with a smile. "For the first time in a long, long time, it feels like we're finally making progress on getting out of here."

After a while, Mila worked up the courage to speak again. "Sir, may I ask a question?"

He froze midway through the stroke he was making on the page. "Is this about Lily?"

"Yes."

He continued the stroke and then set the pencil down. He folded his hands, took two deep breaths, and then said, "Ask."

"Do you think she would have liked me?"

The fox started. "You mean, would she have liked you as a

227

person or would she have been okay with the fact that I'm fucking you?"

"Both," Mila said, with an edge of nervousness in her voice.

Alonso didn't answer right away. He returned to his sketch and chewed his lip as he thought. "I think she would have liked you, although she would probably have thought you talk far too much about numbers for her taste. As to the sex, well, that's something I've wondered ever since I got here. It's not like we were very jealous people, not like some couples I know. I had other relationships before Lily, but when I was with her..." He set his pencil down and looked to the side at nothing in particular. "It's like I didn't see the appeal in other women." He grunted and shook himself, moving to sketch once again. "I'd like to think that she would be okay with the decisions I'd made."

Alonso added some quick short strokes which made Mila think he was drawing her whiskers. "Can I ask you a question as well?"

"Yes, of course."

He flicked an ear at her response. "Are you just saying that because I'm your owner?"

Mila actually had to think about that. There was an impulse to just obey Alonso and permit him to do what he chose, but she also could feel her own separate desires. "No. I also want to answer because I think you're going to ask about BD and maybe talking about the ones we lost is supposed to help us get out of here."

"House, will it help?"

No response.

The fox sighed. "Sounds like it can't hurt at least. Mila, since you've been here, you've seemed to react very emotionally whenever you are told you can be beautiful. Did BD not think you were?"

"No," Mila said sharply. It was harsher than she had intended, but she felt she had to stand up for him. "He told me I was beautiful all the time. It was one of the things I loved about him, because it felt like no one else thought so."

"You *are* beautiful, Mila."

"Thank you, sir." Mila waited to continue, as the fox had his tongue slightly extended while he focused on a careful detail of his art. "How did the rest of your family react, when Lily and the kits died?"

"My parents were already gone by then: heavy smokers, both of them. My sisters, though, I don't think they knew how to deal with it any better than I did. Two of them were so convinced all I needed was another woman in my life that she started setting me up with her girlfriends. The other hated me discussing anything about Lily or the kits and said I was being too morose all the time, which was probably true. I take it it was similar for you?"

"Yes, although it was with my parents. I think the only one who truly understood what I was going through was BD's sister. But eventually I was the one who pulled away from her. She reminded me too much of him and not in a good way."

He focused intently on the canvas in front of him for a moment and drew several lines carefully. There was a small tremor in his hand that hadn't been there a few minutes before. "Mila?"

"Yes, sir?"

"That's enough questions about the past for one evening."

"Yes, sir."

The next day, Mila's cooking lesson ended midday. She had seen a social gathering happening at one o'clock that she wanted to go to: apparently there were several other people from her firm at the Eternal Party. She didn't know any of them personally. (It was a big firm, after all.) Still it was lovely to spend an afternoon chatting lightheartedly about their jobs, sharing funny stories, and talking about terrible bosses they had worked under. Water cooler stuff.

They met in a small room, not dissimilar from Alonso's painting studio, with a small cart of coffee and various cookies. Two of them were feline and two of them were canine, and yet, for the first time, she didn't feel a difference in status. Despite the two felines being nearly naked and the two canines being dressed to the nines, they were all workers in solidarity under the heel of the corporate overlords.

Mila also realized belatedly that it was the first time she had felt confident wandering off on her own in the house without Alonso to protect her.

Afterwards Alonso took her to poker night. It turns out that he was right in what he had said nearly a week ago: strip poker wasn't that popular at the Eternal Party. On the other hand dress-up poker was the game of choice among many canines.

Alonso sat down to a table in a large gaming hall opposite the deaf Dalmatian, who Mila learned was Henrik. She stood to the side next to the silver cat, Alex, while Henrik shuffled. The Dalmatian showed off an impressive ability to manipulate the cards and delighted in performing showy shuffles as Mila watched entranced.

"Don't let him fool you," Alex said. "Alonso is the better poker player."

"How good?" Mila asked.

"Good enough that you'll end up with as much on you as Alonso wants on you."

Alonso had explained the rules briefly to Mila beforehand. The game was Texas hold 'em, and the canines each began with a thousand chips. Each time a player's chips crossed a higher hundreds threshold for the first time, that player got to choose an item from the chest which had to be worn by one of the felines, although certain items could be vetoed. Some tables had a good dozen members surrounding them, but this match was just between Alonso and Henrik.

The first hand Alonso folded early. The next time Henrik bid once, Alonso raised, and Henrik folded. The third hand saw some light bidding, which the Dalmatian ultimately won, bringing him over 1100 chips. He rummaged through the toy chest for a surprisingly long time, selected a remote-controlled vibrator at last, and handed it to Alonso.

The fox turned and beckoned Mila closer. He squeezed the vibrator in his palm to leave some residual heat on the surface before slipping it into her sex and commanding her to hold it. After a quick test to make sure the remote was actually working, Alonso handed it to Henrik, who amused himself with sending it through its paces a few times before settling it on a low thrum deep inside of Mila.

Alonso won a few quick hands in a row coming up above 1200 chips, and letting him select a chastity cage and small butt plug to be added to the silver cat. Then Henrik blew past 1300 chips in a surprising turn. He first selected some wrist cuffs, and then some elbow cuffs, attaching them so that Mila was forced to cross her arms over her chest.

The blinds crept up quickly and the leading player changed just as fast. Alex was soon wearing an armbinder, a muzzle, and a small dangling weight from his balls. Mila received a posture collar, a pair of blinders that meant she could only see directly ahead of her, and small suction cups that tugged at her nipples (after Alonso vetoed clothespins being applied to the same place). Each new item was a new sensation, an exploration, and the fox made sure the dressing process was slow and steady.

The calico squirmed in her binds as Henrik teased the vibrator's remote up and down while he thought about his next hand. "Is it weird that I can't tell who I want to win more right now?" she asked Alex.

"Nn-nnn!" said the muzzled cat.

"I heard that," Alonso said. "You should want your owner to win, Mila, obviously." And without taking his eyes off of the calico, Alonso pushed his entire stack of chips forward and declared that he was all in.

Henrik called, and both players showed their hands. Henrik had a two pair. Alonso had a straight.

Mila felt a twinge of jealousy for the silver cat as he was dressed in more and more items while she was left largely unattended. Henrik thanked Alonso for the game with a quick gesture and dragged the immobilized Alex off to a corner for some fun.

Alonso stayed at the table considering Mila for a while, a finger tapping his muzzle.

"Can we head up to the room, sir?" Mila asked.

He decided at last with a shake of his head. One at a time, he peeled away the items Henrik had selected for her. "I'm not quite satisfied with his selections. Let's keep playing until we find something that works really well."

They ended up playing four more rounds.

Mila and Alonso quickly settled into a routine. Most days Mila went to the kitchen for instruction from Devon and Theo, while Alonso helped Aisha in the library. In the evenings Alonso brought Mila down to his art studio and sketched or painted her. But any activity could and often was interrupted if there was an interesting event happening elsewhere in the house.

With Alonso's encouragement, Mila kept gently nudging her boundaries. She attended demonstrations in the dungeon, and if she liked what she saw, she'd ask Alonso to try it in the privacy of their room. They went to games and social events. Mila forced Alonso to sit through cooking shows (where now she took copious notes on dishes she wanted to try and techniques she wanted to ask about); Alonso in turn managed to get Mila to go to the petplay brunch exactly once. She loved the attention of his constant caresses of her spine, but couldn't stand eating food out of a bowl and crawling around on all fours.

The calico found that she really enjoyed bondage in various forms. Besides Alonso's skill in teasing her bound form to an explosive orgasm, there was the way he slowly tied her up each time, as if wrapping her in a protective shield. It reinforced that feeling of security that had taken a blow when he had thrown Mila out of his room.

Sometimes that sense of security still faltered. Alonso had earned himself a couple of slaps for getting sexual without her consent first, like when he had ordered her to suck him off while he was still waking up or when he had ordered her to crawl onto the bed and present her sex to him after a particularly lusty shibari demonstration. He always apologized, sorry that he had lost himself to the house's influence, and he didn't pressure her.

The calico, mindful of what Aisha had taught her about submissiveness, also volunteered for a few classes on service, much to Alonso's surprise. Other felines gave lessons on how to properly wait tables for meals, how to interact with multiple doms at once, and even how to bootblack. Mila practiced with Alonso in private and found herself quietly enjoying the looks the fox gave her as she knelt down and offered him an evening drink on a tray.

When they were alone, they might discuss Lily or BD. Some days, the words and memories came easy. Other times, they had to force themselves to talk.

A month passed.

Mila became a better cook. She explored her sexuality. She spoke more about BD than she had since his passing. But a worry lingered in her mind.

"Sir," she asked one night as Alonso watched reruns of an old mystery show he liked. "I need to know something."

"About Lily?"

"Kind of. It's more about you."

"Go ahead," he said, keeping his eye on the TV, one hand on the remote and the other on her shoulders.

"Does it stop hurting eventually? Because," she added, before he could answer, "I have Aisha's command protecting me from feeling any pain from losing BD, but I can still feel that it's there. I'm worried that as soon as the command is removed, it's all going to come crashing back."

The fox tapped the mute button and set the controller aside. Mila felt his chest swell as he breathed deep and he moved a hand up to caress a thumb tenderly along her muzzle. "After Lily died, back when I was getting checked out by the shrinks, one of them told me that some people never move *on*, but they figure out how to move *along*. He meant that the pain may not ever fully go away, but you figure out how to deal with it better. That was me, although it took me until I arrived here that I learned that."

Mila slowly lifted her head out of his lap. "But how did you do it?"

He shrugged. "Everyone is different. I can only say what I did."

"And?"

He smiled softly at her impatience. "The problem I had was that I kept associating certain things with just Lily. You know, for the first few months I was here, I brought many women to this room, but I always sent them away before I went to bed. Because I shared my bed with Lily. That was her place."

The calico made a face. She'd been in his bed for weeks now. "Do you need me to sleep on the couch? Or the cage?" She glanced beneath the bed. She'd slept there once and had not particularly enjoyed the experience.

"No. That's changed." He looked at the TV without seeing what was on the screen and for a while said nothing. "It feels so egotistical to say it. I realized that I wanted to have someone in my bed. That was *my* desire. *I* wanted it. It wasn't about Lily, as much as I wanted her. And once I realized that, I could take people to my bed again, and it wasn't as bad anymore." He looked at Mila. "There were a lot of things like that. Things that I loved doing with her, that I had to learn how to love on my own again. But all that and I still haven't found my way out of here."

Mila rested against him once more. She wanted to ask if there was anything he hadn't been able to get over that way, but she was scared the answer was yes. So she simply said nothing at all, and lapsed into silence as he resumed watching his show.

/

Alonso's words stewed in her mind all night. By the time daylight woke them both up, she had made a decision, and when she walked into the kitchen that morning, she asked Devon to not alter Theo's personality that day.

The corgi didn't even miss a beat, asking Mila what she had in mind.

"I'd like you to change me today."

The corgi leaned forward, propping his muzzle up on his arms and wagging hard. Mila had never made a request like this before. "I take it you have something in mind."

Mila's tail wrapped around her waist and she rubbed at it nervously. "And it involves Theo."

The lion, with his animated facial expressions and his sing-song voice, appeared at Mila's side. "Well, now I'm interested too."

Mila stroked her tail several times, trying to smooth it down. Words kept burbling up in her throat and then forming a lump, forcing her to swallow them back down. She had to ask herself again why this was so hard. It didn't hurt anymore; Aisha had seen to that. But she was still jumpy, avoiding the topic that had caused her pain before just in case it might do so again.

Mila bottled up the words the next time they floated close to her lips and forced them out in a rush. "Iwanttobeseductive."

The two men looked at each other then back at her with raised eyebrows.

"It's nothing. Forget—" She cut herself off. She needed to be strong. It was the only way she was going to get out of here. The calico focused her attention down at a spot on the table in front of her, so she wouldn't have to think about Devon and Theo for a moment. "You know how every couple has their little quirks, the games they play that no one else does? With me and my husband, it was flirting. It didn't matter that we'd been married and stuck into a domestic routine: if we had an evening free, we'd flirt like we were oversexed eighteen-year-olds who'd just met. We'd be as sexy as we could and make it clear how much we wanted the other. We'd make games out of it. Sometimes he'd pretend not to be interested, just to see how far I'd go to show I wanted him. We loved that. But since he died, I just haven't been able to do that with anyone else. I can tell Alonso I want him, but I can't... show it."

Mila glanced upwards. Theo and Devon were nodding gently along, their full attention on her.

"Can you help?" she asked quietly.

They nodded in unison. "Of course we will," Devon said. "I take it you want more than just an order to be seductive."

Mila nodded. "That would make me do it, but not feel like I could do it on my own."

Devon crossed his arms, drumming his fingers on his elbow thoughtfully. "So, what's stopping you?"

He asked the question good-naturedly, but it was hard for Mila to answer. She tried envisioning herself trying to entice Alonso and where it would go wrong. "As soon as I start, no matter what it is, I imagine doing it for BD, and then I freeze up. I'm thinking of him and missing him and wishing I could do it for him again, and those are all very unsexy feelings to have, so I can't continue."

The corgi chewed his lip a little as he pondered. Then he held out his hands, the same way he had for Theo. "Let me try something," he said.

Mila placed her hands in his. He started to speak, and she

nodded along with what he was saying, but afterwards could not remember what she had been agreeing with. The next thing she knew, he was handing her a recipe for curry. It was time to get started for the day. She had no idea what changes he made, and she found it hard to think about too much, as if the questions were slipping out of reach before she could get a firm hold on them.

Devon whipped out another recipe card with a flourish and made a show of handing it to Theo, who was looking a bit flustered by the corgi's dramatics. But Mila felt like she was seeing the lion for the first time. In a certain sense she was. It was the first time he had spent an extended period in her presence as himself without being altered in any way. He had a youthful handsomeness, a spirited energy, and that same soft lilt to his voice.

Then there was the adorable way his tail would flick when he was turned away from her, the tip of his tail tapping his ass on one side then the other, as if begging the eye to fixate on it.

Mila wanted him.

Theo, Devon, and even Alonso had made it clear for weeks that there would be no issue with her playing with the lion, but it just hadn't felt right. Now it did. A warmth spread inside her, flowing out from her chest, at the thought of the handsome lion fucking her.

Mila hopped off her chair and stepped over to where the lion was mixing together spices. "Oh, Theo?" she asked, using a singsong tone that reflected his own.

The lion jumped to see the calico so close. "Uh, hi, Mila."

"I'm having a little trouble with this recipe," she said. "Could I watch you?" She pressed close enough for her breasts to brush against him. "I find it helps if I can watch closely."

There was a clatter as the lion fumbled with the spice jars so hard that several went skittering over the table. Mila was distracted as well. The intrusive thought she was worried about sprang forward in her mind: "BD would have appreciated that line." Normally it stood in her head like a roadblock, preventing any other thoughts until she stepped away from whatever she had been doing. But this time, it was a call, waiting for a response, and she knew what it was. "Yes," she agreed with herself. "He would have."

That was all it took. She was able to step past the thought and continue. The calico fluttered her eyelashes at the lion, awaiting his response.

"Uh," the lion chuckled. "I suppose, if Devon's okay with that."

The corgi was watching from a far corner and he eagerly nodded, his head bobbing as quickly as his tail was wagging.

Mila purred softly and kept close to Theo, one hand draped over his backside just above his tail. She could tell he was distracted, making far more mistakes than he usually did and saying of "whoops" or "damn" under his breath each time. Meanwhile his sheath had plumped up quite nicely. When he flicked the gas stove on, the flame burst out around the burner. Mila jumped a little and clung tighter to the lean form of the lion. "I always forget how hot it can be," she said, her hand brushing in between Theo's legs and feeling that sheath pulse.

Again, the intrusive thoughts returned. "BD would have liked a more direct approach," it said. She responded with, "Yes, but Theo and Devon enjoy subtlety." And again, that was enough. The thought left.

Devon coughed. "Mila, as wonderful as it is to watch you, could you perhaps work at your station chopping vegetables for a bit? Distracting people at the stove is dangerous."

She pulled away, leaving her hand cupping the lion's sac as the last touch. For a while, she dutifully chopped vegetables as Devon commanded, but she was keenly aware of every time that Theo checked her way, which was often. She pretended not to notice.

"Oh no," Mila said. She had been preparing a honey drizzle sauce for a side dish of carrots and deliberately spilled a bit of honey onto her chest. "That will be so hard to get out." She pushed her breasts up and bent her head low, running her tongue through her fur. Of course she had only gotten about two drops of honey onto herself, but she ran her tongue in luxurious movements all the way out to her presented nipples, before licking her lips and purring.

The intrusive thoughts barely had time to form in her mind before Devon burst out, "Theo!" The corgi snatched his partner away from the stove, where the tufts of fur on his elbows had gotten dangerously close to the open flame. Devon flicked off every one of the burners quickly. "That's it. No more work at the stove today. Or with a knife."

Theo acquiesced before realizing what that meant. "Oh, sir, not more kneading dough."

"It's a bread day for you, my boy," the corgi said with a fake British accent that would have made Aisha cringe. "Because I would like you to make it through the day unburnt and with all your fingers intact."

So calico and lion were kept at the table for the rest of the day. Mila couldn't tease Theo all the time — she did actually want to learn — but she would inevitably find some way to wind him up about every half-hour or so, whether it was by leaning over to watch what he was doing in a way that put her breasts on display, or subtly brushing the handle of a whisk over her sex, or by cleaning a sampling spoon with her tongue in the most suggestive way she could. By noon, Theo was sporting a near constant erection despite Devon telling him to worry about it later.

Devon seemed to join in on the teasing fun during the later part of the day, finding one excuse after another for Mila and Theo to get close to one another and then for him to look away for just a moment or two, long enough for Mila to sneak in a grope to that twitching shaft, or a brush of her tail along Theo's leg, or pressing close enough to feel his body heat through her fur. Devon would then turn around, admonish the poor lion for being distracted and separate them again.

Theo tried more than once to excuse himself, saying he

needed to go clear his head, and Devon told him he needed to focus and could jerk off later.

The lessons for the day might as well not have existed. Mila found herself forgetting them as soon as Devon spoke them; she was too busy teasing Theo and wrestling with her inner demons. While Devon's tweaks had allowed her to deflect those intrusive thoughts with ease, it didn't stop them. She ended up spending any time she wasn't actively teasing Theo thinking about BD. She thought about him more than she had in the month since she entered the Eternal Party.

She was constantly thinking about what BD would have liked, how he would have reacted, and what he would have done to her in return. But as Alonso had suggested, the nature of the thoughts began to change as the day wore on. They stopped being so much about BD and started to be more about how she, Mila, enjoyed making BD have those reactions. And now she was making Theo react, not quite in the same way, but still.

While her teasing was directed at the lion, it started to work herself up just as well. Eventually the need within her own hips became too much. She started to rub herself not just to tease him but to take the edge off her own desire. She mewled out to Devon, asking if she and Theo could take a break.

"Oh, very well," the corgi said. "It's close to time for Alonso to come pick you up anyway."

Mila started to purr and she brushed aside several items from the top of the table with a sweep of her arm before climbing onto it, stalking towards the lion on all fours. He stood at stupefied attention, unable to take his eyes off her, but his shaft told the story of his need: it pulsed and twitched each time her hips swayed one way and then the other.

When she reached the edge of the table, mere inches from the lion and no longer needing to crawl forward, her hips continued to sway and her tail followed suit. Theo seemed paralyzed by the sight before him and watched as Mila pulled herself up to sit with her legs dangling off the edge. She bent her head and began to groom her fur carefully with her tongue, starting with delicate, light laps along her hands, but quickly progressed over her arms, around the curve of her shoulder, and down to her breasts, where she stayed, lifting them in her hands and drawing her tongue over every visible spot, including over her own now very stiff nipples. The calico alternated from one breast to the other, lifting them one at a time so that there was a constant rolling motion of her chest. When she finally finished the grooming and looked up, she kept the same motion on her chest so that the lion's gaze was transfixed by it.

Theo stared, slack-jawed. The only movement was a flexing of his hips as if some part of his hindbrain thought he was already buried inside her. The intrusive thoughts returned, but this time they only said, "I forgot how much I loved twirling a guy around my finger like this."

Without a word spoken, Mila slipped off the table, dropped to her knees, and pressed her breasts around the lion's shaft. He shuddered and reached out to the table for balance as she rubbed her breasts along his length. She didn't have the kind of massive chest like Jeta that could envelop his entire length, but she could still tease along most of his shaft at once, and leave the tip of his cock out so she could draw her tongue around it.

Theo was so worked up from a day full of teasing that he already showed signs of approaching the edge.

Which was exactly the worst time for Alonso to walk in.

Theo gave out a moan of regret, expecting to be pulled away as the fox regarded them both. Mila pulled Theo's tip into her mouth and suckled on it for just a second before greeting her owner in her huskiest voice possible, "Good evening, Master Alonso."

The fox's brow knitted. He had become very accustomed to Mila's strong resistance to being seductive. His tail curled apprehensively and he looked about ready to intervene.

Using a hand hidden from Theo and Devon by her own

breast, Mila gave the fox a thumbs up to let him know everything was fine.

He relaxed and gestured to the lion. "Go on. Finish up."

Theo breathed a sigh of relief and moved his hands from the table to Mila's shoulder. He had been letting her take the lead but now he started to grind and thrust his cock over her breasts. Mila looked up at him, running her tongue over her lips constantly as the lion got closer and closer to the edge. She watched his orgasm hit in the changing expression on his face: the tightening in his cheeks, the lips pulling back in a half snarl, the pinning down of his ears — and only then did she feel the hot liquid spurt onto the fur of her chest.

Mila kissed the tip of the shaft once before getting to her feet. As she did, she trailed a finger through the sticky liquid in her fur and cleaned her finger off with more slow licks. "Thank you, Theo," she said with a purr.

The lion had stumbled back against the counter opposite and looked about ready to faint with relief. He could only smile in an absent way as a response.

"Back to the art studio?" Mila asked Alonso as the fox took her hand.

He nodded and together they left the kitchen, heading downstairs. While proper submissive protocol dictated that she walk behind her owner, in deference to his status, now she walked out in front, far enough ahead that her naked backside was in full view of the fox and her swaying tail was held high to expose herself.

The stayed silent during the walk, but as soon as they were back in the private room and the door was locked behind them, he asked, "What's going on?"

Mila draped her arms around Alonso's neck, pressing in close but not so close that she threatened to smear Theo's cum all over the fox's shirt. "I asked Devon to make some changes to my personality, sir. I wanted to take this back for myself: I wanted to be seductive again." She batted her eyes at him. "May I choose the pose for today?"

"Go ahead, kitten." He stepped back to watch.

The calico requested two vulpine dildos from the house, silently hoping it would pick up the unspoken suggestion and model them after Alonso's dimensions. It did and offered her two toys whose only significant difference from the fox's shaft was that they both were in stereotypically black rubber. She set one on the ground before the chaise lounge and squatted down over it. Unused to the position, Mila balanced her back against the couch so that she could stay in position with the dildo halfway inside her.

As Alonso sat behind the easel, she angled her hips towards him, making sure her knees were spread to admit a good view. Even when she reached down to tease her clit with a finger, she did so from around the curve of her hip, to obscure as little of the view as possible. She held the remaining dildo in front of her muzzle and reached out with her tongue to just caress under the head of it. Mila let him know she was ready with a look.

"Freeze," Alonso commanded, and immediately Mila was fixed in place, the tension of holding the awkward half-thrust position being borne by the house.

Mila was pleased to note she was having a similar effect on Alonso as she had been on Theo earlier in the day. There was a definite tightness in his pants that had not been present on any of their previous sessions. Although he had steadily progressed into more risqué positions, they had done nothing so direct. As he worked, he had to adjust his erection more and more frequently.

Held in place as she was, Mila had little else to do but think. But instead of the pressing weight of BD's loss, she found herself for once reflecting on a happy memory of him. It had been two or three years ago. In an unusual turn of fate, Mila had a day off while BD was working, and he was texting her every twenty minutes with increasing frustration as work piled stress upon stress onto his head, while she texted back that she had gotten a present for him that he could open when he got home. His day kept getting worse. He got caught in traffic on the way home, adding an extra hour to his commute, and when he tried to stop by the grocery for a few items, he ended up being stuck behind someone whose card wasn't being read. When he finally made it home, she heard him stomping up the hall outside their apartment, then he threw open the front door with a bang, only to drop the grocery bags he carried as he caught sight of Mila. She was standing just inside the apartment, wearing nothing but a ribbon tied around her chest with a bow at her cleavage. "Going to open your present?" she asked.

BD had been so shocked that Mila had to close the door behind him before any neighbors saw her. She kicked aside the dropped groceries and whispered sensually in his ear. "You've had such a hard day. Now just relax and let me take care of everything." He was so tired he sank down right there in the entryway and she kissed him, massaged him, and soon fucked him. He'd had a bad day, but she'd managed to make it a good night. After that, if ever she was already home when he arrived, he'd tease her about not wearing a ribbon.

Mila was so lost in the memory she almost didn't notice when Alonso got up and made his way to her, pulling away the dildo that was at her lips and replacing it with his own shaft. The fox thrust into her muzzle without ceremony, and Mila almost laughed at the unusual sensation of the length entering her while she was unable to move even her lips without focusing. The freeze command kept her locked in place. If he had wanted her to be moving around a lot he would have released her from his command, so she simply let him use her muzzle as a warm hole to get off in, relishing in her ability to work him up.

There was a quick gush of his seed down her throat, which she swallowed away, and as he pulled his length out, he tapped the top of her muzzle and ordered her to return to her usual personality.

Mila stretched and grinned. "That felt good," she said.

He smiled as he tucked himself away. The fox glanced back at his art with a critical eye. "Might be one of the worst sketches I've done in a year or two. You were quite distracting."

Mila got up and put the dildos away, shaking her limbs to return some life to them. "Good. Want to try it again tomorrow?"

He wrapped an arm around her midriff unexpectedly and kissed her forehead. "That sounds like a lovely idea."

Despite Mila herself not getting off, she felt quite content. It was like a long lost part of her life had been restored to her. She even experimented as they returned to Alonso's room, holding her still cum-stained chest out to any passing canines and giving a wink. It had the desired effect; their progress back to Alonso's room was slowed by the many canines who stopped Alonso to ask when his kitten might be publicly available.

They returned to the room to find the door opening as they drew near.

Aisha was inside. "Get in," she said.

They stepped through and Aisha said, "Lock," in a strange ethereal voice. Mila's eyes turned back as she heard the lock click shut behind them, despite Aisha being on the far side of the room.

Mila's eyes went wide. "Mistress Aisha, you did it!"

The jackal held up a hand. Her face was deadly serious. "Yes, I can do basic magic properly now. No, it doesn't work on any of the exits. I've tried. But we have another problem. Sit down, please."

The fox and calico did so. "What's wrong?" Alonso asked.

"I finally managed to extract some more information from the house. Apparently it has an internal estimate of how long it will take you to get out. Mila, the house thinks you're making great progress. You'll probably be out in a few weeks. A few months at the worst."

"And me?"

The jackal's face was a mask of forced impassivity. "When I asked how long it would take you, I got no answer. The house isn't sure you'll make it."

Scherzo

It was Mila who broke the silence that followed. She looked into the fox's eyes and said, "We're not just going to leave you here forever."

Aisha shook her head dismissively. "I have no intention of just leaving him here, but Mila, if you have the opportunity to get out of here, you should take it."

"But—"

"She's right," Alonso said. The fox had taken a seat and was worrying the head of his cane. "We're prisoners, Mila. The most important thing is for us to get out." He forced a smile. "If you get the opportunity to leave, I want you to take it, understood?"

"Yes, sir." She fidgeted with her hands. "It just doesn't feel right to leave if there's more I could do."

He nodded. "I know." Alonso coughed. "Was there anything else, Aisha?"

"No." The jackal stood and smoothed down her dress. "I'll keep investigating."

Aisha left. The air felt heavy, as though some terrible weight hung above them on a frayed rope. After ten minutes of silence, Alonso told Mila to clean off her fur, and once Theo's seed was removed, the fox beckoned her wordlessly to come to bed.

Normally it was easy for Mila to fall asleep in Alonso's arms, but that night insomnia took over. Her mind whirled with thoughts about how they were going to escape the house and what, in particular, Alonso needed to do to escape. But as with most insomnia-driven thoughts, she kept circling back to things she had already dismissed.

The next night was the same, and the night after that, and the night after that. Alonso seemed to have no trouble relaxing — perhaps he had accepted his fate — but Mila rarely got more than an hour or two of sleep. At least the house's magic still ensured she woke up refreshed.

Days later, Mila was roused from her brief nap by Alonso, who was up unusually early. He pulled Mila to consciousness with soft kisses to her breast and a hand cradling her hip in a teasing way. Despite her lingering concerns, she giggled softly and pushed into the touch, encouraging him to be more energetic in his caresses until he was drawing sharp teeth along her nipples.

"Okay, okay," she said. "I'm up."

There was a shuffle of a paper sliding under the door and Alonso gave one more nip before deciding to get the day's event calendar. He stumbled out of bed, pulled on his robe, and then tore up the paper as soon as he had picked it up.

Mila had never seen such a reaction and sat up sharply in bed. "What is it?"

"There's an auction this afternoon."

"An auction?"

"Of felines," he said pointedly. "Canines can put their personal felines up for sale for a day. It transfers ownership, and all that entails, to the buyer temporarily. If you went up for auction, my protections would no longer work and you would be at the mercy of whoever bought you. So we will not be going."

Mila watched as the fox finished shredding up the schedule and chucked it into a garbage can near the door. "Sir," she asked quietly, "who decides on what events will be happening?"

"Why does it matter?"

The calico crawled forward to the edge of the bed. "It's important. Who decides?"

He shrugged. "If people want a particular event to run, they can set up a house committee, put it on a schedule, and have an announcement sent out."

"And if no one has set up an event?"

"There's a common rotation of things which occur."

"But who makes the decision?"

"I... don't know," he admitted.

Mila glanced at a nearby wall. "House, did you set up the auction today?"

Thump.

"Would it be good for me if I went to the auction?"

Thump.

"No," Alonso said fiercely. "Absolutely not. Out of the question."

Mila sat up on the bed, hands on her hips, and summoned every reserve of her strength to fight back against the magic of the house telling her to obey the fox. "You do not get to make that decision for me."

Anger flared in the fox's features. "I am your own—" Alonso froze, realizing what he was saying. He sat down and stared at the floor, tail curled between his legs. "You're right, Mila. I don't. It's the damn magic," he muttered.

Mila slid out of the bed and pulled a comforter along with, wrapping it around her body as she sat down next to him. "I think it'll be okay. The house knows what it is doing."

He gave her a sidelong glance of disbelief. "After everything it's done to us, why would you think that?"

"Well, it's an idea I've had for a while now," she said, not mentioning how much of her sleepless nights this idea had occupied. "My first night here, before I met you, I was wandering all over the house but no one caught me. That shouldn't have happened, unless..." She let the thought trail off for a moment and then addressed the house. "Did you make sure that Alonso was the first canine I would meet?"

Thump.

The fox's ears lifted and lowered as he worked through the implications of that statement. "It knew I'd keep you safe," he said.

The calico nodded. "I think it already knows how today will go if I go up for auction. It knows I'll be safe. Right?"

No response from the house.

"That's less encouraging," she admitted. "But it didn't say I was wrong." When Alonso stayed silent, she asked, "So what do you even bid at this auction? I've never seen anyone use money here."

"Favors," he said begrudgingly. "That's what we call the currency we use in house. All the canines start with a small share, and then whenever we perform a service for another canine, we pay in favors. The house keeps track of how many each canine has."

"Felines don't get favors?"

The fox shook his head. "If I tell a feline to get down and suck me off, they don't get to bargain for the price first. You are assumed to want to serve." Alonso sighed and rolled his shoulders as though uncomfortable. "Working canines in residence, like Aisha, Erik, or Devon, have hundreds of favors they can call on. I have about seventy myself."

Mila remembered the beautiful masquerade dress she had received from Erik and wondered if some favors had traded hands for that. She chose not to ask. "How did you get so many favors?"

Alonso turned his ears away, embarrassed. "I told you. I'm a rather in-demand dominant. Even owned felines want to have scenes with me, and their owners are willing to pay for that. I've done a few classes as well, and I usually get tips for that."

Mila bit her lip. So far as she knew, Alonso hadn't done any of that since she arrived. She'd been monopolizing all his time. "So the effect of this auction only lasts for one day?"

"Yes."

"I can survive one day with someone else."

"No, you can't." Alonso couldn't stay seated anymore. He forced himself to his feet and paced back and forth in front of her, cane cracking against the floorboards on each step. "Mila, I have been shielding you from the worst of this place. Most of the canines you've interacted with have been on the tame side of things. There are many here who will just want to use you and won't care about what you want. They will just assume you will be happy doing whatever they want, even if that means treating you as nothing more than a living sex toy."

"Could it really go that badly?"

"Yes, it could. That is why I ordered you..." He flinched at his own choice of words. "That's why I do not want you to go."

Mila clutched the comforter a little tighter around herself. "Sir, would you..." The words dried up in her mouth as she ran headlong into a command Alonso had given her so long ago she had almost forgotten it had existed. She had to work around the barrier in her mind. "Sir, if I go and things go badly, would you delete the memories of today from my mind?" There. She wasn't asking for her personality to be permanently altered to placate him as he had forbidden.

His jaw worked as he considered. "Only if I would also be allowed to command you to never do anything like this ever again."

"Deal," she said.

"And there's no way I can talk you out of this?"

"No."

"Fine. Then we should go to Erik to get you into suitable attire."

Suitable attire turned out to be leather, lots of leather.

In Erik's costume room, Mila was stripped naked for the first time in weeks. She had barely registered that the collar and corset hadn't come off, not even once. But then, she was unsurprised to see that they hadn't really needed to come off. Whatever magic sustained the house also made sure that its chosen uniform was kept conspicuously clean underneath without need for bathing.

It felt strange. She had gotten so used to walking around with bare breasts and sex, but having her belly uncovered felt naked now. She would have giggled if not for the serious expression on the fox's face.

Erik, assisted by Tricia still in robo-doll mode, brought out a variety of items to compare them against Mila. This time, they let her stay fully conscious and had a mirror placed in front of her so she could consider them as well. Her usual collar was replaced by a model that sported a d-ring at the front. Her new corset dropped any pretense of being latex-like and was clearly made of leather, with extra straps that wound over her shoulders. Some cuffs were added at her wrists and ankles — thin cuffs at Alonso's insistence. Finally a hood was fitted over her head, thankfully with large holes for her eyes, ears, and muzzle: it was decorative rather than restrictive.

Mila had always thought, since arriving at the house, that the standard uniform for felines looked like something out of a particular type of fetish magazine, a high-class one that spoke of cigar smoke and expensive drinks. Now she looked like she belonged in a different type of fetish magazine, one with a grungier vibe.

There wasn't anything they had to do after getting dressed before the auction itself, and Mila didn't feel like going to the kitchen, so they relaxed in Alonso's room. Rather, Mila relaxed, and Alonso remained stiff and aloof, barely speaking with her.

"It's time to go," Mila said, several cooking shows and multiple hastily-scribbled recipes later.

"So it is," Alonso said dispassionately, as if he had hoped the time for the auction would pass and Mila would just forget. He stood and dressed himself in clothes a touch more formal than his usual ensemble — he even added cufflinks — before beckoning her out of the room.

Like on the night of the masquerade ball, there was a steady flow of traffic in the house heading from the various second-floor rooms down towards the grand ballroom, which had been remade once more. The stage was now a simple wooden platform with two tiers. Up on the highest tier, an auctioneer — the same coyote who had introduced Mila to the Eternal Party — stood, warming up his throat with vocal exercises. On the next tier down were several felines leashed to posts with their name on a chalkboard hung above them. All the felines on the auction block were dressed similarly to Mila, in over-leathered versions of the usual house garb, and all the canines were dressed as formally as Alonso. She barely knew the other felines who were up for auction: she recognized Mason, the Sphynx cat she'd first met at the suspension bondage demo, but that was it.

In the crowd, Mila bumped into Vivien and Natalie. The lynx and cougar seemed a bit surprised to see them, but Vivien purred out, "Hello, Alonso," with a simpering smile.

"Ladies." Alonso's voice was monotone and he did not look to either of them. He just continued to march past as Vivien's jaw dropped.

"I'm so sorry," Mila mouthed as she walked past.

Alonso steadily walked Mila up to the auction block. "Last chance to back out," he muttered under her breath, as they grew near.

But Mila kept her mouth shut. She was doing this.

The fox led her to an unoccupied post, took the rope from it, and tied it to Mila's collar. Her ears flicked up as she heard a scratching of chalk and found her name being written (by the house itself, it seemed) on the board above the post. Alonso lingered a moment, squeezing her shoulder, then turned and left her.

Mila took a deep breath and tried to hold back a shiver of

trepidation. The other felines waiting at their posts looked much more excited to be there.

"Ladies and gentlemen!" the coyote's voice, amplified by speakers, boomed throughout the room. "Today's auction is about to begin. If you would all take your seats, the drones will bring out your bidding cards."

At a snap of the coyote's fingers, six felines appeared from behind a curtain. While Mila and the others up for auction were all dressed in excess leather, these newcomers were dressed head to toe in matching black latex. The heels on their identical boots were so high it made Mila's ankles ache in sympathy, and their heads were covered in heavy, feature-disguising masks. It wasn't just that she couldn't tell who was under each mask, she could hardly distinguish the species of each. The only reason she thought one of them was a bobcat was because that one had a shorter tail than the rest.

In perfect synchronicity, the drones began to walk down from the upper platform and out into the crowd, walking down the aisles one at a time and handing out cards. "Remember everyone," the coyote said, "if you try to bid more favors than you possess, your number will turn red and your bid will not count."

Several canines and felines hovered around the periphery of the room, only interested in watching the proceedings. Vivien and Natalie were there, casting worried glances between Mila up on stage and Alonso who was fuming in his seat. A drone approached the fox and offered a card, which he only took when there appeared to be no other way to make the feline move on.

When they had finished, the six drones marched back up to the stage. As one they unzipped their suits over their groin and knelt down over dildos arranged in front of the coyote's podium. Then they went still.

"For our first auction of the night, Mason!" the coyote announced. A buff wolf who would not have been out of place as a bouncer, unhooked Mason from the first post and guided him to a point of prominence where everyone could see the Sphynx. "Starting bid is three favors."

The bidding went quickly, with Mason being purchased for thirteen favors. Next was a tortoiseshell who went for a quick five favors. Then a cheetah who Mila didn't recognize, and who did several cartwheels and splits with the coyote commenting, "Yes, folks, she really is that flexible." She went for an even twenty.

The most ferocious bidding war came for the punk lioness Mila recognized from Alonso's portraits. The big cat ran a pierced tongue over her lips and thrust out her chest to various canines to entice them to bid on her. She ultimately topped out at thirty-five favors.

The closer it came to be Mila's turn, the more her pulse started to race. The sound of her heartbeat started to echo like a drum in her ears, drowning out the sounds of the auction.

And then the piano sounded out.

Mila's ears shot up and she looked around to see if anyone else heard the music, but everyone's attention was on the auction block. The piano played a few notes, a soft half-melody, and then lapsed into silence. "Okay, house," Mila whispered, "I'm trusting you on this one."

Then it was Mila's turn. As the wolf came to undo her lead from the post, his fingers seemed to take longer than usual to undo the knot. "You look scared," he said under his breath.

The calico blinked up at him. His bulk mostly hid her from the audience. So she gave a little nod.

"Everyone gets first time jitters," he said. "Just remember, most people out there want to bid on someone who would be happy to be theirs. So try to enjoy yourself." He got the knot undone but didn't pull the rope away from the post yet. "Ready?"

"Yes, sir," she said.

As he took her to the front of the stage, she tried to remember the feelings Devon had induced in her, feelings of seduction and desire. It was a little harder without the corgi's commands helping to guide her thoughts, but she managed. By the time she made it to the front of the stage, her hands covered her breasts and her tail coiled around her hips to teasingly hide her sex. Mila tried to catch the eye of a few in the audience and wink at them, as though to convey the idea that she'd show them her fully naked body once they bought her.

Noel, the maned wolf, raised his Stetson instantly and bellowed out, "Five!" Belatedly he remembered to hold up his card.

Mila knew the wolf had been trying to get Mila from Alonso since they'd first met. He'd been eager to "try her out" in his words, but beyond that, he hadn't seemed worrisome. Being bought by him wouldn't be too bad.

"Seven," called out a German shepherd. Mila was stunned to realize it was the same one who she had spied on in the dungeon right after being trapped in the house. She didn't recall having seen him any other time since then. Consciously, Mila knew that the command to desire the dog had been long since excised by Alonso, but still a part of her wanted to be with him.

"Ten." It was Erik. The husky gave a knowing nod to Mila. He wouldn't be too bad either, she thought. She'd already been a doll around him once.

So far Alonso's concerns had been overwrought. The first three bidders all seemed like good options to Mila.

"Eleven," Noel declared, but as he held up his number, it flashed red. He growled and threw down his hat.

"That bid does not count," the coyote announced for those who could not see.

"Twelve," said a heavily built dhole.

"Fifteen," countered Erik.

There was a pause, and the coyote auctioneer was warming up his voice, when a trio of college-aged dogs in the front row raised their hands as one and called out a bid of twenty favors. Mila gave the three a flirting bat of her eyelashes. She didn't recognize them, but something about them made her uneasy: they reminded her of drunk frat boys with little care or concern for the women around them.

The coyote auctioneer waited a longer beat this time. "Are there any other bids? Going once."

"Twenty-five." The voice was calm but assertive, and Mila scanned the crowd to find the bidder. It was Zuberi, the painted dog. The jaguar Ingrid was curled up at his feet.

Not to be outdone one of the frat boys in the front row leaned forward and quickly called out, "Thirty."

"Thirty-five," Zuberi said, with no more agitation than he had before.

The coyote laughed. "It seems we have a real bidding war. I will remind the audience that if they do not have enough favors individually, they can pool resources." This was obviously a tip of the hand to the trio in the front row, who conversed with each other quickly, before calling out a bid of forty.

"Forty-five," Zuberi said.

"Fifty."

Someone in the room let out an uncharacteristic whoop. Heads were snapping from Zuberi to the trio and back again. Now they lingered on the painted dog and waited for his bid. Mila herself stood stock still, unsure how to react to this turn of events.

"Fifty-five."

"Sixty." One of the trio was starting to get cold feet and was tugging on the lead canine to stop him.

"Sixty-five."

"Ninety!" The lead frat boy jumped up the bid in an an effort to force Zuberi out.

Someone let out a low whistle. There was a murmur in the crowd.

"One hundred," the painted dog said without concern.

The trio in the front row conversed with one another rapidly. But ultimately there was a sad shake of a head to the coyote auctioneer.

"I heard one hundred favors. Going once! Going twice! Sold to Master Zuberi!"

As the auctioneer's gavel rang down, Mila felt a shift in the world, as though a tinted lens had slid before her eyes. She knew immediately that Alonso was no longer her owner. She belonged to Zuberi — Master Zuberi, she corrected herself. She just had to hope that the house knew what it was doing.

Applause broke out in the room, more enthusiastic than it had been during any of the previous bids: people had seen a bit of action this time and wanted to show their appreciation.

Mila was led back to her post to wait out some finishing announcements from the coyote. She scanned the audience and saw Alonso there, not watching her, but instead staring daggers at Zuberi. The painted dog seemed unruffled, if he even noticed, and he placidly stroked over Ingrid's head.

When the coyote was done, the wolf unhooked each feline from their post one at a time and led them out to their new temporary owner. He worked quickly and efficiently and in a matter of seconds, he had hold of Mila and was guiding her out into the audience, pushing her in front of Zuberi, who was in the middle of an animated conversation with Alonso.

When Mila approached, Zuberi held up his hand. "Enough," the painted dog said with a hint of a snarl. "Alonso, have I ever given you reason to think I have mistreated Ingrid?"

The fox crossed his arms and glowered. "No."

"Then why do you act like I would mistreat Mila?"

"She is different."

"And so she will be treated differently. I will not argue with you. The auction is completed. Mila is mine for the remainder of the day." The painted dog looked sharply to the jaguar and then to the calico. "Follow," he commanded.

It was an order from her owner. Mila was powerless to disobey. So complete was the strength of Zuberi's command that she couldn't even stop and say goodbye to Alonso, but only managed to extend her tail out to him and brush it against his hand before she was led away. She fell into step alongside Ingrid, two steps back from the dog. It was very clear that he led and there would be no questions about where or why. Mila could feel the guiding hand of the house's magic instructing her on what her new owner expected.

Although her head was kept bowed, the calico could still look around. She looked first to her new owner and fellow kitten. Ingrid was wearing the outfit Mila had seen her in most often around the house — lots of cuffs with handy restraining points — but Zuberi on the other hand lacked his usual leather and metal accents. His suit would have been perfectly at home at a high-end business conference. Mila then glanced over her shoulder and tried to find Alonso in the crowd. The fox was being approached by Vivien, but as soon as the lynx tried to touch his shoulder, he jerked away and stalked off in a different direction. At least Natalie was there to console the lynx.

As Mila turned her head forward again, she caught Ingrid's gaze, and the jaguar suggested with a pointed glance that Mila ought to be keeping her gaze, not just her head, lowered as well. She looked down and focused her attention on the painted dog's slim tail.

Although neither Zuberi nor Ingrid said anything, Mila could tell they were headed for the dungeons below. Today the basement was bustling with activity; practically every chamber was in use. Even then, Zuberi was attracting attention. Several couples stopped their scenes to watch the trio pass, and a small coterie began to follow them.

They kept walking deeper into the dungeon, traveling a maze of pathways and passing so many differently themed spaces that Mila lost track of where she was. They finally stopped in a room lined with cement on three sides and a heavy curtain on the fourth. Curiously to the calico, there were targets displayed on one wall. Were it not for the lack of guns or bows, Mila might have thought they were at a shooting range. Instead there were a few throwing implements, knives and axes, as well as a hefty whip that Zuberi picked off the wall.

Mila knew the painted dog gave frequent and very well attended demonstrations in the evening, but she never had an interest in any of the topics. She wasn't going to get a choice in the matter tonight.

Ingrid knelt before her owner, knees on bare concrete, so Mila did the same, wincing slightly at the discomfort.

Zuberi noticed and, in total silence, fetched a small pad for Mila to rest her knees on. While he was occupied, the calico dared to look up and saw that the curtain had been pulled back to admit the small crowd that had followed them. They all stood in silence at the threshold of the chamber, watching intently. Mila's eyes flicked back down just as Zuberi placed the pad in front of her. She wanted to say thank you, but somehow knew that was wrong, so she just moved onto the pad and bowed her head in appreciation.

Zuberi stood in front of her, his hands twisting over the whip and making the leather creak. He held the dangerous-looking item right before Mila's face. "Do you know what this is?"

"A whip, sir?"

"Correct. Do you know what kind of whip?"

"A... bullwhip, sir?"

"Also correct."

A lucky guess on Mila's part. She didn't know any other kinds of whips.

Zuberi let the long cord of leather uncoil in his hands, holding onto the handle only. "This whip was specifically designed to crack. The tip of the whip can move so fast it causes a small sonic boom."

Without hesitation, and giving no prior indication of what he was doing, Zuberi demonstrated by flicking the whip towards the targets on the wall. The shock of the crack made Mila's ears go flat.

"Ingrid. Some candles."

The jaguar sprang to her feet and fetched a series of candles from the supply cabinet in the room, and she placed them on a table near the bullseyes. The jaguar lit each of the candles, bowed, and resumed her place next to the calico.

Zuberi stepped forward. There was a soft intake of breath around the room as everyone waited. Mila felt an invisible hand pulling her gaze up: her owner wanted her to watch.

Zuberi's arm swung out, the whip sailed through the air, there was a sharp crack, and one candle was snuffed out. After a brief pause, the cycle repeated: swing, sail, crack, snuff. Then again, faster and faster, until the last two candles had no pause between them, Zuberi beginning the motion of one before the previous had completed.

There was the lightest, most muffled applause from the onlookers. The display was so impressive, they really had to express it somehow, even though the dictates of the scene would normally want them to be silent.

Mila kept her mouth shut and her hands at her side. Ingrid hadn't reacted except to beam up at her owner, so Mila just smiled in agitated approval.

Zuberi coiled the whip up and made a small flick of one large ear. "Ingrid, the stick."

The jaguar once more leaped into action. She pulled out a small, thin piece of wood that looked like an elongated matchstick and placed it between her teeth, pointing directly in front of her. Then she stepped just to the side of one bullseye, so the stick's tip laid squarely at the center of the target.

Zuberi rolled his shoulders and in one smooth motion, flicked the whip out towards Ingrid. It was hard to tell what happened, other than that the stick was now half an inch shorter. "Step," he commanded, and Ingrid moved with equal precision half an inch forward so that Zuberi's target had not changed.

The whip cracked out again. "Step." The whip cracked. "Step." Faster and faster each time, with the stick growing shorter and shorter.

Mila felt a tension growing in her shoulders. He should be slowing down. The stick was getting too short. He was going to hurt her.

The calico counted: two inches. One and a half inches. One inch. Half an inch. Nothing.

Zuberi's arm wound up for another strike.

"Master Zuberi, no!" Mila flung herself forward, trying to stop him. But it was too late. The whip sailed through the air with the same precision he had demonstrated so many times already. Straight towards Ingrid's muzzle.

Rondo

It missed.

The whip sailed through the air on a direct trajectory to break Ingrid's nose and then, a split-second before connecting, space bent around the whip. It turned to the side as if deflected and cracked harmlessly just in front of Ingrid's muzzle.

A deathly silence filled the room and all eyes turned to Mila. Ingrid, Zuberi, and the entire crowd were watching her. She was clutching at the painted dog's leg like a vice. She let go and sat back, ears flat.

The silence filled in with the sound of the whip being dragged along the ground as Zuberi once more coiled it and held it in front of Mila. "Stand," he said in those deep expansive tones of his.

Mila got to her feet. She forced herself to look into Zuberi's face so she wouldn't have to see the crowd watching them. She shivered, expecting anger or disappointment, but finding instead curiosity in the painted dog's umber eyes.

"Why did you do that?" he asked.

Her owner asked her a question. She had to answer. But while she did feel compelled to answer, there was no haste in the question. She could put together her thoughts and answer with reflection. "I..." she started and then felt the shift of anticipation in the audience watching them. She dropped her voice lower. "I wasn't going to let you hurt her."

He didn't blink. He didn't look elsewhere. He kept staring straight into her. Mila became distantly aware that he was tapping the coiled whip against his leg. Then the spell was broken: he turned to gesture to Ingrid, who was still standing with the tiniest tip of the stick in her mouth. "I've performed this little scenario for many newcomers to the Eternal Party. It is a lesson and also a test. What should you do if you see a dominant endangering their submissive? Most felines fail: they do not try to stop me. They are so wrapped up in the fantasy of serving a master that they believe I have the right to do whatever I want, even if it would harm another or even themselves. Blind, unthinking trust. It is good you did not fall into that trap."

Mila could feel a "but" was coming.

"But..."

And there it was.

The painted dog held up a finger. "You do know that the house prevents injuries, do you not?"

Mila nodded, but something told her that was insufficient and she quickly added, "Yes, sir."

"And yet you tried to stop me from harming Ingrid even knowing I could not?" The question was rhetorical. Mila felt no compulsion to answer. "Your problem is not that you trust me too much, but that you trust me too little, me and the magic of this place."

Mila wanted to retort and say that she trusted the house in ways none of them could understand — after all, she'd trusted it through this auction process — but she said nothing. In part, because she would be speaking out of turn and she knew that was bad, but also because she knew it wasn't entirely the truth. She did trust the house a little, but she had to force herself to take that leap of faith today.

"I'm sorry, sir," she said, staring down at a spot on the floor.

A caress of leather under her chin lifted her back up. The bull-whip, which had seemed so fearsome a moment before, was surprisingly gentle against her fur now. "What do you have to be sorry for, Mila?"

"I failed. Didn't I?"

The painted dog tipped his head to one side, and the ear there flicked down with him. "You did, but in a lesson, failure should only be seen as an opportunity for growth, not a source of regret. Do you understand?"

Mila nodded. "Yes, sir." She felt like she was beginning to understand why the house wanted her here today. She'd thought Zuberi's demonstrations were entirely physical, not psychological. It was part of the reason she'd not attended them before.

Zuberi handed the whip off to Ingrid, who dutifully placed it back on the wall. "While that was a lesson, this is for me. Mila, stand, turn around, and bend forward, tail over your back."

Mila got into position, fully expecting the sharp stinging spanks that followed. She gasped all the same as they landed and when she was allowed to stand back up, she winced lightly from the heat that radiated out from her butt.

"Now, let us retire to my room for some privacy."

There was a disappointed sound from the onlookers, who were clearly hoping for more of a show. Mila couldn't blame them. Minus nearly seeing Ingrid get injured, she would have paid money to watch such a skillful demonstration of the whip.

Mila squirmed and felt the tingling afterimage of the painted dog's hand against her rump. "Sir?"

The painted dog looked up from doing a bit of clean-up.

"Is it possible to pass the test?"

He chuckled. "Of course. Several have. You could have chosen to not stop me because you knew the house would protect Ingrid, or you may have chosen to stop me earlier, concerned that I was demonstrating poor safety standards."

"Really, sir? Someone did that?"

"Jay," he said after a fractional hesitation, unsure if Mila had met Jeta Horowitz. "She had quite a bit of experience before entering the Eternal Party. She knew what an unsafe dom looked like."

Zuberi snapped his fingers, and Mila fell back into step along Ingrid as they left the dungeon and headed upstairs. The calico followed, quiet and submissive behind her Master, but a spark of rebellion had started within her. The docile mindset that the house kept trying to force on her did not match the gentleness that Zuberi had shown. The magic kept trying to make her think that the painted dog was her master now and forever, and she fought to remember that this was all just a play, an act for the day. Alonso was her owner.

The calico took a deep breath and swore to herself that she wouldn't forget that.

Zuberi's room was a stark contrast to Alonso's. Mila had only seen inside one suite — that of the fox's — and she didn't realize how different the decor could be. The layout of Zuberi's room was functionally the same, but beyond that they had very little in common. The furnishings were all black, either in latex or leather. Instead of a comfy reading chair in the corner, there was a bondage chair with more straps than Mila could quickly count. Even the couch had anchor points dotting the sides. A spanking bench dominated the center of the room and a number of vertical suspension devices were fitted against the walls. Where Alonso's fireplace and TV were, Zuberi instead had a massive glass cabinet full of sex toys of all kinds. Mila had seen less stocked sex shops.

The calico once again felt stymied by her lack of knowledge. Sure, her time at the Eternal Party had been educational and she had learned the purpose of many of the items on the shelves, but she'd never needed to consider the price of any of them. She looked at a gas mask on one shelf and couldn't tell if it was supposed to cost fifty dollars or five thousand. It was another blank hole in her knowledge, and she hated that.

While Zuberi waited just inside the door, Ingrid continued on ahead. Ingrid stopped in front of the glass cabinet and with a flick of her tail, indicated a spot on the carpet. Mila silently knelt down there, looking up at the arrayed shelves of items with a quickened pulse.

"Ingrid, dress me," the painted dog commanded.

Mila was surprised to see the dressing command be obeyed with a kiss to start. The jaguar sauntered over to the dog and practically draped herself over Zuberi's front, arms around him, legs entwined with his, lips kissing hungrily, needily along his muzzle. Ingrid had portrayed the role of dutiful silent servant so well tonight that Mila had almost forgotten that her standard role with Zuberi was as his beautiful bound princess and that their affection for each other was barely contained by their rules of propriety in public.

As Ingrid worked her way from his cheek to his shirt collar via kisses, she undid his tie and set it aside. She slipped slowly downward. Buttons came apart along his shirt, one languid kiss at a time, until her lips hovered above his belt and her breathing came harder. Her fingers fumbled for the first time as they tried to pry his belt loose, so engrossed was she in the scent and feel of his fur.

When Ingrid did manage to get his belt off, she tugged his pants down just enough to reveal his sheath and immediately buried her nose in against it, lavishing attention over that spot. But it was over quickly. Zuberi pushed her away with a stern but loving command to focus. The jaguar licked her lips and whined, but did as she was told. She shucked off the dog's shoes so that she could pull off his pants one leg at a time. Then she stood, sliding her arms down along his as she removed his shirt and jacket in one smooth motion. Although many of the items were initially just tossed aside, the jaguar took a moment to neaten the discarded clothes before fetching something new to wear.

Zuberi's new clothes turned out to be the leather Mila associated him most with: boots, chaps, a chest harness, gloves, and to top it off, a cap. When finished, Ingrid gripped the straps of his harness and held him close, pressing her muzzle in against his chest. For a moment, he held her just as tightly, then he spun her around, grasped her by the scruff and shoved her against the nearby wall. A hand slid between her thighs and as Mila watched, inserted three fingers deep between her folds with ease. "You are absolutely soaked, Ingrid. You are too distracted. Mila," he called out, "fetch me the item on the top shelf, farthest to the left."

Mila obeyed, finding a chastity belt in the indicated space, except with two dildos on the inside. She offered it to Zuberi.

"Lube," he said. "In the supply chest." He nodded to a box on the floor not far away.

Mila fetched the lube and, at his insistence, added some to the two dildos before helping to lift Ingrid's legs and thread them into the belt. Zuberi took it from there, grinding the two dildos against her entrances to work the lube over her before pressing them in. Ingrid kept her complaints down to a needy whine. Zuberi turned a key in a special lock, cinching the belt tighter over her hips and then, as he let go of her scruff, he looped the key around a cord on his neck, so it shone there like a pendant.

Ingrid turned around and the couple shared another passionate kiss.

Zuberi patted the jaguar's hips with a push to have her stand to one side. "Now that you are taken care of, and I'm dressed, Mila, stand at attention."

The calico found herself standing forward, stretching herself up to her full height and holding her hands behind her. She didn't know how she knew that particular pose. More magic of the house, she guessed.

The painted dog stood in front of her, one gloved hand running over her side. "Tell me how you are feeling, Mila."

"Overwhelmed," she answered, before she even had time to process the command. "Anxious. Scared. Fascinated."

"All natural reactions. I take it you did not have much experience with kink before you entered the house."

Mila nodded.

Zuberi stepped around behind the calico, his heavy boots

thudding as he moved. "I was like you when I first entered this world. I was terrified by all I saw before me."

"You, sir?"

Ingrid shot her a look, as though Mila had spoken out of turn.

Zuberi ignored it and spread one arm out towards the expansive cabinet. "Can you guess, Mila, what item in here frightened me the most?"

The calico crept forward and looked more closely through the items on the shelves. She struggled to name all of them, but eventually pointed to a sleep-sack that hung on one side of the cabinet.

"Why that one?"

"Claustrophobia is common. And that looks really claustrophobic."

A smile crossed the painted dog's muzzle. "A logical deduction. Fears that exist outside the realm of kink can be brought into it. And you are very near the mark. You just picked the wrong starting fear."

Zuberi reached into the cabinet and picked out a candle, not that dissimilar from the ones he had snuffed out with the bullwhip a short while ago.

For a moment, Mila thought Zuberi was pulling a practical joke on her and she stifled a giggle. Ingrid shot her another dirty look and Mila realized he was being serious. "Fire," she realized.

"Fire," the painted dog agreed. "When I was a pup, my house was always full of candles. And every night, my mother would snuff out the candles by pinching them between her fingers. She would always leave the last one, and ask me to do the same, but I could not. My mind was full of nightmares of my fur catching on fire, being helpless to stop the spread, and dying in agony, burned alive. I feared the candles and stayed as far away from them as I could."

Zuberi handed the candle to Ingrid, who used a match to light it. The jaguar dropped to her knees to grope the dog. Her palm ground against the sheath and she tugged at the dog's sac sharply. Mila watched as Zuberi's shaft slipped into the air and throbbed, requiring only a few moments before becoming fully erect.

Ingrid had been holding the candle far away from him, but now brought it closer. She waved the candle to either side of the dog's shaft, so the heat was near enough to be felt, before sliding it underneath. The tip of the flame danced just out of reach of his cock. The fire flickered and swayed and, one time, seemed to reach up to caress his skin. Zuberi was breathing harder, and he could no longer keep still. His shaft throbbed once, lifting away, but then it rebounded and dipped perilously close to the flame's embrace. The painted dog started to pant heavily.

"Continue, princess," he said.

Ingrid moved the candle away and leaned in to flick her tongue over the tip of Zuberi's shaft, which had formed a bead of pre. She grinned up at him as she swallowed this down, with a look on her face like she had gotten away with sneaking in dessert before dinner.

"I said continue, princess." Zuberi's tone was admonishing, but his demeanor was affable.

She lifted the candle high over the dog's shaft. And then, with a motion so delicate Mila at first didn't notice it, tipped the candle to one side. A bead of wax slipped over the side, forming a small raised path along the side of the candle as it cooled. But a tiny drop survived the descent and dripped down to land directly onto Zuberi's shaft.

Zuberi snarled. His hands clenched into fists. His cock jumped. The wax hardened so fast that even this quick motion was not enough to dislodge it and it stayed stuck to his skin.

More drops followed the first and they formed a small cluster over the bouncing shaft.

Once the growing disk of wax was the size of a quarter, Ingrid set the candle aside and came in so close, her lips almost touched the tip of Zuberi's shaft. She ran a finger along the clean side of his length, and as Mila watched, extended a claw out, which she used to catch under the edge of the wax and peel it off.

Immediately the jaguar leaned in, lavishing her tongue over the spot while Zuberi sighed in contentment. When he relaxed again, his gaze slid to the calico. "Once, the flame was my greatest fear. Now, this is one of my favorite activities. Come," he said and stepped away from Ingrid, whose head tried to move with the shaft, but she was unable to keep up.

Mila fell in beside him, looking out over the massive cabinet.

"Tell me what in here frightens you the most."

It was an order. She had to obey. But again there was patience behind the command. She had time to examine her own thoughts and feelings.

The calico lifted a finger and pointed. "That one."

"Ah, a Wartenberg pinwheel." The device Zuberi picked off the shelf had a thin handle attached to a small wheel covered in sharp needle-like spikes. "Why does it frighten you more than the others?"

"Because it looks like it's meant to peel someone's skin off, sir."

He nodded and held the device up. He also held up a hand, open-palmed, facing her. It was an offering. "I can help you overcome your fear," he said. "But only if you truly trust me. I won't hurt you and I won't let you be hurt, but you need to believe that before we can continue."

He held himself there, hand extended, and waited with infinite patience. Mila could feel Ingrid's eyes on her as well. They were waiting to see if she could trust him, to do what she could not in the dungeons below.

"I don't know if I can," she admitted, and quickly added, "but I do trust you to do your best."

The painted dog's head tilted. He seemed to be considering. "That may have to do," he said. "Are you willing to try?" His hand was still waiting for her.

Mila reached out partway before snatching her hand back. "Do I have to watch?"

"No, you do not."

She squeezed her eyes shut and placed her hand in his.

With no sight, she could only rely on her sense of touch to tell what Zuberi was doing. The heat of his body drew nearer and she felt him place first his hand, then the pinwheel against the thicker fur of her upper arm. His hand moved first, and then the pinwheel followed, drawing a line through her fur up towards her shoulder, but the fur dampened the prickling sensations, so that it felt like an insect crawling over her. That visual was not a helpful one.

But it didn't hurt. She took a shuddering breath as she felt the hand and wheel cross the curve of her shoulder and follow the new leather strap of the corset in towards her chest. There, in the thick fluff of her fur, she could barely feel the pinwheel's progress, and Zuberi pulled his hand away so she could no longer anticipate how it would move. She bit her lip as it headed towards one of her breasts.

Just like Zuberi had described, a nightmare haunted her, of her flinching and driving the spikes of the wheel into herself.

She felt the toy pass through thinner and thinner fur as it progressed up her breast. Each prick was sharper than the last, until she finally felt it touch her bare skin.

Mila couldn't help it. She gasped. And the gasp made her chest heave.

The calico went completely still. She was expecting to feel the spikes plunging through her skin. But she felt... almost nothing.

She cracked one eye open and saw the pinwheel resting gently against her nipple. She cracked the other eye open and watched as the pinwheel moved with her chest as she panted hard. Zuberi's grip on the handle of the pinwheel was so loose that it happily moved with her and even when he added a bit of pressure with his thumb, she felt only like she was being roughly poked, not the needle jab of pain she had been expecting.

A nervous laugh bubbled up through her throat, which became an honest laugh as Zuberi began to roll the wheel back and forth over her nipple, the tiny motions ticklish. She squirmed in place and Zuberi had to order Ingrid to hold her from behind so that he could continue. The laughter grew again as the wheel ran over her other nipple, with Zuberi varying the pattern of the motion so that she was always left guessing.

Then he began to wheel it over her corset (which meant she felt almost nothing), driving it towards her sex. Her breath caught again, but from anticipation, not fear. When he slid the wheel along her clit and then around her labia, she squirmed roughly. It was a curious feeling, somewhere in between being tickled on her clit (that had never happened before) and being teased with claws. She didn't quite know what to make of it.

Zuberi set the pinwheel aside and gave the Mila time to recover her breath. "Are you afraid of this any more, Mila?"

The calico panted and shook her head. "No. Thank you, sir."

The painted dog dipped both his ears in acknowledgment. Then he spread his arms wide, encompassing the whole of the cabinet behind him. "Just think. I made you chose your greatest fear, and ultimately it made you laugh. What might the other implements in here do? Are you willing to let me introduce you to them?"

Mila nodded. "I am, sir."

The next thing Zuberi showed Mila was impact play. The two felines were made to lean up against a bare spot on the wall. Mila could tell it was a frequent order for Ingrid, because there were claw furrows in the wood near where she placed her hands.

Zuberi showed off a flogger first, running the tassels along Mila's back to get her used to them. "I'm surprised Alonso has not introduced you to these. He is quite fond of the art of the swing."

The calico tried to hide how stunned she was. In her month of captivity, Alonso had expressed hardly any interest in whips, crops, floggers, or paddles. It occurred to her, belatedly, that despite all her sexual explorations, there were still notable gaps.

But that was easy enough to fix. She could ask her Master if he would set up a playdate between her and Alonso tomorrow so that the fox could show her how he handled a—

That thought was buried under a weight of righteous anger in Mila's mind. The house was again trying to make her forget that Alonso was her true owner. Zuberi couldn't set up a playdate for her tomorrow; he wasn't going to be her Master tomorrow.

Thankfully, the painted dog was too distracted to notice the agitated ear flicks and tensed muscles in the calico. The calico forced herself to watch as Zuberi ran the same flogger over Ingrid's back, teasing both felines the same way.

Then the flogger behind the jaguar swept away and came down on her shoulder. She stifled a purr of pleasure on her next breath.

Mila told herself not to tense when she felt the tassels leave her back, but she did anyways. It came down with a sensation she could only describe as being clapped firmly on the back. Zuberi continued to alternate striking Ingrid and then Mila. The calico tried to just experience it and not worry about anything. The point where the blows landed crept down her back on one side, then went back up the other. Once he had completed a full circuit, he began to pick up the pace, the strikes coming faster and harder, until there was no pause between a strike to Ingrid and a strike to Mila: it was all part of the same continuous swinging movement. Mila felt like she was getting the most unusual deep tissue massage she had ever received.

The calico jumped a little when the rhythm changed. Suddenly there were two short strikes in a row and a glance over her shoulder told Mila that Zuberi had one flogger in each hand. She wasn't sure when he had picked up the second one. Had it been there the whole time and she had not noticed?

With two floggers and two women before him, the painted dog played across their backs like he was performing a drum solo, with quick snare rolls along Ingrid's back with the occasional sharp base drum strike to Mila's shoulders. His arms swung through the air sometimes, and at others, he somehow achieved quick, wild motions with barely a flick of his wrists.

Mila felt a warmth spreading over her back. The cumulative effect of the blows felt like she had exercised hard and had that pleasurable ache that came with overexerting herself.

She gave a soft sigh when the flogging came to an end and Zuberi simply caressed her. But Ingrid gave out a needy mewl, whimpering for more as she pressed against the wall.

Zuberi patted Mila's shoulder. "One moment."

He stepped away and came back with a weighty leather paddle with several heavy metal studs along its length. Zuberi lunged forward and dug his claws in under the jaguar's collar, jerking her head back just as he delivered a savage string of blows to her ass that all neatly avoided her chastity belt. Mila was worried the house had allowed her to be harmed, but the expression on her face was one of ecstasy. "You little slut," he growled out as he finished his strikes. He continued to hold her close, grinding his slick shaft against her ass as though he regretted placing her in chastity.

Zuberi chuckled as he stepped away to put the paddles back, and Ingrid was left to wave her butt in the air and flex her claws, adding new divots to the wall.

"Sir," Mila called out. She turned her head to watch Zuberi place the paddle into the cabinet.

"Yes, Mila?"

"I was wondering if..." The calico stuttered, unable to give voice to the desire inside her, so she diverted to something else that had been bugging her. "You keep calling Ingrid princess. Is she really?"

The painted dog let out a short bark of laughter. "Those rumors have been going around for years and you are the first to ask about them directly. No, Mila, she's not actually a princess. She is noble though."

The jaguar rolled her eyes.

Zuberi cleared his throat. "She doesn't care much for the title. She's technically the third child of a baron, which as I understand it means she has little chance to inherit anything other than a disdain for us peasant types." He winked at Mila.

Mila giggled and bit her lip. The desire inside her continued to call out and would not be ignored. "I don't think I'm ready for a spanking like that," she said, nodding to Ingrid's backside, "but could I try something a little more intense?"

He paused, and hefted the paddle as if considering her request. "It would be painful."

"But not just painful, right, sir?"

"Never just painful."

She nodded.

Zuberi turned back to the cabinet, ears pricked and sharp. Eventually he selected a small cane from the middle shelf. He tested its flexibility between two hands and then swung it through the air so that it made a soft whistling sound. "I will strike you with this, but only once."

Mila swallowed and nodded.

The painted dog approached cautiously. He put a steadying hand against Mila's spine, making sure her tail was held out of the way, and laid the cane across her ass. "I will strike you here."

Mila closed her eyes and nodded again.

She felt the cane lift away, heard the sharp whistle through the air, and then it landed with a burst of flame that made her gasp. "Fuck!" she yelled out and her claws made their own marks on the wall.

But then the cane was gone, replaced by strong hands kneading the painful line. The pain melted under his fingers, becoming a hot spot that he seemed to push around her body until there was only the slowly smarting spot to remind her of what she had been hit by.

Mila whimpered. "Fuck," she said again, this time out of

desire not pain, as she felt the canine's hot shaft press up against her, smearing pre into her fur.

The next few minutes blurred together. Ingrid helped Mila over to the spanking bench; the calico's legs were surprisingly stiff. She was laid out on the padded surface of the bench and bound tightly into place. When Ingrid slid a small cuff around the midpoint of her tail and attached it to the back of her collar, Mila became aware of how exposed she was. Zuberi caressed up her legs, from the inside of her knees up over back, dragging his thumbs over her slit along the way. Even her breasts were left unprotected. Zuberi's hands continued their progress up over her back and then dropped around her sides to cup each of them. Mila shivered as the position for Zuberi to grope her pushed his shaft right against her folds.

Mila worried that he was just going to tease her, but then he pushed his shaft down and slid inside her in one fluid, powerful thrust. Mila found herself purring in pleasure at the pressure of his body against her. The heat from her earlier flogging and caning spread out to accentuate the warmth from the body on top of her. It tingled and danced over her back and made her feel every roll of his body as he began to thrust.

Until he pulled back out.

Mila tried to move with him and only then realized how tightly she was bound. She whined and tried to wiggle herself to look more enticing in the hope that he'd drive right back in. She thought back to her first night in the house, and the German Shepherd chastising a cat for being too impatient. Now she understood how she herself could be that way.

Ingrid was selecting a variety of items from the cabinet, all in full view of the calico. Mila swore that the jaguar was deliberately taunting her by letting each linger in her view for a moment. Mila couldn't figure out what the objects were for though. They were an oddball collection, which included a hairbrush, a simple piece of silk, and something that looked like — no, it actually was — a simple dinner fork. It was hard to imagine what they were intended for, hard to think of anything really as Zuberi was constantly teasing her by raking claws through her fur and following the paths his flogger took before.

Ingrid set the pile of things behind Mila, so she couldn't inspect it more closely and then fetched two more things from the house itself. Mila did not have long to wonder about what these new items were because she felt plates being placed on her rear, one on each cheek, and then something being added to them. "Hot coals," Zuberi explained. "Or at least warm coals. You could hold these in your hand although it would be quite uncomfortable."

Mila felt the increased temperature sinking into the plates and then into her, suffusing her well-beaten backside. She held as still as she could, not wanting to shake coals, regardless of whether they were hot or merely warm, into her fur.

After a few minutes of Zuberi idly running his claws over her legs, he set the plates aside just before they started to become uncomfortable.

A second later, she felt an ice cube right on her clit.

Mila jump in her bindings and cried out.

It was cold. Not just regular cold, but really really fucking cold. She didn't know ice could be that cold. And she had no idea why it made her feel so gooey inside when she felt her slick juices drip onto the ice cube and freeze it to her skin momentarily. She whimpered and continued to squirm, but the bonds were doing their job well. She couldn't escape the chill of the ice any more than she could escape the heat of the plates. He thankfully took it away before she worked up the courage to ask him to remove it, and filled her with another few thrusts of cock.

Zuberi continued to shower her sex with contrasting stimulation. The prickly Wartenberg pinwheel was brought out again, and then he caressed her sex with the finest, softest silk she had ever felt. He gripped her so tight, she thought his claws might pierce her skin, then he got down on his knees behind her and breathed gently against her, so the air trickled along her folds.

Warming salves and cooling lotions, and a few types of lubricant were all applied to her. Mila was feeling sensations in her vulva she did not realize were possible, sensing nerves that had never had the chance to be so thoroughly used. And in between each round, he thrust his cock into her. She wished he would just stay there, filling her, while he played with her labia and clit, but he always denied her that.

At last, it felt like they had exhausted the pile of toys and Mila felt the shiver of anticipation, thinking of finally getting properly mated. But instead, Zuberi walked around to Mila's front, where Ingrid had been patiently waiting and observing everything. He gripped her roughly by the ears and slammed his shaft into her muzzle.

Mila wriggled on the bench in desperation as she watched the canine's cock disappear completely into Ingrid's muzzle with ease, knot and all. The couple didn't seem to be slowing down. Zuberi's breathing grew deeper. "Sir," she said with a soft whine in her voice, "You could cum in me."

"I'll save that for your owner," Zuberi declared with another deep thrust into Ingrid's mouth.

"But you are—"

The lustful haze fogging her mind vanished. She remembered in an instant, with a realization that snapped against her brain like a blow from Zuberi's whip, that she was Alonso's kitten, not Zuberi's. She had forgotten about the fox completely.

She'd promised herself she wouldn't forget, and she'd forgotten.

The magic had beaten her.

A well of emotions tore open within her and before she could even understand why, she felt tears starting to flow down her face.

Almost immediately, Zuberi was pulling away from Ingrid and starting to undo the bonds holding Mila to the bench, his dripping shaft forgotten.

"I—I'm sorry. I'm sorry. I'm sorry," Mila said, swallowing

around the words, and gasping for breaths between sobs. "I didn't mean to fuck it up."

Mila felt an urge inside her well up, an urge to ask him to fix her, to change her, so she wouldn't be such a disappointment. She had to crush it down. Alonso was right. The house could be terrible in its expectations.

That opened up a whole new set of emotions which slammed straight into the first, making Mila whimper and want to shrink away so no one could see or hear her.

"Shh," the painted dog gently reprimanded. Not an order, just a soothing sound.

As soon as her limbs were free, Mila curled up and tried to hide her head. Two sets of strong arms picked her up, walked her the few steps to the couch, and slid her in between them. She hugged Zuberi fiercely, pressing her head against his chest as she gave in to that urge to hide, to shrink, to disappear. Ingrid stayed close: Mila could feel the jaguar's touch on her back. "I'm sorry," she said again. "I didn't mean to ruin the evening for you."

Zuberi's fingers stroked over her muzzle and brushed against her whiskers. "Hardly ruined," he said softly. "You have done far better than most have on receiving my test."

"I... did?" Mila felt the weight of the jaguar press in behind her, a soft purr rumbling in her throat.

"Indeed. Princess?" One of his large ears turned to Ingrid, who gave a small nod.

For the first time that day, the jaguar spoke at length. "My fear was the sleepsack. It *is* rather claustrophobic, and I've always hated tight spaces, but I wanted to show I could do it. The first time I tried to get in, I ended up jumping out halfway through and vomiting into the toilet. The second time, I managed to get all the way inside, then had a panic attack that it took me hours to recover from. So after that we just talked."

Mila, keeping her head pressed firmly into Zuberi's chest, turned to look at the jaguar. "You just talked?"

"We did."

"It took over a year before she could safely get into the sleep-sack," Zuberi said as he caressed along Mila's ears and brushed a thumb over the delicate fur on its inside. "In the many times I have made an offer to a feline to face their fear, most have refused, unable or unwilling to face their fear. Some accepted, and like Ingrid, could not stomach continuing. You are one of the few who has managed to not only face their fear but conquer it on the very first night. I may be wrong, but I believe it is Alonso's strength that you relied on tonight and his support of you."

At the mention of the fox's name, Mila buried her face deeper into the painted dog's chest.

"Yes," he said softly. "I can see why he chose you. Even when you are worried that you have messed up, it is the feelings of others that are first and foremost in your mind. You, like him, are very sensitive and care deeply about others. You make him proud. I can see it in his eyes."

Mila's ears tried to pull themselves out of the dog's touch, but he did not let them go. "I don't feel like I made him proud tonight."

Zuberi considered her and then reached out to the nearby nightstand. "Call him," he said, pointing to the phone there.

It sounded like an order, but there was no weight behind his words.

Slowly, she pulled away from the pair and stood on shaky feet. Mila reached the phone and picked it up before realizing... "Sir, I don't know how to use this."

"Just say the name of the person you want to contact into the receiver."

Mila held the phone to her ear. There was a soft dial tone on the line. "Alonso Hodgson," she said.

The dial tone clicked over to a ringing. Before the third ring had even finished, the fox had picked up. He sounded breathless, as though he had rushed to answer. "Hello? Who is it?"

"It's Mila, sir."

"Mila? Are you all right? What happened? What did that bastard do to you?" His tone was full of wrathful anger.

Mila's eyes flicked to the painted dog. Zuberi tried to remain nonchalant but there was a stiffness in his spine there hadn't been a moment before, and Ingrid's hackles were on end: they had heard every word.

"I'm all right," the calico said quickly into the phone, cutting off any further ranting. "It's just been very intense. Master Zuberi is very good at making me emotional." She tried and failed to keep herself from calling Zuberi her Master while talking to Alonso. She heard the intake of breath as he prepared to say something, so she cut him off again. "He suggested I call you."

Alonso breathed out slowly. "What do you need?"

"I just needed to know. Are you proud of me?"

There was a brief pause. "Of course I am, Mila. More than I... More than I can really say right now." And she understood that he couldn't say more when others might hear. "Are you sure that's all you need from me?"

"You've done a lot for me, sir. I think Master Zuberi can help me for one evening too."

"All right." He sounded cautious and perhaps a little disapproving. "Take care of yourself, Mila."

"I will."

Mila carefully set the phone back in its cradle and turned around. Zuberi and Ingrid were watching her with interest, but not saying anything. The jaguar was kneeling at her Master's feet, and the dog quietly ran a claw over the edge of her ears.

Mila swallowed. "I'm sorry you had to hear that."

The painted dog's ears flattened, as though he would have preferred the subject not been raised. "I understand," he said with a dismissive gesture. "I consider Alonso a friend but he..." Zuberi sighed. "He has an uncanny ability to place blame on the wrong target. He has more than once blamed me for his own mistake. He is not cruel about it, so I have accepted it without complaint," he said with a shrug.

An uncanny ability to place blame on the wrong target? Mila stood stock still. Icy cold clawed at her stomach as a terrible possibility whispered in her thoughts. "Sir, can I ask you something and have you not repeat it to Alonso?"

"Of course."

The calico struggled to form the worrisome idea into a question she could ask. "Ever since I entered the house, I've been a lot more open about my wants. I've practically shouted out how horny and needy I am before. Alonso told me that's the house's doing, that it makes me act more submissive. Is that true?"

Zuberi glanced down at Ingrid. The jaguar nodded. "It does always come as a surprise to newcomers. Why?"

"Is there a similar effect for you?"

Zuberi's big round ears perked and an eyebrow lifted. "The house has never made me feel more submissive, no."

"No, I meant, does it ever make you act more dominant?"

"Not to my knowledge, and from what Ingrid has told me, the effect on her is quite noticeable. Nor have I heard any other canines discuss this." He lifted a hand and stroked his chin. "But Alonso thinks it does?"

"Yes, sir."

He nodded. "That I think explains some things."

More than you know, Mila thought to herself. Alonso had blamed his desire to rewrite Mila's memories on the house, but it had been him all along. The ice in her stomach melted as anger bubbled up inside, but that too was quenched. He had wanted to do it, but he hadn't. He had been careful ever since. All he had done was keep putting the blame in the wrong place. On the house instead of himself. No wonder the house wasn't sure if he'd manage to make it out: how was the fox supposed to heal when he couldn't admit to his own faults?

"Mila, are you all right?" The painted dog had leaned forward breaking his usual posture to draw slightly nearer to her.

"No, sir. I think I have some things I need to discuss with Alonso." She came to a decision. "But not tonight." She knelt down and rested her chin on the painted dog's leather-clad knee. After a moment, she felt his hand reach out and caress her just as he was caressing Ingrid. "For now, Master, I'd like to continue exploring, but more slowly than before. I don't think I could do anything that intense again tonight."

The painted dog patted her head and smiled.

/

Mila woke the same way she had every morning at the house. She panicked for a moment, not knowing where she was. Then the distinctive light coming in through the windows reminded her. She was in the house. She was at the Eternal Party.

An arm held her tight around chest. She brushed a hand along it and felt thin wiry fur.

For a second time, she was confused as to where she was, until she remembered that she had not returned to Alonso's bed, but had stayed to sleep with Zuberi.

A fleeting thought, barely more than an impulse, flitted into Mila's conscious mind and was stamped out before it could trigger any painful memories. The urge to turn and bury her nose in Zuberi's fur and chase away the thought with his warm scent was tempting, but she knew what he would think of that. He would encourage her, in a softly chiding tone, to face her fears.

The calico took a slow breath and let the thought come back to her. It was a jumble of recollections and feelings. She remembered the way BD's arm used to rest across her, with his thumb teasing at the fur of her belly while he was still fully asleep, and she missed it. She missed him. But she also remembered Alonso's arm around her with its protective, possessive grip and she found herself, to her own surprise, missing that too. Maybe, she thought, it wouldn't be so bad to stay trapped in the house. At least she had those mornings to look forward to.

Creeeeeeeak.

Mila's ears perked. The door to the room had eased open, as if someone were sneaking their way inside. But from her position on the bed, Mila could see there was no one there. Through the crack in the door she heard another door opening with its own groan, and then one further in the distance, beckoning her.

Beckoning her to leave.

Mila's heart suddenly pounded and she whispered so low she didn't hear her own voice. "Can I leave the house now?"

Thump.

Ballade

❧

Mila was so blind-sided by elation that she was frozen in place on the bed.

I can get out, she thought. I can get out. I can finally get out.

And then another thought tickled the back of her mind. "Can Alonso get out too?" she whispered.

Thump thump.

She felt Zuberi begin to stir. Even if she wasn't audible, the house was. The calico rolled over in Zuberi's embrace and nuzzled him under his chin. "Sir?"

"Hmm?" An eye opened and focused on her, sharp despite the early hour.

"I need to go. Alonso needs me."

The painted dog nodded. "Your time with me has ended anyway."

She had noticed. She no longer felt the compunction to think of him as her Master. "Thank you, sir. I need to leave at once."

"Then go." He waved his hand in the direction of the door and offered a small smile like a benediction. "Just remember the strength you discovered last night."

1

Initially Mila bolted through the halls towards Alonso's room to tell him the good news, but her pace slowed and then stopped altogether. "House," she whispered, "I need some place I can talk to you alone."

A door squeaked open about ten feet away. Mila slipped inside and found herself in another servant's passage, with a spiral staircase that led up and down. She could see that no one else was there and so shut the door firmly behind her. She turned to address a wall. "If I tell him how to get out, that doesn't mean he'll be able to, right?"

Thump.

"He has to figure it out for himself, doesn't he?"

Thump.

"Fuck. But can I at least help him figure it out?"

Thump.

Mila sat down on the staircase and thought. The house still would not confirm how she was able to leave, but she was pretty certain she knew. She tried to put together everything she understood about the house and a few things she had guessed to come up with a plan to get Alonso out. When she had it fully formed in her mind, she told it to the house.

"Will it work?"

Silence.

"Please. I need this to work. I need to help him." She pressed her head to the woodwork and willed the house to give her some sign, some clue that she was on the right track.

The ethereal piano sounded out again in the stairwell, chiming uplifting chords, but that wasn't all this time.

Suddenly, Mila was not alone. There was a pair of slim feminine arms wrapping her up in a hug and a purr rumbled against her spine.

Mila whirled around. The stairwell was empty, but just for an instant she could see the flickering afterimage of a presence that had been there.

The calico held perfectly still, even her tail was rigid, expecting something else to appear or for the piano to return. When nothing happened, Mila bolted up the stairs two at a time, heading for the library.

Aisha wasn't alone in the library. As Mila approached, she found the jackal in deep conversation with a malamute she recognized from poker nights. She remembered what Jeta had told her about Aisha not being properly respected by others in the house, and the calico was determined to have everything go perfectly today.

She approached demurely, tail down and head low, waiting several steps away until she was acknowledged.

Aisha saw her and there was a curious glint in her eye. She waited until the malamute had finished what he was saying and turned her head to the calico. "What is it, Mila?"

Mila took a few steps forward and bowed. "Mistress Aisha," she said in clear, enunciated tones, her best talk-with-a-VIP voice, "I have a private message from Alonso when you have some time."

The jackal nodded and looked to her companion. "We'll have to discuss this later, Michel."

The malamute gave a quick goodbye and waved at the pair of them.

Even before the door shut behind him, the calico had dropped to her knees and begun to lean in towards the jackal's feet. "May I greet you properly, Mistress Aisha?"

A finger on her forehead stopped her. "Mila, do you really want to lick me out?"

Mila glanced around to make sure they were alone. "Um, not personally, no, Mistress Aisha."

"Then don't. When you desire to bury your head between my legs, then you may do so." She lifted her finger from Mila's forehead. "Now stop delaying. What's Alonso's message?"

"That was just to get you alone," she said, and then added, "I can leave the house, Mistress Aisha."

The jackal's eyes went wide. "Then what are you still doing here?"

"I think I can get Alonso out too, Mistress Aisha."

The jackal gripped the calico by the arm and started to pull her towards the door. "Mila, get out of the house now. No delays. Once we're outside, you can tell me how you did it and I will see to it Alonso gets out as well."

Mila's heart fell as her feet began to turn and she started to walk towards the door with the jackal. She summoned all her internal strength, forced her feet to stop moving and shouted, "No!" She rounded on the jackal and snapped, "I have to try!" Before the jackal could order her again, she spoke quickly. "I think it has to be me. I have to be the one to get him out. If I just leave, that might be what traps him here forever. So I have to try," she repeated.

Mila looked up, hopeful that the jackal would see it her way.

Aisha stared straight through her.

In the month she had known the jackal, she had seen many expressions on her face, but the shock and bewilderment were brand new. "Aisha?"

The jackal shook herself as if waking up suddenly. She looked down at the feline as if seeing her there for the first time, and then she slowly extended a solitary finger. "One try, Mila. No more."

The calico nodded slowly. "If it doesn't work, I'll leave. I promise, Mistress Aisha."

"All right." The jackal rolled her shoulders and cleared her throat as if trying to refocus herself. "Now tell me, how did you figure out how to leave?"

"I'll tell you, I promise, but first I need to know something. Is the house haunted?"

Thump thump.

Mila and Aisha turned to look at a bookshelf where the house had given its response. "That seems quite definite," the jackal said, then she turned her attention back on Mila. "Why do you think the house is haunted?"

"Because I saw her." Mila gestured up to the portrait that hung above the entrance. The snow leopard Lady Yasmin sat there, as regal as ever, leaning against... Mila squinted up at the portrait. She had thought the snow leopard had been leaning against a railing, but now that she paid close attention, she realized what else it might have been. "A piano," she whispered to herself.

"Mila?"

The calico took a breath before trying to explain. "I've been hearing piano music off and on ever since I arrived, music that no one else can hear. I think it's Lady Yasmin's piano. It's really only been there when I was connecting more with the house, like on the night Alonso threw me out. But just now, I didn't just hear her. I saw her too. I'm sure it was her. She was wearing the collar and corset; I just know it was her."

To Mila's relief, Aisha didn't contradict her, nor did she admonish the feline for forgetting to use her title. "Tell me everything."

So Mila told her the events of that morning, including the ghostly presence she had felt in the stairwell.

"I've never heard of anything like that happening," the jackal admitted. She considered. "Let's try to recreate the circumstances of the appearance. Mila, stand against the bookcase there, just as you were before you saw her, and put your thoughts back to how they were at that moment."

Mila stepped up to the bookcase and... *pressed her head to the woodwork and willed the house to give her some sign, some clue that she was on the right track.*

The ethereal piano sounded out again in the stairwell, chiming uplifting chords, but that wasn't all this time.

Suddenly, Mila was not alone. There was a pair of slim feminine arms wrapping her up in a hug and a purr rumbled against her spine...

Mila whirled. Aisha's face was stricken. "I saw her too. Lady Yasmin," the jackal confirmed in a quiet voice. Then her face brightened. "Of course! I can't believe I didn't see it before."

"What?"

Aisha slumped back against a bookcase and tried to articulate her thoughts. "All the notes on magic say that every spell has four parts: the will and the word, the wind and the world. I thought the will just meant intention. I've found so many admonishments of young mages, telling them to be careful of their intention, because the spell would replicate all of it. But other places talked about spells like they had a life of their own, separate from the intentions of the caster.

"It must be that when a spell is cast, the mage infuses it with their own will. That's the reason why the house almost feels like it's alive: we're literally interacting with an echo of Lady Yasmin's personality. We were able to see her because you were resonating so closely with her that her echo could actually manifest physically. Maybe we could even converse with her if we find the right emotive reference point..."

While the jackal ran through the possibilities this opened up for her research, Mila tuned her out and looked around at the walls of the library with new eyes. She'd been feeling more and more like the house had been looking out for her, protecting her in a myriad of tiny ways. And now it made more sense. The snow leopard herself was watching over her, but... "Why did she trap me here then?"

The jackal's expression softened from manic academic interest to something approaching sorrow. She turned her back to Mila and spoke quietly, directly to the house, just loud enough for Mila to hear. "Did Lady Yasmin lose her partner before creating the Eternal Party?"

Thump.

"Was she thinking about that loss when creating the Eternal Party?"

Thump.

The jackal took a deep breath and looked back at Mila. "The spell copies all intentions, conscious and unconscious. If she wanted this place to be a haven from her own grief, then that became a part of the spell. The house will try to help you, whether you want it to or not."

That only fired up Mila's determination. "I'm going to get Alonso out of here. Will you help me, Mistress Aisha?"

"What do I need to do?" There was unwavering steel in the jackal's voice, and it occurred to Mila that if ever she was in a life or death situation, there was no one she'd want in her corner more than Aisha.

Mila thought back to her plan that she had made in the stairwell. "I'm going to make a perfect evening for Alonso, but — and this is important — he can't think that any canine has influenced me to do this. That includes himself. So the first thing I need is for you to talk to him, Mistress Aisha. Make it clear I am preparing something of my own volition and that he is not allowed to give me any orders or ask me any questions today."

The jackal considered. "That should be doable. I can claim you are preparing a surprise for him and that you deputized me to make sure he didn't accidentally spoil it by ordering you around."

"And house... or Lady Yasmin..." She looked to Aisha and grimaced. It didn't feel right to call it that. "House, you want Alonso to get out too. So you cannot influence me on today's plans at all. Can you do that?"

Thump.

"Thank you. And then I know I'm going to need Erik to make me an outfit and Devon and Theo to cook something. Can you call in some favors to make sure Erik doesn't interfere? I don't think Devon will need any special prodding."

Aisha nodded.

"I'll have some other instructions later. But now I need to convince Vivien to help."

The jackal waved a hand dismissively. "I'll do that."

"No!"

Aisha's fists clenched and her eyebrows knitted together in an expression of "How dare you."

"Mistress Aisha," Mila said, trying to keep her tone sharp and commanding. "If this works, Vivien will have to say goodbye to someone she cares about, possibly someone she loves. You will not force her to do that. You will not force her to be happy about it. Or so help me, I'll... I'll hit you." Mila put her hands on her hips and held her head high, trying to look as authoritative as Aisha herself was.

The jackal stared at her levelly for a moment. "You really don't do intimidating well, Mila. It is not one of your strengths."

"Aisha," Mila said with a whine.

The jackal held up a hand. "I won't do anything to Vivien. I swear. Go on and get her. Meet up with Erik afterwards."

Although Mila had comparatively little to worry about from the other felines at the house (despite a few residual feelings of jealousy over her being with Alonso), Mila had not once visited the rooms set aside for them. When she went to find Vivien, she stayed near the center of the building. Rooms here weren't given to a single person, but to several at once. Mila was surprised to see that right under Vivien's name on her door was Natalie, and when she knocked on the door, it was the cougar who opened it.

The tawny feline blinked sleepily before lighting up when she saw who was there. "Well, hello, Mila. I was wondering when you were going to come visit us."

The calico felt embarrassed that she hadn't spent more time

getting to know the cougar in her time at the Eternal Party. They'd barely seen each other since that first encounter. "Sorry. Alonso's been keeping me busy."

The cougar's face drooped. "Right. How is he?"

Mila really wished she was wearing a big hoodie or something she could pull over her head and disappear into. She still felt responsible for how poorly he had acted yesterday. "He's okay," she lied.

The cougar smiled in a way that suggested she knew Mila wasn't telling the whole story. "All right. And what can I do for you?"

"Actually, I was looking for Vivien. I had no idea you lived together."

The cougar looked more surprised than disappointed: Mila had made no secret about not wanting to be around the lynx. "Yeah, we do. Sorry. I know she wasn't the nicest to you when you arrived. I promise you there is a wonderful person underneath that prickly exterior. Anyways, she's here, I'll go get her."

Natalie let Mila into their quarters and the calico was impressed by how nice they were. The apartment, for that's what it felt like, had a central living area with doors leading off into adjacent bedrooms. The base decor of the room was upscale suburban tenement: hardwood flooring, marble countertops, plush sofas and armchairs, and elegant crown molding that was stained instead of painted.

Covering almost every wall were photographs, some blown up to poster size, that showed Natalie, Vivien, and a serval Mila didn't know visiting a variety of locations outside the house, all in the nude. Mila was surprised how extra nude the photos felt when the felines in it did not wear their corset or collar. The destinations included beaches, mountaintops, forests, and even a few spots in the city (late at night, of course). If she paid close attention, the calico could see a progression: earlier pictures showed a shier Natalie at the start of her transition, tagging along with her more extroverted friends, and later pictures showed a confident Natalie, standing just as tall and proud as the other two.

Mila jumped in the air, tail straight out, when Natalie started banging her fist into one of the bedroom doors. "Hey! Vivien! You've got a guest!" The cougar then lowered her voice and looked apologetically to the calico. "She's a heavy sleeper. I've literally watched someone try to wake her up with a spanking and fail."

From the door opposite, the serval poked her head out, lifting a pair of headphones off her ear, but nothing came from Vivien's room, not even a sound to suggest she was moving about.

"One moment," Natalie said and slipped into the bedroom, closing the door behind her. The serval tilted her head and turned her ear to face directly to the door. Mila did the same.

There was a bit of shuffling, a grunt of effort, a scream followed shortly by a thud, and then the sound of running. The door swung open and Natalie dived through, followed a second later by an angry Vivien. "Damn it, Nat. You don't have to throw me out of bed. You can just knock — oh, hi Mila." The lynx's expression spun on a whim and she grinned at the calico. "What are you doing here?"

"I need your help."

The lynx's ears perked. "Something for Alonso?"

Mila nodded.

"Of course." She seemed to have forgiven him for his demeanor yesterday without a second thought. "Whatever it is, I'm happy to help."

Mila winced. This was going to be harder than she thought. She glanced at the Natalie and the serval. "Can we talk in private?"

The serval shrugged and Natalie, with a quick wave, led her out, chatting about taking a visit to the dungeon to see who might be down there. Mila watched them go. The serval was already sneaking a hand between the cougar's thighs and stroking her sheath.

"Okay, now what is it?" the lynx asked, slightly impatient.

"Let's sit down."

The lynx shrugged and slouched into a seat, collapsing into it sideways with the grace only a feline could manage. She started to lick at the back of her hand and groom herself, as her fur was quite messy from having been in bed, despite Mila staring at her. "Seriously, Mila, if it's about yesterday—"

"It's not."

The lynx's short tail shivered at the interruption. "Then what is it, really? Enough beating around the bush."

"I'm preparing a surprise for Alonso," Mila said slowly. "I need your help because you know him much better than I do. But I didn't want to ask this of you unless you knew: if everything goes right today, Alonso will be leaving the house."

Vivien stared at her. Her head shook a little, her lips moved without sound, and when she finally found her voice, she spoke in tones quiet and hollow. "You're taking him away, aren't you?"

Mila couldn't meet her eyes.

The lynx took a quick shuddering breath and tried to hide a sniffle in the crook of her arm. She drew her legs up to her chest and shrunk into her seat. "What did I do wrong?" she asked with a soft whine. "Why didn't he ever want me?"

Mila felt her heart breaking. "It wasn't you. There was nothing you could have done."

The lynx's jaw was quivering.

"Vivien, you like being here, don't you?"

"What kind of fucking question is that?" Vivien spat, anger rising in her voice. "The house doesn't let you in unless you want to be here. That's one of the rules."

Mila quietly shook her head.

The lynx's mouth hung open. "He's... he's not supposed to be here?"

"No. Sometimes the house lets other people in and then doesn't let them out. He's been trapped here for years." The lynx still looked at her like she couldn't believe it. "Come on, Vivien, you know he's never acted like any of the other canines. He's different. He's different because he's not supposed to be part of the Eternal Party."

Vivien looked away, then her eyes went wide and she turned right back to the calico, pointing with a wavering finger. "You," she said with a gasp of surprise. "You're not supposed to be here either. That's why he chose you."

Mila nodded. She'd hoped Vivien wouldn't figure that part out.

"Fuck, and I was such a bitch to you too."

"It's okay," Mila said. "I've figured out how to get out. I need your help to get Alonso out too."

The lynx didn't say anything for a bit. She sniffled and rubbed her nose. "He will come back every now and then, won't he? He won't be gone forever?"

"I don't know. I think we can come back."

"Will you keep him away from me?" the lynx asked fiercely.

"No, no, of course not. Vivien, if we can come back, what am I going to do? Tell my owner no?" She offered a smile.

Slowly, the smile was returned.

Erik did not look pleased to see the pair of them. He was surly and grumbled under his breath, while Aisha, sitting behind him, looked like the proverbial cat that had caught the mouse. "I'm paying you ten whole favors so you do nothing but what I asked of you. That is an enormous fee and you know it."

The husky looked from calico to lynx and back again with an expression of longing. "Can't I at least have them be in display mode?"

"No," Aisha said firmly.

"But—"

"No."

"At least let me use Tricia!"

"Oh, by all means, silence her jabbering however you most enjoy, but Mila and Vivien are off limits."

Tricia grinned widely as this conversation went on, and when she caught Mila looking her way, she winked back at the calico.

It occurred to Mila that the cheetah was being significantly less airheaded than she usually was. Maybe it was an act, to encourage the husky to dollify her. The Eternal Party really took all types.

Erik continued to mutter under his breath but accepted the terms. He put Tricia in wind-up mode which had her moving even more robotically than normal, all jerky movements with a placid and unmoving smile fixed onto her muzzle. He continued to curse and swear as he took notes on what Vivien suggested for him, sending out the robotic Tricia into the rows of fabrics to look for what he needed. He had all of Vivien's measurements — in intimate detail — already, but Mila had to stand and let Erik get more precise details before they could leave once again.

Mila and Vivien burst into the kitchen. "Devon! Theo! I need your help," Mila said.

The corgi and lion looked up sharply. For a second, they were confused, then Devon sprang into action, leaping in front of Mila with the posture of a caricature butler. "Of course, fair maiden. Our kitchen is open to you and we are but your humble servants." He bowed.

Theo followed behind him, his back hunched and his gaze always down. "A-as he said," the lion stuttered, "w-we are b-b-but your humble servants."

"And I need him in his usual set of mind," Mila said, jerking a thumb at Theo.

Devon glanced at his partner. "Why?"

"No distractions today, Devon."

The corgi looked a little disappointed, but snapped his fingers. "Theo, reset," he said.

Immediately the lion stood up straight. He was as disappointed as his partner. "What's this all about?" he asked.

"I'm making a dinner feast for Alonso and I need your cooperation, and," she added before the corgi and lion could look too excited, "I need absolutely no questions about it beyond that. No orders either."

The corgi just smiled at these conditions. "We do need to know what we're helping with, dear."

"So do I." She turned and addressed the nearest clear space of countertop. "House, I need the dish that Lily made that Alonso liked the best."

Thump.

Mila reached into a nearby drawer and pulled out a recipe card. "Looks like we're making a sausage pot pie."

"Tricky," Theo said, taking the recipe from her. Vivien pressed in close to the lion and read over his shoulder as he planned. "We'll need a lot of good side dishes to make it appropriate for dinner."

While lion and lynx were distracted, Devon slipped in close to Mila. "I know you said not to ask any questions, but I do feel I need to know who this Lily is."

Mila considered and whispered. "House, show me the photo."

Thump.

She pulled it out and handed it to Devon.

The corgi initially smiled at the sight of the younger Alonso, but that smile quickly fell when he realized the implications of the photo. "Oh Alonso, you poor, poor man." He tucked the photo back away into a drawer so Devon and Vivien wouldn't notice it. Then he snatched the recipe card out of Theo's hands. "We're not making this," he declared.

"What? Why?" It was Vivien who complained.

"Yeah, why?" Mila echoed. She had the plan all laid out in her mind and didn't want anything to interfere with it.

The corgi tapped a foot. "This dinner of yours, I trust it is meant to be a romantic dinner for two this evening? Something special to be treasured and remembered?"

Mila nodded.

Devon flicked the recipe card. "This is going to make him cry. Very unromantic." He slipped the recipe into a drawer. "Instead, house, could we have a light steak dinner; appropriate wine pairing; soup, salad, and dessert; an eclectic assortment of sides; and one small element that would remind him of Lily."

Thump.

The corgi pulled out a handful of recipe cards. "This is what we'll be doing."

"Who's this Lily you keep mentioning?" Theo asked.

Devon, without missing a beat, pointed a finger at both lion and lynx. "Both of you forget any mention of Lily." It was one of the rare times Mila could remember ever having seen Devon make such an immediate and serious command of anyone. But the pair returned to their dissection of the recipes without a word crosswise.

Mila tapped Devon's shoulder. "I would like to make a good amount of this myself."

The corgi nodded and bowed. "I would have expected nothing less. We are at your disposal, chef."

The day rushed past. Mila spent most of the time in the kitchen, practicing the recipes so that dinner would be perfect. She stepped out on occasion to do test fittings with Erik, check in with Aisha, or to brainstorm ideas with Vivien. The lynx proved invaluable. The fox had hidden far more of his desires from Mila beyond "the art of the swing" that Zuberi had mentioned.

A little before sunset, Mila began cooking dinner in earnest; the time for practice was over. She got things to the point where only the finishing touches were needed and then handed off control of the kitchen to Devon and Theo.

The next stop was to Erik, who dressed them in the most irate silence Mila had ever experienced. While Mila trusted Erik to create a spectacular outfit, it had again been designed with significant input from Vivien. The first item of the new outfit were shoulder-length latex gloves and thigh-high latex stockings, both of which the lynx insisted were Alonso's favorites despite him never mentioning them around Mila. Their corsets were replaced by a more decorative set with thin strips of silk attached, two of which looped over their shoulders and two of which ran over their hips, but still left their breasts and sexes exposed. The silk on Mila's was bright orange to complement her fur while Vivien's was sky blue to complement her eyes. Finally a freestanding broach nestled low into the fur of their chests to draw the eye into their cleavage. With that, at least, she could understand how it would appeal to Alonso.

Now fully dressed, Mila didn't just look sexy, she felt sexy. As she and Vivien left the tailoring room and headed down the hall to the library, Mila's walk turned into a sensuous strut. Beside her, Vivien was swaying her hips in time with Mila and checking the calico out more than she ever had before.

In the library, Mila checked with Aisha that the remaining orders of business had been taken care of. Aisha had rented out the observatory for the evening with a few more favors, so that they would not be disturbed there, and she had prepared the room to Mila's specifications.

After that, the calico and lynx climbed up to the observatory. Mila had timed it just right: the last remnants of dusk cast the sky in deep purples and stars were beginning to twinkle to life. The observatory itself had been largely cleared out, with a single large table in the center of the room set for a candlelight dinner and a curtained partition in the corner. Then there was nothing to do but wait, rocking on their heels until she heard the distinctive tapping coming up the stairs and the door crept open.

Mila felt her heart leap into her throat. There was no turning back now. It all had to go right or Alonso would be trapped here forever.

Nocturne

Alonso had a smirk hidden indiscreetly at the corners of his mouth as he made his way up to stand before the pair of felines. He didn't say a word.

"Did Aisha tell you the rules for the evening?" Mila asked in what she hoped was a playful tone that hid her nervousness.

The fox cleared his throat and held up a hand, ticking off the instructions one by one. "First, I am not to give either of you any orders, no matter how small. Second, I am not to ask either of you any questions, no matter how simple. Third, at the end of the evening, I will be given three questions to ask you, and then you will ask me one question which I must answer fully honestly." He lowered his hand. "Aisha had me repeat them twenty times to make sure I knew them."

"And...?"

The fox rubbed the handle of his cane. "And I agreed."

Mila nodded to Vivien.

The lynx took a step forward with a small bow. "Welcome, Master Alonso. Your kitten has prepared a night of entertainment for your pleasure. Please follow our instructions so that you can enjoy the full totality of it."

Alonso tipped an ear to her. "Follow your instructions. That's coming dangerously close to ordering a canine around." He winked. "All right, you two. What's fi—?"

"Sir!" She tried to keep her tone respectful even as she interjected. "That's a question."

"This is going to be tougher than I thought." He paused and tapped a finger on the cane. "I would like to know what is first."

"We are going to start with some additional clothing selections."

The fox's eyes roamed over both of them, and the broach did its job of encouraging him to ogle their chests. Mila nodded again to Vivien, who stepped behind the curtain and came back with a tray to present before Alonso. The tray gleamed like silver, the kind normally used to offer a selection of fine cocktails or canapés at a party, but it instead held about ten different options of piercing. Mila held out her chest as Vivien offered the tray to him. "Please select the item you would most enjoy for your kitten's nipples."

Alonso seemed to have an immediate desire in mind, reaching towards one, but then hesitated and moved his hand away.

"Sir," Vivien pressed, "each of these was cleared by Mila in advance. You should choose the one you want."

Alonso's gaze flicked over to the calico, who nodded in confirmation of Vivien's statement.

Alonso picked up the item he had initially gone for: it was a simple bar piercing, but a small chain and weight hung from it, with a little gemstone inlaid so that it could pass as kinky jewelry.

Alonso picked up a pair of the items and brought them up to Mila. "Take a—"

"Sir!"

He blinked. "Right. No orders. Sorry. I hope you know you should take a deep breath first."

She grinned and took a deep breath, feeling the pinching pressure as the magical piercings were applied. Then he let go and the sudden weight tugging her nipple down made her shiver. It was far less than the cardboard sign Alonso had hung from her breasts weeks ago, but it was still surprisingly effective at teasing her. That was probably why he chose it.

Vivien smiled. "Anything for me, sir?"

Alonso picked up a simpler ring piercing and added them to the lynx's nipples, demonstrating this toy by tugging each of them with his claws.

Vivien purred in appreciation, then took the tray behind the curtain and came back with some clamps which she handed to Mila. The calico got down on her knees and gently ran a thumb over Vivien's slit. Unlike how Mila had been with Jeta, who she found very attractive, there was something almost clinical about the way she teased the lynx: it was a thing she had to do rather than a thing she enjoyed. All the same she made sure the lynx was having fun, brushing her thumb back and forth over the lynx's folds, which were far bigger than Mila's own. The calico carefully attached one clamp to each of Vivien's labia — just how the lynx had shown her how to do earlier that day — and then attached the connected elastic strip to the top of her stockings. It held her sex spread apart and Vivien demonstrated how the clamps moved as she walked. (Vivien had explained earlier that day that Alonso loved being able to see how aroused someone was getting without impediment. Another thing Alonso had never told Mila.)

The lynx stepped behind the curtain and came back with a second tray. "We have a variety of clamp strength, size, and connector elasticity for your kitten," she said.

Visually there was not much difference beyond the size of the clamps, so Alonso picked up each item and tested it between his hands. Mila was less certain about this than she had been about the piercings, and was relieved when Alonso picked a well-padded clamp whose strap was loose. She shivered as Alonso attached it and demonstrated walking with it attached just as Vivien had done. The clamps themselves weren't turning her on: the rhythmic tugging felt like someone was fumbling awkwardly with her sex. The effect it had on Alonso, who could not take his eyes off her, made her feel so much better. She took a second lap around the observatory and added additional sway to her hips.

Once more Vivien went away and came back with a new tray, this time of butt plugs. There were some of rubber and some of metal and even some of glass. Mila saw him test several in his hands, as he had with the clamps. He stopped on a smaller metal plug that he tilted back and forth, feeling the second heavy weight inside which bounced and jiggled freely inside a hollow chamber.

"This one," he declared.

Vivien held up a bottle of lube. "Would you care to do the honors?"

The fox set his cane against the table and took the lube from her, slicking up the plug with practiced, sure motions. He didn't need to even give Mila an instructive look; she knew what was expected. She bent forward against the wall, lifted her tail, and spread her legs, feeling the extra tug on her labia as she did. Metal touched her pucker and sent shivers along her spine. Mila tried to relax, she really did, but the plug was cold. Alonso had to grip her hips to prevent her from constantly pulling away. And then it slipped deep inside in one quick motion that made her claws extend. Mila groaned and waited for the toy to warm up inside her.

"And for me?" Vivien asked, holding the tray a little higher. She was biting her lip softly and subtly indicating the larger toys with the tilt of her ears.

Unlike how carefully he had decided on things for Mila, the fox quickly selected the thickest, heaviest plug from the mix, coated it in lube, spun Vivien around, and shoved it in roughly. The lynx did a good job of keeping her composure. The only sign Mila could see of her reaction was how her little tail was flicking faster than usual. Alonso finished with a playful slap on the lynx's rear which got a soft purr from her.

As Vivien strutted back behind the curtain, staying there for a while this time, Mila took Alonso's hand and guided him to the table set out for dinner. In objection to tradition, she pulled out his chair and helped him be seated.

Before joining him at the table, the calico angled her chair for him to see. There, in the middle of the seat, was a dildo, once more vulpine in nature. Carefully Mila positioned herself above it and began to lower herself down. She gave full voice to her desire, cooing and groaning without reservation as the toy slid inside her. She stopped halfway impaled to sway and shift about as though she needed to readjust herself, but in reality was just adding motion to the many teasing toys on or inside her. Then she continued sliding down until her lips met the knot.

Although Mila and Alonso had practiced a lot with her taking his knot, it was still something she had to work up towards and didn't always happen. Tonight had to be perfect though. She just remembered what Zuberi had taught her, trusted in the house, and handed over all power to gravity, sinking fully onto the knot with a quick plop.

Alonso stared at her in surprise.

Vivien came out with a bottle of wine and began filling up their glasses, but it was at this time that Mila realized there was a slight flaw in her plan. To help position herself onto the dildo, she had pushed the chair away from the table, and now she needed to pull the chair forward without getting up. She awkwardly began to scoot and scrape the chair forward in little bursts that sent pleasurable jolt tingling up her spine. The piercings swayed, the plug bounced, the clamps tugged, but worst of all was the dildo, which stayed quite firmly fixed in place. All motion was relative after all, and Mila's short, sharp movements made her feel like the dildo was bucking into her in firm, needy thrusts. She was panting by the time she got the chair into position. The calico accepted the wine and downed several swallows to calm her nerves.

"There is…" Mila began and needed to take another steadying sip. "There is a remote next to you that controls the vibrator inside the dildo," she explained.

Alonso looked at it and without hesitation flicked it to max.

Mila's knees clacked together under the table and she gripped the edge of the table tight as the dildo sprang to life within her and buzzed so hard it made her teeth chatter. It was raw electric pleasure, a live wire straight into her deepest pleasure center. "S-s-sir," she mewled out. "Please don't make me cum just yet."

He waited a moment more before sliding the vibrator down to its lowest setting. "A pity I can't simply order you not to cum."

She took deep gulps of air through her nose and shivered from tailtip to eartip.

There was a ding from behind the curtain, which made Alonso turn in his chair, staring curiously.

"We had the house set up a temporary dumbwaiter," Mila explained. "That will be dinner, fresh from the kitchen."

Alonso nodded and turned back, clearly wanting to say several things, but being stopped by the rules he had agreed to.

Vivien came sauntering back out with the food, laying a plate first in front of Alonso then in front of Mila until all the dishes had been laid out. She then stepped back and held her hands together just at her waist. "Tonight," she announced, "Chef Collins has prepared for your dining pleasure a steak, cooked medium rare, asparagus with jus, mashed purple potatoes, a side salad made with roasted butternut squash, gazpacho, crème brûlée, and a buttermilk biscuit. Your drink tonight is a '73 Chateau Galliard." ($300 a bottle, Mila thought.) "We apologize that all courses are being served simultaneously, but your waiter will be preparing other entertainments. Enjoy."

Mila watched Alonso attentively and with growing worry as he picked up the biscuit and turned it over in his hand. His expression was surprisingly intense when he finally set it down. "I do hope you are not going to be making a habit of this."

"Sir?"

Alonso checked over his shoulder, and lowered his voice so Vivien would not hear. "Lily made these all the time. Didn't matter what else was on the menu. She'd even make pizza and biscuits."

"I know, sir." Mila squirmed on the seat and not just because of the dildo still buzzing gently away. "I asked the house for a little accompaniment to dinner, something of hers. I hope that's all right."

Alonso said nothing and bit into the biscuit. He chewed, swallowed, and set the remainder down. "Damn," he said, his tone even. "You really made those well."

"Sir? Is it all right?"

He glanced up as if suddenly reminded of her presence. "Yes, Mila. It's fine. Just don't—" he stopped himself and rephrased. "I would prefer if you didn't make a habit of digging up her recipes. There's one or two I want to be just hers."

"I understand, sir." She made a mental note to thank Devon for helping her avoid that particular pitfall.

He glanced down at the meal in front of him.

"Shall we?" Mila offered.

He nodded and together they began to eat. Only about a minute into the meal, while Mila was still working on the soup, Vivien sat down on yet another dildo-augmented chair in the far corner of the observatory and began to play the cello, a soft romantic piece that matched the atmosphere of the candlelight perfectly.

Mila coughed gently and whispered, "The second button on the remote controls her dildo, sir."

Alonso picked up the remote and held it so Mila could see as he manipulated Mila's vibrator, sending it in wild spasms and sudden surges that left the calico panting and squirming in her seat, clenching down as tight as she could to try and hold off an orgasm. She was squeezing her spoon so hard she was worried it might bend.

Then the fox showed himself performing a near identical motion on the remote for Vivien. The lynx played her song without the slightest sour note or missed rhythm. She didn't even shift her position.

Mila lowered her ears. "She has a lot more practice dealing with that than me."

"She does," Alonso agreed and left Vivien's vibrator on medium and Mila's on low as they continued to dine.

Later, Alonso slipped the remote under the table and ate the rest of his meal one-handed (except for the steak which required the knife). Every now and then Mila felt the vibrator pick up pace, or suddenly die away completely. It kept her always on edge, anticipating the next action of the toy buried within her. She was sure he was doing the same to Vivien, but the lynx didn't let on that anything was changing.

Alonso finished his meal a little before Mila did, and he sat back with the glass of wine in one hand and his remote in the other, teasing Mila while she finished. She hurried through the last few bites of asparagus (never her favorite vegetable) and pushed her plate aside. "May I prepare the second dessert?"

He glanced at his crème brûlée ramekin, which was polished spotless, nodded, and set the remote aside. After climbing out of her seat, Mila didn't go to the kitchen, but instead slipped under the table. It was a bit more cramped and awkward than she anticipated but she nevertheless slid in between Alonso's legs, undoing his pants and pulling them and his underwear down enough to expose him. His sheath was full but not revealing any more of his shaft than the tip. Mila was annoyed and slightly worried: she thought she'd done a better job working him up than that.

The calico tried to reposition herself for better access and had to pause and shut her eyes for a moment at the way that movement had shifted the plug inside her. She reached out and traced along his sheath with a single finger, claw extended just enough to brush through his fur. Even that was enough to make his tip start to push into the air; her muzzle was there to slide around it. The calico suckled and slurped. She felt the shaft stiffen and push enthusiastically deeper. However, despite practice, deep-throating was still not a skill she had picked up. In a moment she had to pull back, gasping. But she was pleased by how long she had held out; she saw a fully hard shaft twitching in the air, waiting for her.

"Mila," Alonso began.

"Shh," she said. "Not done yet, sir."

She wriggled out from under the table and turned his chair for extra room. With a kiss to his cheek, the calico slid into his lap. The heat of his shaft pressed against her spread-wide sex. There was a part of her that would have been so content to grind her hips against him in slow, gentle pleasure until she drifted off to sleep, but the conscious part of her brain said no. She had a duty she needed to perform right now. She positioned his tip at her entrance.

Mila waited for the right time in Vivien's lyrical cello piece to punctuate her drop down over the fox's length. She wriggled her hips from side to side as she fell and felt the plug and nipple weights bounce around as she did. Given the expression and soft twitches on Alonso's face, she guessed he could feel the plug a bit too.

When she pressed down far enough she could feel his knot pressing against her spread labia, she took a deep breath and prepared to sink onto it. But Alonso's arms held her up. "Mila," he said, "you don't need to do this to prove you're as good as she is."

The calico blinked. She hadn't intended for him to take that interpretation on tonight's events. "This isn't about her," she said. "She'd be able to take you far better than I ever could. This is about you and what you enjoy." Before he could interrupt her again, she let her weight drop and slide herself over Alonso's knot.

This time he gasped, and he did so again when she eased herself off and dropped low a second time. She built into a steady rhythm of thrusting down over his whole length, but the rhythm hitched and staggered every time she sank over the knot. The calico's body still instinctively clenched to try and push it out, so her fucking wasn't as smooth as what she had seen Vivien accomplish with Noel back at the masquerade.

Alonso lowered his muzzle to rest against her neck, breathing heavily as they mated. At first he simply let her move, but once he got a feel for the rhythm, he pushed up to meet it, holding her hips so he could angle in deeper and harder on every thrust.

She pressed her forehead to Alonso's and could feel the panting of his breath against her chest. Tremors ran along her tail: the calico had been so focused on his pleasure that she'd almost not noticed how good it felt to have that cock deep within her, or those fingers gripping her ass, or those teeth teasing her nipples.

"Mila," Alonso said in between quick breaths, "are you—"

"No questions," she interjected, struggling as much as him to get words out.

He grimaced and tried to focus on his words. "I want to know if you are close," he said after half a dozen more eager thrusts.

She shivered. She was and she really wanted him to rub at her clit, because she was sure that would send her over the edge right now. But instead, she said, "That doesn't matter, sir. What matters is your pleasure. Use me as you want."

He looked into her eyes as if making sure she meant it, then, with a tremendous effort, he lifted them both out of the chair and shoved Mila onto her back on the table. Dishes and decorations went flying. Mila had a moment of panic as the candles dropped to the floor, but they snuffed themselves out halfway down.

Alonso pinned her down, growling down at her. He thrust in full body motions, once, twice, three times before he erupted within her. Mila clutched to him as she felt his warm seed flow into her sex. It wasn't enough to get her off and despite how desperately she wanted to, she pushed that thought aside. She just held Alonso and caressed him as he recovered from the intense orgasm. (And was it just her, or had Vivien's cello song faltered just a little at the sight of the two of them going at it?)

"This evening," the fox said and then grunted as he eased his knot out of her, "has been wonderful."

"There's still one thing left," Mila said, while suppressing a groan at how empty her sex now felt.

Alonso nuzzled in against her cheek and his hand crept down her flank, headed to her hips.

"No, sir. I'd like you to take a seat."

The fox looked puzzled, but too heady with afterglow to worry about it. He practically fell back into his chair and shook himself a little so he could pay attention better.

Mila sat up on the edge of the table. She could feel his seed leaking out of her spread sex and she saw his gaze fixed there. "Okay," Mila said, as much to psych herself up as to draw Alonso's attention. She pulled out a trio of envelopes that had been hidden amongst the flowers on the table. Thankfully they had not been knocked off. "There are questions in each of these envelopes. You need to ask me the questions exactly as written."

"All right," he said hesitantly. The fox took the envelopes with a glance over to the still playing Vivien. "I trust you know what you are doing."

Alonso flipped the first envelope open while tucking his softening cock away with the other hand. He glanced over the message inside with growing concern. He didn't say anything.

"Sir," she reminded him, "you agreed to follow the rules for the night."

"Yes, it's just..." He swallowed and looked at her. "Mila, who is your owner?"

"No one," she said honestly. "I've been unowned since early this morning."

"But..." She could see the questions written on his face that he knew he could not ask. How? Why?

"I promise I'll explain everything later," she said. "You shouldn't be surprised though. Taking ownership requires full consent without the house interfering. Removing ownership is the same. I chose this morning to be an independent feline. That's all." She shifted a little on the edge of the table. "I promise it is intended to be temporary."

Alonso cast another, more worried, glance at Vivien. His voice dropped too low for the lynx to hear. "That's extremely dangerous."

"I know the risks. I've had Aisha and the house looking out for me all day."

"But—"

"The next envelope, please."

His throat clenched tight as he held back a growl and he flicked open the next one. "Have you been ordered or influenced by any canine or the house today?"

"The only orders I have received today from canines were from Zuberi telling me to go when our time was up and to remember the lessons he taught me, and from Aisha telling me to leave her presence and then later commanding me to explain things." She thought that nicely encapsulated Aisha recreating the circumstances of encountering Lady Yasmin's ghost without needing to go into detail. Nevertheless, she cringed at misdirecting Alonso about Aisha's command to get out of the house: technically leaving the house was leaving her presence, but it still felt like she was lying to her owner. If the fox noticed that anything was wrong, he didn't show it.

The calico took a steadying breath and continued. "The house has not influenced me in any way since this morning. I specifically requested that from it." She gestured around. "All this was my idea, although I did get a lot of help from Vivien on the particulars. You never told me how much you like latex stockings." Mila ran a finger along them but Alonso seemed too preoccupied to care.

"The house did not influence you," he said, modulating his voice so it was a statement of disbelief rather than a question.

"I impressed upon it the importance of this evening. Next envelope, sir."

He opened it, and the furrows of worry in the fur of his face only grew deeper. "Mila, do you love me?"

"No," she said, compelled to honesty by the house.

"Good." He seemed relieved although his tightness in his

shoulders and the cant of his ears still spoke of nervousness. "Otherwise that would have been awkward as I don't love you either."

Mila leaned forward. "Now I get one question, and remember, sir, you promised to answer it completely honestly."

He nodded and sat up straight.

"Sir," she said and then had to swallow before continuing, "when we both manage to get out of here, would you consider letting me still be your kitten, at least from time to time?"

He blinked. It was not the elated response the calico had hoped for, but she had prepared for that. "You don't really want that."

"I do."

"I'm your owner. It's just the house making you fit the role."

"You're not my owner, remember?"

"It doesn't matter. The house will make you submissive regardless."

"It said it hasn't influenced me all day."

"It lied!" A sour note hit on the cello and so Alonso whispered. "It lied."

"But I have to tell the truth. And I told you it has not influenced me."

The fox's eyes searched left and right, searching for another target to blame. But she hadn't left him one.

"No," he said, barely above a whisper. He stood and walked to the railing surrounding the upper level of the observatory. He tilted his head back to stare up into the stars.

Mila sat there shocked. He'd said no. He wasn't going to leave. The plan had failed.

The calico swallowed and silently pleaded with the house for help. If there was something she needed to do, she didn't know what it was.

The table bucked suddenly underneath her, propelling her to her feet, and then the floor twisted, forcing her to take a few more awkward steps towards Alonso. It wanted her to go to him.

A brief quavering note hit on the cello. Mila glanced back to see Vivien looking as panicked as she felt. Silently, the calico gave her a signal to keep playing.

Mila paused one pace behind Alonso to sort out a quick plan. She couldn't just tell him what he needed to do to get out, so she couldn't make this be about him: she had to focus on herself and lead him by example.

Most of all, she had to be honest.

"I'm scared, sir."

His ears flicked around. "Of me?" he asked, his voice defeated.

"No, not you." She stepped up beside him on the railing. He had a hand resting against it, but pulled it further away when she placed her own next to it. "I'm scared of what might happen when I finally leave. You said you had gotten over the worst of the pain, but I haven't. It's still raw, and it's waiting for me the moment I leave the house." *The pain is waiting for you too*, she added silently, *even if it isn't as bad.*

"You've gotten stronger," he said, refusing to look at her.

"I have, but I know I'm not strong enough yet." *Neither are you.* "I keep thinking about all the cooking that I've been doing. I've really loved learning from Devon and Theo. I want to keep experimenting with new things, and I could. But I also know how easy it would be for me to go back to the way things were" — *and how easy it would be for you* — "back when I was getting delivery for every meal just so I could avoid talking to other people." She laughed ruefully. "I had cheap ramen watered down with tears three nights a week."

"Mila," Alonso tried to cut in.

"It's true!" The calico could feel her own chest tightening as she spoke. "Do you know what I did for dinner the night before I was trapped here? I just stopped at a local pharmacy, picked up a premade sandwich, and went through the automated checkout, because my eyes were bloodshot and I didn't want to have to explain to yet another stranger why they were. And I'm scared because that already sounds like a good idea again." *Aren't you tempted as well?* Mila stopped and forced herself to take a deep breath. "It would be easier if I had someone there I could cook for on occasion, someone who would push me to keep doing it."

Alonso said nothing, but his hand returned to its place on the railing and this time he didn't flinch away when she touched it.

"The reason I set all this up today is that I had a terrible, awful thought. What do I do if I get out of here and I want to keep playing like this? Can you imagine the personal ad I'd need to put up? 'Recent widow seeks dominant man to tie her up. Must be prepared to deal with emotional outbursts and lots of crying.' No one would even respond to me." *Would anyone respond to you?*

He sighed.

"Alonso."

The fox tore his eyes away from the skyscraper-impeded horizon with great difficulty. He looked at her.

"Alonso, it's me. It's not the house. It's just Mila. The same scared cat you met weeks ago. Except I've grown to like some of these things." *Just like you.* "And I hope I won't lose them the moment I set foot outside." *You don't want to lose them either.* "I'm hoping I'll have someone to keep me from forgetting." *You need someone just as much as I do, maybe more.* "And I'm hoping that someone will be you." *Don't you want me to still be there?*

She'd done it. She'd bared her heart to him. She'd laid down the path to escape. Now it was on him to follow it.

The fox's eyes moved away from hers, glistening with tears. "Our relationship would be highly inappropriate."

Mila tried not to smile. He wasn't agreeing yet, but he actually considering it. "Oh really?"

"We're not the same species."

"So we can't have children. I'm okay with that."

"I'll be away on work most of the time."

"I can wait."

"I'm too old for you."

Mila couldn't help herself. One soft giggle escaped her throat. "A month you've been fucking me and now you're worried you're too old."

For a fraction of a second, genuine happiness broke through his grim expression. "I'm just struggling to see what you'd want in a washed-up man like me."

She pressed close to his side, her head against his shoulder. "You mean besides the awesome sex? Because you've been where I am, and because you were kind to me, when you didn't need to be."

The fox tipped his head back and stared straight up into the night sky, in the gap between the skyscrapers. "I suppose I've never given much thought to what life after the house would really look like. It feels so impossible, like starting my whole life over again. I suppose if I have to start over..." He looked down at Mila with a small smile. "It might as well be with someone I like."

Click.

Creeeeeeeak.

Alonso's ear flicked back. "What was that?"

Mila's vision was suddenly blurred by the presences of some stray tears. She wiped them away and said softly. "We can go."

"Go where?"

"We can leave the house."

For a second, Alonso was stunned. Then he whirled around. "We can leave?"

Thump.

There was a second, discordant thump as the cello was carelessly thrown aside and Vivien covered the intervening space at a dead run. She latched onto Alonso and buried her head in his shirt. "Promise you'll come back, sir."

Alonso didn't react to the lynx. In a quiet voice, he was repeating, "We can leave," as his muscles seemed to give out. He collapsed to his knees, and Vivien fell with him. The jolt of her body hitting his finally woke him from his stupor. He looked at her in a panic and then at Mila.

"I told her that we couldn't leave," the calico said. "I didn't tell her why."

The fox ran a hand comfortingly down the lynx's neck. Vivien didn't loosen her grip. "But how? What changed?"

Mila went back to the table and picked up one of the discarded envelopes. She handed it to him. "Ask me again, but ask for the whole truth this time."

For once, Alonso didn't hesitate. "Mila, do you love me? And tell me the whole truth."

"No," she said, "but I realized this morning that I *could* love you someday."

"And that's what did it?"

Mila shook her head. "Alonso, in all the time we've been together here, we've never really talked about what we wanted to do once we got out of the house, outside of that one burger you wanted to have."

The fox protested lightly. "We've talked about work."

"Work, sure, but that's not something to look forward to. That's not something to hope for." She knelt down beside him. "Since Lily and BD, neither of us have had that. Tomorrow was just another day that would be full of grief and hurt. But this morning, for the first time, I really, really wanted to wake up and I wanted to wake up in your arms. That's all the house has been trying to show us: there's still something to hope for. I realized that this morning, and I set all this up so that you'd realize it too."

Tension seemed to drain from Alonso's features. "It took all this just to convince me?" He was almost laughing.

"We'll talk more about why it took all this later." She still had Zuberi's words about Alonso's misplaced blame lodged in her head. It was going to be a very long talk.

"All right," he said. He looked down at Vivien, who hadn't loosened her grip an inch. "I promise I'll come back," he assured her with pats over her head. "Uh, house, I can come back can't I?"

Thump.

"Will I remember this place after I leave?"

Thump.

Vivien didn't seem to care that Alonso was conversing with

the house. She squeezed him once and then stood up and aside. "I'll miss you every day until you come back."

He stood slowly and patted her cheek. "I promise not to be gone too long." He collected his cane from where he had left it leaning up against the dinner table. His claws traced along the hatchwork pattern on its head thoughtfully. Then he looked to Mila. "Shall we?"

"Please," she said with a sense of urgency. She didn't want the house to think there was some other reason to keep her.

As much as Mila wanted to make a beeline straight for the front door, Alonso insisted on saying a few goodbyes first. Mila had only been a prisoner for a few weeks. Alonso had been there for years. He said goodbye to Aisha, who told him that he was always welcome back in her library. He said goodbye to Devon and Theo, who made him promise to visit their restaurant once it was up and running. He said goodbye to Zuberi, who gave the pair of them a queer look but accepted the goodbye in the spirit it was offered. He said goodbye to a few others that Mila either didn't know or had minimal contact with.

And then, finally, they were headed for the front door.

It loomed in front of them, and Mila almost couldn't believe that she was going to be able to leave. She reached out and gripped the handle.

It didn't turn.

It jiggled, which was far more than it had ever done before, but the door itself stayed firmly shut. "What's wrong? I thought we were supposed to be able to leave."

Behind her, Alonso let out a quick bark of laughter. "You can't leave the house looking like that!"

Mila glanced down at herself. She was still wearing her outfit for the evening, spread-open sex and all. "Right. House, my clothes from when I arrived."

Thump.

Mila opened the closet next to the door and started to redress, but Alonso looked suddenly thoughtful. "House, the flower too."

thump

The sound was so quiet, Mila only heard it because her ears were turned in the right direction.

Alonso pulled out the flower from where it had been deposited and handed it to Mila. "Remember," he commanded.

It wasn't necessary: Aisha had let her remember weeks before. Still, having the purple hyacinths in her hand once more made the memory and all its associated emotions that much stronger. "I was going to his grave," she said softly. "I was going to put this on it. I suppose I still should."

Alonso placed a comforting hand on her shoulder. "When you leave, Aisha's command is going to drop. You'll feel the pain all over again."

"I know." Now fully dressed, she placed a hand on the door. "Will you come to his grave with me?"

"I will."

The handle turned easily this time. The door opened.

In the time since they had left the observatory, it had started to rain. Water poured from the sky with frightful intensity. It looked almost identical to the night Mila had entered the house. Together, they crossed the threshold of the door and stood outside.

Mila clutched so tightly to the hyacinth flower that it threatened to be torn apart. Her breath came in a shaky rasp. A horrid hollow feeling burrowed through her as she contemplated the existential void of her life without BD. It hurt like a dagger driving into her side. It hurt like an ice cube forced down her throat. It hurt like—

Alonso wrapped an arm around her.

And it started to hurt a little less.

Epilogue: Coda

Mila squirmed impatiently in her seat as she waited to get off the plane. Part of her squirm was due to anxiousness: she had no idea where they were going and Alonso hadn't even told her the flight was to LA until they had to show their tickets at the airport. The other reason for her squirming was that just before they had boarded, Alonso had ordered her to go into the bathroom, take off her panties, and stick them into her carry-on.

Of course, she obeyed. Not because she had to, but because she wanted to. Because the soft fabric of her dress and the occasional breeze brushing over her naked folds filled her head with idle fantasies of Alonso ravaging her in the airplane restroom. Because she knew it excited him just as much as it excited her. Because she trusted him to protect her when she gave up control. Mostly.

The pair of them had developed a silent signal in the months since they had left the Eternal Party. It had begun as a nervous tell of Alonso's. He had tried to arrange a surprise party for her birthday, but had a terrible poker face: every time she would question him about what they were doing for her birthday he would always turn one ear — and only one ear — back as if he had heard something behind him. That was how she knew he was hiding something. So they turned it into a signal. The ear-turn, as Mila called it, meant, "I know this is unexpected, but trust me."

The fox was ear-turning a lot on this trip. He had been ear-turning in the weeks before the trip when he often spent an hour a day on a private call and wouldn't tell Mila who else was on the phone.

And he'd also left his cane behind. That was unusual too.

Mila followed submissively behind Alonso as they got off the plane and tried not to think of how her dress was brushing against her mound with every step. She was hoping that as soon as they got into the terminal, he would tell her to go put her panties back on, but he didn't. He just took her by the hand and led her to the baggage claim.

All the while he held her hand, his pinky was extended to brush the leather bracelet she wore as a discreet public alternative to her collar. No one had to know she was a good obedient kitten following her Master's lead, but she knew and he knew and that was what mattered.

Thankfully they were able to pick up their bags quickly and Alonso hailed a cab to take them to their destination.

The cabbie did a double-take when he saw the address. The dachshund glanced at the couple in his backseat through the rear-view mirror. "You're sure this is where you want to go?" he asked in a heavy Chicago accent that was out of place in California.

"Very sure," Alonso said.

"Something wrong with the address?" Mila asked, trying to wheedle a little information out of someone besides Alonso.

"You just don't look the type," the driver said as he started to pull out.

Alonso did another one of his ear-turns. "We're traveling incognito."

"Ah, I get it. Well, don't you worry. Your secret is safe with me."

"Incognito?" Mila whispered in his ear.

Alonso ignored the question and whispered back. "Tailtip on your sex."

The calico bit back a grumble about Alonso's secrecy and adjusted her seat to curl her tail around her leg and brush the tip of it between her inner thighs. One of the advantages dresses held over pants was that so much more could be hidden by them. All the same, the slight chance of discovery added an extra thrill to the commanded masturbation. He hadn't told her to rub herself hard or make sure she was wet, so she only distracted herself with flicking a bit of fluff back and forth over her sensitive parts.

They left the airport and turned away from the city, heading through a residential area before turning along a steep hill that led into an upscale residential area, then into an even more upscale residential area. They came to a gate. Alonso handed over the entrance code to the driver, who tapped it in, and drove them into a neighborhood full of what Mila could only call estates. These weren't million-dollar houses: these were multi-million-dollar houses. This was the spot for some of the richest in the entire LA metro area.

What the hell were they doing here?

"This is it." The cabbie hopped out and got their luggage out of the trunk. While accepting a very large tip from Alonso, he whispered something about "an incognito trip back to the airport whenever they needed one." Then he drove off.

Mila and Alonso stood in front of an elegantly crafted modern house. It stood on a sloping hill and had a single roof that sloped down with it. The wall of the house facing the street was an almost featureless blank gray slate, although the garden in front of it was well-tended and beautiful. Mila counted three bays in the garage.

"How did you afford this?"

"I didn't buy the house," Alonso said with a laugh.

"I was wondering how you would have afforded renting this, even for a day."

The fox gave her a look and pinched her rump. "Come along, kitten."

"Yes, sir," Mila said, following as the fox walked up to the front door.

There was no keyhole on the handle, but there was a numerical pad next to the door, and Alonso quickly typed in a code.

The inside of the house was even more jaw-dropping. Mila lost count of the number of bespoke features she saw. The only thing which appeared to be straight from a hardware store were the walls, except when she looked close, she saw they had a rough, hand-crafted texture to them. This house contained everything she had ever convinced clients would be too expensive to maintain. Sure enough, she was even standing on a genuine hand-woven rug in the front foyer.

They were on the middle floor of a split-level house. In front of them were a dining room and kitchen. To their left, stairs led down to a living area, with sumptuous couches and mini-bar on one side and a small performance space surrounded by instruments — including an out-of-place viola — on the other. To their right, stairs led up to what Mila assumed were bedrooms. Everywhere the decor was distinctly rock-themed: thundereggs, geodes, and fossils decorated tabletops, table lamps consisted of lights underneath crystal formations, and huge chunks of petrified wood hung from the walls like banners.

Before Mila could drool over too much, Alonso called out, "We're here!"

There was a slight commotion in a side room before a tigress burst out. It was Jeta Horowitz. "Mila! Alonso! You made it." The tigress swept both cat and fox into a bear hug.

Alonso gave a mock growl. "Jeta, behave yourself."

The tigress released them both and took a bashful step back.

Alonso placed a hand on his spine. "You may not have been able to crush me back at the house, but you can here. I am delicate."

"Could have fooled me last night," Mila said with a snigger. "Why didn't you tell me we were coming to see Jeta?"

An ear-turn. "I just wanted to keep some surprises for you."

Surprises, Mila noted, not surprise. There was more to this than the fox was letting on.

"You didn't tell her she was coming to see me?" Jeta sounded as jokingly irritated as Mila felt.

"No, I didn't. She mentioned how you wanted her to come see you after she got out and I said I'd try to find a time to make it work. That's what I did."

The tigress had her hands on her hips and rolled her eyes. "Well, I want to hear everything that you two have been up to since I've been gone, because clearly this is still a thing." As she said "this" she gestured between the cat and fox.

"I promise I'll tell everything, but can I borrow you in private for just a minute?" the fox asked.

"But you just got here." Jeta looked to Mila. "We have so much to catch up on and—"

"It will only take a moment," the fox said insistently. He had his hands on the larger tigress's shoulders and was already steering her towards the upper floor bedrooms.

"If you say so..." The tigress let herself be directed away, looking over her shoulder and giving a shrug of what-is-going-on back to the calico.

Mila returned a shrug of her own.

Then the calico was alone and exquisitely aware of how expensive every single thing around her was. She was conscious of each of her claws. She felt if she nicked something it would cost more than her monthly salary to repair it.

Thankfully, that thought barely passed her mind before the tigress and fox returned.

Jeta was laughing at something Alonso had just said when she caught sight of the calico again. Her jaw dropped. "Mila!" the tigress exclaimed in shock. "What are you wearing?" Jeta looked genuinely horrified. "No, no, no, this will not do."

Mila held her hands up defensively as the tigress stomped towards her, but was unable to stop the much bigger feline from forcibly undressing her, yanking off her dress with a squeal and an embarrassed flattening of her ears. The tigress didn't bother to comment on her lack of underclothes. She left the calico standing naked in her house and hoping that the massive windows on the far wall were one-way.

The tigress stepped back, looking the calico up and down with a smirk. "Much better."

"Still a little off I think," Alonso said with a gesture downwards.

The tigress followed the gesture until she was looking down at her own shirt and pants with an expression of disgust. She gave a grunt of annoyance before yanking all her clothes off and tossing them into a corner. "There," she declared, standing naked and proud. "Much better."

Mila had expected Jeta at home to be different from the Jeta at the Eternal Party. The tigress wasn't under any magical personality-altering compulsions out here. But she was not expecting the tigress to be an adamant nudist.

"What about him?" Mila asked, gesturing to the still clothed fox.

"What about him?" Jeta repeated.

"He's not naked."

The tigress looked at the fox, then back to Mila. "So?"

"Why doesn't he have to strip down too?" Mila tried to put her hands on her hips and look intimidating, but Aisha had been right. She couldn't do that well. Instead, she was pretty sure that the pose, while naked, just made her look especially revealing.

"Cause he's a guy."

Behind the tigress, Alonso ear-turned.

But for once, Mila ignored that. "So? What does that have to do with anything?"

"He's a guy. There's nothing wrong with him being naked, of course, but he hasn't had centuries of puritanical obsession with nudity try to make him dress demurely. In my house you are not going to hide any of this sexy body, got it?"

"Got it," Mila said, although in truth she didn't. Not just nudist, but feminist nudist? She shrugged and then flushed as she realized Jeta Horowitz had just called her sexy.

"We have a lot to get caught up on. Let's take a seat in the living room," Alonso suggested, and the three of them stepped down the stairs into an exquisite circular conversation pit — yes, an honest-to-goodness conversation pit — lined with a leather couch and centered around a hefty wooden table that Mila was sure, given the tigress's proclivities, doubled as a bondage point and sex table.

Jeta had a preternatural ability to look like she was ready to fuck someone just by lounging on the couch. She looked between the calico and fox. "Now, you two, how has your reintegration with the normal world gone?"

Mila found herself sitting next to Alonso and draped her tail over his lap. He rested a hand on her inner thigh, tantalizingly close to her sex.

"It's gone well all things considered," Alonso said. "I ended up quitting my job. After ten years out of the skies I didn't feel like it'd be safe for me to be a pilot again without a lot of retraining, and I wasn't about to go through all that again. But Mila is encouraging me to try art full-time."

The calico nodded. "We're fine on money," she said, feeling a need to justify her economic status when surrounded by the signs of Jeta's wealth.

"More than fine," Alonso agreed. "Apparently Aisha, in her role as the Eternal Party's accountant, had been diverting some house funds to pay off my mortgage, worried that since I wasn't a usual guest, the house might not take care of things while I was away correctly. Now that I've sold it and moved in with Mila, we're set for quite a while."

"You moved in?" Jeta batted her eyes and purred. She leaned

forward so her breasts spilled out above her folded arms. "Awfully fast, even for you, Alonso."

"We... tried being separate at the start. Didn't work."

"Totally didn't work," Mila agreed. "We just collapsed at my place the first night we got out," she said, eliding over the long emotionally fraught visit to BD's grave and how grateful she had been that Alonso had stayed by her side the entire time. "And then — can you believe it? — the next day was a Monday. We had to go in to work."

The tigress gave the knowing nod of someone who always aimed to leave the Eternal Party on a Friday afternoon.

Mila went on. "It was so weird. I had to pick back up on projects that I hadn't touched in a month. Everyone had carried on like I was out sick, but no one talked about it."

"It was even worse for me," Alonso said. The fox rolled his shoulders uncomfortably. "First thing that happened was I got a call telling me there's been a glitch in the system and I need to 'retake' some training. I showed up and everyone there is twenty years my junior. Even the instructors I didn't recognize. And then I get another call from IT wondering why I haven't updated my phone in 10 years."

Mila giggled a little. "But we made plans. We wanted to try meeting each other the right way this time. So after work, we accidentally-on-purpose bumped into each other at a café." Mila took a deep breath and let it out in a groan, her head falling forward into her hands. "It was a disaster."

"A train wreck," Alonso agreed. "It was like I didn't know how to have a conversation in any place that wasn't a kink club. What do people who just met talk about, if not talk about sex?"

"And I kept wanting to call you sir," Mila said, nuzzling in against Alonso. "Actually did once too, right in front of the waiter as we were paying. I almost ran out of there, I was so embarrassed."

Alonso wrapped an arm around her waist and squeezed. "But

then we went to your place and things got much better. We had sex, of course, but we also talked a lot about what we wanted."

It had been far more difficult than that, Mila thought. Free of the house's compulsion to answer honestly (and confess her horniness at every other opportunity), she found herself wanting some privacy. And Alonso had never been fully comfortable discussing his wants. But they had, with some difficulty and spurred on by their own desire to get to the fucking, talked.

The hardest part of the evening had been when Mila told Alonso about why he had been trapped at the Eternal Party for so long. She was worried he wouldn't believe her, but the fact that they had escaped made it easier for him to accept it. He even agreed with her suggestion to start going to therapy again.

Alonso carried on, heedless of Mila's internal dialogue. "We kept up the attempts at dinner dates for, what, a week? Two? But it was always awkward and we always ended up fucking at her place afterwards anyways. Honestly, I never thought I was going to be hornier out of the house than in it."

Jeta purred quietly and raised a hand to cup one of her breasts. "Well, stress can dampen sexual desire, and I imagine being trapped at the Eternal Party was quite stressful for you both."

Mila found her eyes tracking the movements of the tigress's chest. "Well, we dumped the idea of trying to start from scratch and just admitted to ourselves that we were a couple. But then we spent another week trying to figure out what kind of couple we were. We tried just being boyfriend and girlfriend, and that was another disaster."

"Less of a train wreck this time," Alonso said. "We kept dancing around what we really wanted: that I wanted to order her and she wanted to be ordered."

"At least some of the time," Mila said with a nudge. "So we tried a dominant and submissive relationship, but only in the bedroom, and that wasn't enough. Then we tried being owner and kitten like we were at the house, and that was too much. And now we're Master and kitten, and that's working out for us so far. We've been exploring the contours of what we want and when and how. It's been good."

"It has," the fox agreed. He kissed her, and with one hand caressed the bracelet on her wrist, and with the other gently spread the folds of her sex as if showing her off to Jeta. "Good kitten," he whispered in her ear.

Mila purred softly. It still felt good, even if she missed the way those words had made her feel so good back at the house.

"Any trips back to the house yet?" Jeta asked.

"Several actually," Alonso said. He held Mila's gaze a moment more before turning back to the tigress. His hand pulled away too, to Mila's mild frustration. "When Mila originally encouraged me to try art full-time, I thought she meant doing watercolors of fruit in bowls, but it turns out there's a surprising demand for erotic portraiture."

"I can imagine." Jeta languidly pointed a finger back upstairs. "Your drawings of me are hanging in the master bathroom."

Mila was suddenly overcome with a fit of giggles.

"What?"

The calico had to cover her face with a hand. "You are way too submissive to call your bathroom the master bathroom."

Jeta joined in the laughter. "That's completely fair."

Mila turned back to Alonso and ran a hand up his inner thigh. "And Vivien has been happy you've returned so often."

"She is a wonderful model," the fox admitted.

"And that's all you've been doing back at the house? Painting?" The tigress waggled an eyebrow suggestively.

Mila was glad Jeta hadn't asked her about going back to the house. She was a little embarrassed to admit she hadn't returned, not even once. The calico had more than one nightmare about being trapped there again, this time without Alonso or Aisha to protect her. Whenever she had to go past it on the way to work, she crossed the street to be along the opposite sidewalk.

"Not everything. I've actually had a number of conversations with Aisha, Devon, and some others. Turns out there are a lot of secrets about the house that we've only just started to uncover. Jeta, why don't you come over here?"

He beckoned, and the naked tigress drew closer. The calico scooted to one side to make room.

Mila almost missed what Alonso did next. He snapped his fingers sharply, in such a way that only his index finger was left pointing up. He swayed that finger back and forth in front of the tigress.

Mila opened her mouth to ask what was going on, but for once there was no ear-turn, but instead a sharp glare from the fox to command her silence. Jeta, however, seemed to be utterly fascinated by the finger and could not look away.

Slowly the fox moved closer to the tigress, keeping that one finger upright. Her eyes continued to track it, even to the point where she started to go cross-eyed to keep watching it.

But it was more than that. The closer Alonso got, the more Jeta's jaw went slack. Her normal upbeat perky personality seemed to drain away and leave behind a befuddled expression in its place. When the finger was within an inch of touching her, the tigress's hips began to squirm and her hand dipped between her thighs.

Alonso darted forward and up to tap her forehead. The tigress's eyes rolled to follow the movement. The tigress gave out a tiny mewl and there was a distinctive shlck sound of fingers diving into and out of a wet slit.

The fox sat back, hands folded over her lap, but Jeta continued to stare into a spot just in front of her forehead. "Hello, kitty," he said.

"Kitty," Jeta repeated brainlessly. She was panting a little as her hips kept grinding against her hand.

"Do you remember telling me what was so important about kitties?"

"Kitty," Jeta repeated. A look of concentration tried to break through on her placid face. "Kitty w-wants..."

"Go on."

"Kitty wants... Kitty wants..."

"It was a certain kind of kitty. Do you remember what kind of kitty you are?"

Another attempt at concentration that kept being smoothed over into blank nothingness as the tigress fingered herself. "K-kitty... Kitty..." Then blissful happiness spread over her face. "Slutty kitty!" she said proudly.

"Yes, you are a slutty kitty. And what do slutty kitties want?"

Jeta kept trying to formulate a full sentence. "Slutty kitty wants... slutty kitty wants... sex?" She tried to finish off the sentence in some way that made sense, but Alonso shook his head.

"No, silly kitty. Think hard. What is it you really really want?"

A light bulb seemed to go off in the tigress's head. Her eyes finally focused on something besides the spot in the air before her. "Pretty titty! Slutty kitty wants pretty titty!" Her hands pulled away from her thighs with a wet shlorp and immediately gripped her breasts, brushing her fingers along her nipples.

"That's right, good kitty!"

It wasn't quite the same as the "good kitten" phrase he had used with Mila, but close enough that it made her smile.

"Now," the fox said sharply. "What does a kitty want?"

"Slutty kitty wants pretty titty!" the tigress enthused.

"What does a kitty crave?"

"Slutty kitty craves pretty titty!"

"What does a kitty need?"

"Slutty kitty needs pretty titty!"

By this point, Jeta's hips were lifting up into the air as she tried to hump at nothing. Her hands were too preoccupied with teasing her own breasts and her mind was clearly not working at full power.

The fox put a finger on his chin thoughtfully. "Kitty, what are these?" He pointed to Mila's naked chest.

"Pretty titty!" the tigress exclaimed and she lunged for the calico before Mila could stop her, bowling the smaller feline over on the couch as she started to kiss and suck and tease all over Mila's breasts. Most distractingly, the tigress was grooming her with her thick tongue, which was big enough to nearly encapsulate a third of a breast at once.

Mila giggled hard and waved frantically at Alonso. "Make her stop!" She hadn't realized how her brief play with Zuberi had left her so sensitive to ticklish sensations, but this was definitely ticklish. She was having trouble getting the words out due to laughing too hard.

The fox waited for a while before snapping his fingers twice.

Immediately Jeta was back to normal, although she returned midway through licking all over Mila's breast, and when she sat up, her tongue still hung out of her mouth for a moment. She slurped it back in and wiped off her drooly jowls. "You controlled me," she said, more surprised than anything else.

"I did."

"But we're not back at the house." Jeta looked back at Mila, still pinned underneath her, for confirmation.

"I don't think we are," Mila said, but she was unsure too. "House, are you there?"

Thump.

For a second, Mila's heart leaped into her throat. Then she saw Alonso's leg sticking out towards the central table.

"You ass!" She wriggled out from under Jeta and came over to swat the fox on the shoulder. "Don't scare us like that."

"But wait." Jeta picked herself up, looking a bit dazed. "If we're not at the house, how did you control me?"

Alonso held up his hands to ward off more attacks from Mila. "I promise I'll explain everything if you both sit down."

Mila glared at him playfully and gave him one last mock kick before sitting next to the tigress.

"Very well, I hypnotized you, Jeta."

"When? How?" the tigress interjected.

"Check your phone logs."

The tigress gave him a queer look, but stood up and picked

her phone off the kitchen counter, scrolling back through it. Her jaw dropped. "You've been calling me for weeks. I don't remember any of this."

"You are, as it turns out, very suggestible. We experimented with various hypnotic effects over the phone and one time we tried wiping your memory of the session. It was so successful that you suggested I do that regularly, so that this meeting would be as much a surprise for you as for Mila."

Mila felt she knew where Jeta's militant nudism had come from as well. She jerked her thumb towards the tigress. "That's who you've been calling?"

He nodded. "As to the how, that's the second surprise. You've both probably noticed how your time in the house intensified certain desires."

"Yeah," Mila said, petting the tigress's tail as she sat down beside her again. "Like with corsets. Before the house, they were eh, but now I own a dozen and find any excuse I can to wear them."

"That was the same way for me too," Jeta agreed. She traced a claw over her naked belly as if wishing she could put one on right now.

"Aisha has her theories as to why, something about being exposed to a new desire in an idealized setting."

Mila groaned silently. Alonso was still bad at explaining things, but this time, at least, he seemed aware of the fact, and tried again.

"Basically," he said, "when you put on a corset now, part of your mind is reliving the experience of wearing a corset at the Eternal Party. It's easier to ignore the negative aspects like the difficulty of lacing it up or when it pinches, and the positive aspects feel so much better, because you are focused on that ideal time."

"Oh, I get it." Mila couldn't help but rib her Master. "I think your dick is just about perfect not because it is, but because I remember being at the house and the magic making me think that."

"No, it's because my dick is just about perfect, you brat." Alonso stole a quick kiss on her throat while pinching her ass. "As to the hypnosis, it was Devon and Theo's experiments that are responsible for that. They still wanted to engage in their personality play after leaving the house. Devon thought it was impossible, but Theo suggested hypnosis, as he'd tried it before unsuccessfully. Turns out after living in the house for a while, he became a natural subject and maintained his suggestibility even when they left the house. After a bit more experimentation, Aisha has determined that all felines who have visited the house have that same suggestibility. She thinks that the power of command inside the house is really due to felines being in a naturally hypnotic state while they are there."

"But none of the felines were wandering the halls like zombies and saying, 'Yes, Master, I will obey,' in monotone." Mila paused to consider what she had just said. "Okay, no one but Tricia."

Jeta laughed.

"Hypnosis doesn't typically work that way," Alonso explained.

The tigress pulled legs up to sit criss-cross and scanned her phone. "You called me a whole bunch of times. Even if I assume a couple of those were to arrange this visit, and a couple others were for induced amnesia and being fascinated by Mila's tits — not that you needed a trigger there — that leaves a lot more post-hypnotic suggestions, I bet."

"Oh yes," the fox said with a grin. "Want to try out some of the others?"

"Hell yeah!" Jeta pumped the air with a fist.

"Sure," Mila said. "Although I'd like to know what triggers you put in me, first."

The fox rubbed the back of his neck and didn't meet her gaze. "I actually haven't even tried anything with you yet, Mila. Jeta was an experiment, to see if she might be as suggestible as Aisha thought. I didn't want to try anything with you in case it didn't work. You weren't at the house nearly as long as Jeta has been."

Mila almost felt disappointed at that. There were a few aspects of the house she missed, even if she wasn't willing to go back just yet. One was the sheer assortment of toys it contained that she couldn't purchase on her budget. Two was the lack of injuries inside its walls, as she had strained herself on multiple occasions trying to replicate positions she'd managed with ease there. But three was the ability to truly relinquish control. She didn't want to lose all control all the time, but there were moments when she wished she could just hand over herself to Alonso. After experiencing the total control offered by the house, their play felt like just that: play. Getting even some of that back would be wonderful.

Mila hid her feelings and asked, "So what did you install in Jeta here?"

The fox considered and snapped his fingers. Immediately the tigress fixated on them once again. "Jeta," the fox said, enunciating carefully, "serve."

Wordlessly the naked tigress slipped off the couch to stand before them. Her arms were held straight at her side and she kept her head bowed. "Sir, miss, you honor me by coming to my home. What can I do for you? A drink, perhaps?"

The calico, interested to see where this would go, considered for a second. "Coffee, as dark a roast as you have."

"Will an americano be sufficient?" the tigress asked with a slightly apologetic tone.

"That's fine."

Alonso, however, bent forward with a grin and said, "A rum and coke with a blowjob chaser would be great." He winked at Mila.

"As you wish," Jeta said and turned to move into the kitchen.

Mila leaned over and whispered low. "Her accent changed. It's Swedish now I think."

"I know. I noticed it when I set up the trigger the first time, but it wasn't something I meant to happen. I think she subconsciously connects a maid or other service role with Sweden. It may be from an early movie she was in. I haven't looked it up."

The couple watched as Jeta prepped the drinks. Even after a month of watching Devon play with Theo's personality, Mila had never witnessed a transformation as total and complete as what she now saw: gone was the bombastic sexuality that shouted to everyone around to look at the tigress, and in its place was something so simple and quiet that you could almost forget she was there. The tigress worked with quick, efficient movements: she turned on the espresso machine and electric kettle, ground the beans into the filter, tamped them down, locked the filter in place, got a mug and glass of ice as the water continued to heat, poured in the rum, poured in the coke, stirred, set the drink aside as she pulled a shot, and finally added the hot water to Mila's americano. There was an aura of infinite patience around her as she worked, as though she would have been happy standing at the espresso machine for an hour if that's how long it took to warm up.

Then she was bringing the drinks over on a tray, setting Mila's on a saucer on the table, and handing Alonso's to him directly. The empty tray was whisked into the ether so quickly Mila couldn't tell where it had gone. The tigress got on her knees. She worked with the same efficient method she had employed when making drinks, as if the act of sucking Alonso off was no more exciting or important than any other duty she might perform: his zipper was pulled down, the button was undone, the two wings of the pants were folded to the side with definite creases, and a claw hooked under the band of Alonso's boxers and pulled them down. She even took special care to make sure the fox's sac was not irritated by the elastic band. As businesslike as Jeta was being, Alonso was already standing at full mast, his shaft throbbing with desire. The tigress pressed her lips to the tip of the fox's cock and slid over it in one smooth motion.

It was the quietest blowjob Mila had ever witnessed. Jeta's head bobbed silently without a single smack of her lips or noisy breath. The only part of her that moved was her head, as the tigress tried to be as unobtrusive as possible. But it was clearly still a good blowjob, because soon Alonso was lifting his hips to meet Jeta's mouth and groaning under his breath.

Mila sat in silent jealousy but wasn't sure who she envied more: Alonso for having the beautiful tigress servicing him or Jeta for getting to service Alonso.

The tigress pulled off the shaft and looked up at the fox. "How would sir like to deposit his seed?"

"In your mouth," he said, "swallowing so you don't leave any mess. And speed things up."

The tigress obeyed. Her hand stroked over his knot as she bounced her muzzle in his lap. Alonso must have been as worked up as Mila had been feeling, as it took very little time for his hips to shudder and thrust in climax. Jeta suckled the shaft until it stopped twitching, carefully cleaned him with soft licks of her tongue, and began to tuck him away. "Is there anything else sir or miss would like?"

Alonso took a moment to recover his breath and then snapped his fingers sharply. "Jeta, reset."

A full body shudder ran through the tigress and she stood. "Wow. Really, wow." Another shudder went through her and she dropped into the seat next to Mila, hugging the calico. "Can you believe this?"

Mila had to carefully balance her barely-touched americano so that the weight of the tiger didn't make it spill. "It's pretty incredible," she said. "Could you try hypnotizing me?"

Alonso shifted in his seat. "I would like to test a few more things first."

"Oh. Well, could I hypnotize her?"

"No." The fox's hands came up quickly. "Mila, playing with someone's thoughts is something potentially dangerous. You have to be very careful as we do not have the house here to protect us. Much of what I've been doing on those phone calls has been reinforcing a lot of safety precautions. That, and I have been studying and practicing. Once you've done all that, maybe. Besides," he said with a wave, "Jeta is extremely suggestible and that means we would need to be extra cautious."

The tigress made a face. "Am I really?"

Alonso slid closer, taking Jeta's wrist in his hand and looking her straight in the eye. "Jeta," he said slowly, and then jerked her hand forward, as he commanded sharply, "drop!"

The tigress slumped forward, eyes unfocused staring at a spot on the couch, her whole body still except for deep heaving breaths.

"Are you hypnotized?" Alonso asked.

"I am hypnotized," the tigress responded in near monotone.

"Are you deeply hypnotized?"

"I am deeply hypnotized."

Alonso reached up to turn the tigress's ears down and whispered to Mila. "Take a step outside for a few minutes."

"But I'm—"

"Mila." He gave her that look that suggested he was not going to take no for an answer.

The calico swallowed her concerns that she was butt-naked except for the strap of leather on her wrist and carried her drink to a nearby door, stepping out onto the deck. Thankfully from this lower side of the house, there was a high privacy fence in all directions which meant she was completely secluded. The porch extended into a pool, so Mila sat on the side of it and dipped her toes into the water as she sipped her americano. Skinny dipping had never been on her list of wants, but now there was something appealing in the thought. The only thing that kept her from diving in was the thought of how long it would take to dry her fur out properly.

That, and the memory of a pool party from many years ago.

Her friends had pressured her to go. Mila didn't want to be there: the only bikini she had revealed too much of her pelt for her comfort. So while her friends were diving into the deep end and sipping hard lemonade, Mila hid in a pool chair under a massive umbrella and hoped no one would notice her. Someone did, of course. A cat about her age tread water just in front of her. He kept calling out to her, cajoling her to join him. He said it was a perfect day for a swim. He said the water felt great, not too warm or too cool. Mila looked around and realized that there was no one else nearby. He wasn't interested in the party either: he was interested in her and he didn't care how she looked. So she took a chance. She ran up to the pool and jumped in with a splash that made both of them laugh.

It had been the day she met BD.

There was no stab of guilt, no hollow icy feeling coring her out from the inside. There was just an ache in her heart that never fully went away.

Since leaving the house, she'd had good days and bad days. Some days she and Alonso were able to regale each other with stories of their former partners, like BD's disastrously bad hot pot birthday party, or the way Alonso and Lily came up with their kits' names. (No literary names, he had insisted.) Some days, though, Mila wanted nothing more than to wall herself off from the world, press herself in to Alonso's warmth and protection, and cry.

It hurt less now, or perhaps Mila was better about dealing with the pain. Or perhaps there wasn't a difference between the two.

The calico's ears perked as she heard the door open, and she turned to see the tigress there dressed just like she had when Mila had first met her: in nothing but a corset and collar. Mila flicked her head away, hoping to blink away the stray tears and clear her throat before Jeta noticed anything was wrong, but she wasn't fast enough. The tiger slid in beside her, one hand on Mila's back. "We don't have to continue if you aren't ready," she said.

One sob escaped Mila's throat, but only one. "Sorry," she said. "I think I need a minute."

The tiger's response was to wait and make sure Mila was okay with the touch, before moving closer, into a full-bodied hug.

"Thanks," the calico said. She set her drink to the side. "I don't think I ever told you how I ended up being trapped at the house, did I?"

"Aisha told me," the tigress said, her voice a little lower as if she wasn't sure that was something that should have been done.

Mila nodded, glad to not have to go through the entire story again. "I was just thinking that BD — my husband — he would have loved to have met you."

The tigress purred in response. "I'm sure I would have loved to meet him too."

"You don't have to say that." Mila wiped away one more tear as her eyes dried. "It's not like he was someone famous or special like you."

"He was special to you."

"He was, but that's not what I—"

Jeta cut her off. "And you are very special yourself. Aisha certainly thinks so, and I trust her judgment." The tiger tilted her head back and considered for a moment, then she reached out with a claw and gently touched it to Mila's chin. "Mila, I know we have not spent that much time together yet, but may I make a guess about you?"

Mila's ears flattened and then came back up unsteadily. "Okay," she said, curious to know what the tigress had in mind.

"My guess is that in your relationship with your husband, he was the reliable one. Now," she held up a hand to stop any protestations, "I don't mean to suggest that you were unreliable, but that when something went wrong, you always went to him to fix it."

Mila nodded. "How did you know?"

The tiger looked off into the distance. "If I understand it right, you were trapped in the house because the weight of the grief was too much and you did not have the strength to bear it, and yet you found the strength to stand up for Alonso and fight to get him out of the house as well."

Mila felt a little embarrassed. "It's not like—"

"You did magic."

"What?" It was all Mila could think to say.

"Aisha told me. She gave you a direct order to leave the house. A canine gave you a direct order at the Eternal Party. And you said no. You disobeyed. You can't do that just because you want to. The only way to fight the magic of the house is with your own magic."

Mila struggled to find words. "Aisha didn't say anything."

The tigress gave her a somewhat mournful smile. "She worries that magic is disappearing, but what terrifies her more than anything is the thought that she won't be fast enough or clever enough to save it, that it will be her fault when the last trace of magic vanishes. Every feline at the Eternal Party, myself included, has been tested by her for the slightest spark of arcane talent, and you're the first to manage anything. Aisha wanted so badly to ask you to stay at the house with her, but she knew that was not where you would want to be."

Mila pulled her knees up to her chest and rested her head down on the soft fur of her own knees. She remembered the strange look Aisha had given her when she had told the jackal no. "What does that have to do with BD?"

The tigress sat back and stretched her legs out as she watched the wisps of clouds going by overhead. "In my view of the world, we are not just ourselves: we are a reflection of all the people we have ever seen, heard, or met. We are the clearest reflection of those we held most dear. I think it was BD's strength you relied upon to fight for Alonso, his strength that let you perform magic." The tigress turned to look at her, staring deep into her eyes. "So yes, I do think I would have loved to have met your husband."

Zuberi had also said that Mila had displayed incredible strength, but he thought it had come from Alonso. Maybe it had come from BD instead.

Mila smiled at this. So many well-meaning friends and family had told how wonderful it was to have such great memories of BD, but Mila was keenly aware of how she would never be able to make any new memories. This, however, felt different. The way Jeta said it, it was like there was a piece of BD that was still within her, guiding her, helping her, just as he had always done. "Thanks," she said, after a while. Then she nudged the tigress. "I suppose we should get back to whatever that fox has planned."

The tigress nodded and stood, gesturing to the house. "If you're ready, Mila, Master Alonso requests our presence in the playroom."

Master Alonso, not just Alonso, Mila noted with a slight pang of jealousy. The tigress's tone spoke of her complete acceptance of her place in the world, and Mila found herself wondering if she really ought to have plucked up her courage and returned to the Eternal Party, if only to experience that again.

The calico started for the door but Jeta held her back. "We need to get you properly attired first." She gestured to some items sitting on a table just outside the house. A towel, but also her own favorite collar and corset. They must have been tucked away in Alonso's luggage. Mila dried her feet off while the tigress laced up the corset. It was direct from the house, so fit her perfectly, but it did not go on with the same invisible feeling of corsets put on in the house itself.

The collar made Mila a little worried. The act of Alonso sliding the collar around her neck had come to signify the change from their public life of boyfriend and girlfriend to their private life of Master and kitten. It was extremely personal to her. But Jeta, without needing to be told, treated it with the same reverence Alonso would.

"So, are you going to tell me what the deal is?" Mila asked.

The tigress smiled. "Apparently you confessed a fantasy to Master at some point of both of us serving him at the house, being owned together. So he has hypnotized me to be his property for the remainder of the day."

"And you know that?"

"Did knowing you were under the house's compulsion make it any easier to resist it?"

Mila shook her head.

Jeta smiled. "Come along. Master is waiting."

Mila fell into step behind the tigress as she stepped around the conversation pit and up to what Mila had assumed to be just a bookcase on the wall. But with the press of a button, a secret door revealed itself and together they entered the playroom.

It was not as well supplied as the house. There was no way it could have been. But all the same, Jeta had amassed a sizable collection of bondage gear, slings and crosses, suspension points, and enough rope to supply a rodeo. A Sybian and several other fucking machines sat in a corner. Mila had done her homework since leaving the Eternal Party. She knew how much all those items cost now; she'd made plans for purchasing one or two.

In the center of it all, like an oasis in the midst of debauchery, was an elegant Persian rug on which sat a high-backed leather chair. Currently it had Alonso as its sole occupant. "Kittens, inspection," he said as he watched the two come in. He did not comment at all about how long they had taken. He understood that sometimes Mila needed time.

Mila hopped to obey, standing before the fox with her legs spread slightly, her arms held crossed behind her back, and her chest lifted to hold out her breasts. Jeta came up alongside her and mimicked the posture.

The calico glanced to the side: she hadn't set up this scene with Alonso beforehand and wasn't sure how formal he expected it to be. She was relieved to see Jeta's posture loose and casual.

Alonso had been reading a book when they came in, a guide on shibari. He thumbed through a page or two more while his kittens waited patiently. Mila was used to waiting. The fox liked to pause just before things got intense and let Mila's own imagination fire her desire into the stratosphere. Currently her fantasies were filling up with thoughts of the beautiful tigress at her side. By the time Alonso put his book aside, Mila was sopping wet. But he still took his time, investigating his two kittens thoroughly with caresses, pinches, teases, and more than one firm smack to an ass. "Kitten," he said, and it took Mila a second to realize he wasn't talking to her, "I need your help to test the strength of this new hypnotic power. Will you assist me?"

"Of course, Master," Jeta said with a soft purr.

"It could be... strenuous."

"I know you will watch out for your kittens, Master."

He nodded. "Kitten, tell me how I would make you have the quickest, most intense orgasm."

The tigress thought and just before responding, there was a slight shift in her hips, like she was resisting the urge to bring her hands to her center and start to rub. "Something big and thick in my sex, a vibrator held just under my clit, and someone playing with my nipples, Master."

"Very good. Mila, would you collect toys to assist with that while I get Jeta set up?"

"Yes, sir," the calico said and stepped to the side of the room that seemed devoted to storing all manner of toys and implements. Jeta's selection was far less varied in overall purpose than Zuberi's collection. Jeta had no sleepsacks for starters. But in what she did have, Jeta had variety. There wasn't just one dildo. There were close to twenty, different sizes and shapes, including one bigger and thicker than Mila's forearm. For a second, Mila gawked, unable to believe that Jeta could take that. But then, she thought, maybe the tigress couldn't, and it was there merely to be aspirational.

The calico inspected the toys closely for signs of wear and tear to their surface. One was clearly more well loved than others and Mila decided to go with a toy slightly larger than that one. It had no species signifiers: it was just a thick tapered cylinder.

For vibrators, Mila skipped over the bullet vibes and the vibes attached to other toys and instead picked up a magic wand, grinning at the number of settings it had.

She took a pair of simple clamps connected by a chain and headed over to the fox and tigress. They had been occupied on the far wall of the room, getting the tigress into a sling well supported by heavy metal chains. The position they had opted for had Jeta sitting upright but with her legs lifted and splayed to the side to give full access to her sex. Cuffs held her wrists up and away as well. She looked on the items Mila brought with a smile.

"Get her set up," Alonso ordered, and Mila understood what he meant.

She slipped into the space between Jeta's thighs and first ran the dildo's tip over her folds a few times before sliding it in with a slow twist. The tigress was as eager as Mila was, and it slid in easily. The nipple clamps came on next with the tigress barely reacting to the pinch, but instead purring at the touch, so Mila snuck in a few gropes as well. She laid the vibrator first on the tigress's clit and then, remembering what Jeta had said, slid it down slightly. "She's all ready, sir."

"Yes, she is." The fox agreed. He stepped up to the tigress's side and wound the nipple chain around a finger to tighten it. He gave an experimental tug which earned a wider smile from Jeta. "Tell me, kitten, from here, how long do you think it would take you to climax, once Mila turns the vibrator?"

"Less than a minute, Master."

He nodded, and then his expression became serious. "Jeta, you are not to climax until I give you permission. Do you understand?"

"Yes, Master."

"And you are to inform me the moment you are edging."

"Yes, Master."

He held up his phone with the stopwatch app at the ready. He glanced at Mila and she understood. The instant his thumb came down on the start button, she clicked the vibrator on.

There was a tug from Jeta in surprise at the toy's activation. She lifted away for a moment, but then she settled in against it with a deep moan of contentment. Alonso played with the chain going to her nipples, moving his finger around so it tugged them in all directions.

By fifteen seconds, Jeta had begun to grind in earnest up

against the vibrator and Mila had to work to keep the dildo deep and the vibrator on target.

By thirty seconds, the tigress had begun to pant, and her thighs were trying to clench around the toys at her hips, but the chains held her fast.

By forty-five seconds, she had said, "I am edging, Master."

Mila watched wide-eyed as the seconds continued to tick by. Alonso said nothing and did nothing except to mark time and keep tugging the chain. Mila could feel the quiver running through the tigress's muscles as the orgasm approached but didn't hit. Her panting, however, had stopped. She hardly seemed to be breathing at all, until her voice escaped with a keening whine of raw need.

At two minutes, the tigress's body suddenly jumped, flinching away instinctively from the vibrator and its overstimulation.

"Keep it on her," Alonso commanded and Mila struggled to obey on the now squirming tigress.

She eventually had to push herself in against Jeta's hips, taking away some of the tigress's leverage. The whine in Jeta's throat came out as a whimper as she struggled to escape.

At three minutes, she gave up trying to free herself. Her body simply shook as it was unable to stop the tremors that ran through her arms and legs.

At four minutes, she started to growl.

The sound started deep in her chest and built over time. She was staring into Mila's eyes with fierce determination. The tension was building in her body. Mila could feel it in the tigress's thighs which were straining to shut and could see it in her arms which were struggling against the chains holding them. Suddenly Mila was very very grateful that Alonso had chosen such a sturdy frame for the tigress to be bound to, as she was reminded that the tigress was an apex predator who could snap her in half with ease.

Jeta took in a quick breath, and the low growl shifted to a deep-throated snarl. Her lips curled over sharp fangs and her body began to thrash against her bindings, the powerful predator caught in the trap.

Alonso's orders couldn't have kept Mila standing there, but what did was the realization that Jeta wasn't snarling at her, but rather at herself, at her own traitorous body's attempts to disobey the order she had to obey.

Jeta took a quick breath and snarled again, her whole body going tight, making every binding sing with tension. The breaths came faster and faster, but just before Mila thought the tigress would either hyperventilate or injure herself, Alonso said sharply, "Stop."

Mila yanked the vibrator away and stepped back. The dildo, slick from Jeta's constant edging, slid out and flopped onto the floor.

Jeta's snarls turned to whimpers, which pitched upward as Alonso took the clamps off her nipples and tossed them aside. He wrapped her in a hug, pulling her head against his chest as she shook. Steadily the whimpers died away into purring, as Alonso cradled her.

Mila understood what the tigress was experiencing, that mix of frustration and satisfaction, but ultimately the knowledge that Alonso would take care of everything and she was safe.

"That was seven straight minutes of edging, kitten," he said. "How do you feel?"

The tigress was still taking heaving breaths. "I'm okay. But I can't do that again today."

"No, no. Don't worry about that." He caressed her cheek. "But there is another test I'd like to run."

She nodded and stiffened slightly as she tried to pull herself into an attentive posture, which was rather hard in the sling.

The fox caressed over her chest, playing with the rich fur between her breasts. "I want you to focus on the most satisfying orgasm you have ever had. Not the strongest or most powerful or the longest, but the one which made you feel the most contentment. Remember it. Remember how it felt. And when I snap my fingers the next time, you will have that orgasm again."

She nodded and despite still struggling to control her breathing, she smiled. "Yes, Master. I have it."

Alonso glanced to Mila, then to the tigress's sex, and Mila, heeding the silent order, stepped forward and placed her hand there.

The fox snapped.

Another tremor ran through the tigress's body, starting at her tailtip and ending at her ears, which flickered as she gasped. A second later, Mila felt the telltale clenching under her fingers as Jeta came. "Wow," she said silently.

Jeta hung limp in the chains, purring constantly, and Alonso had Mila help him to get her free. The tigress's legs were understandably wobbly and even with an arm around the shoulders of both fox and calico, she struggled to stumble forward. Alonso had her kneel down against the chair and took his seat there, so she could lean up against his leg. Mila took the opportunity to plant herself next to his other leg.

"Now, what other tests to run?" the fox muttered to himself.

"Do you really need to run more tests?" Mila interjected.

"Technically, no."

"Then what are we waiting for?" When this got no response, she put her hands on her hips and tried to be intimidating again. "Alonso..."

"Master Alonso," Jeta corrected in between dreamy purrs.

"Not until he hypnotizes me, it's not." Mila was still trying to be stern. It didn't appear to be working.

The fox grimaced and tried to look away. "It's just that you and I were never supposed to be at the house. The magic may not have influenced us the same way. The effects could be... weaker for you."

"Weaker? You just made her hold back an orgasm for minutes just by ordering her to, and then you made her cum with a literal snap of your fingers. Even a fraction of that would be amazing."

The fox chuckled a little but didn't relent.

"Alonso, you're not worried that I'll like you less if it doesn't work, are you?"

"What can I say? Old anxieties die hard." He tried to pass it off as a joke, but he couldn't meet her eyes. "I don't want to let you down," he said with a more somber tone.

Mila got to her feet and slipped herself into his lap. She kissed him gently on the cheek. "Well don't worry about it. Even if it doesn't work as well as it does for Jeta, we could have a lot of fun trying to get me to her level."

He nodded and gently took her hands in his own. "All right. Are you ready to try?"

The calico squirmed and squeezed the fox's hands. "I am."

There was a jerk forward and Alonso's commanding voice said clearly, "Drop, kitten."

And Mila fell forward into her Master's embrace.